RIOT

A 1960s Love Story

CHARLES S. ISAACS

HARPERS FERRY PRESS

ISBN-10: 0692486968
ISBN-13: 978-0692486962

For Carole
my own love story

"To read dispassionately the hundreds of statements describing the events… is to become convinced of the presence of what can only be called a police riot."

-- Chicago Study Group Report on Disorders During the 1968 Democratic National Convention, submitted to the President's Commission on the Causes and Prevention of Violence (December 1, 1968)

Chapter 1

September 4, 1967 – Chicago

"Imagine yourself now a South Vietnamese peasant, a woman." *A simple challenge*, I thought at first. But that "simple challenge" would soon redirect the path of my life.

For me, the entire Labor Day Teach-In was a revelation. Students, faculty and invited speakers debated topics concerning the war: "Is It Winnable?" "What Would 'Victory' Look Like?" "Why Are We in Vietnam Anyway?" "The Draft: Fair or Not?" I'd been on campus for only a few days, but my education was already under way.

A presentation on the Tonkin Gulf Incident astonished me. In 1964, President Lyndon Baines Johnson announced that North Vietnamese torpedo boats attacked an American ship in international waters without provocation. Citing this incident, he persuaded Congress to almost unanimously authorize going to war. At the time, 23,000 American "advisors" were stationed in Vietnam. A year later, there were 184,000 combat troops. Now, almost half a million. But the president, one speaker convincingly argued, invented the Tonkin Gulf attack and lied about it. Lied to the Congress, to the American people, to the world. I'd never heard anything like this.

Later, the topic was, "Is It Good for the Vietnamese?" The pro-war speaker, a law professor, offered some abstract notions regarding democratic governance and free markets. The opposing speaker was introduced as Emma Gold, triggering enthusiastic applause from one side of the room.

A short gray-haired woman, dressed in a Russian peasant blouse and skirt, with a colorful shawl draped over her shoulders, took the podium. Emma Gold smiled, acknowledging the reception, and surveyed the crowd. Without speaking, she reached into her bag and pulled out not notes, but a pack of Newport menthol cigarettes. Slowly, with calm deliberation, she shook one out, lit it up and took a deep drag. After exhaling, she began to speak, in the gravelly voice of a chain smoker. Her speech was like no other.

"Here at Midway University, this wonderful institution of deep thinking and brave experimentation," she began, "I invite you to join me in a little thought experiment. Please indulge an old woman for a few moments and close your eyes." Looking around, I saw that most of her listeners were giving her the benefit of the doubt. So did I.

"Imagine yourself now a South Vietnamese peasant, a woman. Your husband fought to drive out the Japanese during World War II. In 1945, he came home to join in celebrating the end of colonial domination. Together, you worked your family's little rice patty. You gave birth to two healthy sons. But his patriotism called him to fight once again, this time to expel the French invaders. In 1954, he returned from the Battle of DienBienPhu without his left arm, but joyful that Vietnam's last occupying power had finally been defeated. Peace and independence at last."

"A dozen years after that historic victory, armed men arrive in your village. With them are a few white men with red, white and blue emblems on their uniforms. A Vietnamese officer calls the villagers together. He announces that your beloved country has been cut in half, that your hero, Ho Chi Minh, is president only of the North. Someone else is president of the South, and the two halves are at war with one another. He claims it is the patriotic duty of the Vietnamese of the South to fight the Vietnamese of the North. After conferring with one of the white men, he nods to his soldiers. They point their guns at ten young men, pull them to their feet and line them up. He proclaims that these men, some still boys, will be your village's contribution to this 'great patriotic war.' He snaps his fingers. His soldiers surround the young conscripts. They all march out of the village and down the path. Soon, they are out of sight."

"Your first son is gone. You feel it in your bones that you will never see him again. You are heartbroken. You don't understand what's happened. Why has your nation been broken in two? Why are Vietnamese fighting other Vietnamese? They called your 'Uncle Ho' a Communist. You don't know what that is, but you do know him as the national symbol of independence. To you, he *is* Vietnam."

"Weeks later, when you have no more tears to mourn the loss of your son, another band of men arrive. These have guns of various types, but no uniforms. They too call the villagers together. They explain that the Western powers imposed a temporary division of the country after the French were driven out, but promised a national election leading to reunification. They say the United States blocked that election to prevent

Ho's certain victory. Instead, the Americans installed a puppet government in the South, and began training an army. Now, American troops are pouring into the South to prop up their puppet regime, and their warplanes are bombing the North."

"Someone asks, 'Who are you?' 'We are the Viet Cong,' one replies. 'We fight under the banner of the National Liberation Front, to throw out the Americans and reunify our homeland.' Your remaining son stands up and announces, 'I will join you.' 'No!' you cry. 'You are my only son now!' But your husband understands him. 'We must let him go,' he says. 'It is now his generation's turn to resist the foreign oppressors.' You embrace your boy. Then he and five others head off with their new comrades, down that same jungle path. Tears flow once again."

By now, you could hear a pin drop in the big hall.

"Without the young men," she continued, "times become very hard. Everyone works, young and old, but there isn't enough manpower. Your husband strains to do the work of two men with his one arm. One day, overcome by the labor, his heart screams in protest. He dies in your arms."

"Now you must leave the village of your ancestors and find a new life. You begin walking toward Saigon, where you hope to find paying work. It's a long walk, taking many days and many nights. You pass old forests, now reduced to cinders. You see children with scarred and discolored skin, and villages that have been burnt to the ground."

"You come to one village where no-one is in sight except a single woman, sitting on a box. You ask what happened. 'Foreign men came with machine guns one night,' she explains. 'They split into small groups, and charged into every hut. They shot everyone: Men, women, old people, little children. They said nothing to us, but shouted to one another. I did not understand their language, but they kept yelling 'Commie Gooks,' whatever that means. I survived by pretending to be dead. When I finish with the burials, I don't know what I'll do. Maybe I will die too.' You wish her well and continue on your journey."

"Finally, you reach Saigon. You find work, mopping floors in a dance hall. Every night, it's filled with loud, rude American soldiers. Many get drunk, throw up, even pass out. Others leave with young, sometimes very young, Vietnamese women who tell you the only way they can feed their families is to sell their bodies. You mop the floors.

You observe closely the corruption of your homeland, the debasement of your people. Every night, you cry yourself to sleep. Alone."

Emma Gold paused, then said in almost a whisper, "Now, please open your eyes." As she scanned the audience, I felt her eyes burning right into my own.

"Here in our comfortable surroundings," she continued, "we can't truly feel the searing pain of this woman's life. We cannot truly know her sorrow. But we can share her one remaining dream, and fight to make it a reality. We can *fight* to end the abomination being carried out by *our* government, carried out *in our names*. We can *fight* to bring the troops home, and, once and for all, leave Vietnam for the Vietnamese. *We can do this*."

She waved her hand across the room, and whispered into the microphone, "We can do this... *for her*."

Following seconds of silence, as though we were emerging from a trance, the applause began. People got to their feet. A long standing ovation. Emma Gold leaned into the microphone, raised her fist and called, *U.S. Out! U.S. Out!* The cry rang out across the hall: *U.S. Out! U.S. Out!*

She strode quietly off the stage, made her way down the aisle and walked out the door. Once the clamor settled down, the program continued. After that experience, though, I didn't think I could handle any more, so I left. But now I understood that it wasn't enough to stay out of this war. I absolutely had to *do something* to get my country out of it, to stop the atrocities. *But what could I do?*

Chapter 2

The day after the Teach-In, I registered as a math major, since it was my best subject in high school. I signed up to take Math, Computer Science, English Composition, Western Civilization, and Logic. Now it was on to the campus bookstore, with the cash I'd saved for it.

Midway's acceptance letter had come with a generous financial aid award. Grants and loans would cover the tuition, but the grants required me to maintain a B average. My parents offered to cover the dorm costs. The price of college textbooks, though, came as a total shock. I left the store with only the Western Civ textbook.

Once classes began, that was the only course I didn't like. I couldn't accept that the evolution of Western civilization could be understood through tracing the births, deaths, rivalries, intermarriages and wars of the European royal families, all of which I was expected to memorize. And it drove me crazy that so many kings had the same names: Henry, Edward, Philip, Charles, John, William and, most egregiously, Louis. (France had eighteen of them.)

I still didn't have the other books, or enough money to buy them all. When I mentioned this conundrum to an upperclassman, he pointed to the north campus gate. "Head out there, walk two blocks, hang a right, and look for a store called Previously Perused," he advised. "That's always the first place to go for books."

I followed his directions and found myself on High Street, where the buildings typically had stores on the ground floor and apartments on a floor or two above. Number 147-149 was Previously Perused. A bell jingled as I stepped inside and looked around. Used textbooks occupied half the shelves, hardcovers and paperbacks the rest. A jam-packed bulletin board advertised campus activities, tutoring services and things for sale. The used books were marked at half or less of their list prices.

I stacked the books I needed on a desk in a corner. As I began mentally adding the prices, I heard steps coming from behind. A woman's gravelly voice asked, "May I help you with something?"

When I turned, I must have looked like an idiot, wide-eyed with my mouth hanging open, not responding to her question. "Are you all right?" she asked.

"Oh, uh, sure," I stammered. "I'm new at Midway. Steve Harris."

She gave me a firm handshake. "Emma Gold."

"Well, yes, I know. I mean, uh, well, I was at the Teach-In and heard your speech. It was only a few minutes long, but it changed the whole way I think about the war, or rather about me and the war. By the time you finished, I was on the verge of tears. I never felt the horror of this war the way I do now. Am I talking too much?"

Her eyes peered at me a little more closely. "Would you like a cup of coffee?"

"Sure," I replied.

"Come." She motioned toward the back room. "Oh, are these your books?"

"Well, yes. But I'm pretty sure I don't have enough cash."

She turned, beckoned a young woman over to the desk and asked, "Cat, would you please add these up and bring me the tape?"

This "Cat" was about five-three, slender, with long, thick black hair, high cheekbones, full lips, a small, slightly broad nose, and large, deep, almond-shaped eyes. Her skin brought to mind the deep tone and creamy texture of butterscotch pudding. She smiled, and either my mind or my hormones, maybe both, told me I'd like to get to know her a little better. But now wasn't the time. I introduced myself quickly, and awkwardly, before following Emma to her back office.

She poured the coffee, lit up a Newport and asked, "So, what was your overall reaction to the Teach-In?"

"I didn't understand until then," I explained, "that it's not enough for me to just use my draft deferment to avoid participating in this war. Now I know we have a moral obligation to get our country *out* of Vietnam."

"Oh, but we do participate in it, whether we want to or not," she objected. "You might find ways to avoid being drafted, but it's still our taxes that pay for the war. We're complicit in its devastation, in this way and in many others we're not even aware of. By taking action to stop the war, we can at least try to strike a balance."

"We could refuse to pay those taxes," I suggested.

"Well, Henry David Thoreau tried that act of conscience. He was protesting the Mexican War, which was an outright bloody land grab."

"And what happened?"

"He was sent to prison. One day, his friend, Ralph Waldo Emerson, asked through the bars of the cell, 'What is a man like you, a man of letters, doing in a place like this?' And do you know how Thoreau responded?"

I did not.

"He asked, 'What are *you*, a man of conscience, doing *out there*?' "

"A good story, which might even be true," she continued. "But there'll never be enough Americans willing to spend years in prison if they can avoid it. That's why Muhammad Ali got so much attention this year when he refused to be drafted, and why they're using him to set an example. Even if he manages to stay out of prison, he's already been stripped of his heavyweight championship, his license to fight in most states, and his passport. This is not a decision one takes lightly."

"I agree," I said. "But then what *can* we do?"

We were interrupted when Cat came in with the adding machine tape. I knew I was making a fool of myself, but I couldn't take my eyes off her. Emma showed me the total.

"Uh-oh," I groaned. "Your prices are terrific, but I still don't have enough money."

"On your way out, just pay what you can. Sign the tape and leave it with Cat. You can pay the rest whenever you're able. Okay?"

"Well, sure."

"Let's continue our talk over dinner. How about Friday at seven, my apartment?"

I eagerly accepted, and asked for the address. Emma pointed at the ceiling and said, "Second floor."

Cat had my books already packed. I paid what I could, and she wrote out a receipt with the balance circled. I tried hard not to stare as she did it. On my way out, I wondered if it was possible to be bewitched by two women in a single day.

Chapter 3

Emma's apartment was the size of the double-wide store downstairs, with a stairway door on each end. It was furnished modestly but comfortably, and decorated with a few exotic works of art. What caught my attention most were the books. Books, on shelves lining the walls. Books, piled on the floor. Books, even on furniture. Emma noted my interest.

"Now, you can probably guess how 'Previously Perused' came to be," she explained over wine and cheese. "When I inherited this building five years ago, it was vacant. I bought library shelves for the store, filled them with books I'd accumulated over the years, and put up a sign. Before long, students began bringing in books they wanted to sell. I never expected it to become a real business."

"Is that what you'd call it now?" I asked. "Does it make money?"

"Well, not very much," she admitted, "But that's not the point. I don't need a lot of money. The store gives me an opportunity to do something for the students. Most of all, it gives me a way to meet interesting, intelligent young people. Like you."

"Well, I don't know about that!" I stammered, blushing.

Dinner was delivered from Sal's Pizzeria, right down the block. Emma's interests, I was to learn, were many and varied, but the culinary arts were not among them.

I wanted to know more about her, but she wanted to talk politics. I did gather that she was a widow, living alone; that her daughter, Ellie, was studying at Columbia for a Ph.D. in History; and that she was only in her early sixties, not as old as I'd first thought.

Soon, we got down to business. "Do you remember where we left off?" she asked.

"Sure I do. We agreed that the war machine won't be stopped by guys like me avoiding the draft, or by a few people risking prison by refusing to pay taxes. Beyond that, I'm kind of at a loss. There are antiwar marches and rallies, though. Could they make an impact?"

"Yes, they might," she agreed, "and there'll be a big one, an important one, in Washington next month. You'll be hearing about it very soon. It's good to hold national mobilizations a few times a year. But that's not enough. People need to be involved on the other 360 days too."

"But how?"

"Everyday organizing. Everyday acts of resistance. Here's an example. Have you examined a telephone bill lately?"

"Not really. It's pretty complicated, and I don't even know what all the little nuisance charges are for."

"Of course. It's designed to be difficult. If you look closely, though, you'll find a 10-percent excise tax, which has a very specific purpose. You see, those funds are specifically earmarked for the Vietnam War. It's a hidden tax that nearly everyone pays without knowing it. That's an example of what I meant when I said we all participate in this war. Every time we dial a phone number, we make a small contribution to a bullet, a grenade, a bomb, a child's death."

"I bet millions of people would object if they knew," I said. "But what can we do about it? People can't live without a phone these days."

"It's easier than you think. Court rulings prohibit the phone companies from cutting off your service for refusal to pay that tax, as long as you send them a note explaining why. This is one war tax that people can legally withhold."

"It's that simple?" I asked. "If people knew that, lots of them wouldn't pay."

"So then what would happen, Steve?"

"Well, there'd be less money for the government to wage war," I quickly answered.

"Yes, it would make it a little bit harder to pay for the war. A very good thing. But of course, only one small drop in a very big bucket. Something even more important might happen, though. What do you think that might be?"

I was stumped. "I have no idea," I admitted.

"Forget the money. Focus on the level of consciousness," Emma prompted. "Put yourself in, say, a young mother's shoes. You don't like the war, and certainly don't want to raise your children to be warriors.

But you have no way to do anything about it. You have too many obligations at home to join rallies and marches, especially if they're a thousand miles away. But somehow you learn that you can refuse to pay this war tax, and you even get a chance to tell the phone company why."

"Right."

"And after she does that," Emma asked, "what happens? Does she see herself a little differently once she's taken this little step?"

"Well, I guess she'll be glad to have done something about the war."

"Yes, and how important is that! Perhaps for the first time, she's engaged in political action. She has stood up for her values and said '*NO!*' to the government. She's no longer a passive observer. She has *taken action*, without even leaving her kitchen table. And now what does she do?"

"If she feels good about it, I guess she'll tell her friends." My next thought made me smile. *Maybe she'll tell them over the phone!*

"So you see how this can trigger a ripple effect," Emma continued. "But there's even more. Once she's taken her first step, others may follow. Another phone bill the following month. Another refusal to fund the war. Another note to the phone company. Another one the next month, and the one after that. With each action, she sees herself more and more as a person who's put her hand on the wheel of history. And when the next march on Washington comes along, maybe she'll find a way to get there, even with the whole family in tow. She might start a local peace group. You see, once political consciousness is awakened, *anything* can happen."

My mind raced. I had visions of telephone lines burning up with concentric circles of political awakening, letters flooding in to the phone companies, government officials panicking over the drying up of war funding, suburban moms packing up their families to picket the White House. I must have appeared lost in thought.

"Are you with me?" Emma asked with concern. I snapped back to the real world.

"Yes," I assured her. "Is this what you meant by 'everyday organizing?' "

"That's the essence of it. Engage with people's daily lives. Encourage even the smallest actions. Actions breed activists. On the big stage, by itself, the telephone tax protest is insignificant. But it adds up. And, if we keep building the base for a mass movement, big changes can happen. Ending this brutal war might be only the beginning."

"Emma," I said, "this has really got me thinking, but I also think it's keeping us up too late. I should go now, but I hope we can continue this conversation."

"Of course," she responded. "How'd you like to continue it in a group? I meet with Midway students on the first and third Tuesday of the month, in what we call 'The Circle.' Want to give it a try?"

"Sure. When and where?"

"Next Tuesday at seven," she said, pointing at the ceiling.

"Third floor?" I asked. She nodded.

Chapter 4

I spent the weekend with the royal families, trying to memorize names, dates, intermarriages and wars. I tried making notes on the paths of the Tudors, the Bourbons, the Hapsburgs, the Windsors, the Hanovers, the Brandenburgs and the Hohenzollerns. By Sunday night, I had twenty pages filled, along with a splitting headache.

Mostly, I was looking forward to Tuesday night at 147 High Street. That afternoon, though, I was so consumed with writing computer code that I lost track of time. When I looked up at the clock, it was already almost seven. I left everything where it was on my desk and rushed over to Emma's. I found the front door unlocked and took the stairs two at a time. The door on the third floor was wide open.

This apartment had been converted into a meeting space. All the interior walls, except for the bathroom, had been removed. Folding tables and chairs were stacked against the back wall, and about twenty-five chairs were arranged in a circle. The session had already begun. I spotted Emma and Cat, but the seats near them were occupied. I unfolded a chair and tried to slip quietly into it.

A young man with a thick beard and intense dark eyes had begun a presentation. Before I even caught on to the subject of his talk, it was obvious how passionately he felt about it. He spoke standing up, jabbing and pointing his fingers, often pausing for emphasis as he fixed his eyes on individuals, as if to drill the material into their heads.

His subject was our country's use of chemical warfare in Vietnam, particularly Napalm, which he explained was a jelly-like mixture of gasoline, benzene and polystyrene plastic. It was a kind of liquid fire, striking the skin at a temperature of 2,200 degrees and burning into the body, feeding on human tissue and melting the flesh.

I didn't want to accept that the country I grew up pledging allegiance to would ever use such a weapon. But a magazine called *Ramparts*, circulating around the room, featured photographs of Vietnamese children mutilated by this atrocity. Their skin looked like swollen raw meat. Some had eyelids so burnt that they couldn't be shut. I was glad I'd skipped dinner, because I didn't think I could have kept it down.

But that wasn't the end of it. He moved on to Agent Orange, a toxic defoliant our helicopters, airplanes, trucks and boats were spraying over the Vietnamese countryside.

"The Pentagon's openly stated objectives," he explained, "include depriving the Viet Cong of both jungle cover and food supply, and driving peasants off the land into the government-controlled cities. Millions of acres of forest and farmland are being destroyed in the process, and the cities are bursting with disease-ridden shantytowns."

The active ingredient in Agent Orange, I learned, was called Dioxin. Fatal in certain doses, no-one had calculated how many thousands, perhaps tens or hundreds of thousands, had died from contact with it. In lower doses, it caused birth defects. It got into breast milk and caused genetic diseases, not only in humans, but also in the food chain: cattle, pigs, water buffalos. I was learning a lot, very quickly, about what my country was capable of doing.

To make it even worse, both Napalm and Agent Orange came out of America's university laboratories. The Pentagon contracted their manufacture to an American corporation whose everyday consumer products were present in nearly every household: the Dow Chemical Company.

Before the session broke up, Emma said, "We've talked about base-building through everyday organizing. Now let's consider an 'everyday' anti-Dow campaign, maybe a boycott of one of its products. If you have an apartment, see which of them are in your kitchen. If you're in a dorm, check the cafeteria. Call your parents and ask them to look through their cabinets. Let's see if we can come up with a focus, a small action ordinary people can take every time they shop for groceries, an everyday protest against the destruction Dow brings down every day on the Vietnamese people."

As we prepared to leave, I thanked the speaker for the information. He introduced himself as Larry Graff, a grad student in Chemistry. "If I'd gotten my degree five or ten years ago," he mused, "I might've become one of Dow's chemists."

The evening was an eye-opener for me, but my eyes often drifted over to Emma's stunningly beautiful assistant named Cat. Beginning the next day, my daily routine included a walk before dinner, a walk that inevitably took me to High Street, where I hoped to "accidentally" run into Cat, when she might be closing up for the day.

One evening, it happened. As the store came into view, its lights went out. I stopped in my tracks. Cat emerged from the doorway and headed in my direction. Her eyes met mine.

"Oh, hi, Steve. Remember me?"

Oh, did I remember! But, for I don't know how many awkward seconds, I stood there, mute. I was so afraid of embarrassing myself that I didn't respond.

"Steve? It is you, isn't it?"

Finally, I recovered. "Sure it's me, Cat. I didn't expect to see you. What a nice surprise!" *(What a lie.)*

"I'm heading over to the campus café," she said. "Want to join me?"

"Sure. That's where I was going too." *(Another lie.)*

Walking to the café, we made small talk about the weather and about school. We were surprised to discover we were both math majors at Midway, although she had a dual major in physics.

"I haven't seen you in my classes, though," I said.

"That's probably because I started two years ago. I'm a junior now."

"Oh. So what are you taking? Calculus?"

"No, I did that in high school," she replied. "This semester, it's Advanced Probability and Number Theory."

I'd studied a little probability theory, but found it difficult. *And she's into the advanced version,* I thought. I didn't even know what Number Theory was.

During dinner, I asked about her name. I thought Cat might be short for Catherine.

"Oh, my name." She looked up and smiled.

Oh, those teeth, I marveled. *Oh, those eyes.*

"You wouldn't be surprised," she began, "to hear that my dad was African-American. My mom was from the Philippines. When she got pregnant, a doctor told her she wouldn't be able to carry to term. She prayed every night he was mistaken, and insisted on giving her unborn child a name in her native language. Well, I came along in '48. Everyone calls me 'Cat,' but my full first name is Ca-taca-taca. In Tagalog, it means 'amazing.'"

Perfect, I thought. And now I knew she was a year older than me, but two years ahead in school.

"Do you see your parents often," I asked, "now that you're at Midway?"

Cat's countenance suddenly darkened. Her eyes closed for a moment and her face seemed to droop. She looked up at the clock and said, "I have to go now."

We stood up and walked outside. No more words were spoken. She turned and headed for the library. I stood and watched, wondering what dumb *faux pas* I'd committed.

Chapter 5

I called home in the morning, and asked my mother to help me with a research assignment on "Market Saturation by Brand-Name Consumer Products," by looking through her kitchen cabinets and making a list of anything manufactured by Dow Chemical. I used the same ruse with the dorm's Food Service Manager, asking him to let me poke around his pantries. Both agreed. Encouraged by their cooperation, I used the same story at the campus café and a few local restaurants.

On Sunday, I was knocking on doors in Midway's off-campus residential buildings. When I said I was on a research assignment for the campus antiwar movement, most of those doors opened. I explained what I knew about Napalm, Agent Orange and Dow Chemical, which didn't take long because all I knew was what I'd learned that one evening. Few of them knew even that much, and most thanked me for the information. We conducted many joint investigations of kitchen cabinets and pantries.

By late afternoon, I thought I'd identified our target, a product found in nearly every kitchen. Just as people referred to tissues as "Kleenex," nearly everyone referred to the material used to preserve leftovers as "Saran Wrap." This had to be Dow Chemical's best-selling product. Everyone used Saran Wrap.

Except for one, my last call of the day. Will Whitman, tall, lanky, with long, straw-colored hair and a small beard, invited me in and listened to my pitch. He knew much more about this than I did. There was no Saran Wrap or any other Dow product in his apartment.

"Folks call me Whit," he told me. He'd graduated from the University of Wisconsin's Madison campus, and was now working on a Master's in English Lit.

"Man," he explained with a slight southern drawl, "We had a anti-Dow campaign goin' on at Madison all last year, and it'll heat up again this year. Folks at other colleges are on it too. In fact, a national network's developing." Whit spoke not only with his mouth, but with his hands as well, waving them around as though conducting an orchestra.

I asked, "Would you consider helping a group of us put together a campaign at Midway?"

"When and where? I'd love a chance to slam them baby-killers."

I told him about The Circle. Later, I called Emma and related my adventures, including my encounter with Whit. She said I'd done good work.

"And you, my young friend," she added, "have now become what Movement people call an *organizer*."

That sounded like a compliment, so I thanked her. I'd attended only one session of Emma's Circle, but already it felt like where I belonged.

I arrived for the next session with more than politics on my mind. I desperately wanted to repair the connection with Cat that I'd somehow broken as it was only beginning. I tried to make eye contact with her from across the room, but she only looked away. I was bewildered.

It quickly became apparent that Saran Wrap was an ideal target for a boycott. Hands shot up to form a committee to draft a leaflet, contact other student organizations and write a press release for *Midway Magenta*, the campus newspaper. Sabrina Martin, the graphic artist on this newly formed committee, said she already had ideas for the leaflet.

Then I asked Whit to tell us what's been going on at UW-Madison.

"We targeted Dow Chemical a year ago," he began, "and it would be hard to find anyone on campus today who didn't know something about that corporation's war crimes."

"But when I called over there yesterday," he added with his trademark wave of the hands, "I got exciting news. Two weeks from now, on October 18th, Dow will be sending recruiters there. Since they first found out, students have been organizing for a big demonstration. They might even blockade the building. I'll be joining them, and I have room in my car if any of you want to come along. It's only a two-hour drive."

This sparked a debate about whether blocking Dow's recruiters would be either effective or ethical if we did it too. Some were opposed, arguing that a blockade would violate constitutional rights to free speech and free association. A law student pointed out that since corporations were treated as "persons" under the law, they had First Amendment rights.

"Bullshit!" came a retort. "Do corporations have skin that burns and melts under contact with Napalm? Do corporations shed tears, mourning the deaths of their stillborn children? Do corporations even have a conscience? And what do we call *actual* persons who calculate personal gain, monetary profits, in terms of the deaths of innocents? We call them *monsters!*" This view seemed to carry the room, but the consensus didn't go as far as Larry Graff's proposal did.

"Let's give them what they dish out," he argued. "We can manufacture a little Napalm in our own chemistry lab. When Dow's recruiters show up, we can give them a taste of their own medicine!"

It surprised me that I saw a cold logic to this, but many others found it repulsive. The discussion by that time, though, was getting a bit muddled.

Emma brought it to a merciful end, at least for the time being. "This is an important debate," she said, "but we don't have to decide tonight. Midway's corporate recruitment won't be until spring, so we have plenty of time. Does that make sense?"

Heads nodded in agreement.

"There's one more item on tonight's agenda," she added. "Nicky Jarvis of Students for a Democratic Society is here to share some information with us."

A short, thin young man, Nicky's blondish hair was long enough for a ponytail. He wore a blue work shirt, jeans, heavy-looking boots and an army surplus field jacket.

"Thanks for having me tonight. I know it's getting late, so I'll be quick," he began. "After six months of meetings, virtually all the national antiwar and civil rights organizations have agreed to co-sponsor a national demonstration in Washington on the 21st of October. The rally will be at the Lincoln Memorial. After that, we'll march to the Pentagon and confront the beast in its lair."

He passed out copies of a four-page pamphlet titled, *From Dissent to Resistance*. "This is the National Call for the march," he explained. "Please bring it home and read it. We'll hold an organizing meeting Thursday night at seven, in the main student lounge. There's a ton of work to do in less than three weeks, so we'll need all the help we can get. Thanks again."

The pamphlet's back page caught my eye before I put it into my pocket. It was signed by the "National Mobilization Committee to End the War in Vietnam," with a long list, in smaller type, of co-sponsoring organizations, from SNCC and SDS to Communists and Maoists, to the NAACP and a variety of religious and pacifist groups. There were more than a hundred. Inside, one sentence read in bold type, "We Americans have no right to call ourselves human beings unless, personally and collectively, we stand up and say *"NO!"* to the death and destruction being perpetrated in our names."

I was anxious to read the rest of it, because this theme echoed my own thinking now. It wasn't enough to disagree with this war. *We had to end it.*

As I got up to leave, there was a tap on my shoulder.

"I owe you an apology," Cat said. "Can we go for a beer or something?"

Chapter 6

As we got settled at Pete's Tavern, I said, "I think it's me who owes you an apology. I know I must've said something to upset you, but I honestly don't know what that was."

"Well, I guess you did," she replied. "But there was no way you could've known. I need to explain. Can I tell you a story?"

"Sure."

"Remember, I was born after the doctor told Mom she couldn't have a baby. She and Dad treated me like a gift from God. They denied me nothing. Mom quit her job to stay home and care for me. That meant Dad had to work more overtime, but he spent lots of his time off playing with me, taking me places, telling me stories, teaching me things. They sent me to an expensive private school because they thought the public school didn't challenge me enough. Later, I found out they borrowed a ton of money to pay the tuition. Daddy had a good union job at the GM plant, but they never had the luxuries his co-workers enjoyed. We lived in a small rented house in Detroit, and never owned a new car."

"I was their only child, and the focus of their lives. They called me their Little Flower. The three of us were a loving, devoted family. I couldn't have asked for more. My only complaint, if I had one, was that they were overprotective. At the playground, while the other moms chatted on the benches, mine hovered near where I played. I was the only kid on the block who had to wear a football helmet riding my bike or my scooter. Mom or Dad brought me to school and picked me up every single day, even though I could've taken the bus by myself."

"Got the picture," I said.

"So, when it came time to apply to colleges, they assumed I'd be going to Wayne State or some other commuter school. But I wanted to go to Midway. I didn't tell them when I applied, because I didn't want to have that discussion until it was absolutely necessary. I thought I might not even get in."

"Once the acceptance letter came, along with an offer of a full-tuition academic scholarship, I asked for a family meeting. I showed them the letter and pleaded with them to let me go. Mom looked devastated. 'You're only sixteen,' she said through her tears. 'You're too young to be on your own.' I argued I wouldn't be on my own. I'd live in a dorm with supervision. And, by the time classes began, I'd be seventeen."

"Finally, Dad relented. 'Honey,' he said, 'it's time to let our Little Flower bloom.' Mom eventually gave in, but she insisted on two conditions. 'First, you have to promise to call home at least twice a week,' she said. 'And second, when it comes time to go to Chicago, we want to drive you there and see exactly where you'll be living. I'm not going to stick you on a bus and wave good-bye.' I told her Chicago was almost 300 miles from home. But they didn't care, so I agreed."

"A few months later, when they dropped me off at the dorm, Mom opened every drawer to inspect for insects, bounced on the bed to test its sturdiness, even interviewed the floor's resident assistant. Dad and I cheerfully humored her. It was getting dark when they said good-bye. As Dad drove, Mom and I threw kisses until the car was out of sight."

She paused, sniffled, and dropped the bomb.

"A blinding thunderstorm blew off Lake Michigan onto I-94 that night. A tractor-trailer flipped over into oncoming traffic. Mom and Dad were both killed in the crash."

"Oh my God," I exclaimed. "I'm so sorry!"

Cat began to weep. I handed her a napkin, and took another for myself.

"Even worse," she added after composing herself, "I didn't know what happened until a week later. I didn't know why no-one answered the phone. But I was consumed with the beginning of classes, meeting other kids, all of that. Once I found out, I stayed in my room crying for two days. When I pulled myself more or less together, I knew I'd have to leave school. I had nothing to go home to, but also no way to pay for expenses like the dorm."

"But you're still here," I said. "How'd that happen?"

Finally, a slight smile.

"Before I left campus, I had to sell the textbooks I'd already bought. Someone told me about Previously Perused, so I met Emma almost the same way you did. She noticed right away I was very upset and took me into the back office."

"When we sat down with our coffee, she asked what was troubling me. At first, I couldn't get the words out. I broke down crying. But eventually, I blurted out what happened to my parents and why I had to sell my books."

"Emma reached over, holding my hands in hers. She asked whether a part-time job and an apartment would help. I told her I couldn't make enough money working part-time to rent an apartment. 'That's no problem,' Emma told me. 'I have an extra one, and I could use some help down here.' So that's how I'm still in school. Emma pays me to help out at the bookstore, and I live on the third floor of 149 High Street, adjacent to her meeting space. It's been two years now, and she's never asked me to pay any rent. And when I need books for school, I simply borrow them from the store."

"What a lifesaver," I responded.

"It sure is. It was like Emma adopted me on the spot. I'd do anything for her. Anything. And now that she's made it possible for me to stay in school, I'm determined to make the most of it. That's the least I owe my parents. Emma too."

We walked together back to her door, and she put her key in the lock. I asked if I could give her a hug. As we parted our brief embrace, I said softly, "I'll always be there for you, Cat."

"Somehow," she replied, "I know you will." She reached up and gave me a peck on the cheek, then turned and went inside.

Chapter 7

A few dozen students eventually drifted into the student lounge Thursday night. The young man leading the meeting didn't look like SDS. Dressed casually but neatly, in chinos and a cotton sweater, his moderately long hair and small beard were both neatly trimmed. He also looked vaguely familiar. "Who's that?" I asked the person on my right.

"Jeff Rosen," came his quick reply. "First-year law. A couple of weeks ago, he started Law Students Against the War. Last year, he led a two-week student strike at a college in New York City. It made all the papers. Even national TV."

I remembered seeing news coverage of that strike during the past spring. I'd probably seen Rosen's picture too, in the papers or on TV. He opened the meeting confidently, with an infectious air of enthusiasm that generated momentum for action.

"October 21st can be a historic day," he began, "but only if people like us make it happen. Meetings like this one have been taking place at colleges, churches and union halls all over the country. But Midway is coming to it late in the game. We need to fill as many busses as we can, two weeks from tomorrow night. That'll take a lot of work, so tonight we'll organize to get it done. Okay?" The response indicated assent.

"We have no time tonight for debate," he continued. "If you're here, we can assume you've read the call and you agree with the campaign's theme. Don't just oppose the war. Resist! Resist the draft. Resist the taxes. Block recruitment. Stop the troop trains. Get in the way of the war machine. Am I right?"

Applause. Raised fists. Shouts of "Right on!"

Rosen was good at this. In barely a half hour, he recruited a committee to design a leaflet, distribution captains for each dorm, and squads of campus leafleters. There was no shortage of enthusiasm, and he sure knew how to marshal it.

I volunteered only to leaflet my dorm, though. I was falling behind on my schoolwork, and that bothered me. As urgent and exciting as I found antiwar work, I didn't want to take on more than I could handle. When I got back to my room, I filled a blank piece of paper with a big, bold "**3.0**," and taped it to the wall. This would remind me every day of the B-average I needed to keep the financial aid package that was keeping me in school. I really liked being at Midway, and couldn't afford to screw things up.

Sunday night, I blanketed the dorm with the flyers. It took longer than I thought it would, because many students wanted to talk about the war, and had questions regarding the march and its theme of resisting, versus just opposing, the war. Some, of course, didn't want to deal with anything but their own schoolwork, and more than a few were too drugged out to care about either. But I did my best to get it done. I was sure I'd be seeing at least some of them on the bus to D.C.

With the leafleting done, I promised myself I'd spend the next two weeks focusing on schoolwork. My vow didn't hold up for very long, though. It was only Tuesday afternoon when I found myself on High Street. It was as though Previously Perused exerted a powerful magnetic force, and I was a helpless steel ball.

As the door closed behind me, I spotted Cat helping a customer. When our eyes met, I blew her a kiss. *Why'd you do that?* shouted a voice in my head. *Stop being a jerk!*

I walked through to Emma's office, where she looked up from her paperwork and greeted me with a smile. "Good to see you, Steve. Have a seat. Can I get you some coffee?" I told her I was okay, but she got up to pour it for us anyway. It seemed the electric coffeemaker was always perking back there, and at least one Newport was always burning.

Emma was pleased with my report on the organizing meeting. She told me a couple dozen students had already been in to buy bus tickets.

"How's our Saran Wrap committee doing? I asked.

"It's been only a week," she replied, "but they're very enthusiastic. They're planning to start the boycott campaign right after the big march."

"I'm getting the feeling," I said, "a lot of things get started up there on the third floor."

Emma suddenly convulsed in a fit of wheezing and coughing. I didn't know what to do. Cat rushed in and poured her a glass of water. I held Emma up, and Cat helped her get the water down. The coughing subsided after a few minutes.

I helped her up to the apartment and got her comfortable on the couch with a pitcher of water at her side. When the crisis eased, I came back down.

"This has happened before," Cat told me. "But she refuses to see a doctor. Water and rest seem to help, though. It's closing time now, so you can go. I'll close the shop and make sure Emma's okay before I leave."

I offered to stay, but Cat insisted. I was uneasy, though, walking back to the dorm.

During that week, Emma had good days and bad days. Sometimes, she was her usual talkative self. Other times, coughing made talking, and even breathing, difficult. I began helping out at the shop, which provided an excuse to spend time with Cat. We used some of the downtime for studying, but we spent most of it either talking or reading each other poems or short stories. I couldn't get enough of her.

Emma was home, resting in bed, during the next gathering of The Circle. We discussed the Saran Wrap boycott and the upcoming march, but our concern about Emma's health put a damper on things, and we adjourned earlier than usual. Nearly all of us were signed up for Friday night's convoy to Washington.

When I arrived at the bookstore late Friday morning, though, an ambulance was double-parked in the street. Emma was being carried out on a gurney, her face covered with an oxygen mask.

"Before I opened the shop," Cat told me, choking back tears, "I went upstairs to see how Emma was doing, like I usually do if she's not there ahead of me. She was flat on the bed, wheezing and gasping for air. I sat her up and called the police. They sent the ambulance."

"You did the right thing," I said. "You might've saved her life." Cat began crying and fell into my arms.

Downstairs, a small crowd had gathered. Sal, the old pizza guy, came over. "You gotta go with her," he declared, handing me a set of keys. "Take my car. It's right across the street."

It was a short drive to the Midway Medical Center. We left the car, emblazoned with "Sal's Pizza" advertising, right in front, hoping Security would think a delivery was in progress, and rushed inside.

Emma was already being examined by a doctor. After a few minutes, he came out to talk.

"With the oxygen, she's breathing nearly normally now," he explained. "But I want to admit her, so we can keep an eye and run some tests. If you want to, you can come see her after, let's see, around three this afternoon."

Sal said to keep the car as long as we needed it. "I got another one and," he winked, "if I need any pizzas delivered, I'll let ya know."

We got back to the hospital at three sharp and located Emma's room. We found her sitting up in bed without the oxygen mask, leafing through a magazine and scowling. "There's nothing worth reading in this place!" Clearly, she was feeling better. "Please, can you bring the books on my nightstand at home? The doctor says I'll be here at least overnight, and I'm already going out of my mind."

Cat stayed with her while I went to get the books. When I returned to the room, I told them, "The busses are leaving in only a few hours. They'll have to go without us."

"No, they won't!" Emma insisted. "I've got doctors and nurses to look after me. You two go on and stop the war. That's much more important."

Cat and I objected, but she insisted. This was no time to argue, so we settled on a compromise. Cat would bring her schoolwork to the hospital and stay with Emma, and I would have to represent the three of us in Washington.

Chapter 8

Boarding the second bus in line, I spotted Whit and sat down next to him. He already had his head in a collection of poetry. I'd brought along W.E.B. Du Bois's *The Souls of Black Folk*, the only one of Emma's recommendations slim enough to fit in my jacket pocket. I wondered, though, how much reading either of us would get done on this trip. I asked about the protest in Madison.

"Man, it was great," he replied. "We ran Dow Chemical right out of town. No-one expected 3,000 protesters. The whole campus got shut down and, from what I hear, it still is. Oh, and Larry Graff came with me. Quite an interesting fellow."

When Whit got excited, the hands got even busier. I leaned back a little to avoid getting hit in the nose. I envisioned him and Larry having a conversation as they drove: Whit letting go of the steering wheel to wave his arms around, Larry jabbing and pointing. It must have made quite a sight for passing motorists.

"Sounds like a hell of an impact," I responded. "But why was the campus shut down all week?"

"Well, the university president called in the cops, hundreds of them, armed with billy clubs and tear gas. This morning, I heard seventy people are still in the hospital. But the crackdown only broadened the protest. There've been big demonstrations against police brutality yesterday and today, including lots of students who didn't support blocking the recruiters in the first place. Loud picket lines at both the president's home and the police station. Talk of a student strike too. Other UW branches are also getting involved. This is gonna be one helluva year."

When the bus hit the highway, an amplified voice asked for everyone's attention.

"Welcome, war resisters! I'm Jeff Rosen, and I'll be your bus captain tonight. After I share some important information, you can get back to whatever you're doing. I'll start with the most important: The bathrooms are at the back of the bus!" That got laughter, hooting and applause. When it settled down, he continued.

"At Midway, we didn't have time to organize for the Week of Resistance encouraged by the national call, but that wasn't the case everywhere. Here's an update, and it's far from complete. On Monday, a big rally on the Boston Common, where a few hundred draft cards got burned. This, you probably know, can trigger a five-year stint in federal prison. But these guys stuck it right in the government's eye. That's what 'resistance' is all about!" More applause.

"On Tuesday, thousands of protesters blocked the Army's Draft Induction Center in Oakland. They even blocked the surrounding streets. Nearly the same thing happened in San Francisco. In both places, they came under attack by helmeted cops."

"Then on Wednesday, thousands rallied to toss Dow Chemical's recruiters out of UW-Madison. They got attacked too. From now on, we better be prepared for this type of response."

"This morning, over a thousand young men turned in their draft cards at the Department of Justice. Their statement said they were 'ending their relationship with the Selective Service System.' Yes, that's what 'resistance' is all about. Also, nearly 500 professors, clergymen, writers and public intellectuals handed the federal marshals a petition in support of those men, where they volunteered to share whatever punishment the government lays on them."

"And just before we left, the Mobe got a call from New York City, where the Navy had a recruiting day planned at all the public colleges. The recruiters ran into big protests at every one of them. At Brooklyn College, students shut the whole place down. And it's a big place."

"And what's been happening in Congress? Yesterday, it passed a bill making it a crime to picket the Capitol Building without permission. The penalty: automatic six months in jail. That's no joke, folks, but now the First Amendment is. They say LBJ will sign it into law tomorrow morning. None of them seem to care that it's absurdly unconstitutional."

"Why did they do this? Because they're scared shitless. Because our movement is growing. Resistance is spreading. We're gonna stop this fucking war. And tomorrow, we get to flex a little muscle. On to the Pentagon!"

More cheers. A chant rose up: *One, two, three, four. We don't want this fucking war! One, two, three, four. We don't want this fucking war!*

When it subsided, Jeff continued. "Now, you've might've heard there are plans for civil disobedience at the Pentagon. It's no secret, and it came up during the Mobe's negotiations with the Feds for the parade permit. Here's how it's supposed to go down. The building will be guarded by soldiers, and there'll be a line we're not supposed to cross. Crossing that line will trigger an arrest, a small fine and probably a night in jail."

"At least that's what's been agreed to. It's what the Fed's chief negotiator even told the press. But we each have to decide for ourselves whether we want to take this risk, and whether we trust them to keep their side of the bargain. That's up to you. So think it over."

"Now, please listen carefully to this. By contract, our return trip has to start at 10 p.m. sharp, no matter what, from the Pentagon's south parking lot. So you'll want to get there earlier to find bus G22. We don't want you waking up in Nova Scotia Sunday morning!"

"There's one more thing. You might not want to hear this, but it's important. A rumor's floating around that there's marijuana on this bus." That brought laughs, as bags of weed waved in the air. "Here's the bad news. Highway Patrols across the country are on the lookout for chartered busses this weekend. They'd love an excuse to pull us over and arrest everyone on board for drug possession. Across state lines, no less. So think of the rest of us as well as yourselves. No pot smoking 'til we're off the bus in D.C. Then it's up to you." Good-natured groaning met that message.

"Now, please relax and enjoy the trip. Oh, and what was that chant again?"

One, two three, four...

After a while, singing broke out. Steve Andrews, an occasional drop-in at The Circle, strummed his guitar. Others added the beat of bongo drums. Bags of food got passed around: sandwiches, nuts, fruit, candy, potato chips. I'd gone to the busses almost straight from the hospital, and hadn't even thought about eating. Lots of others had, though, and the first thing they wanted to do was share. I felt like peace, music, caring and sharing were all linked in my generation's DNA. I was grateful for the snacks since I hadn't eaten all day. The bus was bursting with high spirit. I wished Cat could have been there to enjoy it with me.

A few hours later, the hustle and bustle and singing and chanting gave way to snoring. I was exhausted, happy, and able to put my worries about Emma away for the time being. Soon, I drifted off too.

I woke when the motion of the bus came to a stop. The sun was up, and we were at a highway rest area. "Time for breakfast," Jeff announced. "It's seven now. We roll again at eight." I joined the rush off the bus, hungry for breakfast, but just as anxious to find a real bathroom.

On the way in, I grabbed a newspaper. It was the *Pittsburgh Post-Gazette*, so I guessed we were in western Pennsylvania. Whit and I freshened up, brought egg sandwiches and coffees to a table and looked at the paper. We were in it, but not in the way we expected.

"Government Mobilizes to Protect Capitol," read the front-page headline. "Reds and Anarchists Head for DC." Whit and I scanned the article.

> *U.S. Government agencies are coordinating resources to protect its landmark institutions from a potentially massive onslaught of Communists, peaceniks and assorted malcontents expected to mass in Washington on Saturday.*
>
> *Official spokesmen refused to provide details, but sources speaking off the record have told the Associated Press there may be 2,000 Capital Police and 1,800 National Guardsmen assigned in the District of Columbia. On the Virginia side of the Potomac, stationed to protect the Pentagon, will be 3,000 soldiers, along with several hundred federal marshals. In addition, according to these sources, the Army has positioned an additional 6,000 troops at nearby military bases, and has put 20,000 more on alert, up and down the east coast.*

That was the theme of the news coverage on the morning of the big march. There wasn't even passing mention of the reason these "malcontents" were coming in from all over the country. Not a single interview with any of the Mobe's leaders. Even worse, the Associated Press byline meant this story was appearing in newspapers everywhere. My sense of exhilaration was suddenly tempered by deep apprehension. I wondered what might be lying in wait for us in Washington, and whether our message would ever get out to the country. I wasn't the only one getting back on the bus a bit more somber than when we stepped off.

As we drew closer to D.C., though, it was easy to rekindle the excitement of the day. The roads were choked with busses like ours. They came from all corners of the country: from Michigan, Maine and even Mississippi; from New York, New Jersey, and even one from New Mexico; from South Dakota, south Florida, even South Carolina. As we got bunched up in traffic, clenched fists thrust out the windows. Fingers formed V's for victory. Songs burst forth. Once again, we were happily on our way to make history.

Chapter 9

It was almost noon when we reached the National Mall. I stood on a bench to look out over the crowd. I'd never seen so many people in one place. And still they came, from all directions. Protesters filled the Mall from the Lincoln Memorial to the Washington Monument. Even the reflecting pool was occupied, mostly by hippies in various states of undress, puffing away. From the speakers' platform, on the steps of the Memorial, came an announcement that we were a quarter million strong.

The air was festive. I sensed a collective joy over how the sheer size of the crowd amplified our individual and small-group voices. On the fringes, where the speeches could only faintly be heard, there was music, singing and dancing. Jugglers juggled. Mimes mimed. Picnickers picnicked. Vendors were selling antiwar buttons, shirts, hats and banners. On this crisp, sunny afternoon, surrounded by antiwar protesters from all walks of life, it looked to me like the dawning of a new day.

The ominous drone of military helicopters, regularly hovering overhead and occasionally drowning out the speakers, was not nearly enough to dispel the celebratory mood. Nor was the rush up the steps, knocking over the podium and a dozen microphones, by some lunatic in a Nazi uniform. He was quickly wrestled to the ground by the Rev. William Sloane Coffin, Jr., the pacifist chaplain of Yale University. This brought a huge roar from the crowd.

The many speeches were often stirring. Civil rights groups, pacifist groups, various Old and New Left organizations were all represented. Dr. Benjamin Spock, pediatrician to our generation, gave a terrific, passionate speech. So did David Dellinger, the middle-aged longtime militant pacifist who served as the Mobe's chairman. I sensed, though, that the speech-making was only the opening act. The big event, the one everyone anticipated, would be the March on the Pentagon.

The leaders must have recognized the restlessness in the air. Cutting the speeches short in mid-afternoon, they announced the march was about to begin. We formed ranks of forty or so, arms linked together for as far as the eye could see. In fits and starts, we moved across the half-mile bridge that took us over the Potomac to Virginia, almost directly into the Pentagon's huge parking lots. One chant led to another. *End the War in Vietnam! Bring the Boys Home! Hell No, We Won't Go! Hey, Hey, LBJ. How Many Kids Did You Kill Today?* And of course, *One, Two, Three, Four...* Near the end of the bridge, a young Black man was standing atop a rise, holding a banner emblazoned, "NO VIETNAMESE EVER CALLED ME NIGGER."

As the goal came into sight, the march turned into a stampede. Demonstrators who'd been waiting for this moment all day, all week, all month, broke ranks and charged ahead as though they'd been waiting for it all their lives. The most organized group I saw at that point was a couple of hundred young men, trotting in neat lockstep ranks of eight, waving Viet Cong flags and chanting, *Ho, Ho, Ho Chi Minh! The NLF is Gonna Win!*

There was a high speakers' stand in the parking lot everyone was charging across. Carl Davidson, a national SDS official, was making perhaps the most militant speech of the day. I stopped to listen.

"Repression must be met, confronted, stopped *by any means necessary*," he shouted into the bullhorn. He targeted the army induction centers. "We must tear them down. *Burn* them down, if we have to." I thought his speech matched the mood that characterized the crowd. Hordes of people, though, charged past the speaker's stand as though it wasn't even there. The time for speeches had apparently passed.

Up ahead, I wandered toward a gathering of Yippies. These were hippies with a joyful brand of revolutionary politics, led by a charismatic comic genius named Abbie Hoffman. They danced, passed around reefers and chanted mystical incantations aimed at the Pentagon. One told me they were performing an "exorcism." If it succeeded, the six-million square-foot building would rise up off its foundations, glowing with a bright yellow light. And then the war would end. Just like that. This didn't strike me as a practical plan, so I moved on.

The Pentagon itself was protected by lines of rifle-bearing soldiers. Periodically, protesters ventured over to talk to them, trying to persuade them to join us, but they remained mute and stoic. A girl planted a kiss on a young soldier's cheek. He didn't respond, but federal marshals swooped in and arrested her. A group arrived with a big box of chrysanthemums. They planted them in the barrels of the soldiers' rifles, where they remained. It seemed the march had concluded with an impromptu antiwar festival, right there in the shadow of the Pentagon.

With the onset of darkness, people began streaming away, many to catch long-distance busses with looming departure times. The massive media presence was also thinning. About ten thousand protesters still remained when the soldiers with their flower-loaded rifles unexpectedly withdrew into the building. Many in the crowd wanted to follow them and stage a peaceful sit-in. Some even fantasized about seriously disrupting operations inside the behemoth office complex.

With the sentries gone, no obstacles remained between the crowd and the building's second-story entrances. Stone steps on both sides led to a small plaza at the front doors. The wall between the steps also appeared scalable. *Could a sit-in actually be possible,* I wondered, *in the actual "belly of the beast?"*

As the moon began to rise, I spotted climbers quietly scaling the wall. When they approached the top, dozens simultaneously surged up each of the two stairways. Miraculously, they made it up to the entry plaza. Then into the building, through unlocked doors! It was working!

Now, hundreds moved toward the stairways, some warily, others charging ahead. *What to do? Had I come this far just to watch? Could I go home and tell Emma and Cat I opted out of this historic moment? Was this a time for cowardice?* The crowd around me gathered itself and surged toward the building. I went with the flow.

Before I'd gotten far, though, my forward progress ground to an abrupt halt, as I'd run into an obstacle. I stepped back and looked up. A tall, muscular Black man held his hands out, shouting to anyone who would listen, "Stop! Stop! It's a trap!"

Many charged past him. Some of us hesitated. "Just wait," he urged, "and watch." I did.

Within minutes, demonstrators crowded the entry plaza, gathering themselves for a charge into the building. Suddenly, it seemed from out of nowhere, helmeted soldiers and marshals swarmed them, wildly swinging clubs, pounding down with rifle butts. Screams filled the night. As they subsided, bodies were dragged into the building. I couldn't tell how many were still conscious.

It was a struggle to process the sight of American soldiers luring Americans into what the stranger prophesied was a trap, then beating them to a pulp. It seemed the brutality of the war had come home.

I looked around. The stranger was gone. Someone behind me sniffed, "At least they got inside." I wheeled, swung, caught him in the jaw, and knocked him down. The shock brought me to my senses. I reached down, helped him to his feet and mumbled an apology. With tears forming, I slowly walked away.

Sitting alone on a grassy rise, I surveyed the scene. A group of about thirty gathered nearby, discussing their next move. They didn't look like militants. They weren't young. A few were white-haired women. After a while, they split in half, each contingent moving toward one of the stairways, raising the white banner that universally indicated the absence of threat. They slowly ascended the steps, sat down in the Pentagon's entry plaza, and began to sing.

> *Amazing grace,*
> *How sweet the sound,*
> *That saved a wretch*
> *Like me...*

They met with the same fate. Soldiers and marshals pounced. This time, no resistance was offered, not even screaming from pain and fear. Only the terrible sound of wood and metal shattering human bone, until all went silent. I leaned over and threw up on the grass.

Only a few months before, my big concerns were girls, rock 'n' roll, borrowing Dad's car. Now, everything was about that war, halfway around the world, the war I hadn't wanted to have anything to do with. I'd put my hand on the wheel of history for the first time, and it got pulverized.

And why am I so alone, sitting here now? I asked myself. But I knew the answer. It wasn't as if other people weren't nearby, probably willing to offer support. It was that my connection with the nation I'd been brought up to love had become strained to the breaking point. I didn't only feel lonely. I felt betrayed, lost, ungrounded.

After a while, I dried my eyes and looked at my watch. *Time to go.* Only a few thousand remained now, and it looked like the night would bring more sacrifices. But I'd seen enough. I pulled myself together and focused on finding the right bus to get me home.

Chapter 10

Glancing around the half-empty bus, I spotted the stranger who'd kept me from the Pentagon assault. "Mind if I join you?" I asked.

"Not at all."

I reached out my hand. "Steve Harris." He gave me a firm handshake and a warm smile. "Marcellus Theodorus Hopkins. At your service."

"Well, you were dead right that it was a trap," I said, sitting down. "I sure owe you one. But how'd you know?"

"Did you notice the double-A patches on their uniforms? That's the sign of the 82nd Airborne. They're no security guards. LBJ sent them into Detroit this summer to squash the riots. Before that was over, forty-three Black people were dead."

I asked, "How do you know about them?"

"The 82nd trains at Fort Bragg. That's where I got my Army Green Beret training."

"Green Beret? And you're protesting the war? At the Pentagon? When the theme is resistance to the government?" I wondered whether he might be making this up.

"Correct on all counts."

"So, were you against the war when you joined the Army?"

"This was in 1960. There was a little trouble with Cuba brewing then, but I'd never even heard of Vietnam. See, there were no jobs in Chicago, or at least none that high school prepared me for, and the recruiter said they'd teach me a trade. I did learn a few things, but not that. During Basic Training, a Black instructor gave me two books, one written by a man named J.A. Rogers, the other by W.E.B. Du Bois. I learned more from them about me and my heritage than I ever did in school."

I pulled DuBois's *The Souls of Black Folk* out of my pocket, and showed it to him. That brought a smile.

"One day, this was in '63," he continued, "I got called into the Colonel's office. He told me I'd been chosen to train for Special Forces, the Green Berets. I almost fell off my chair, but he stood up and so did I."

"He stepped around his desk and shook my hand. 'Congratulations, boy,' he said. 'You're a credit to your race.' Credit to my race? Boy? Hah! I was still a niggah to him, but I had to think fast. I didn't know what this new adventure would bring, but I figured it had to be better than the brig. So I simply said, 'Thankya, suh,' and shuffled on out the door."

"Two weeks later, I'm at Fort Bragg, in the most intensive training program imaginable. It was so total that it took over not only my body, which was being molded into a lean hard weapon, but my mind as well. I'd never been so focused in my life. They taught me how to kill a man with my bare hands in a dozen different ways. In '65, after two years at Fort Bragg, I got my green beret. And off I went to Vietnam. By then, the war was heating up."

"What happened there?"

"Well, the dozen guys in my unit were sent to the Mekong Delta for, they told us, "special targeted missions." A CIA agent said the Viet Cong was infiltrating villages, terrorizing civilians and establishing bases. He claimed that was the reason the peasants were turning against us. Our unit's first assignment was to eliminate the VC leadership in one village. The next night, a Vietnamese guide led us there, and pointed to a big hut. Our orders were to sneak in, spray everyone inside with automatic weapons fire, then disappear into the jungle. Our guide would lead us back to the base."

"I was in the rear as we burst into the hut, guns blazing. *Rat-a-tat-tat. Rat-a-tat-tat.* The only light came from those bursts of fire, but that was enough for me to see women and children, and a few old people, huddled together. Screaming, bleeding, dying. For a few seconds, I was paralyzed, still standing at the entrance. These weren't VC guerrillas. Maybe their families? Did they have anything to do with the VC? Did it matter? No, it didn't. I couldn't do this, so I stepped back into the darkness."

"Then what?" I asked, wide-eyed.

"The shooting ended. The only sounds now were weak cries and moans of pain. I backed away. When my buddies came out, we followed our guide into the jungle. A grenade blew up what was left behind, including any survivors. As we approached base camp, I heard a bang and felt excruciating pain in my leg. One of my own guys had inflicted the consequence of disloyalty: a shattered knee."

"And that, my friend, ended my illustrious military career. They flew me to a military hospital in Germany where I got a new knee, an honorable discharge, a medal, veteran's benefits and some cash. It seemed they couldn't turn me into a contented civilian fast enough. That was fine with me. My basketball days were over, but I was still alive and mostly intact. I never did get any civilian job training. But this Green Beret had learned enough to hate this war. Does that answer your question?"

"It sure does."

"Good, because I'm ready for a nap."

So was I. When I opened my eyes, the bus was pulling into a highway rest stop. Back on the road after a quick breakfast, I asked, "What did you do when you got back?"

"At first, not much at all. My big brother Cassius got sent to prison while I was away, and my mom moved in with her sister, down home in Memphis. I knew the South would be another war zone for me, so I stayed in Chicago on the streets I knew. I still wasn't qualified for much of a job, though, so I spent much of my time walking those streets. One day, I ran into an old friend, James Watkins, who'd helped keep me out of trouble when I was a kid. He was working at the South Side Organization. He showed me around there, and I was impressed. The SSO is run by community people, folks who are trying to empower that community. Everyone there is Black, even the Board of Directors. Outside of church, I'd never heard of such a thing. James offered me a part-time job, teaching martial arts and working with young people. I jumped at the opportunity."

"A few months later, a delegation of Midway students came in and told me about their new organization, the Black Student Union. They asked me to be their advisor. So now I go back and forth between the SSO and the BSU. I try to mix the two groups whenever I can. They can learn a lot from each other."

"So what about you, Steve?" he asked. "What's your story?"

"Not much to it," I said, and gave him a thumbnail sketch of my life back home in Waterloo, Iowa. "So you can see," I concluded, "not very interesting. But since I got to Chicago, all that changed." I told him about the Teach-In, about Emma and Cat, about what I was learning in The Circle.

"After last night," I continued, "I wonder if my life is getting *too* interesting, maybe more than I can handle. You saw what happened out there the same as I did." I described the pangs of alienation that overtook me while I was sitting on the grassy slope, sensing the fading away of the deep connection I'd thought I had with my country.

"Listen," he interjected, "You've just stumbled onto a tiny sliver of the Black experience. 'Alienated' is the least negative way to describe my people's relationship with the USA. So welcome to the club."

I said, "I hadn't thought of it that way."

"Of course not. Why would you? So now, go and read that little book you showed me last night, *The Souls of Black Folk*. That'll help you understand a few things."

Back at Midway, I thanked Marcellus again, promised to read the book, and said I hoped to stay in touch. We shook hands and headed our separate ways.

Walking to the dorm, rumblings of change heaved deep in my gut. *Was it grief over the disillusionment? Or was it fear of what might lie ahead?*

Chapter 11

The first thing I had to do was check on Emma. After three rings, I recognized her raspy voice.

"Hello?"

"Emma, it's Steve. I just got back. How are you?"

"Steve, we've been so worried. Are you all right?"

"Yes, yes, I'm fine," I lied. "But I want to know about you. How do you feel? What do the doctors say?"

"They say I'm okay to go home. In fact, Cat's getting me ready now. I'll be there in an hour. Come over and tell us everything."

"Cat is there? Can you put her on?" Emma passed the phone to her.

"Steve, oh my god, we saw some of it on TV. We didn't know what happened to you and it sounded so awful."

"It was awful, but I'm sure what you heard wasn't everything. Anyway, I'm okay, at least physically. But what about Emma?"

"I'm taking her home, and I'll stay with her until at least tomorrow morning. Can you come over? We can all catch up."

"I'd be no good to you now," I replied. "Not until I get a short nap and a long shower. I'm exhausted and I smell like a dumpster. How about I get there around seven? I'll stop at Sal's on the way and pick up something for dinner. I need to thank him for helping us out anyway."

"That sounds great. Emma needs to get settled in too."

Back in my room, I took off my shoes and fell into bed with my clothes on. It must have been an internal clock that woke me with a jolt. It was almost six, and now I smelled like a sewer. I tore off my clothes, threw them into a pile, grabbed a towel and ran off to the showers. I set the water to nearly scalding, soaped up and leaned against the wall. Slowly, with my eyes closed, I slid to the floor.

The scenes at the Pentagon flashed before me, like in a dream. When they faded away, what replaced them was an actual dream I first had when I was a child.

I was four years old, having a wonderful time at a carnival with my parents. I went on the rides, played the games, and took in the festive sights and sounds. Mom was on one side, Dad on the other. In the dream, I couldn't see their faces, but I knew it was them. I was using both hands to hold a big ice cream cone. Then, all of a sudden, everything changed. The scenery I'd been enjoying seemed to melt, like my ice cream. The wonderful upbeat music became distorted, slowing down to a dissonant whine. I looked up in panic. My parents were gone. Strange, scary creatures surrounded me, threatening...

I snapped out of it as though struck by lightning, the same way I did when I first had this nightmare, and whenever it recurred. I switched the water to barely tolerable cold and rinsed off. Ten minutes later, I was on my way to High Street, still disturbed but at least clean and awake.

Cat rushed me at the door, grabbed me around the waist and held tight. The pizza box and the six-pack I was carrying almost flew back down the stairs, but somehow I managed to wrap them around her too as we made our way into the living room. I put them down on a coffee table and kissed Emma on the forehead.

"First," I pleaded, "The medical report. What did the doctor say?"

"Well," Emma explained, "It seems I'm in the early stages of a lung condition called emphysema. My coughing and wheezing are classic symptoms that can come and go. The doctor gave me some medicine and told me to drink lots of water, rest for a couple of days, and get a checkup in a week or so."

"What about these stairs? Will they be too much for you?"

"No. He said the exercise would be good for me."

Cat was giving her a hard look. She rose up to her full five-foot-three, placed her hands on her hips, and demanded, "And what else?"

"Oh yes, I'm supposed to cut back on my smoking."

"Not quite," scolded Cat. "Come on now."

"All right, all right. I'm supposed to quit."

"And what's that in the ashtray?"

Emma held out both hands in mock surrender. "I'm doing it gradually. Okay?"

Quickly and strategically, she changed the subject. "Now, Steve, tell us everything. We've seen the TV and we read the morning papers, but now we need the real story." Cat sat back down and turned to me.

I recounted all of Saturday's events, even the carnival nightmare they triggered. The only thing I left out was the vomiting. As I recalled the brutal attacks on the protesters, I found myself wondering whether these events had actually occurred. I saw them in my mind's eye, but now in dreamlike sequences. After answering their questions, I asked, "Is that what was on the news?"

"No," Emma replied. "The coverage showed patriotic soldiers defending the homeland from attack by commies, anarchists and hippies."

"So then, what was the point of it all?"

"This was a movement-building event," she explained. "You had all those people bonding together, absorbing the strength of their numbers. The concept of escalating, 'From Dissent to Resistance,' took tangible form. And when the Iron Heel struck down at the Pentagon, many thousands, including you, began your education into the underbelly of U.S. power. Now, people are coming back home with stories to tell, some with scars to show for it. And the Resistance will be stronger for that."

She reached for a cigarette, but Cat grabbed her wrist. Clearly, she had taken charge of Emma's recovery. Her love, devotion and concern struck me as absolutely beautiful.

"Okay, okay," Emma surrendered. "But now, Steve, do you think you would've been so shaken by all this if you hadn't grown up *white* in America?"

Her question brought back my encounter with Marcellus. I summarized our long conversation on the bus, and his remark that I'd discovered "a tiny sliver of the Black experience."

"I know this has been painful," Emma said, "but consider it a gift. You have a new pair of eyeglasses now. When you wear them, you'll see the world as it truly is, instead of how you've been conditioned to see it. But you must remember to keep those glasses on, even if they're uncomfortable, even if they hurt, if you really want to penetrate the fog."

"By the way," she added, "Marcellus Hopkins is a remarkable young man. If he's invited you to stay in touch, do it. You can learn a lot from him."

"How do you know Marcellus?" I asked.

"He visited the shop right after the BSU brought him on. I spotted real leadership potential right away. Since then, he drops in every once in a while. We talk, and we pick out books together. I've come to really value his insights."

Coming from Emma, this was quite a recommendation, but it only reinforced what I already thought. Now, though, Nurse Cat decided this had gone on long enough.

"Emma," she said, "you've had a long, stressful day, what with the hospital and the news reports and all. It's time to lie down, maybe with a good book. I'll bring you a glass of warm milk."

"Well, I am getting a little tired," Emma conceded. "But let's make our next Circle gathering an evaluation of yesterday's events. We still don't know what happened to those who got arrested, but I'm sure some were from Midway and hopefully they'll be back. Invite your new friend, Marcellus, to join us."

Cat led me to the door, and gave me a hug. "Emma's a very lucky girl," I remarked.

"And so am I," came her quick response.

Now I was feeling lucky too. That night, I stayed up late, reading *The Souls of Black Folk*.

As the week unfolded, Emma seemed to be on the mend. She was spending more time each day in the shop and hardly coughing at all, except when she was smoking. She tried to minimize that when Cat was present, but to little avail. Once, while I was visiting, Cat got so frustrated and angry that she suddenly walked out, slamming the door behind her. Emma said I should go too.

"I can handle things here now," she said. "Midterm exams are coming, and you need to study." She was right about that, since schoolwork was sometimes the last thing on my mind. I wondered, though, whether she really just wanted time alone with her Newports.

During the next few days, I did concentrate on studying. The only break I took was to pop into the BSU office to see if Marcellus was there. He wasn't, but one of the members told me he was at the SSO.

Chicago's South Side began only a block from the Midway campus, but it was in another world. The houses here were walk-up tenements, and it seemed every block had a building advertising "Hotel: Hourly Rates," with at least one letter hanging off or missing. Small liquor stores, poolrooms and storefront churches also abounded, sometimes side by side. Jukebox music poured out the open doors of tiny bars. Much of the commercial activity was not in the stores at all, but out on the corners, where drugs and prostitution seemed to be big business.

The SSO building occupied almost half a block. Inside, I spotted Marcellus sitting in a corner, talking with three young men. I sensed suspicious eyes on me as I walked across the floor, apparently the only white person in the place. Marcellus welcomed me, though, and invited me into his office. Behind the desk hung a poster of Muhammad Ali, with a quote dated April 1967:

> *My conscience won't let me shoot some poor hungry people in the mud for big powerful America. And shoot them for what? They never called me nigger.*

I told him I did read *The Souls of Black Folk*, and summarized some of Sunday night's discussion with Cat and Emma. "It all fits in with what you said on the bus," I concluded. "I wanted you to know."

"I guess you got a lot to think about," he responded.

"I sure do. Emma says I've been given a new set of eyeglasses, and I'll see things a lot more clearly if I keep them on."

"I like that," he said. "But don't be surprised if they pinch at times."

I asked if he would join us at Tuesday night's gathering of The Circle. He accepted the invitation, and asked, "Would it be okay to bring someone along?"

"Of course it is. Do you have someone special in mind?"

"Sharon Sheppard. You should meet her."

"Who's that?"

"Well, she's an International Affairs major, absolutely brilliant, and the new president of the BSU. She's also a single mom. I don't know how she does it."

As I was leaving, he asked, "By the way, did I mention who gave me my copy of *The Souls of Black Folk*?"

"No, I don't think so."
"That was Emma Gold."

Chapter 12

Even though it was midterm week, Emma's meeting room was packed. It was standing room only.

Next to Marcellus sat a tall, slim, attractive woman who I supposed was Sharon Sheppard. Her skin tone was café au lait, her hair natural, cut short. Surprisingly, what struck me most was her posture. While most college students tended to slump into a variety of slouches, she sat ramrod straight, legs crossed, hands folded on a knee. Her bearing imparted a powerful, confident presence.

Emma kicked things off. "We have a full house tonight and limited time. Also, we have an agenda. We need to get to an understanding of what happened in Washington, and what it means for the antiwar movement's future. So I've asked Jeff Rosen to chair this discussion. I'm told he's very experienced at this kind of thing."

As she sat back down and Jeff stood, someone called out, "Right. He's the chairman of everything!" Jeff glared while others laughed or clapped. "Let's start," he began, "with reports from the front. By now, we know what happened at the Lincoln Memorial and on the march to the Pentagon. Let's hear what happened after the arrests. Nicky?"

Nicky Jarvis's left arm was in a sling. "After the soldiers and marshals beat us up," he reported, "they dragged us to a loading dock and threw us into paddy wagons and troop transports. We rode for about half an hour to what looked like a big warehouse."

"Once we were inside, they separated out the wounded and took us to a small field hospital. We got patched up, and our broken bones got set. We were about a thousand, mostly young, but not all. A famous author got arrested with us: Norman Mailer. Anyway, they marched us deep into the building to a huge room filled with cots, a mega-dormitory. It was attached to a big bathroom, like the ones at the highway rest stops. Then they locked the doors."

People called out questions. "How long were you there?" "How'd you get out?" "Was there food?" "What'd you do?"

After Jeff calmed things down, Nicky continued "The prisoners' mood was buoyant at first. We were together, we were alive, and we were warm. We quickly adopted a policy of non-cooperation. That led to singing, kidding around and game-playing. But we were exhausted, and people started dropping off to sleep."

"In the morning, they herded us into a big cafeteria. After breakfast, it was straight back to the dorm. That's when the arguing began. Some said we'd already made our point, and we should give them our names so we'd get released. Others yelled that would be selling out, and we should stay there until they gave up and let us go. One faction even argued for a breakout. It was getting crazy."

"Even Jeff couldn't get this under control. There were too many of us, and everyone had an opinion. By Thursday, the only consensus we'd reached was that we were getting sick and tired of one another. Finally, two men in suits came in. One was an attorney for the Mobe who told us he'd struck a deal with the feds. If we plead 'no contest' to a misdemeanor charge, we'll be fined ten dollars and get suspended ten-day jail sentences. Thanks to a donor, the Mobe could cover our fines and we'll be on our way home."

"Some called this a sellout, but that didn't get anywhere. We were bored, we were tired, and nearly all of us wanted out. The other suit was a federal judge. He told us to line up at the tables out front and sign a paper. Then we'd be free to go."

"So that's how it ended. Depending on our destinations, the trucks took us to either the bus station or the train station, and we had to figure out our own way to get home. For some, that meant hitchhiking, but we all got out of that town as fast as we could."

Jeff retook the floor, and invited a few questions. Once those were answered, he moved on. "Now that we're up to date on what happened, let's talk about what happens next. Where does the Movement, the Resistance, go from here? How are we gonna stop this fucking war?"

There was no shortage of ideas. Listening, I roughly divided the debaters into two schools of thought, which I labeled the "Base-Builders" and the "Fifth-Columnists."

The Base-Builders pushed building the mass movement as the main priority. "Once our movement reaches a critical mass," one said, "the pressure on the politicians will be too much to resist. If the president doesn't end the war, Congress will refuse to fund it. In the meantime, we need to keep getting people involved, in whatever way they can. We need boycotts, like the one around Saran Wrap. We need tax refusal. We need draft resistance. We need a million people demonstrating in Washington, and ten million letters to Congress."

To the Fifth-Columnists, this was a fantasy. "Do you have any idea how many billions of dollars the big corporations are making off this war?" asked one, rhetorically. "Congress is accountable to the money, not to the people. And letters to Congress ain't worth the paper they're written on. They'll only end this war when the cost of dragging it out is more than what they and their corporate clients get from it. That means we have to *bring the war home*. No war-related corporation should be allowed to recruit, on or off campus. Same for the military. Banks that handle blood money shouldn't get the people's money. Chase ROTC off the campuses. We need to turn young people against imperialism, against their parents, and in support of the Viet Cong."

"You can't build a mass movement in this country," someone interjected, "by waving around the flag of the country's enemy."

"You can build your mass movement, if you want," called another, "but that'll never end the war. The war will end when the Vietnamese win it, which they eventually will. How does that happen? It happens when the body bags pile up so high that the U.S. can't sustain it any more. Wars are won and lost on the battlefield, not on the National Mall. We need to help the VC right here."

I found myself agreeing with both sides, even though they weren't compatible. I hoped Emma might reconcile the differences. She and Cat got up from their seats, though, and headed for the door. As they passed, Cat whispered, "She's drained. I'll help get her settled downstairs and then I need to study for an exam tomorrow. Can you close up?"

I agreed, and looked at my watch. It was past eleven. I remembered my Western Civ midterm was at nine in the morning.

As the debate wore on, people started drifting out. The arguments continued, but nothing was resolved. It was well past midnight when everyone remaining agreed we should call it a night.

But when I got into bed, I couldn't fall asleep. The world around me was crumbling, and my lifelong supports were disappearing. The last time I looked at the clock, the hour hand was on the five.

At 8:30, I woke with a start. However groggy I was, I had a half-hour to wash up and get to the exam. I managed to stumble through the door seconds before the teacher locked it and handed out the tests.

I was on time, but something didn't seem right. Some of the material was completely unfamiliar. I looked up and noticed my professor wasn't in the room. I looked around, not recognizing my classmates. Suddenly, it hit me. I was in the wrong room!

I approached the teacher and asked, "This isn't 304, is it?"

"No," he replied. "It's 302."

I handed him the exam book, unlocked the door and let myself out.

The door to 304 was, as I expected, locked, so I waited in the hallway until the class period ended. Then I explained to Professor Lane what happened.

"Missing in action gets you a zero," he asserted, "whatever your excuse."

In a panic now, I pleaded with him to give me a break. I argued I was there on time, only not in the right place. I told him I'd studied hard, and I'd lose my financial aid if I failed the course. He seemed irritated.

"All right, here's what we'll do," he said. "You get yourself here tomorrow morning at eight, and I'll give you a makeup test. However, the highest grade you can hope for on a makeup is a C."

I did more studying, took the exam, and got a C-minus. Fortunately, I did better in my other classes, so at mid-semester, I was tracking at least in the neighborhood of my holy grail, the 3.0 average. I knew I'd have to manage my time more wisely, but I had no brilliant ideas how.

Cat got A's on all her exams. I suspected she'd never gotten anything less.

Chapter 13

Now the Thanksgiving weekend was approaching. This was a "command appearance" in my family, and I'd have to go back to Waterloo for the long weekend. Emma had planned a New York City trip to visit friends and spend time with her daughter. But Cat had nowhere to go. I couldn't leave her all by herself, with no family, alone on a big family holiday.

So I called home. First, I asked Mom what we had planned. I hoped the answer might be, "Nothing this year," so I could stay in Chicago.

"Oh, there'll only be a few of us," she answered. "Your Uncle Harry and Aunt Belle will be here and, of course, Cousin Richard."

I thought that was just peachy. Harry was in some kind of money business, and loved to talk about how much of it he claimed to be making. Belle came to family gatherings draped in tasteless, gaudy, glittery things that Harry's money could buy. And Richard was the older cousin I'd always been compared to. I thought he was a jerk, but somehow I always came up short in the competition. How many times had I heard, "Why can't you be more like Richard?"

I suppressed a groan and asked, "Would it be okay if I bring a friend?"

"Of course! No-one's used the guest bedroom in years, and we'd be happy to meet one of your new friends."

I reported this to Cat and invited her to go with me. I also warned her about the family dynamics, and said I'd appreciate some support.

"So would I," she responded. "Family holidays without my parents have been tough. I'd love to spend this one with you, and meet your parents."

On Thursday, we talked through the entire five-hour bus ride. It was late afternoon when the door of the house I grew up in flew open. My mom stood there, beaming, her arms spread for a big "welcome home" hug. Then she saw Cat.

I got the hug, but it felt more tentative than expected. I introduced Cat.

"So nice to meet you. Please come in." I detected a drop in temperature. "Steve, why don't you show Cat – is that right, Cat? – to her room."

Upstairs, Cat wanted to needed to freshen up after the trip. I told her to take her time, dropped my bag in my old room and returned downstairs.

Mom grabbed my arm in the kitchen. "You didn't tell me," she whispered sharply, as though the neighbors shouldn't hear this, "you were bringing a *girlfriend*."

"Just a friend," I cheerfully explained, while hoping that would soon become a lie.

"Really!" she exclaimed. "And that's not all, is it?"

"What's not all?"

"Never mind. Go ahead into the dining room. Dinner's almost ready, and the family is waiting."

No surprises there. Rich Uncle Harry was carrying on about some big deal he closed, commanding the total attention of not only my dad, but also his wife and son, who'd probably heard this story a hundred times. I gave Dad a quick hug and took a seat.

"Well, the prodigal son returns!" bellowed Uncle Harry with a self-satisfied air of originality. "How's Chicago treating you?"

"Not bad," I replied. "Winter is only beginning, and school, you know, is school."

"I guess it is. Speaking of school, did you know Richard got accepted at the Harvard Business School? Yup, he'll be a Harvard MBA!" Richard sat there smirking. I didn't have a good reason, but still I wanted to slap it right off his face.

"Wow, gee, terrific," I squeezed out. "Congratulations, Richard."

He nodded. I was wondering why I couldn't simply call him *Dick*, when Cat appeared. In only a few minutes, she'd done something with her hair and makeup, and put on hoop earrings, a simple necklace and a long black dress ending at a pair of high-heeled boots. She looked like a movie star, and I felt like a *schlump*. I stared for only a few seconds, then took her arm, led her to a seat and introduced the family.

"This is my good friend, Cat." Time froze for a moment. So did the room's temperature.

"Welcome to our little family," said Aunt Belle as Cat sat down. "So tell me, what kind of a name is Cat?"

She picked up the vibes right away. "Oh, it's short for Catherine," she answered breezily.

"Oh, that's cute. And where are your people from?"

"From the United States: California and South Carolina. I grew up in Detroit, though."

I already regretted bringing her here, but she was more than holding her own. Thankfully, Mom came in with the turkey and trimmings, and the evening turned to the holiday rituals of carving, passing dishes, piling plates and gluttony. Cat only picked at her food, but remarked at how delicious it all tasted. Me, I was getting nauseous.

After enduring the dinner, Cat helped clear the table for dessert. Dad called me into the den.

"What's the matter with you?" he demanded, again in a strong whisper, the necessity of which I still wasn't able to fathom. "You say you're bringing a friend. Then you show up with a girlfriend. Not only a *shiksa* you bring us. A *schvartze*, yet! And on a big family holiday, in front of Harry and Belle and Richard! Your mother is very upset."

"*Schvartze*." The word resounded in my head. I'd heard this Yiddish term all my life. Its literal translation is "Black." But this was the first time I heard the ugly racist contempt it harbored.

So now it was out in the open, at least between the two of us. I made a spot tactical decision to retreat.

"Sorry, Dad, I guess I should've warned you."

I headed back to the dining room, thinking about what to do. I knew putting Cat in the middle of a family confrontation would do more harm than good. So I came up with what I thought was a better idea, an exit strategy.

When I got a moment alone with Cat, I related the brief aside with my father.

"What's a *shiksa*?" she asked.

"That's a non-Jewish girl."

"Oh. And a *schvartze?*"

"It's the Yiddish word for *nigger*," I replied without thinking. "Cat," I blurted, "I'm so sorry I put you in the middle of this. We shouldn't have come here. I expected the usual family tensions, but I never, ever thought you'd be treated so shoddily." She put a finger on my lips to stop me.

"I wasn't all that surprised," she said. "I was ready for it. I've been dealing with those attitudes for as long as I can remember."

"Well, you sure dealt with this group, and you sure made me proud to be at your side. But we can't stay here through the weekend. We'll escape in the morning. Here's my plan..."

Dessert wasn't any better. Cousin *Dick* asked, "What are you studying at Midway, Catherine?"

"Well, it might change, but right now I'm studying to become a mathematician."

"Really? What do they do? Financial analysis? Stock predictions?"

"Well, not that I know of. What interests me the most are theoretical problems that have defied solution for centuries. Sometimes, at the highest levels, the challenge is to determine whether they can be solved at all."

"Where's the money in that?" challenged one-dimensional Uncle Harry.

"Good question," she conceded with an innocent look. "Maybe when I grow up, I'll give that more thought. For now, I'm just fascinated by the puzzles of the universe."

"But I do know," she added, "that we can trace all technological and scientific advances back to pure thought, which at first appeared to have no practical application. Look at how relativity theory and quantum physics are changing the world right now."

No-one at the table wanted to get into that, so they simply nodded and mumbled recognition of something they knew nothing about. At the first opportunity, I launched my exit strategy. "Cat doesn't live entirely in the world of theory," I told them. "She also has a job helping a sick old lady who doesn't have any family."

She caught on right away. "Yes, Miss Ella's very nice, and I'm happy to be there for her. I arranged a fill-in worker for this weekend, but I did promise to call each morning to make sure everything's okay. Would you mind, Mrs. Harris?"

"Oh, of course not," said Mom. "I'm sure she's lucky to have such a responsible aide. Use the house phone anytime."

After breakfast Friday morning, Cat asked for the phone to check up on her "client." She dialed random numbers and held the receiver to her ear. A few seconds later, she spoke some words, stopped as though to listen and registered alarm. We watched as she tearfully hung up the phone.

"Miss Ella has taken a turn for the worse," she reported. "And my fill-in doesn't know what to do. I told her I was coming back, and to call for an ambulance if she needs one. Steve, can you come with me? I might need your help."

I hesitated. Looking pained, I said, "Of course I will."

Then, to Mom and Dad, "I'm sorry we have to go so soon, but it does sound like an emergency."

"No problem, son," Dad said. "Get your stuff together, and I'll drive you to the bus station." They looked as relieved at our quick exit as we were.

Chapter 14

The ride back to Chicago began quietly. Neither of us had slept well overnight, and we soon dozed off. I loved the warmth of Cat's lean little body tilting into mine as she slept. I was troubled, though, by my failure to anticipate what I'd gotten her into. She suspected what might lay ahead, she came with me anyway, and she played it like a violin. But that didn't excuse me. Why did my own parents' racism take me by surprise? I knew I'd never feel the same way about them after this.

When I woke, Cat was reading quantum theory. I remembered Emma had loaned me a new book: *The Man Who Cried I Am* by John A. Williams. I pulled it out of my bag and began reading too. I always enjoyed reading, and sharing that pleasure with Cat made it even better. But now, concentrating was difficult. I closed the book.

"Cat, I'm so stupid," I said. "I should've known this would happen. It's all my fault."

She closed hers too, and asked, "Why are you blaming yourself?"

"Can I tell you a little story?" She nodded.

"About a year ago," I began, "I got a Saturday job unloading produce trucks at a supermarket. The rest of the crew was three Black guys: Eddie, Junior and Quinn. At first, they ignored me. That made me uncomfortable, but I focused on the work. After a few weeks working as a team, though, we did start talking, and soon began hanging out together after work. They were all a little older than me and none of them finished high school, so we didn't have very much in common. But we sort of 'clicked' together."

"Where do your parents come in?" Cat asked.

"I'll get to that. When summer came, I started working with them full-time. One of Eddie's cousins, a trucking company dispatcher, lined up jobs for us. When we weren't working, we played cards, shot pool, pitched coins, all the stuff guys did together. I met their families too."

"Did they meet yours?"

"That's the thing. My parents didn't approve of any of this. They said, first of all, I shouldn't be doing manual labor. And secondly, I should have friends who are 'on my level.' They were sure this 'phase' of mine would end when I left for college. 'Then you'll make friends who are on your level,' Dad once said.

"So I thought when they saw I had a friend as brilliant and articulate, as beautiful, as you, someone so clearly *above* my level," I continued as Cat blushed a little, "it would make them happy. When they behaved so cold and awkward with you, it confused me at first. I guessed they weren't expecting to see a girl. I didn't really get it until I heard that word, that ugly, awful word."

"*Schvartze?*" Cat asked.

"Right. They didn't object to my friends because they were uneducated. It was because they were Black. Why didn't I see that? I'm so stupid."

"Think about it, Steve. Why didn't you see it?"

"I don't know. We watched the civil rights movement unfolding on TV together. They never made openly racist comments, or at least I didn't hear any. I guess I didn't want to hear any of that."

"That's what it was, Steve. You weren't stupid. But you were deaf to things you didn't want to hear, and blind to things you didn't want to see, things that would've damaged your respect for your parents."

I gave her words a moment's thought, then concluded, "That's it, Cat. Deaf and blind. Deaf, *dumb* and blind."

Cat patted me on the cheek, and we returned to our reading. After a while, though, I noticed her book was closed, her eyes half-shut. She was frowning and, I thought, trembling a little bit. I asked if something was wrong.

"Please hold me, Steve." I did. The trembling got worse at first, but it subsided after a few minutes. She pushed away and sat back up, wiping her eyes.

"Cat, what is it?" I asked.

"I'm so frightened," she replied.

"Frightened of what?"

"You had a choice to make back there, and you chose me. You didn't have to."

"So that scares you? I don't get it."

"Look, you know I miss my parents every day. Besides them, the only people who ever really cared for me are you and Emma. Now Emma's sick. I know she's had a pretty good week, but I also know she has a disease that doesn't get better."

"I know that too," I said, "and we'll do the best we can for her. She's important to me too. But I told you I'd always be there for you, and you just told me that's what I did back at the house. So why is this scary?"

"Why? Don't you remember what happened at the Pentagon? I couldn't sleep that night, up worrying you might've gotten your head cracked open. Or worse. If Marcellus didn't block your path, that's what would've happened. And there was all that revolutionary talk at The Circle. You're attracted to that. I saw it in your eyes. I didn't leave early to study that night. I left because it scared me you'd get involved with something dangerous. It was too much for me. I can't handle another loss. I don't think I could go on living with that much pain."

After I looked into her eyes and promised I wouldn't let that happen, she curled up in my arm. We quietly moved together with the bump and roll of the bus. Hearing Cat tell me I was that important to her filled me with contentment and warmth. I felt I wasn't completely in control of my life, though, and hoped I'd be able to make good on my promise.

Chapter 15

On the way from the bus station, first on the subway and then a short walk, Cat grew silent again. I sensed she was wrestling with herself about something, and that I shouldn't intervene. When we reached her front door, it was time for me to go. But that was the last thing I wanted to do. What a relief it was when she asked, "Would you like to come in?"

Would I ever! "Sure," I answered quickly. "Here, let me carry your bag up the stairs."

Cat's apartment was simply furnished. The living room had a couch, two chairs and a coffee table. Opposite was a desk made of a hollow door spanning two small file cabinets, with a typewriter in the center and flanked by bookcases. A TV sat on a rolling cart in a corner. There was an open eat-in kitchen. A closed door led to, I guessed, a bedroom.

I asked, "Was this furniture here when you moved in?"

"Yes, it was. Emma told me the tenants recently disappeared. They left a note of apology, telling her they were leaving the country. She thought they were drug dealers in some kind of trouble. Anyway, they took some clothing and personal items, but left everything else behind. The closet was full of clothes in my size, so I sort of inherited them too. And some of those things must've been expensive."

Asking about the furniture was mainly a way to fill the empty space of my unease. I didn't know what I was supposed to do. Now that I'd brought her bag upstairs and seen the apartment, was it time to say good-night and leave?

"Make yourself comfortable," she said. "I'll bring you something to drink." That made it easier. I sat down on the couch.

Cat came back with two glasses of white wine. We both drank, me on the couch and her still standing, looking down at me with an expression I hadn't seen before. I put the empty glass on the table. *Now what?*

She emptied hers too, then came over to the couch and sat down. *On my lap!* She wrapped her arms around me and buried her face in my neck. Instantly, I sprang to attention, wondering if she could feel it through my jeans. Next, her lips found mine, her tongue snaking its way in. We held that kiss until we had to come up for air. I took her head in my hands and gently kissed her forehead, her eyelids, her cheeks, her nose, her ears, her chin. She pulled away and stared into my eyes for a moment, then stood up and took my hand in hers.

"Come," she said, leading the way to the bedroom.

I was bursting for action by now, but Cat first whispered, "Slowly, slowly, please. My first time."

I undressed her piece by piece, anointing each revealed body part with caresses, soft kisses and occasional little nips. Naked, we tumbled into the bed. My fingers, lips, and tongue explored every square inch of her body. It was everything I'd imagined it to be. Pert little breasts and the sweet valley between them, the gentle curve of her tight belly, firm buttocks sculpted perfectly to fit my hands. From the crown of her head to her tasty little toes, nothing escaped my attention. The phrase, *Butterscotch Goddess*, zoomed across my brain. The torture was exquisite. After a blissful eternity, Cat whispered, "Now," and we became one.

Waking the next morning, I at first didn't know where I was, but I had a memory of a most beautiful dream. Cat came through the door with two steaming mugs of coffee, and sat next to me. We kissed, breathed in the aroma of the fresh coffee, slid over until our bodies were touching, and sipped. *So this*, I thought, *is what heaven must feel like.*

As I set the empty cup down on the nightstand, reality broke in. Cat reacted to the change in my expression when I turned back. "What's wrong?" she asked.

It took a moment until I responded. "This just hit me. We had no protection last night. I don't even keep a condom in my wallet. I might've gotten you pregnant. What are we gonna do?"

"Sure we had protection," she replied, calmly.

"We did? How?"

"When I was with Emma in the hospital, waiting for you to get back from Washington, not knowing what might've happened, Emma noticed how worried I was. We had a talk about my feelings for you, how I was trying to resist them, how my resistance was already breaking down."

"I didn't know any of this was going on," I said.

"Of course not. You were the last person I'd have wanted to know. Anyway, Emma insisted I go downstairs to the clinic and get a prescription for birth control pills. 'Just in case,' she said."

"And you did?"

"Of course I did. That was no time for an argument. I've been taking the pills for over a month now."

"It sure didn't seem like you had last night planned."

"Oh, I didn't. Not at all. You saw me wrestling with my feelings yesterday. But by the time we got here, I wanted to be as close to you as I could get."

"I've wanted that for a long time, Cat. But I thought it was only a fantasy. Come here. Come to me."

Our bodies intertwined, I ran my hands up and down her back, marveling that this was happening. Once again, we made sweet, gentle love.

Resting afterward, I had an idea. "Let's do something fun today."

"Something fun?" she asked with a raised eyebrow.

I laughed. "Something else fun."

After breakfast, we visited Renoir, Monet and Van Gogh at the Art Institute, where we picked up brochures. Cat suggested, "Let's be tourists all weekend."

We moved on to the Planetarium, the Field Museum and the new Museum of African-American History. We took a long walk through Grant Park, and a short one on the shoreline. We never left each other's sides, and never ran out of things to talk about. We celebrated each morning and each night by making love. Rising from the ashes of the Thanksgiving Day debacle, it became the greatest weekend of my life.

After Sunday dinner, though, it was back to the dorm for me. We both needed to get ready for school. I hadn't gotten a block from High Street when I became aware of an aching emptiness in the pit of my stomach. This, I instinctively knew, had to be the downside of love.

The big "3.0" poster I'd hung on my wall jolted me back to reality. I tried finishing a computer program, but my mind kept drifting back to Cat. Conceding I wouldn't be able to concentrate on the program, I put it away and moved on to a math assignment. The result was the same. Next, I tried Logic, but found myself reading the same paragraphs over and over again. I didn't even try opening the hated Western Civ book. Instead, I got into bed with a collection of short stories and fell asleep.

I did get to my Monday classes, but found myself unable to focus much better. As soon as the last one ended, I made a beeline for Previously Perused, hoping Cat would be there. We'd been separated for almost twenty hours. For me, that was far too many.

Emma was shelving books. "We were expecting you," she said. "Cat's in the back, studying."

I asked, "How was your weekend?"

"Very good, although a little tiring. It was great having mother-daughter time with Ellie, and I got to see some old friends. And how was yours?" she asked, flashing a wide smile.

"Better than I could ever have expected," I replied, my face lighting up. Obviously, she already knew something. I told her she looked well, and asked about the coughing.

"Much better, thanks. The medication does seem to be helping."

"And the smoking?"

"Still working on it." I rolled my eyes.

"I'll leave you two alone," Emma said. "Cat's in the office, and it's time for my prescribed walk around the block." She locked the door on her way out.

"Hi, Stranger," I called cheerily when Cat was in sight. She looked up but stayed seated, not even happy to see me, it seemed.

Before I got halfway around the desk, she said, "Steve, please sit down. We need to talk." I sat.

"First of all," she began, "you made me happier this weekend than I've been in a long, long time."

"Me too," I blurted. "That's why I ran over here right after class. I haven't been able to concentrate on anything else."

"The same thing happened to me. And in this morning's classes, I was unprepared for the first time. That's why we have to stop seeing each other, at least for a while. If we don't keep our grades up, we'll be out of Midway. For me, that would be a betrayal of my parents' memory, and of everything Emma's done for me. For you, it might mean a one-way ticket to Vietnam."

This was devastating. "Why can't we do both?" I pleaded.

"I hope we'll be able to one day. But for now, we need to slow things down, get some distance so we can get our school lives in order."

"Was this your idea," I asked, "or Emma's?"

Cat put her elbows on the desk and leaned her chin on folded hands. "It sort of grew out of our conversation today. When I came in, she sensed that I was excited and worried at the same time. I told her about our beautiful weekend, but also my worries about school. She suggested we'd both benefit from what she called 'balance'."

I knew I wouldn't be able to talk her out of this, not when the two of them were lined up on the same side. So I tried to mitigate the damage.

"How about we keep apart until the weekend, and then make time to be together? We can see how it works out."

She considered my plea and responded, tentatively, "Well, okay. We can try weekends, but we'll still have schoolwork to do." I thought I detected a note of relief in her eyes, but wasn't sure whether that was wishful thinking.

"But now, you should go. I need to get this work done today."

I forced myself up from the chair. "Can I at least get a hug?"

I did get that. But when I moved to kiss her, she gently pushed me away saying, "Please, Steve. Go now." I looked down and saw her eyes misting over.

I left the shop without looking back, wondering how I could get through the week on my own.

Chapter 16

I decided the only way to survive this arrangement was to plunge into my schoolwork and try not to obsess about Cat. After classes every day, I also spent an hour or so pumping iron at the school's gym. The physical exertion cleared my mind and helped me plan a studying strategy for the evening. When I got back to my room after dinner, I was focused and able to be reasonably productive. Falling asleep was more difficult, so I read until my eyes closed. By Thursday, I'd almost caught up with my classes.

That night, I got a call from Whit. "Turn on the news, quick," he said.

I ran down to the dorm's Common Room where the TV was already on. The breaking news was that a U.S. Senator from Minnesota named Eugene McCarthy announced he would challenge President Johnson for the 1968 Democratic nomination. His overriding issue was opposition to the Vietnam War. "There comes a time," he said, "when an honorable man simply has to raise the flag."

The TV anchor's tone indicated he considered this a quixotic quest, since McCarthy was hardly known nationally and had neither a campaign chest nor an organization. To me, though, this was very big news. It gave us something positive to rally around, a presidential campaign that would be an antiwar crusade.

When the report ended, I called Whit back and asked what he thought about it.

"I'm not completely sure," he said. "I don't know much about him, or how far he'll go. But I heard he'll be making a big speech here in Chicago, tomorrow at five. It's open to the public. Want to go?"

"Sure."

"I'll pick you up at 3:30, so we get there early."

Friday's *Chicago Tribune* reported that McCarthy was a poet in addition to being a politician, and had once been a college professor. In Congress for the past eight years, he wasn't known as a dissenter or a crusader. He'd even voted in favor of war appropriations. I didn't hold that against him. This war was changing how many people think. I knew because I was one of them.

I asked Cat if she wanted to join us.

"I can't," she replied. "I need to take Emma for her checkup. I want to make sure she gets a stern lecture about smoking."

"Hard for me to imagine anyone giving Emma a stern lecture about anything," I remarked.

"I know, but I have to do what I can. This is life or death. You go to the speech. I'll try to catch it on the radio. When it's over, come to me. I'll have dinner ready. Oh, and one more thing."

"What's that?"

"Bring your toothbrush." It had never occurred to me that the mere mention of a toothbrush would trigger a bulge in my pants.

Whit and I got to the Sheraton-Blackstone just in time to get seats in the rear of a large ballroom. The opening speaker was Allard K. Lowenstein, a New York lawyer who'd once led the National Student Association. His speech was a stem-winder, blasting the President and the war, not only for its ever-escalating brutality, but also for its cost, which was draining money from Johnson's own anti-poverty programs. After forty-five minutes, he left the crowd fired up for Senator McCarthy, who received a standing ovation.

When the applause died down, McCarthy gave a speech that could only be described as anti-climactic. The words were fine, but he delivered them in the voice and cadence of an academic, not a politician, and certainly not someone likely to lead an antiwar crusade. It was easy to see why Lowenstein was on the program. His speech, in fact, ran fifteen minutes longer than McCarthy's.

On the way back, Whit asked for my reaction.

"For me, the most important thing is that he sticks with this," I replied, "and makes getting us out of Vietnam the campaign's central issue. He might not be the perfect candidate, but he's going way out on a limb. He deserves to be supported."

"But you know," responded Whit, "he didn't say he'd run in all the primaries, or how he expected to win. We don't know if he even sees a way to win. And a presidential campaign might co-opt all the other antiwar work that's going on."

"I see what you mean. But look, Whit. This war is making me ashamed to be an American. I hate that. If there's even a chance McCarthy can shorten the war, we should go with it. I want to be proud of my country again. I remember when I was, and it felt a lot better than how I feel now."

Later, Cat and I embraced like we'd been separated for four months, not four days. I asked what happened at Emma's doctor visit.

"He told us she's holding her own, and should keep taking the same medicine."

"And the smoking?"

"He was very firm. He even said each cigarette is shortening her life by the amount of time it takes to smoke it. She listened respectfully and thanked him. But as soon as we got outside, she reached for a Newport. I stopped her, but it drives me crazy."

"I know it does. Me too, but we can only do the best we can. I guess Emma will only quit when she really wants to, or has to."

"Yes," Cat tentatively agreed, "if it's not too late."

"What's her opinion of McCarthy?"

"She's kind of skeptical, but said she's looking forward to hearing from the young people at The Circle."

The weekend flew by, much too quickly. Sunday night, it was once again back to the dorm for me. I didn't see Cat again until Tuesday night, at a crowded gathering of The Circle, where opinions about McCarthy's candidacy abounded.

Larry Graff waved around a newspaper. "It says here," he said, "that LBJ is ahead of him by a 4-1 margin."

"It means nothing," countered Emma. "First of all, the campaign has hardly begun, and people don't yet know who he is. Second, McCarthy doesn't have to win. Just a strong showing might trigger enough political pressure to push the president into changing direction. It's a long shot, but it's something."

"Also," added Jeff, "the primaries go state by state. If antiwar forces can focus on each of them, one at a time, we can have a serious impact."

"But Illinois doesn't even hold a primary," said someone, "and most of us are too young to vote anyway."

"Right," called out another. "We can get drafted when we're eighteen, but can't vote 'til we're twenty-one!"

"But we can campaign and help turn out the antiwar vote," said Whit. "The first primary will be in Wisconsin. That's not too far from here, and it's only three months away."

"Whit, why don't you check in with your friends up in Madison?" asked Emma. "See what they're planning to do. Ask if they need help." He agreed.

"Here's what worries me," argued SDS's Nicky Jarvis. "We've built a big antiwar movement based on two things: education and *action*. If our actions weren't having an impact, McCarthy wouldn't even be running. But if they stop because all our energy is focused on an electoral strategy, the movement will dry up and we'll be weaker than when we started."

This sparked a lively discussion. A consensus emerged that it would be a mistake to give up any antiwar activity because of this campaign, and that we needed to put pressure not only on LBJ, but also on McCarthy to stay the course.

"But if we go too far, like that attack on the Pentagon," asked someone, "won't it turn people against us and discredit McCarthy?"

"No, it will probably strengthen him," Emma responded. "McCarthy won't associate himself with violence, or even militancy. If people are turned off by such tactics, they're likely to see him as the more acceptable alternative. Moderate civil rights groups get lots of money from white liberals afraid that Blacks might turn to SNCC or the Black Nationalists. Dr. King even raised that dynamic in his *Letter From a Birmingham Jail*. It's the same thing. Anyway, most of the antiwar work is perfectly peaceful."

"That reminds me," said Sabrina. "Our Saran Wrap Boycott committee has been leafleting shoppers at the supermarket. We're getting a great response. People who never heard of Napalm are horrified when we tell them about it. We want to make this an everyday thing, from four to six o'clock, but we need more people for that."

I announced, "I can do Thursdays," and others joined in.

After the meeting ended, I left with Cat, but got no further than her door. "School night," she said, kissing me on the cheek before she went inside and closed it. *So near and yet so far,* I thought.

Chapter 17

Sabrina was right about the Saran Wrap campaign. Many peak-hour shoppers were in too much of a hurry to talk to us, but most accepted our leaflet. Among those who gave us a moment for explanation, the reaction was overwhelmingly positive. We even persuaded some people who were ambivalent or apathetic about the war itself to live without Saran Wrap. No-one we met tried to defend burning the skin off children.

Sabrina, a tall, slim redhead, very attractive, whose artistic sensibilities extended to her choice of clothing and accessories, was particularly effective with the men. Some seemed flattered when she approached them, and she periodically attracted knots of listeners. Few were too busy to stop and talk to her, and most walked away holding the leaflet.

Whatever the shoppers' reasons for considering our campaign and joining the boycott, I hoped Emma was right about a small step like this leading possibly to larger actions.

Friday night, I arrived at Cat's door with both my toothbrush and my books. She'd invited Emma to join us for dinner, on condition that she leaves her Newports downstairs. We phoned in an order to a Chinese restaurant. When it arrived, we worked our way through a maze of little paper containers, passing things around and eating way too much.

At one point, Emma said, "By the way, Cat, we have a little mystery. A private detective came in today, asking where you lived. Of course I asked why. He said he wasn't at liberty to tell anyone except you, but he needed your address so the matter could be explained in writing. To me, it sounded a little suspicious. I told him I couldn't divulge any personal information, but that you get your mail here at the shop. He said his employer, a law firm, would be in touch. Any idea what this could be?"

"Absolutely none," Cat replied. "I don't even know any lawyers."

When Emma tired, I offered to walk her downstairs. I wanted to make sure she'd be okay, but I also wanted to talk to her alone. She took the steps very slowly, her breathing a little labored, so I didn't say anything until we got inside her door.

"Emma," I blurted, "this 'balance' thing with Cat is driving me crazy. And she can be so strict enforcing it."

She seemed to know this was coming. "Look," she responded, "I know you two are madly in love. I can see it, and I support it. You're very good for one another. And, God knows, she deserves some joy in her life."

"So what's the problem?"

"I'm not too old to forget the obsessive nature of new young love. That's where the problem is."

"How?"

"Each of you have three very important things in your lives: your education, ending the war, and each other. If these three things aren't kept in balance, they'll all suffer. Right now, if you and Cat spend as much time enjoying each other as you'd like to, you'll both flunk out of Midway. Chances are, if that happens, you'll one day blame each other for it. Let your imagination take it from there. And remember, for you two, failure isn't averaging a D or an F. It's B-minus."

"Of course, your antiwar work would suffer too. On the other hand, if you poured all your energy into that, your relationship would die on the vine and, again, you'd be out of school. But if you spent every minute of every day on schoolwork, you wouldn't have much of a life at all."

"I can see your point," I said. "But this is so hard. How do people do it?"

"With difficulty, if they have to deal with it at all. This level of passion doesn't touch everyone, you know. But the problem you're having now is temporary. The crazy obsessive phase will pass once you're more settled together. You won't love each other any less, but you'll be able to handle life together without artificial rules. The balance will come more naturally."

"But when will that be?"

"You'll know when it happens."

"Thank you, Emma," I said, not quite satisfied. "I'll sure be looking forward to that day."

I took the stairs two at a time going back up. "What took so long?" Cat asked. "I was getting worried."

"I needed to talk to Emma, and it took a little longer than I expected. She explained this 'balance' thing to me, and said we won't need these rules forever."

"Anything else?"

"Yes. She said you and I are madly in love with each other. I realized I haven't used those words."

"No, you haven't."

I looked straight into her eyes. "Listen carefully, Cat. I. Am. Madly. In love. With you."

"And I'm madly in love with you," she said. "Now, let's go to bed."

It was a glorious weekend, even with a little bit of "balance."

Shortly after I arrived back at the dorm, Marcellus rescued me from the Western Civ book with an invitation to join him for a beer.

"First of all," he began once we got settled at Pete's Tavern, "I have a book for you." He handed over Richard Wright's *Native Son*, which he told me was set in Chicago. I thanked him.

"No thanks necessary," he said. "When you're finished with it, just return it to Previously Perused."

"I don't know how Emma makes any money," I wondered out loud. "She's supposed to be selling books, not loaning them out for free. I hope she doesn't do this with everyone. Do you get there often?"

"Oh, I drop in every once in a while. I like talking to her."

"So you've met Cat?" He said he had.

When I told him she and I were a couple now, he remarked, "You're a lucky guy. She's really something."

"Right on both counts," I agreed. "Are you seeing anyone now?"

"Sharon and I have been spending time together, but I don't know where it's going. I'm attracted to her, but I don't think she's gotten over Sammy yet."

"Sammy?"

"This is a sensitive subject," he explained. "People see Sharon raising her daughter on her own. They make assumptions: promiscuity; paternal abandonment; drugs; prison. But Sammy was a good husband and a good father too."

"So what happened?"

"He worked as a para-legal at South Side Legal Aid. One day, he was explaining to some knucklehead why he'd lost custody of his kids. The guy pulled a gun and shot him point-blank. Their little Arielle wasn't even two years old."

"My God! Can you ever get over something like that?"

"I don't know. Luckily, Sharon got an insurance settlement that allowed her to go back to school, though. Otherwise, she might still be a waitress."

"With her height and looks," I suggested, "I'd think she could've been a model."

"You're right. She certainly could've been, if she was white. But she's a strong, resourceful woman and a great mom. Arielle is everything to her now. I'm just happy to be her friend."

"Anyway," he continued, "let me tell you why I wanted to get together tonight. The South Side Organization got a federal grant to run an after-school program for junior high school kids. We've been recruiting tutors for about a month. But we need help with math, so I thought of you."

"But don't you want real math teachers doing this?"

His eyes flashed as he pounded the table. I hadn't seen him like this before.

"That was our original idea for the whole program. But it went nowhere when we approached the teachers! We did recruit a few Black teachers, but there aren't many of those to begin with. Most of the white teachers scoot out of the neighborhood as soon as the dismissal bell rings. And when we met with parents, they brought up something I should've thought of in the first place."

"What was that?"

"One mother summed it up best. She said, 'Our kids are behind 'cause their teachers don't teach'em nothin' during the school day. What makes you think somethin' different will happen after school?' I had no answer for that. So we have a few Black teachers, some parents, and a few students from the BSU. Where we've come up empty is math. Interested?"

"I can try it," I replied. "But not until after final exams."

"The program starts in January, so that's fine. How about giving it a try during intersession? Let's say from three to five, Monday, Wednesday, Friday, and Saturday?"

"Okay," I agreed, "except for Saturday." I was willing to cut into studying time, but not into my limited time with Cat. "If it goes well, I'll try to schedule next semester's classes around the after-school sessions."

"That's a deal," he said, grinning and standing to shake hands. After we parted, I realized I never asked what this job pays.

The Christmas break was coming, and final exams would begin right afterward. The only subject that worried me was Western Civ. The textbook and lectures were mind-numbingly dull. I needed to do well on the final, though, after landing a C-minus on the makeup midterm. I went to see Professor Lane in his office, hoping to get some studying tips or at least show him I cared about the course, which I really didn't except for the grade.

"I'll tell you what to do," he growled, "but you won't do it."

"What's that?"

"The best way to prepare for the final is to outline the entire textbook, and use that outline for studying. Since you'll have written down the important facts, you'll be more likely to remember them. But, like I said, you'll never do that."

I thanked him and left. I had no idea why he disliked me. I wondered if he'd taken the midterm mix-up personally. His idea sounded like a good one, but it would put a huge dent in the vacation time I'd been looking forward to. The textbook had 834 pages. Big pages.

Anyway, it was Thursday night, and soon I'd be with Cat again. I fell asleep anticipating the weekend, and forgetting about Professor Lane and the royal families.

Chapter 18

Catching up with the news Friday morning, my mood darkened. The U.S. was still escalating the war, boosting troop strength to 485,000. More than 11,000 American soldiers had been killed during 1967, plus Vietnamese in the untold hundreds of thousands. My country was destroying theirs, sacrificing our own young men along the way. *The antiwar movement might be growing,* I thought, *but it wasn't even slowing the war.*

After classes, I rushed over to Cat's place. I found her sitting on the couch staring at a piece of paper. I sat next to her and asked what it was. She handed it to me.

Once I read the letter, typed on expensive law firm stationery, I knew why she seemed to be in shock.

> *Dear Miss Crawford,*
>
> *On behalf of this firm's client, the Central Life Insurance Company, I write to apologize for the two-year delay in delivery of the proceeds from your late father's policy. Herewith enclosed is the check that is due to you as its beneficiary.*
>
> *A brief explanation is in order. The policy was discovered by your family's landlord, Mr. Henry Milstein, while cleaning out the house after the tragic accident. Mr. Milstein had neither an address nor a telephone number for you, so he put the policy in a safe place, hoping you would contact him about it. After a few months passed, he mailed it to the company.*
>
> *Central Life, though legally obligated to issue you this check, was unable to locate you. It forwarded the check to my firm, which held it in*

escrow and assigned an investigator to the case. He asked Mr. Milstein if he was saving any other papers for you. Among those was a letter of acceptance to Midway University. Our investigator visited the university, and was directed to the bookstore on High Street. I have taken the liberty of giving this address to Mr. Milstein, who will forward the remaining papers that he has held for you.

I trust this letter finds you well, and that you will put your insurance proceeds to good use.

Yours truly,
Truman J. Winston III, Esq.

I looked up at Cat, and she handed me a check for two thousand dollars. "I didn't even know Daddy had life insurance," she said. Her eyes were misty.

"This is great news," I said. "Why do you look so sad?"

"It brings back the grief. And how can I can accept that money? It would be like profiting from his death."

"Wait a minute," I said, taking her hand. "Why did your dad buy life insurance? He wanted you to have something in case he couldn't be here for you. It was his wish that your life be a little easier now. So, by accepting this check, you'll be honoring his memory."

"I don't know. It doesn't feel right."

"I understand. You do need to cash the check, though. Otherwise, it'd be like giving it back to the insurance company. Then put the money in a drawer until your emotions settle down."

"Okay," she said. "Come, let's have dinner."

While we ate, I told her about my meeting with Professor Lane. She supported his suggestion to outline the book. I knew her mind was elsewhere, though.

When we got into bed, she snuggled up close, rested her head on my chest, and began softly weeping. I held her, caressed her and whispered loving words, until a merciful blanket of sleep overtook us both.

In the morning, I made breakfast while Cat was in the shower. She came out wearing a towel wrapped around her hair and a white terrycloth bathrobe. When Cat wore white, the image it evoked for me was butterscotch pudding topped with whipped cream. Luscious, either way.

"Steve," she began as we dug into the pancakes, "I've been thinking, and we need to talk about a couple of things. One is studying during the break, and the other is the insurance money."

That was Cat, consumed by emotion one moment and totally practical the next. I sighed and suggested, somewhat apprehensively, "Let's start with the school thing."

"I have a paper to write," she explained, "and you have 834 pages to outline, besides whatever else we need to do, right?" I suspected where this was going, and was in no hurry to get there.

"What's your paper about?" I asked.

"It's the story of Fermat's Last Theorem. Do you know about that?"

"No. I don't think I ever heard of it."

"But you certainly know the Pythagorean Theorem."

"Sure. In a right triangle, the square of the hypotenuse is the sum of the squares of the two other sides: $x^2 + y^2 = z^2$. Pythagoras proved that an infinite number of combinations exist for x, y and z."

"Yes, and it was a beautiful, elegant proof, the very definition of a classic. Pierre de Fermat was a 17th-Century French mathematician who wanted to take it a little further, and examined this equation: $x^n + y^n = z^n$. He hypothesized there were *no* whole number combinations of x, y and z that worked if n was greater than two. After he died, someone found a note he'd left behind, referencing his proof of that proposition. It became known as his Last Theorem."

"So that was it?"

"No. It was only the beginning. You see, Fermat's actual proof was never discovered. For mathematicians, proving that theorem became an obsession that's lasted over 300 years. Teams have worked on it without success. Modern computers haven't done any better."

"You mean it's never been solved?"

"Not yet. It's become the holy grail of Number Theory. My professor questions whether Fermat really proved it in the first place, and whether it can be proven at all. On the other hand, no-one's been able to demonstrate that it can't be proved. The object of my paper is to trace the mathematical evolution of this mystery. There've been many published attempts at the proof, but they've all been found to be flawed.

All these attempts have built on one another though, and one day someone might solve it, if it can be solved. A European mathematician named Grothendieck may have only recently opened the door to a solution. This is fascinating stuff."

Excitement gleamed in her eyes. "Maybe you'll be the one to solve it someday," I said. She laughed. I asked to read the paper when it's finished, wondering if I'd understand any of it.

"I'd like you to," she responded. "But first I have to write it. And you need to get your outline done and memorized. So we need to focus on those projects and keep to ourselves, even on the weekends. This is crunch time."

Holding my panic in check, I calmly countered, "Can't we work on these things together? You do your thing, and I'll do mine? I don't want to be away from you the whole time."

"Neither do I," she said. "But we'll never get the work done if we're together, certainly not if we're here."

My inner negotiator kicked into gear. "We can work at the library," I suggested, "where there's no distractions." After a minute of thought, she agreed to that. *Good. Now to the next step.*

"But we can't live at the library," I continued. "Let's set work hours and be flexible about the rest."

She considered that thought, and countered, "What matters is results, not time. If we're in a quiet, non-distracting library environment, can you cover a hundred pages a day?"

"Sure I can."

"Okay. As long as I'm making progress too, we can work until you've done your hundred pages. At night, back at the dorm, you can cover more pages. After a week or so, we might have a day or two for us. I hope we do."

I had no choice but to agree.

"But no faking it," she cautioned, her eyes narrowing. "I want to see the work."

"Of course," I sighed. "Now, what about the money?"

"I wouldn't be here except for Emma," she explained. "I've been living rent-free for over two years, and she's been more than generous in paying me for helping out in the shop. This is my chance to pay her back."

An hour later, Emma was reading the lawyer's letter. "This is wonderful," she commented.

Cat held out an envelope filled with cash and said, "I want you to have this. It's to repay at least some of what you've done for me."

Emma smiled and quietly said, "Of course not. This is for you, not for me."

The two of them locked horns, the irresistible force and the immovable object. I knew enough to stay out of it. After fifteen minutes of this, as Cat was tearing up in frustration, Emma proposed a solution.

"Look, we've got a long, cold winter coming, and it'll be easier for all of us if you have a car. So why don't you use some of that money to buy one?"

Now I stepped in. "That's a great idea, Cat. It'll be much easier for both of you going to doctor visits."

"Well, okay," she conceded. "But, Emma, even though the car will be mine, you'll always have first dibs on using it."

"Fair enough," Emma agreed. "Just make sure it has a heater."

Before we left, Emma stood and spread her arms. The three of us embraced. To me, it felt the embrace of a family, more so than I'd ever felt with my parents.

Chapter 19

We decided to postpone shopping for a car until after final exams. Nothing was to interfere with our assignments during the break. Each morning, we met at the library. I worked on my history textbook, while Cat took notes on articles in mathematics journals. By the time I finished outlining my hundred pages, it was usually dinnertime, so we ate at the school cafeteria. Then she walked home, and I headed for the gym, hoping to burn off my pent-up lust.

On the fourth day, I'd only gotten through eighty pages when the closing chimes rang. I said I'd have to finish up at the dorm.

"Oh no," she objected. "We'll pick up a pizza on the way to my place, and you'll finish it there. I told you I want to see the work." No argument from me about that.

We did go back to work after dinner. She typed at her desk, and I worked at the kitchen table. I was tired, though, and I made slow progress, reading some pages several times before making any notes. By the time I announced my quota was done, it was past ten. I began gathering my stuff to leave.

"Wait, Steve," she said. "It's late. Spend the night with me."

It was only an hour before we both fell asleep, but what a glorious hour it was.

"See, we can be together and still get our work done, if we're disciplined about it," I suggested over breakfast. "Why do we have to spend our nights apart?"

"You might be right," she conceded. "Last night kind of surprised me. Okay, let's try it."

"Yes, let's try it," I agreed, my face lighting up.

"But," she added, "no touching until your hundred pages are done!"

"Not even a good-morning hug?"

"Well, all right."

After that, my productivity at the library shot way up. I was getting more proficient at outlining, and I had a real incentive to get through my daily assignments as efficiently as possible. Most nights, we were able to enjoy each other. It wasn't only sex. We read together and we read to each other. We watched TV. We even went to a movie.

Emma invited us for Christmas Eve dinner. "I've invited Marcellus and Sharon too," she told us. "And Ellie will be here for a few days."

"We'd love to," I said. "Do you need any help? What can we bring?"

"No, Ellie will be all the help I need, and the cooking won't be a problem."

Cat baked an apple pie anyway. Emma introduced us to Ellie as soon as we arrived.

"I've heard a lot about you two," she said. "I'm so grateful to you for taking care of my mom. I couldn't have stayed at school if she was all by herself now."

"There's no chance she'd be all by herself," Cat responded. "She has too many friends and admirers. And has she told you about what she's done for me?"

"I don't know anything about that," replied Ellie.

Cat took her arm and led her into the kitchen. "Well, I have a story to tell you."

"Dinner will be ready soon." Emma announced. "Let's have a drink in the living room." She poured the wine, and we began nibbling on the snacks she'd laid out.

"I got a call this morning with exciting news," she told me. "You've heard the Democrats will be holding their national convention here in Chicago next year?"

"I heard something. When is it?"

"End of August. The Mobe is planning a massive antiwar demonstration right outside the convention. We'll be hearing more once the staff is in place."

Marcellus and Sharon arrived with four-year-old Arielle, all dressed up for a party, her hair decorated with ribbons and bows. Cat and Ellie came in from the kitchen, and Emma made the introductions.

Arielle thought it was wonderful that there was a person named Cat. "Mama," she asked through her giggles, "could you change my name to Gerbil?"

I got down on the floor with her, and she introduced me to her dolls as she took them out of her bag. "Here," she said, "you be this one... and this one... and this one." Once she set up the storyline, we helped the dolls act it out. Arielle was a delight.

Soon, Sal and his assistant brought in trays of food: eggplant parmigiana, veal scaloppini, lasagna, linguini and garlic bread, enough for a dozen people, plus two bottles of Chianti in straw baskets.

"I told you the cooking wouldn't be a problem," Emma whispered.

Once we began eating, I asked Ellie what was going on at Columbia.

"Well, the antiwar movement is growing very strong," she began. "But there's something developing closer to home."

"What's that?" asked Cat.

"You see, Columbia is sort of an expansionist power. It keeps growing into the surrounding communities. Thousands of neighbors have been evicted from their apartments to make way for students and faculty. Blocks have been razed for new academic buildings. Its money and political clout have steamrolled every objection. And now, it somehow pulled off a deal to build a new gymnasium on the site of a Harlem park. We're determined to stop it, one way or another. It's disgraceful that a public facility serving poor Black children can be snatched away by a private, 95 percent white university."

"Who's 'we'?" asked Sharon.

"So far, it's only SDS and the Afro-American Society. But Harlem community groups are beginning to organize around it, and we're just beginning to make it an issue on campus. There's something big brewing here."

"Midway's expansion into the South Side has been an issue for years," Marcellus interjected, "but it hasn't stolen a public park."

"What's the BSU working on here?" asked Ellie.

"We've decided to focus on two issues," Sharon explained. "First, we want to force the university to diversify its student body. Midway is also 95 percent white, and that's ridiculous in a city like Chicago. The other issue is the educational program. You could spend years at Midway without ever hearing about W.E.B. DuBois, about Toussaint L'Ouverture, about Frederick Douglass or Nat Turner. We're gonna push hard for more Black professors and a Black Studies program."

"We won't be able to get either of these on our own," she added, turning towards me. "We'll need support."

"And you'll get it," I said. "White students should support this. The world we'll be graduating into isn't 95 percent white, like Midway is. And if we don't know something of African-American history, then we don't know American history."

Marcellus smiled. "Now you got it."

The conversation turned to the embryonic McCarthy campaign. Sharon said the single-issue focus on the war wouldn't spark enthusiasm among Black voters unless it broadened to address the web of racism and poverty that afflicted the inner cities. But Ellie thought those problems would never be addressed until the war was ended. We explored and debated, back and forth, all of us searching for answers.

Emma beamed. Christmas Eve, and the children were here together, talking politics.

Except for Arielle, who'd climbed up on my lap and was intently focused on dropping linguini into my open mouth, one hilarious strand at a time.

Chapter 20

Cat and I spent Christmas Day working at her place, since the library was closed. But it was a huge effort for me to stay focused on history when she was so tantalizingly close. At around two, I padded over to the desk and began gently massaging her neck.

"Ste-VEN!" she called sharply, her emphasis and inflection rising on the second syllable. "How many pages?"

"More than sixty."

"Come back when it's a hundred."

By dinnertime, I'd done more than a hundred pages, and Cat finished the first draft of her paper. We didn't need to cook, because Emma had sent us home with enough leftovers for a week. Later, we snuggled up on the couch, shared a bottle of wine and watched "It's a Wonderful Life" on TV. Later in bed, we gave ourselves to each other for Christmas.

After another few days, I finished my outline. Cat handed me her term paper and asked me to read it. The content was over my head, but the brilliance and elegance of the presentation was unmistakable. It occurred to me that becoming a real mathematician probably wasn't in the cards for me.

We didn't have much studying to do for our other courses, so she spent the next two days drilling me on the 130 legal-size pages that comprised my outline. By New Year's weekend, I had it committed to memory. At last, we had time for ourselves.

We spent that weekend the way we'd spent our first one, posing as tourists and making love at every opportunity. The weather was surprisingly mild on New Year's Eve, so we took a ride on the Water Taxi, and a tour of Chinatown that included a delicious dinner. After the midnight fireworks at Grant Park, we brought in the new year back home.

Final exams were the first week of January. Grades were posted the following Monday. I got an A in Logic, a B-plus in Math, B's in English and Computer Science, and a C-minus in Western Civ. I was furious that all the work I did during the break turned out to be a waste of time. Cat said she thought Professor Lane put a ceiling on my final grade back when I screwed up on the midterm, and I should settle for passing the course at all.

"He was probably hoping you'd fail," she added. "But you didn't."

The bottom line, though, was that I hit my target 3.0 grade-point average right on the button.

Cat got an A in everything.

The rest of January was Intersession. We were opening the store on the first morning when a long-haired, bearded young man, wearing a tie-died shirt and bandana, came in,. He handed me a flyer he hoped to post on the bulletin board. It advertised a four-year-old VW Bug for $500. I brought it over to Emma.

"Of course, it's all right," she said. I turned away, then turned back.

"What do you think about driving a bug?" I asked.

"Oh, I think that would be great fun."

"Stick shift okay?"

"Honey," she replied with a smile, "I'm from the days before the automatic transmission was invented. As long as the engine doesn't need to be cranked, I'm fine with it. Just make sure the heater works."

I showed the flyer to Cat, who responded, "Let's take a look."

The car looked good. The mileage was low and the tires had plenty of tread. "Let's give it a test drive," I said. "If it rides as good as it looks, it'll be a great buy."

"Okay," she agreed. "Ask Emma if she can manage without us for a little while. I'll go upstairs and get the money, just in case."

When she came back down, I passed her the keys.

She handed them back. "No, you drive. I took Driver Ed in high school, but I was too young to get a license. Also, I don't know how to drive a stick shift."

"Are you sure you want to buy a car you can't even drive?"

"Sure. You and Emma can be the drivers until I get a license, and you can teach me how to drive it."

The car started right up, everything seemed to work, and the heater was more than adequate. A half hour later, we had new plates on our new car, and Miss Ca-taca-taca Crawford had a learner's permit. She insisted on registering the car jointly. On the way back to the shop, I asked why.

"That's how I want it," she replied. Her eyes narrowed, and she got quiet. I'd seen that look before, and knew it would be best to let her be.

After I parked the car and reached for the door handle, she grabbed my arm. "Wait," she said, "There's something else."

"What's that?"

"I don't want you going back to the dorm next semester. I want you with me." This came as a shock.

"You mean move in? What about that 'balance' thing?"

"We passed that test during the break. I'm not worried about it anymore. And I want to wake up next to you every morning."

I squeezed her with all my strength. Who knows what might have happened, at that very moment, if that damned stick shift wasn't in the way.

Chapter 21

Emma ground her cigarette out as we came back into the shop. Pretending not to notice, we told her about the car, and also our new living arrangement. I prayed she wouldn't bring up that 'balance' thing again. But she smiled broadly and responded, "That's wonderful. You two are perfect together." It occurred to me that she and Cat might have already discussed this.

"Now that there's two of us there," I added, "we should talk about rent."

"No, not today," Emma replied as she rose to greet a customer. "Too busy." I wondered if she would ever not be "too busy" for that conversation.

When it neared the time for my first after-school class, Cat said, "Take the car. Dinner will be ready at six." I kissed her quickly and tore myself away.

Five eighth-graders awaited me in a small conference room, notebooks at the ready: Three Black boys, one Black girl and a Puerto Rican girl.

"Let's get to know one another," I said. "We can start with our names." Henry, James, Robert, Brenda and Sonia introduced themselves.

"My name is Steve," I said.

"We should be callin' you *Mister* somethin'," said Brenda. "You the teacher."

I replied, "I'm not really a teacher. Think of me as a 'learning-helper.' And besides, I'm not all that much older than you."

"But you a white man," she insisted.

"I'll try to get past that if you can," I replied. Brenda shrugged her shoulders.

"So what's going on with your math classes?" I asked.

"Algebra," said Henry. "We all in the same class, and none of us are gettin' it."

"Right," added James. "Last year, we did okay, but this algebra is hard."

"Algebra," I explained, "is a game. It should be fun." Sonia and Henry rolled their eyes. "So what's the problem?"

"In class, we get confused," Henry explained. "And the book, it seem like some other language."

I asked to see the textbook. It was so old that the pages had turned yellow, and its presentation was as dry as dirt.

"I think it the teacher," offered Brenda. "Sometime it's like she don' get it neither."

"Could be she don't," added Henry. "Remember, last year she taught art? But this year, we got no art classes. No music neither. So they made her a math teacher."

"You said algebra should be fun?" asked Sonia. "We hate it. We only came here today because Marcellus said you was his friend and you was good at math."

Behind Henry was a small bookcase with a box of dominoes on top. That gave me an idea.

"Well, let's give it a try," I suggested. "Henry, would you put that box of dominoes on the table?" He looked puzzled, but complied.

"Dominoes ain't math," argued Brenda.

"When we're finished," I said, "you can decide whether or not we're doing math. But let's start with a magic trick. Do you like magic?" All five murmured agreement. Magic sounded more promising than math.

"All right," I instructed. "Everyone open your notebook and pick out one domino. Stand it up in front of you, so you can see the two numbers, but I can't."

They did as directed, and James asked, "Now what?"

"Now," I announced, "I'm going to tell each of you what those numbers on the domino in front of you are."

"Without seein' 'em?" blurted Henry. "No, you can't!"

"That's the magic. But I'll need a little help from you. Okay?" They nodded.

"Pick one of the two numbers and write it down. Okay? Good. Now multiply that number by 5. But don't let me see it."

I waited a minute, and then said, "Now add 7."

Then, "Now multiply by 2"

Finally, "Add your second number."

"I don't get it," said Robert. "First you said it'd be algebra. Then you said it'd be magic. I don't see neither one. This is 'rithmetic."

"Here it comes, Robert," I replied. "What did you get for your final answer?"

"66."

"The numbers on your domino are 5 and 2," I told him. "Turn it up and show everyone if I'm right." The kids looked at the domino, then up at me, then back at the domino.

"Maybe a lucky guess,"offered James.

"Maybe so. What did you get?"

"45."

"Here's another lucky guess, James. Your numbers are 3 and 1."

Eyes wide in wonder, he showed the group his domino. Now, there was a little buzz in the room. Quickly, I repeated the trick for the other three kids, with the same result. They insisted I tell them how I did it. "And what about the math?" demanded Brenda.

I asked to borrow her pencil and notebook, and for all of them to come up to my desk.

"Let's call your first number 'a'. If we multiply it by 5, like I said, what do we get?"

"5a," they called out. I wrote it down.

"And if we add 7 to that?"

"5a + 7."

"And if we multiply each part by 2?" A moment of silence.

Sonia got it first. "10a + 14," she called out. They all agreed when I wrote it down.

"Now, let's call your other number 'b' and add that to it."

I wrote "10a + 14 + b." "And that," I said, "was your final result, depending on what your 'a' and 'b' were. So, Robert, when you told me '66,' I simply subtracted 14, and there were your two numbers: 5 in the tens place and 2 in the ones place. 52."

"But how?" asked James.

I pointed to the expression: 10a+14+b. "If we subtract 14 from this," I asked, "what's left?"

"10a + b."

"Right. So if 'a' is 5 and 'b' is 2, then '10a + b' is 50 + 2 = 52. And it's right there. So, you decide. Was this algebra, or was it magic? Or was it just a little fun? But now let's take a look at the problems in your book."

With ten minutes left, I asked that they close their books. I pulled a deck of playing cards out of my pocket and asked, "How about a little card trick now?"

When the session ended, I asked, "See you Wednesday?"

All five heads bobbed up and down. "Oh, yeah."

I had them. It felt terrific.

After a quick workout at the gym, I headed home for dinner. "Home for dinner," I repeated to myself over and over, "with Cat." That felt good too.

Early the next morning, I checked out of the dorm and moved my stuff to Cat's place. "No, to *our* place," I reminded myself. Later, she had her first lesson on the stick shift. We had lurches and stalls while she learned to operate the clutch, but she quickly got the hang of it.

"This car is fun," she said. "We should give her a name."

"Okay," I replied, perfectly willing to accept Cat's determination of the car's gender. "Any ideas?"

"Let's call her Tooter," she suggested, turning to me. "No, I don't know where I got that."

"Well then, Tooter it is."

I looked out the window, watching the howling wind bending trees and blowing garbage cans down the street. "Emma was sure right about needing a good heater," I remarked. "It's brutal out there today."

Cat asked, "So why aren't you dressed for such a cold day?"

"My winter clothes are still in Waterloo. I thought I'd be going back there during one of the breaks."

"You need to go get them," she instructed. "The coldest part of winter hasn't even gotten here yet. And you better go today. You've seen this week's weather forecast."

"I might have to stay overnight," I replied. "Remember, it's five hours each way."

"Do what you have to do," she said. "I'll miss you, but it's better than seeing you freeze to death."

After the driving lesson, I went upstairs to tell my parents I was coming. Mom asked, "Will anyone be with you?"

"No. Only me."

Her voice brightened. "I'll get your room ready. Try to get here for dinner."

Tooter and I hit the road at noon. When I got to the house, no-one was home. I let myself in, packed up my stuff and squeezed it into Tooter's little trunk, back seat and passenger seat. It barely fit.

Mom came home from the market while I was finishing. I gave her a hug and told her to go ahead inside. "It's cold out here," I said. "I'll bring the packages."

While we put the groceries away, she asked about my grades. She was pleased with the report, but then asked, "So how's your little friend?"

I disliked the tone of that question. "Do you mean Cat?" I asked.

"Yes, that one. Catherine, wasn't it?"

"Sure, okay, Catherine. Anyway, she's doing great. Straight A's last semester."

"Really?" She sounded surprised, but shouldn't have been after having met Cat.

"By the way," I added, "She's much more than a friend now. We're talking about getting married." Actually, Cat and I hadn't talked at all about this or anything else long-term. We were loving and living day to day. I didn't know where that sentence came from.

Mom's jaw dropped open for a moment. She said, "I need to call your father," and hurried upstairs.

Heading to my room for a final check, I passed Mom's door. She was on the phone. "Yes," she yelled into it. "It's that *schvartze!*"

I stood there for a minute, unsure what to do. Back downstairs, I found a pen and notepad. "Here's my new address and phone number," I wrote. "No dorm bill this semester." I left the note and my house key on the kitchen counter and left.

Along the way, I stopped for dinner and called Cat. I told her what happened, and that I'd be back around midnight.

"I'll be waiting," she said. "But drive carefully. Please."

Exhausted when I got back, I left my stuff in the car and trudged up the stairs. The apartment was dark, except for a faint glow from the bedroom. Four scented candles threw off just enough light for me to make out Cat's naked form under the bed sheet.

"Hurry," she said softly. Suddenly, I wasn't so tired anymore.

Chapter 22

Wednesday's class had three additional girls: Tootie, Angela and Cherylle-Veronica. I asked what brought them.

"Yesterday," Cherylle explained, "Brenda asked the teacher if she could show the class a math trick. She did it, and it worked. Then she showed us how it worked. After school, we asked where she got it, and she told us about you. So we wanted to come here too. Is that okay?"

"Sure" I answered. "The more the merrier. And Brenda, good job!"

I structured the session the same way, beginning with a "magic" trick and explaining the algebra behind it, transitioning to homework help and finishing with a card trick. They loved card tricks. At the end of the session, Henry burst out, "This ain't Mathematics, this Mathemagic!" Everyone laughed, but the term stuck.

A handsome, conservatively dressed, middle-aged man stopped me at the door when I arrived for Friday's class. He introduced himself as James Watkins, the SSO's executive director. "Eighteen kids are waiting for you today," he told me. "I've set them up in our training room, and found a rolling blackboard you can use. But no more recruits. We don't have any more room." I agreed, and promised to tell the kids.

"By the way," he added, smiling, "our reimbursement is per-student, not per-hour, so your pay has about tripled." The best part was, I'd have done this for free.

The session went great. With more kids calling out answers, and sometimes debating the possibilities, it was even livelier than the first two sessions. It felt like conducting an orchestra.

After my workout, I rushed home for dinner. I was glad to see Emma there with Cat. I was bursting with my news. I also got an idea at the gym that I wanted to run by both of them.

"You'll never guess what happened at SSO today," I began.

"Well, I'll guess your class has grown to eighteen," Emma said.

"How on earth do you know that?" I asked, taken aback.

"Marcellus dropped in at the shop, around an hour ago," she explained. "He was as excited about it as you are. He says you're already one of the most popular teachers in the program. And that's in a place where, as he put it, 'white folks are not very popular.' "

"Well, I'm having a ball," I said, and related what happened in the class. "I'm a little worried, though, that I might empty out my bag of tricks pretty soon. I can always invent more 'Mathemagic,' but it'll get redundant after a while. I need to find fresh material. And I only know maybe a dozen card tricks."

Emma looked amused. "You may have heard, Steve," she said in a conspiratorial whisper, "that there's a *bookstore* downstairs!"

"This has given me an idea," I told them when the laughter settled down, "and I want to know what you think."

I turned to Cat and asked, "Do you remember asking me to read your paper on Fermat's Last Theorem?"

"Sure."

"And I didn't have much to say? Certainly nothing useful."

"Well, you didn't have much time to analyze it."

"The fact is," I explained, "it was way over my head. I kind of decided right then that I'm not cut out to be a mathematician. It would take me ten years to get where you are now, if I could ever get there at all."

"Steve," she said, "you have to remember I had four years at a high-level academic prep school, plus two years at Midway before you got here. So, of course my math is a little ahead of yours."

"Anyway, here's what I'm thinking," I continued. "Even if I could become a mathematician, I know now I'd be mediocre at best. But I might become a decent math *teacher* one day. I sure enjoy what I'm doing now, and the kids seem to like it too."

"If you'd rather be a teacher," responded Cat, "that's what you should do."

"It's a wonderful idea," added Emma. "I saw how you and Arielle enjoyed each other on Christmas Eve. Children and you seem to be a good combination."

"Midway has a major in Mathematics Education. Maybe I should switch over."

"Now, that might be going too far," warned Emma. "Keep in mind that most of those terrible ghetto schoolteachers you've been hearing about got their training at schools of education. They were trained to fail, and that's just what they're doing. Why not try one course next semester, and decide after that?"

"Good idea. If I want to switch my major, there's plenty of time to do it."

Later, lying in bed with Cat, I said, "You know, Emma was right. Next after being with you, I do love being with kids."

"That was obvious to me on Christmas Eve," she replied. "My heart swelled watching you and Arielle playing together."

"Maybe," I mused, "we could have one of our own one day."

"Maybe so," she said. "But we better finish school first. Imagine what a distraction that would be!"

"Oh, I can barely even imagine. Anyway, I know what we should name her when the time comes."

Cat looked puzzled. "What would that be?"

"Kitten, of course!"

"And what if it's a boy?"

"Hmm. How about Tom? "His middle name would be Cat. Tom Cat."

After we finished laughing, Cat climbed up to straddle my body, and smothered my face with kisses. Then she buried her face in my neck and we held each other, gently rocking a few degrees back and forth. By the time she slipped me inside, we were both ready to explode.

Chapter 23

Intersession flew by. I had my classes to prepare for and teach. Cat spent every weekday with Emma in the bookstore. I helped out as much as possible, and I did discover a few good books with math tricks and puzzles, along with two books of card tricks.

I noticed that Emma, from time to time, accepted signed adding machine tapes as IOU's, like mine. One day, I opened a desk drawer and found a fat envelope filled with those tapes. Lots of these were never going to be paid. Also, I never knew how many books she loaned out for free, but I guessed there were plenty.

The information available at registration included course titles, descriptions, times and locations, but not the names of the professors. When I signed up for the second required semester of Western Civ, I hoped I wouldn't draw Professor Lane again. English Comp and Math were also extensions of the fall semester courses. Next up in introductory Philosophy was Ethics, which I thought would be interesting. Instead of continuing with Computer Science, I decided to try Sociology of Education.

Cat signed up for Differential Equations, Quantum Physics, Game Theory, Symbolic Logic and Romantic Era Poetry. I was glad she wouldn't be needing my help with any of those.

The next weekend, a blizzard hit Chicago. We spent both days indoors. I got to read *Native Son*, and Cat read *The Man Who Cried I Am*. She also showed me how to make a pot of soup by combining whatever happened to be in the fridge and pantry. While the soup simmered on the stove, we melded on the couch.

The snow came down from Saturday morning until late Sunday. Our car was parked right in front, but she was invisible from the window, buried under a mountain of drifted snow. "Poor Tooter," murmured Cat.

Sunday night, we heard the plows scraping their way down the street, and it was clear for traffic when we woke in the morning. I found a snow shovel in the basement and cleared the sidewalk. Down the block, I saw Sal shoveling in front of his pizzeria. I thought he was a little old to be doing this, so I walked over and finished it for him. He sent me back with his thanks and a large mushroom pizza, lunch for Cat and Emma and me.

I returned *Native Son* to the stacks, and Emma loaned me two others to read: DuBois's biography of John Brown, and Eric Williams' *Capitalism and Slavery*. I'd been trying to finish one of Emma's books every week, learning more from them than from any of my classes.

When the time came to leave for the SSO, Emma suggested calling first. I hung up after a dozen rings. "They're probably closed because of the snow," she guessed. I spent the rest of the afternoon excavating Tooter.

On Wednesday, I called again. Still no response. I decided to drive over and see what was going on. I had my answer as soon as I crossed the boulevard separating Midway from the South Side. The streets there were impassable. I had to turn around and go back.

It wasn't until Friday that I made my way to the SSO. Marcellus told me the plows didn't arrive until Thursday night.

"How could that be?" I asked. "High Street got plowed out on Sunday, as soon as the snow stopped falling."

"That's the way this city works," he explained. "The Black ghetto is last in line for everything, and I mean everything, from school supplies to garbage pickups. We have the slowest fire response time, and cops who only get out of their cars to arrest people or take payoffs. We even have leftover teachers, incompetent rejects from white schools. Instead of getting fired, they get transferred down here."

"Who's responsible for this?" I asked.

"Well, here in Chicago, everything's controlled by the mayor, Richard J. Daley. Nothing gets done, or not done, without his okay. He controls every politician, and the City Council is his rubber stamp. He's The Boss."

Only eight students showed up that day. They told me the neighborhood schools had been closed all week. After class, I decided to skip the gym because it was a busy day at the shop. Classes were to begin on Monday. I was glad I went to help out. We even stayed open an extra hour. As we were leaving, Emma handed me an envelope with cash inside.

"What's this?" I asked.

"It's for your work during intersession."

I put the envelope down on the desk, and put my hands up, palms out as if to keep it from jumping back at me. *This*, I thought, *is one I can win*.

"Emma," I asked, "did I ever apply for a job here?"

"No."

"And did you ever hire me?"

Again, "Well, no."

"So you can't pay me, since I don't work here. I was just a friend doing another friend a little favor. We don't pay friends for favors. In fact, I'm wondering if I should feel insulted. What do you think, Cat?"

"Oh, I don't think so," she replied, her eyes twinkling. "It was only a little misunderstanding."

"You two get out of here," scolded Emma, "before I throw you out!"

On our way upstairs, Cat said, "That was good, Steve. You got her to give in."

"Yes," I agreed, "and it may never happen again."

With intersession ending, it was time to figure out how we, and especially I, could stay focused on schoolwork while we were living together. Cat brought it up the next morning.

"What may help make this work," she said, "is a consistent schedule, at least for the weekdays."

"We already have our class schedules, Cat. Plus, there's my after-school sessions, and Saran Wrap leafleting on Thursdays. And you have your bookstore hours. Isn't that enough?"

"What I'm thinking about is how we start the day. You've been working out in the late afternoons. That's good, but how about switching to early mornings? Set the alarm for six. Throw something on and get to the gym. Then back here for shower and breakfast. That'll set you up for a productive day."

I thought about it for a few minutes. I didn't like the idea of getting up so early and rushing outside during the cold winter, but I saw her point.

"What about nights and weekends?" I asked.

"Same as during the break. We'll decide how much work we need to accomplish. Once that's done, our time is our own."

"I don't know about getting up so early, and leaving while you're still asleep."

"I'll get up too," she offered. "In fact, I'll come with you if that'll make it easier. I could use some exercise too."

That brightened the picture considerably. I agreed to try it.

Like most of Cat's ideas, this turned out to be a good one. I'd have preferred to start my days nuzzling with her in bed, but at least we were together. The only part I didn't like was the male attention she got at the gym in her leggings or shorts and halter tops, with that tight, sexy midriff in between. She told me to ignore it, but I still made sure to stay close. When I caught a guy looking her over, I stepped between them. Sometimes, I'd stare back at the potential predator until he moved on. Other times, I'd give Cat a little pat on the butt or a kiss, as if to signal, "This one is mine." I did enjoy that.

By now, the war had been dominating the news for months. After a B-52 raid obliterated an entire village, the *Tribune* quoted a U.S. military officer trying to justify the devastation by claiming, "It became necessary to destroy the village in order to save it." Every week, we read of "body counts," reporting small numbers of U.S. casualties and enormous numbers of "enemy" casualties. In my mind, the math didn't add up, since the North Vietnamese and Viet Cong resistance never showed any signs of either shrinking or weakening. I wondered whether someone in the Pentagon was making it all up. No way to tell. But it was obvious they were being used to convince the American people that U.S. troops, through victory after victory, were winning the war.

That's what President Johnson claimed in the State of the Nation address we watched on TV. "The enemy has been defeated in battle after battle," he announced, citing "continuous heavy losses." He conceded that the war still raged on, but insisted, "America will persevere." He concluded this part of the speech with what we considered a piece of unintended irony. "Aggression," he intoned in his deep Texas accent, "will never prevail."

The Big Lie began to unravel soon afterward. First, the Viet Cong attacked the big Marine base at Khe Sanh. As audacious as that was, it turned out to be a diversionary maneuver. The U.S. forces, tied up there, were clearly unprepared when the resistance unleashed what became known as the Tet Offensive. On January 31st, 1968, we woke to learn that insurgents had launched simultaneous surprise attacks on government and U.S. installations in 134 South Vietnamese cities and towns, including the thirty-six provincial capitals they'd been infiltrating for months.

Two news clips summed it all up for me. In one, a young man stood in a public square, his arms tied behind his back. The South Vietnamese police chief approached, pulled out a silver revolver, extended his arm and calmly shot him, point-blank, through the forehead. The victim was identified as Nguyen Van Lem. For many Americans, his execution became the brutal face of the regime our troops were fighting and dying to protect.

The second startled me even more. In a televised raid, a dozen Viet Cong guerrillas stormed and took over the U.S. Embassy in Saigon. It took eight hours for American soldiers to dislodge them. After all the Pentagon propaganda claiming that "we" were winning the war, Americans had to be shocked, I thought, watching U.S. forces lose control of their own embassy.

At the new semester's first gathering of The Circle, excitement was rampant. When Emma suggested this might be the turning point of the war, we hoped she was right.

It certainly seemed that way. Even Walter Cronkite, the news anchor known as "the most trusted man in America," reported on CBS TV that this war was "unwinnable." Not only news commentators were changing their opinions. Congressmen, including Democrats, were turning against the president. New York's Senator Robert F. Kennedy said the Tet Offensive demonstrated that,

> *Despite all of our reports of progress, of government strength and of enemy weakness, half a million American soldiers, with 700,000 (South) Vietnamese allies, with total command of the air, total command of the sea, backed by the huge resources and the most modern weapons, are unable to secure even a single city.*

On February 18th, the State Department released its highest ever weekly toll of American casualties in Vietnam: 543 dead and 2,547 wounded.

It took the U.S. forces two weeks to regain control of Saigon, and two more weeks to capture the other cities. Their primary weapon was the bombing raid. Most of their victims were civilians. By the time the Tet Offensive ended, though, it had more than accomplished its main objective. Only delusional Americans could go on thinking this war was being won. A poll showed LBJ's approval rating, as high as 80 percent early in his term, had now dropped to 30 percent. Only 6 percent said they approved of how he was handling the war.

Chapter 24

At The Circle's next gathering, Larry Graff delivered a report.

"The Placement Office posted Dow Chemical's recruiting visit," he announced, "and I got the first appointment. It's two weeks from today at one o'clock. Conference Room 101 at the Business School."

This was exciting news. Now it was time to plan our protest. We soon agreed that all the campus antiwar groups needed to be involved. We made a list, and a few people volunteered to make calls.

Sabrina also had a report. She'd been approached by a *Sun-Times* reporter who requested a sit-down interview about the Saran Wrap boycott. "What do you think?" she asked.

A chorus responded, all to the effect of "Do it!" Sabrina agreed, but asked Larry to join her in the interview, since he was our expert on Napalm. He agreed as well.

Before we adjourned, Emma told us that the Mobe would be calling for marches in various cities on April 27th to protest the continued bombing of Vietnam, and to build support for the August demonstration at the Democratic Convention.

"Here," she continued, "the Chicago Peace Council is working on getting permits for a parade and a downtown rally. We'll be hearing more very soon."

I wondered how Emma seemed to know about these things before anyone else did.

Two nights later, fifty students met in a lecture hall to plan the anti-Dow protest. Besides Larry, who still thought we should douse the recruiters with home-made Napalm, two factions quickly emerged. One wanted to organize for a rally outside the Business School or a peaceful picket line. The other wanted more than that, arguing that Dow's recruiting had to be physically prevented, by a sit-in or some kind of sabotage. I agreed. Talk wasn't enough. We had to *do* something.

The main objection to a sit-in was that it would violate Dow's First Amendment rights, and also those of the students who signed up for interviews. The debate was peppered with charges of opportunism, adventurism and other isms. These were the same arguments I'd heard at The Circle months before. Reconciling them would be difficult. After an hour, I got an idea that I hoped would break through.

"It won't only be a protest against Dow," I said. "It will also be a protest against Midway. This is our university hosting the recruiting. It's collaborating with Dow and its Napalm factory *in our name*. That makes every one of us complicit in Dow's war crimes. That's why we have to stop it. That's why it's our responsibility to stop it."

As the debate wore on, this argument gathered some support. Without a consensus on a sit-in, though, a committee was formed to plan only a rally. When we got up to leave, Cat said, "You made a very good point there, Steve."

"Too bad it didn't convince enough people," I replied, a bit glumly.

"No, but it convinced me." My mood instantly brightened.

Out in the corridor, Nicky Jarvis pulled me aside. "SDS office, tomorrow at five."

When we met there on Friday. Nicky got right to the point.

"We were there last night, and we heard all the arguments. I still think a rally, no matter how big, will be a waste of time if we don't stop Dow's recruiting. Who agrees?" Everyone did.

"Then let's do it. The rally will get started around 12:30. At a little before one, when the interviews are scheduled to begin, we'll go inside and block the conference room."

"But there's only a dozen of us here," I said. "That's not enough."

"You're right. We need to get the word out, but do it quietly. Only tell people who you trust, and have them tell others. We don't want the administration to get wind of this, and I'm sure there were infiltrators at last night's meeting. But don't worry. We'll have enough people."

I told Cat the plan for a blockade over dinner.

"I thought that was the purpose of the meeting," she said, "and I've been thinking about it all day. It might be dangerous, you know, since the Chicago cops won't be very sympathetic to the cause. So I talked it over with Emma."

"What did she say?"

"She pulled a book by Frederick Douglass off a shelf, opened it and pointed to a paragraph. It read, 'Power concedes nothing without a demand. It never did and it never will.' Then she said, 'Any demand has to be backed up by bodies. If people don't put themselves on the line, nothing will ever change.' I saw her point."

"So you're in?"

"I think I am," she said. "No, I know I am."

"After all," she added with a little smile, "*Someone's* got to be there to keep an eye on you."

It turned out that Dow Recruiting Day was the same day Sabrina and Larry's interview was reported in the morning *Sun-Times*. It seemed to me that Larry must have scared the reporter by the way he threw his hands around while he talked. He came off as a possible madman. But equally obvious was the reporter's attraction to Sabrina. The overall tone of the article was generally positive regarding the boycott, and very much so about her. She even got a plug in for the rally, which turned out to be even larger than we'd hoped for.

Cat and I got there a little late because of class schedules. About a hundred students had already broken off, and were charging up the steps to the Business School. We were the last ones inside before security guards locked the building down.

Larry, who knew exactly where to go, led the way. At his signal, we all sat down, blocking the entire corridor from wall to wall. He opened the conference room door and called in, "Sorry, guys. Today's interviews are all cancelled." One of the recruiters peered into the corridor. Quickly, he slammed the door shut and turned the lock

Steve Andrews, who never left home without his guitar, started singing a popular song of the labor and civil rights movements. We joined in.

> *We shall not,*
> *We shall not be moved.*
> *We shall not,*
> *We shall not be moved.*
> *Just like a tree that's*
> *Standing by the wa-ater*
> *We shall not be moved.*

After a few verses, a red-faced older man in an expensive-looking suit approached, accompanied by four security guards.

"I'm George Rice, Dean of the Business School," he announced. "I received a call from the conference room. What's going on here?"

"We're waiting for our interviews," someone called out. "With Dow Chemical."

"Right," called another. "But the door's locked. Can you get it open?"

Dean Rice's face got even redder. "Who's in charge here?" he demanded.

A chorus rang out, all with the same answer: "No-one."

Rice snorted, turned and walked away. We resumed our singing. He returned, without the guards, fifteen minutes later.

"Please listen to this," he said, holding a hand in the air. We quieted down.

"I've spoken to President Kent and to the recruiters. We prefer not to bring in the police, but this has to end. The recruiters have agreed to cancel today's interviews and leave the campus if you will peacefully exit the building first."

I thought this was a good development, but we needed to talk amongst ourselves. Since I'd been the last one to get into the building, I was face to face with the Dean when I stood up. "Come back at two," I told him. "We'll let you know."

"All right," he said, reaching into his pocket for a pen and a little pad. "By the way, what's your name, son?"

"Nguyen Van Lem," I replied. He dutifully wrote that down, turned and left. I wondered whether he recognized the name of the Vietnamese prisoner whose summary execution had been broadcast around the world.

Our flash meeting was a little chaotic. Most wanted to accept the offer and claim victory, but some argued we should stay. Eventually we reached consensus.

When Rice came back, I told him, "Here's the deal. We're not going anywhere until the recruiters do, but we'll clear a path so they can get out. No-one will bother them."

Rice returned to his office, and came back five minutes later. "Your terms are accepted," he said. "Now clear the way."

We formed a single-file line on each side of the corridor, stretching almost to the front door. The recruiters walked nervously through what must have seemed a gauntlet. When they got outside, we followed.

The rally had dwindled, but the crowd was still substantial. Nicky claimed the microphone and announced, "The baby-killers are leaving. We won! Now, let's all make sure they get away safely."

The recruiters had hundreds of escorts accompanying them across campus to their car. A chant rang out. "Out with Dow! Out with Dow!" Marc Lorenzo, the only SDS member who also belonged to the marching band, pulled out his trumpet and started playing "Battle Hymn of the Republic." Those who knew the words sang them. The rest of us clapped to the rhythm. Now we had a parade, led as it was by the only two unhappy people in it. Our ranks swelled as people hanging out on the quad fell into line and joined us.

As we watched the recruiters jump into their car and speed away, Whit called out, "Y'all come back soon now. Don' be a stranger!"

Our parade reformed and marched back, with Lorenzo now playing "When the Saints Go Marching In." The singing was joyful, and dancing broke out. Cat and I whirled and twirled our way back through the quad. Our victories were few and far between. This one deserved a celebration.

"That was great," Cat said, clearly excited. "But now I have to get home. Emma's coming for dinner. She wants to hear about what happened. And isn't it your Saran Wrap Day?"

"I can skip that this one time," I said. "I've done enough for Dow Chemical today. We'll cook dinner together." We walked home happy, my arm across her shoulders, and hers around my waist.

"But first," I added when we got close, whispering into her ear and painting it with my tongue, "I'm gonna need a little appetizer."

Chapter 25

We enjoyed our "appetizer" interlude for an hour, until Cat announced it was time to make the spaghetti and meatballs. When the meal was almost ready, the phone rang.

After the call, she told me, "Emma's doesn't feel well enough to come up here. I said we'll bring dinner to her. I hope she's not getting sick again."

Downstairs, Emma was sitting on her couch, smoking a cigarette and drinking a glass of water. She looked pale. We asked if she was all right.

"Sure I am," she replied. "But I got a little winded coming up from the shop. I didn't know if I'd be able to make it up another flight."

"So the mountain came to Mohammed," I said with a bright smile, patting her on the back.

In the kitchen, I told Cat in a low voice, "Emma really needs to see her doctor."

"I know," she agreed. "I'll call first thing in the morning."

As soon as we sat down to eat, Cat told her all about the Dow Chemical protest, down to the smallest detail. I had nothing to add to her narrative, although I thought she was exaggerating my own role in it.

While Cat talked, the color came back into Emma's face. She was savoring every bit of this story. When it ended, she clapped her hands and exclaimed, "A people's victory! Wonderful! No, stupendous! You've exercised real leadership in this, Steve."

My face reddened. "Cat exaggerates," I objected. "I didn't do much at all."

"Don't be too modest. Cat told me what you said at the strategy meeting, bringing up Midway's complicity. That was instrumental in making today happen. This university has to be held accountable for what it does, and what it sponsors. And at the sit-in, you facilitated a good, smart decision. You didn't dominate anything, but you helped make things happen. That's what good leaders do."

"Well, okay," I mumbled. Probably sensing my discomfort, Emma changed the subject.

"So tell me, you two. It's almost midterm time. How are your classes going?"

Cat said she was working hard, but keeping up. She mentioned one problem in Quantum Mechanics she was struggling with. I had no idea what she was talking about, and I'm sure Emma didn't either, but we both called up signs of encouragement. Then Emma asked, "What about you, Steve?"

"Well," I replied, "I'm doing fine with Math, English and Ethics. I'm enjoying the readings, and the philosophical arguments over ethics are fascinating. But I drew Professor Lane again, so I don't have high expectations for Western Civ. I'm outlining the text as we go along so I won't have to do it all at the end, but it's really a drag."

"I understand," she responded. "That textbook they require isn't even good history. Ellie's dissertation will argue that history is made from the bottom up, not from the top down. But aren't you taking something else? I don't remember."

"Yes. And that's a different problem. It's Sociology of Education, which I'm finding very disturbing."

"I'm not surprised," she said. "I did warn you, didn't I? What in particular is bothering you?"

"The course's emphasis is on what the professor calls 'The Culture of Poverty.' He teaches that the poor performance of the ghetto schools is the fault of the Black families. He says they have too many children, don't get married, don't eat breakfast together, are passive and dull, lack curiosity, provide no verbal stimulation, and don't value education. So that's why the kids don't learn. He makes everything seem so hopeless."

"That is such bullshit!" Emma exclaimed, pounding the table and rattling the dishes. She looked ready to explode, and I got worried. She calmed down, though, and asked, "Is this what you see on the South Side? You've spent enough time there to have an opinion."

"Well, I don't know which families eat breakfast together, or what that even has to do with anything, but one thing that's struck me is how important education seems to be to them. The kids in the after-school program come because they want to, not because they have to. Some of their families have invited me into their homes, where the first thing they tell me is that education is their kids' only hope of having a future."

"Of course," Emma said. "Black people have been in a continual struggle for education since the days of slavery, when reading was outlawed. This thread runs all through their history."

"I don't understand. What's going on here?" I asked.

"Instead of training their students to teach," she explained, "these so-called Schools of Education provide them with excuses for giving up on the kids. Their graduates come into the ghetto schools expecting the children to fail, and that's precisely what happens. It's a self-fulfilling prophecy. This 'Culture of Poverty' crap lets the teachers off the hook and puts the blame on the victims."

Before we left, Cat took hold of Emma's arms and told her, "We'll see the doctor tomorrow." Emma nodded in assent.

While we cleaned up our kitchen, I wondered out loud if we'd gotten Emma overexcited during dinner.

"No, I don't think so," Cat said. "The struggle for social justice is what keeps her going. And isn't her passion for that a big part of what attracts us to her?"

"Yes, it is," I agreed, putting the last dish away. "And, speaking of passion, are you ready for dessert?" We headed for the bedroom.

In the morning, Cat started calling the doctor's office right after we got back from the gym. When she got through, she learned the only opening was at 10:15, when she had to be in class. I told her to book the appointment, and I'd bring Emma to it. She agreed and picked up the phone.

When I came back from my shower, Cat told me, "When I told Emma about her appointment, she said she was much better and didn't need to go. We had a big argument."

"How'd it turn out?"

"I told her I was gonna hold my breath until either she gave in or one of us died. I don't know whether she believed me, but she did give in."

I found Emma sitting at the kitchen table with a cup of coffee and a pile of newspapers.

She didn't move. "Steve," she began. I knew what was coming, "Is this trip really necessary? I'm feeling much better than yesterday."

"Yes, it is," I answered firmly, walking over to the phone and lifting the receiver. "Do I have to call Cat?"

"Oh, all right," she grumbled, standing and reaching for her coat.

At the clinic, I followed her into the examining room, where the doctor asked, "What seems to be the problem?"

"Oh, nothing much," she replied. "I got tired a little early last night, so my two wardens insisted I come see you."

This was the reason I had to be there. "It was more than that," I interjected. "She got wiped out climbing a single flight of stairs, and she looked pale as a ghost afterward."

The doctor frowned while examining her.

"Mrs. Gold," he began, looking up, "what happened yesterday is typical of chronic emphysema. If it's ever worse than that, you should go straight to the E.R. If it's fairly mild, rest will usually be good enough until it passes. These episodes are reminders that you have this condition, and that you need to take care of it. I'm giving you a new prescription, and I want to see you again in two weeks. Have you stopped smoking yet?"

I knew, to the word, what her answer would be.

"I'm working on it."

When we got to the shop, I still had an hour before my next class, so I helped open up while Emma brewed a pot of coffee.

"The New Hampshire primary is coming up in a few days," she said. "Have you been following it?"

"As much as I can. There's been a lot more press coverage since the embarrassment of the Tet Offensive. But the experts still don't expect McCarthy to get more than 20 percent."

"They may be right," she speculated, "but they also might be in for a big surprise."

"That would be nice, but LBJ has the whole party machinery behind him, all the newspaper endorsements, and plenty of money. His ads come close to charging McCarthy with treason."

Emma interjected. "But what he lacks is a believable message. The issue is Vietnam, and he can't talk his way out of that. Americans don't like losing wars, and they especially don't like wars without endings. Did you know we've already lost more boys than we did in the entire Korean War?"

"I didn't know that, but I did read somewhere that we've dropped more explosives on Vietnam than we dropped in Europe during all of World War II. And I read that the generals want 200,000 more troops there."

"At some point, all this has to register with the voters," she continued, resting her elbows on the desk. "The college students are turning out in force for McCarthy. They've been coming into New Hampshire from all over. And, from what I've read, the Johnson camp is completely misreading the tea leaves. They're not even taking the challenge seriously. I wish McCarthy's speeches fired people up, though. He could put you to sleep."

The bell attached to the front door jingled as a customer came in.

"You go on to your classes now," she said. "I'll handle this."

"And," she added, grabbing my arm, "thank you, Steve."

As I walked out the door, I wondered whether she'd be lighting her next Newport before, or right after, dealing with the customer.

Chapter 26

It shocked the nation when the president fell short of a majority in the March 12th New Hampshire primary. Eugene McCarthy received 42 percent, double what was generally expected, to Johnson's 49 percent. The difference was only 3,500 votes. To sweeten the news even further, a stupid mistake by party officials caused 20 of the state's 24 convention delegates to be awarded to McCarthy. Antiwar forces would be in the house!

We would be outside the house too. The Mobe's call for a demonstration, though not yet official, was gathering endorsements and shaping up to be a huge event. I knew it wouldn't be neat, but it would certainly be loud. Different groups might bring conflicting agendas, but they'll all be under the banner of ending the war. I looked forward to it.

After Tet and then New Hampshire, the press took the McCarthy campaign more seriously. Even though few established party organizations pledged support, it was powered by countless enthusiastic, optimistic college students. On campuses across the country, they shaved their beards, cut their hair, tried dressing like normal people, and joined what became known as "Clean for Gene" campaign teams. Next, in three weeks, would be Wisconsin. Whit and a few friends had a table in the Student Union every day, signing up volunteers.

Meanwhile, we had midterms to deal with. I studied my Western Civ outline, and made sure to be in the right room at the right time. At least Lane couldn't hold *that* against me. Math was no problem. I actually enjoyed the English exam. To my great delight, the midterm in Sociology of Education was primarily multiple-choice. For most of the questions, I simply gave the professor what I knew he wanted to hear. This course was irritating, but not very demanding. The Ethics course had no exams. Its only requirement was a term paper that would be due in May.

Once the exams were graded, I was still stuck with a C in Western Civ. The others were B and B-plus. To keep my 3.0 average safe, I'd need to pick up my game a bit and do well with the Ethics paper.

Cat got an A in everything.

During the next weekend, Senator Robert F. Kennedy threw his hat into the ring. I wasn't sure what to make of this, and postponed taking a side until after the next gathering of The Circle.

Cat and I, mostly Cat, decided to keep up a disciplined schedule during the week-long spring break. After gym-shower-breakfast, a certain amount of work had to be done before fun time began. My only real work was the Ethics paper, which was to present the age-old conflict between free will and determinism, and argue a conclusion that the professor would hopefully find reasonable. I started in the library Sunday morning, planning to read works by Kant, Sartre, Rawls, William James and Aristotle. When I came home, I told Cat what I'd read. She said, "Emma has all those books on the shelves. Why not do your work there?"

I thought that was a great idea. I'd be able to help Emma out when she needed it, and Cat would have more time for her much more demanding coursework. I told Emma I'd be at the shop all week, except when I was teaching my after-school classes.

Kennedy's candidacy was the The Circle's main topic. As usual, opinions were both mixed and passionate. Some accused him of being an opportunist, jumping in to compete against McCarthy, who'd been the one to take the risk of clearing the way. Others argued for supporting Kennedy because he had better name recognition, access to more money, and a stronger chance to win the general election.

At one point in the debate, I zoned out. A thought popped into my head of how lucky I was to be here, in the midst of these very smart people, all trying so hard to find a path to ending this awful war. Every one of them had other things to do with their time. But they chose to be here, engaging with one another to make their lives about more than just themselves. How lucky I was to find Emma, who'd taught me so much! Marcellus too. *And what*, I wondered, *had I done in some previous life to deserve Cat in this one?*

It was her elbow that interrupted my reverie. "Are you all right?" she whispered.

"More than all right," I said with a smile, squeezing her hand. She gave me a quizzical look.

Before the group broke up, Whit asked if anyone would be able to go to Madison and make phone calls for the primary. "This is the next hurdle," he said, "and we've got LBJ on the ropes."

Cat, Emma and I caucused for a few minutes. I suggested, "Tomorrow, I have my after-school class, so let's do this on Thursday. Once classes get going again, it'll be hard to get away."

"I'd like that," Emma responded. "I can close up for the day."

Cat demurred. "I have way too much work to do. It would be on my mind all day. You two go. I'll keep the shop open, and study during the downtimes."

When Emma and I arrived at the Madison Teachers Guild, a coordinator led us to a long, narrow room, with counters lining the two walls and one window at the far end. Chairs and telephones were spaced four feet from one another, down the two sides.

"Welcome to our phone bank," said the young man, handing each of us some papers. "What we're doing today is identifying people who are likely to vote for Gene in the primary. Once their names have been flagged, we'll go back to them in two weeks with our 'get-out-the-vote' effort."

I found an empty seat, and looked through the list of registered Democrats and their phone numbers. The instructions said to numerically indicate the voters' probability of pulling the lever for McCarthy, with "1" being "least likely" and "5" being "most likely."

We also had a script, with branches depending on the person's responses. For voters who indicated enthusiasm for the cause, it said to simply thank them and promise to get back in touch. For the undecided, it called for asking a few preset questions or reciting talking points. When we encountered voters hostile to the cause, we were to simply thank them for their time, hang up and move on. The idea was to get as much relevant information as possible as quickly as possible. I began dialing.

I focused intently on my lists, and made good progress. Many people weren't at home, so they would get another call from the evening shift. The many people I did speak to expressed a wide range of views, so I was using all the numbers between 1 and 5. I wrote more than enough 4's and 5's, though, to fuel a degree of optimism.

When I took a moment to catch my breath, I sat back and looked around. A dozen people were dialing, talking, making notes, like I was.

Two-thirds of the way down the other side of the room was Emma, though, following her own script. She was standing, sometimes pacing, holding the phone in her left hand and a lit Newport in her right, speaking animatedly into the receiver. I knew right away what she was doing: persuading those on the other end of the line to cast a vote against the war. She was, of course, violating the established protocol, since we were supposed to be only gauging opinion. But I knew no-one would interrupt her, and no-one did.

By five o'clock, my index finger felt ready to fall off from dialing all those numbers, and I was getting hungry. I was glad to be playing a small role in the campaign, but I was also glad to see the next shift taking over the phone bank.

My last call was to Cat. I told her there was heavy rush-hour traffic, and we'd have to stop for dinner along the way. She didn't take it well.

"Be sure to call me if you'll be home past nine," she said glumly. "And drive carefully. Please."

Emma and I ate quickly at a highway rest stop, but the rest of the drive was through pouring rain. Visibility was bad and the traffic was slow. There were accidents along the way. By the time I got home, it was 9:15. I was late.

Cat stood in the doorway, a welcome sight. Her crossed arms and tight visage, though, warned of trouble ahead.

"Where have you been?" she demanded when I reached the landing. "You said you'd be home by nine! You promised to call! You know how I worry. You promised!"

I hemmed and hawed my way through an apology, with little effect. Closing the distance between us, I stopped talking and wrapped her in my arms. At first, her body was stiff, unyielding. After a minute or two, though, it softened. She squeezed me around the waist, sobbing against my chest.

"I missed you all day," she said through her tears. "After you said you'd be late, I had this awful sense of déjà vu. The two most important people in my world out there on the interstate, in a storm at night. I tried pushing it away, but it wouldn't go. All I could do was sit here alone, watching the clock and wondering if you'd ever come back."

"We're all home safe now," I said, stroking her hair, "and I promise it won't happen again. I really mean it." I held her tight against my body. When she calmed down, I asked, "Want to hear about my day?"

"That can wait until morning," she said, taking a step back. "You must be very tired. Come." She took my hand and led me into the bedroom. I really was tired. But not too tired.

Chapter 27

Sharon called the next day to invite the three of us for an early Sunday dinner. She said there was something important to discuss, so we quickly accepted.

Arielle squealed as we came through the door. "Come on, let's play!" she pleaded, grabbing my wrist and pulling me into her room. She had the dolls lined up and the storyline already prepared. A half hour later, when dinner was ready, she tried negotiating for more time, but without success. As a compromise, Mommy allowed her to bring along her favorite doll, a big one named Flossie.

It was during dessert when Sharon got to her agenda. "Do you remember, on Christmas Eve, we talked about the BSU's new goals?" she asked.

"Sure," I responded. "More Black students. More Black teachers. A Black Studies program. How's it going?"

"Well, we did get a meeting with President Kent. He called in the Director of Admissions and told him to work on a program to recruit qualified Black freshmen. We suggested going after transfer students from the Southern Black colleges, and he agreed to look into that too. Something might come of this, but we'll see."

"What about the other two things?" Emma asked.

"We hit a wall with those. Kent insisted that Midway's hiring process was color-blind. We pointed out that this so-called 'color-blind' process produced a lily-white faculty, so it must not be so color-blind after all. When we brought up Black Studies, he said academic policy decisions originate in the Faculty Council, so we should approach its chairman, Professor Lane of the History Department."

I groaned. "I bet I know where that went. Nowhere."

"You're more than right about that, Steve. First, he refused to meet with us, but we persisted. When he did hear our demands, he called them 'reverse racism,' and insisted that he'd never dignify them with consideration by the Faculty Council."

"So now what?"

"When we talked about this before, you said you thought some white students would support us. Do you still think so?"

"Sure I do."

"Well, it's time to find out. The Faculty Council's next meeting is Thursday afternoon. We're going to take it over, and make sure they at least hear our case. If white students are there in support, they won't be able to isolate us, or pigeonhole the BSU as a bunch of angry, ungrateful Black militants."

"We'll get right on it," I promised. "We developed a telephone tree for the Dow Chemical protest, and there were no leaks. We can put it to use for this."

"Wonderful," Sharon said. "The meeting will be in the Midway Theater at four. We'll gather at the far end of the rear parking lot a half hour earlier. That'll give us time to assign battle stations without being noticed. We have to surprise them."

"But listen, Steve" Marcellus added. "Sharon's asking only for support behind the BSU strategy, not for suggestions or arguments. Following Black leadership will be something new for some of the people you contact."

In each of the calls Cat and I made, we stressed that point. When the time came on Thursday, Sharon stepped up on a box and gave us our marching orders. There was no discussion. At precisely 4:05, she announced, "Now!"

Silently, we poured through the back door and onto the theater stage. The Black students formed four ranks of twenty, facing the audience. Cat was among them. Down the stairs on each side of the stage streamed more than a hundred white supporters. We lined the walls on both sides of the auditorium. At the same time, the lobby doors opened. A dozen uniformed Black Panthers entered and stood with their arms folded, blocking the exits.

Professor Lane, standing at the podium, was dumbfounded. "What's going on here?" he demanded. "This room has been reserved for a very important meeting of the Faculty Council. You must all leave. Immediately!" No-one moved and no-one spoke.

From backstage came the sound of drums, first very faint, then rising. I saw panic register on some of the professors' faces. When the drumming got low again, the ranks on stage parted in the middle. Sharon strode through the opening, flanked by two more Panthers, straight to the podium where she calmly told Lane, "Excuse me. I will take the floor now." Everyone heard this, because the microphone was on. Lane looked around and backed away. The drumming rose again, then suddenly stopped.

Sharon was now the center of attention. She'd changed into colorful African garb, complete with an elaborate headdress. Almost six feet tall to begin with, the headdress and, I suspected, high heels, had her towering over the podium. I'm sure I wasn't the only one struck by the regal bearing she projected, standing so straight, so quiet, so elegant, until the buzzing in the audience settled down.

"My name is Sharon Sheppard," she began. "I will not use much of your time, but you will hear what I have to say. I represent Midway's Black Student Union, which will present you with a proposal." I wondered whether she was as confident as she appeared.

Among the hundred or so Faculty Council members, all but two of them white, the buzzing renewed. One stood up and shouted, "Young lady, this is a scheduled meeting of the university's most important academic body. It is not to be hijacked. If you have something to say, you must go through the proper channels. This is outrageous, and we will not have it!" Expressions of support rang out.

Sharon did not respond, except to raise her right hand toward the ceiling. The drumming resumed, beginning low and rising to a fever pitch. She lowered her arm and it suddenly stopped. Silence reigned once again. Sweat formed visibly on the faces of professors sitting near me.

"But before I present you with this proposal," Sharon continued, "I will yield the floor to Brother James Watkins, Executive Director of the South Side Organization."

Watkins got right to the point.

"I want to thank the BSU for inviting me to Midway University," he began. "In all my years at the South Side Organization, which is headquartered only six blocks from this very spot, I have never before been invited here. To my community, Midway may as well be on a distant planet."

"We have reached out to your university, several times, for assistance that could've been easily provided. The results of this outreach have been pathetic. I know many of you are afraid to walk our streets. I know what goes through your minds when you see our young men. Midway's only connection with the South Side has been the purchase of real estate for its own expansion."

"But I'm not here today to beg Midway University to suddenly adopt a Good Neighbor Policy. I am here in support of the Black Student Union. Your response to Sister Sheppard's proposal will be a test of whether even the best and brightest of my people are welcome at this institution, or if your only recognition of their talent and hard work is token tolerance. Be informed that the BSU has the full support of the South Side community, and that we will be watching. You would do well to remember this as you consider its proposal."

With those words, he turned and strode off stage. As instructed, we remained silent. Apprehension hung in the air.

"This university was founded seventy years ago," Sharon announced. "Since then, the world has changed. African colonies have thrown off the shackles of European colonialism. The Civil Rights Movement has reshaped the social and political landscape of the United States. Yet here at Midway, *nothing* has changed. The Black experience does not exist in its curriculum. Its students, both Black and white, are taught *white* history, *white* philosophy, and *white* literature. *Our* writers, *our* thinkers, *our* scholars, *our very history*, which is central to the history of this country, are passed over. In the required freshman World History course, Africa does not exist. This is not only an incomplete education. It is an *insult*. And now it's time that it ended. The BSU's proposal challenges you to take three steps in beginning to right these wrongs, and to complete them by the beginning of the Fall Semester."

"First, we propose the hiring of no less than twelve African-American professors. This will not occur through the normal course of events. Since Midway's racial reputation makes Black scholars reluctant to apply here, they will have to be actively recruited."

"Second, we propose the formation of an autonomous Black Studies Department, chaired by a prominent Black scholar, with a budget equal to that of the History Department."

"Third, we propose that completion of a course in African-American History, to be offered by the new Black Studies Department, become required for the B.A. degree. A requirement for *every* Midway student."

"Finally," she concluded, "let me inform you that these proposals are not mere requests, presented on bended knee. They are *demands*. When we return in the fall, we will expect them to have been met. If not, we will be prepared to be more persuasive."

The drummers went to work once again. That was our cue. As we streamed back up the steps and through the stage, still in single file, the Black students chanted to the drumbeat, in unison, "Power concedes nothing without a demand." In response, we chanted, "It never has and it never will." The Frederick Douglass quote was repeated over and over until we all spilled out into the parking lot. There, as the drummers jammed, jubilation reigned. When Sharon emerged from the building, everyone applauded. Cat and I charged at each other. I lifted her up and swung her in circles. Then, surprised to see Emma joining the festivities, we ran over.

I asked, "Did you see what happened?"

"Marcellus and I were up in the balcony, with Arielle," she replied breathlessly. "We saw the whole thing. It was absolutely magnificent!" It looked to me, at that moment, like Emma had shed about twenty years.

Marcellus, Sharon and Arielle joined us. Arielle began jumping up and down with her hands in the air. I reached down and picked her up.

"Sharon, that was an amazing performance" I gushed. "How'd you come up with such elaborate orchestration?"

"Well, Midway wasn't my first college," she explained. "After high school, I went to a community college, but dropped out after I got pregnant. I had a different major there."

"Oh. What was that?"

She looked down at me, smiled and softly replied, "Drama."

Chapter 28

The month of March 1968 had been such an exciting one for me. We drove Dow Chemical's recruiters off the campus, and an embryonic Black-white alliance drew a line in the sand for the Faculty Council. Meanwhile, both the McCarthy and Kennedy campaigns gathered steam. Polling for the Wisconsin primary was looking good for our side. The month would end on an even higher note.

On Sunday, March 31st, Cat turned the TV news on while we cleaned up after dinner. We were surprised to hear that President Johnson was going to address the nation later that night, pre-empting all the networks' regular programming.

"What do you think he'll say?" she asked.

"Who knows? Could be another escalation of the war. The generals are saying they can't win it with *only* half a million troops on the ground. But how can LBJ give in to that while his approval numbers are crashing? I heard on the news he's down to, like, 30 percent."

Nicky Jarvis called to tell us, "We'll be gathering on the quad to hear the speech. The college radio station will broadcast it over the P.A. system. If LBJ announces more troops or more bombing, we need to respond right away. Look, there's no time for planning. How about we march over to the ROTC building and burn the motherfucker down?"

"Sounds good to me."

When Cat and Emma and I got to the quad, hundreds of students were milling around, wondering what to expect. Promptly at nine, the broadcast began. The first substantive things Johnson said were that he was suspending the bombing of North Vietnam's northern cities, and that he would open negotiations to end the war. The crowd applauded, with varying degrees of enthusiasm. Then came the blockbuster, delivered almost as an afterthought.

"I shall not seek, and I will not accept, the nomination of my party for another term as your president."

The campus exploded in celebration. Students who'd been watching TV in the dorms poured out onto the quad. Musical instruments appeared, and improvised bands joined together to play protest songs and dance music. We were sure now that our next president, either Kennedy or McCarthy, would finally withdraw U.S. troops from Vietnam.

Optimism was still running high when The Circle gathered two nights later. The Wisconsin primary results weren't yet in, but we had reason to expect good news in the morning. Emma opened the session by asking if any of us knew of a turn-of-the-century short story called, "The Monkey's Paw." We all shook our heads, puzzled.

"Let me give you a brief synopsis," she began. "A British couple's adult son works in a nearby factory. One night, an old friend pays the couple a visit. He gives them a wooden box which he says was given to him by an Indian mystic. Opening the box exposes a mummified monkey's paw which, he claims, can grant its owner three wishes. Before saying good-night, though, he warns them not to tempt fate with it."

"The couple opens the box one more time before retiring for the night and, mostly in jest, they wish for a gift of two hundred pounds. The following afternoon, a factory representative visits to tell them their son got ensnared in some machinery and killed. He explains that the company disclaims any responsibility, but presents them with a compensatory check... for two hundred pounds."

"I don't think I need to tell you the rest of the story," she concluded, "except that next two wishes also backfired."

"So what," she asked, "is the moral of this little fable?"

It took a few moments until someone called out, "Be careful what you wish for?"

"Precisely. LBJ's abdication is a vindication of our movement, and perhaps it will provide an opening to peace. But let's consider it in context." Whit asked her what she meant by that.

"Shift your focus to domestic policy," she explained. "Remember, during just his first two years, LBJ got the Civil Rights Act and the Voting Rights Act passed. He got Medicare and Medicaid. He declared a War on Poverty, and isn't that a war we've all supported? He signed the Immigration Act, repealing four decades of racist laws. And for the past two years, he's been trying to get a law passed to outlaw racial discrimination in housing."

I knew Emma was right, but couldn't put the pieces together in my head. I asked, "So were we wrong in opposing him?"

"Of course not. The Vietnam War wasn't his when he came into office, but he made it his own. The escalation, the bombing, the Napalm, the deaths, they add up to a human and historical sin. But the abdication is a little more complicated than it seemed Sunday night, when we celebrated. Given time for reflection, I see it as tragic, even though it was necessary. LBJ's war advisors hijacked what was shaping up to be the greatest presidency since FDR. This is no small tragedy either. It's of Shakespearean proportions. Also, we can't be sure of what's coming next."

Emma's monologue kind of deflated us that evening. I knew she was right, but the euphoria that followed in the wake of LBJ's address felt so much better.

The good feelings returned on Wednesday, though, when we learned McCarthy won the Wisconsin primary with 56 percent of the vote. Johnson, whose name was still on the ballot, got only 35 percent. Kennedy, a late ballot entry, got 6 percent. Even though the president was no longer a candidate, I viewed that primary as a referendum on the war. And we won it, by almost a two-to-one margin. Everyone I met that day was in a sunny mood. It wasn't long, though, until the darkest of clouds rolled in.

That night, I turned the late news on while Cat was getting ready for bed. The big story was about Martin Luther King, who was in Memphis to support the striking sanitation workers. It broadcast the closing paragraph of the speech he was delivering to a packed church rally. As soon as it began, I yelled for Cat to come and watch. I was having a terrible premonition. The words he spoke burned themselves into my memory.

> *We've got some difficult days ahead. But it doesn't matter with me now, because I've been to the mountaintop... Like anybody, I'd like to live a long life... But I'm not concerned about that now. I just want to do God's will. And He's allowed me to go up to the mountain. And I've looked over and I've seen the Promised Land. I may not get there with you. But I want you to know tonight, that we, as a people, will get to the Promised Land. And I'm happy tonight. I'm not worried*

about anything. I'm not fearing any man. Mine eyes have seen the glory of the coming of the Lord.

Cat and I turned to one another. I squeezed out, "My god, he thinks he's gonna be killed." Haunted by Dr. King's words, I hardly slept that night.

At a little past six the following evening, April 4th, the whole country learned of the assassination. The ghettos erupted in rage. Riots, looting, arson, and open battles with police broke out in 125 cities. We heard sirens wailing through the South Side. The late news reported that twenty square blocks of the West Side ghetto had burned completely down, and that the Chicago police were overwhelmed, unable to stem the tide of the uprising.

In the morning, Mayor Daley appeared on TV. He said he ordered his cops to *shoot to kill* any suspected arsonist, and *shoot to cripple* any looter. The newscaster reported that more than 12,000 National Guardsmen and 5,000 regular Army troops would be dispatched to Chicago by the end of the day.

Marcellus called to tell me, "Don't come down here today. It's not safe. We've closed the after-school program, and we're trying to keep folks indoors." He had no time for questions.

That night, thousands of Chicago's Black citizens were randomly rounded up and thrown in jail. Nine were reported killed. This only fueled the anger. While Cat and I were watching it on TV, Nicky called.

"Are you guys going to the march tomorrow?"

"What march?" I asked.

"It's an emergency action in solidarity with the Black community. We're marching on the National Guard armory, starting tomorrow at two."

"Don't you need a permit for something like this?"

"Yes, and that's the surprising thing. The city is stonewalling the Peace Council on permits for the antiwar parade on the 27th. But the Mobe got this one in a matter of hours. We're restricted to the sidewalks, but otherwise we shouldn't run into any problems. The staging area will be in a park about four miles away."

Once I wrote down the details and thanked him, I told Cat what he said.

"I don't know, Steve," she responded. "The armory will be full of soldiers, and the whole city's on edge. It sounds dangerous."

"Yes, but this'll be a peaceful march," I argued. "The city even granted a permit. And it won't be like the Pentagon, where people tried to break inside. It's only a march through Downtown and then around the armory's perimeter. Maybe a few speeches. That's all."

"Okay, but let's get Emma's take on it. Give her a call."

"It's the least people can do," Emma agreed a few minutes later, "and I wish I was up to a four-mile walk. I'm surprised the permit came through so quickly, but it's certainly good to have it. Before you decide, though, I suggest checking in with Marcellus or Sharon. Get their perspective too."

Marcellus didn't answer his phone, but Sharon did.

"This sounds like a good thing," she said. "Any outside support our people can get is super important. Things are getting crazy down here. We have tanks rolling down our streets. Cops are going nuts. They're shooting people, breaking heads, arresting anyone they can get their hands on. The noise is terrifying Arielle. But I need to talk to Marcellus. He's out with the Panthers, trying to cool things down. Can we call you in the morning?"

"That would be fine," I replied. "Meanwhile, stay safe."

Cat and I fell asleep watching the cities burn on TV. I woke an hour later, and carried her into the bedroom. Neither of us slept well. During one of my waking episodes, I reflected on the week that had opened with such hope, ending now in apocalypse.

Sharon called early to say they would join us. I told her we'd pick them up at one, and stumbled into the shower. I woke Cat when breakfast was about ready.

"So we're going, right?" I asked, after telling her about the phone call.

"I guess so," she responded, picking at her cheese omelet. Looking up with a little smile, she added, "Like I said, *someone* has to keep an eye on you!"

Chapter 29

Driving to the staging area, I asked Marcellus about his night out on the streets.

"At times, it was scary," he reported. "We had to keep from getting shot or arrested ourselves. But we did convince people to get indoors, and I'm sure we saved a few lives."

"Sharon said you were with the Panthers. They weren't part of the uprising?"

"No. Their position was that it was self-destructive. The people in these cities were burning down their own communities and inviting military intervention. It's understandable because of the anger, the disorganization, the impulse to strike out at whatever's close by. But the Panthers regard spontaneous outbreaks as counter-revolutionary, because there's no possibility of victory. They're armed and they're willing to fight, but only in self-defense or when there's a chance of winning."

"So you were with them last night, and there were Panthers at the BSU's confrontation with the Faculty Council. Is there a connection?"

"Nothing formal. I grew up with some of them, and my martial arts classes are popular with the South Side chapter. A few members had even been in prison with my brother Cassius for a while."

"Have you given any thought to joining?"

"They recruited me, and I did consider it. They do good work, like their free breakfast program for kids, and their structure and discipline make for positive role models. They encourage self-respect. But the life of a Black Panther is a little too regimented for me. I had enough of that in the Army."

We had to park Tooter a block from the staging area. The police vehicles surrounding the small park led me to think this march would be a big one.

But it wasn't. Apparently, the same concerns Cat had voiced kept many people away. Fear was thick in Chicago's air. Heading out toward the armory, not even a thousand strong, we seemed to be outnumbered by the police.

I soon sensed something else wrong with this march. The mood was somber, not defiant. There was no singing, no chanting of slogans. They sky was depressingly gray, and smoke still rose in the distance from smoldering overnight fires. Also, we were still grieving the loss of Dr. King. Whatever the reason, the usual energy was missing. The police, gripping clubs in their hands, their faces uniformly menacing, herded us onto crowded sidewalks as we slowly made our way toward the armory.

In a weak attempt to lighten things up, I asked Sharon, "So how's your little angel doing?"

She smiled. "Oh, Arielle is great. Her fifth birthday is coming up in two weeks, and she's excited about going to 'big-girl school' in the fall."

"Any plans for the birthday?" Cat asked.

"I know she'd love a party, but that's kind of a problem," Sharon explained. "She spends her weekdays at Midway's preschool. Her friends from there are all children of Midway faculty and students."

"How's that a problem?"

"They're mostly white. And they're not going to bring their kids down to the South Side for a birthday party. Not to my place, not to the SSO, not anywhere. They seem to be decent people, I guess, but they'd be too scared."

"So you need another place. I'll ask Emma. She might know of one. And you be sure to call me the next time you need a babysitter. I come cheap." Cat squeezed my hand a little tighter.

As we moved down a small hill, the East Chicago Avenue Armory came into view. Ahead of us, the forward ranks of the marchers were massing on the street, which was closed to traffic at both ends. Before we were able to join them, the huge armory doors burst open. Hundreds of soldiers in gas masks swarmed out, pointing bayonet-fitted rifles. They charged forward. There was no escape. Tear gas canisters flew. People coughed, wheezed, screamed they couldn't see, fell to the ground.

Marcellus called, "Let's go!" We turned and followed him back the way we'd come. His prosthetic knee caused him to run with an odd gait, but he was still fast. He kept checking to make sure we were keeping up.

I looked back down the hill. The police were also in attack mode now, clubbing the fleeing marchers, throwing some into paddy wagons, leaving others bleeding in the street. My mind was racing along with my legs. Suddenly, I knew why the permit was granted so readily, and why the police made sure we got to the armory. "This whole thing," I shouted, "was a trap!"

Marcellus led us into a block-through alley. No cops followed us in, and it seemed for a moment that we'd escaped. When we made it halfway through, though, a canopied troop transport pulled up at the far end, blocking the exit. Two soldiers climbed out of the cab and walked toward us, hands resting on their sidearms. Soldiers on one end, cops on the other. Nowhere to run. Worst of all, there was terror in Cat's eyes. I held her close.

Marcellus remained calm, though. "Stay here," he ordered, strolling confidently toward the two soldiers. I noticed he was wearing his old army field jacket and combat boots. As he walked, he pulled a green beret from a pocket and put it on.

I couldn't hear the conversation he struck up with them, but it seemed to begin well. I thought he might be able to talk us through this. But one of them raised his voice and pointed at us. Whatever Marcellus was selling, they weren't buying it now. The guns were coming out of their holsters. I started forward, but Sharon grabbed my arm.

"Wait," she said. "He can handle this."

Sharon was right. Marcellus suddenly morphed into a whirl of chops, jabs and kicks. In less than a minute, the two soldiers were on the ground, one obviously unconscious, the other dazed. At his beckon, we ran forward.

"Get in the back of the truck," he ordered. "I'll drive." At that moment, if he'd told us to jump on a flying carpet, we'd have done it.

We rushed to the rear of the transport and parted the curtain. Six more soldiers were sitting on benches. I froze, but Cat, as usual, grasped the situation instantly.

"Hurry!" she called. "Two of your friends are lying in the alley. They look hurt."

The soldiers grabbed their rifles and jumped out of the truck. One turned back and asked, "Did you see what happened?"

By then I'd recovered. I answered, "No, but four guys ran past us as we were coming through. Big white guys. They looked like bikers."

When all six were in the alley, we jumped into the truck and closed the curtain. Marcellus fired up the engine and off we went. Ten minutes later, he drove it into the park where the march had begun. The weather was getting nasty now, and the park was deserted. We ran over to Tooter and headed for home.

Once we caught our breath, I said to Marcellus, "I guess that Special Forces training really came in handy today."

"I guess it did," he agreed.

"But how'd you know the keys were in the truck's ignition?"

"I didn't, and they weren't. I hotwired the truck to get it started."

"You hotwired it?"

"Yeah. Cassius taught me how when I was a kid," he explained, adding "I guess I've had a varied education. 'Interdisciplinary' is the college word for it, I think."

Now we could laugh, releasing some of the day's tension. A few minutes later, I asked him if they'd be looking for us.

"I don't think so," he replied. "They'll retrieve the truck and cover this all up, along with what else happened today. They'll never admit charging into civilians with bayonets. And it'd be too embarrassing to admit they lost two soldiers and a truck."

After dropping them off at Sharon's place, we parked Tooter on High Street and rushed down the block. At our door, I paused and asked, "Shouldn't we tell Emma what happened?"

"Later," Cat said firmly, pulling me inside. Upstairs, we went at each other with an adrenaline-fueled lust that bordered on violence.

Once we were spent, we rested, with her head on my chest, my arm wrapped around her. After a while, she said, "Now, make that call."

Emma was relieved to hear my voice. "I was worried something might've happened to you," she said. "I've been hearing terrible stories."

I apologized for waiting so long to call, and told her we had a story of our own for her.

"I want to hear it," she said, "but let's save it 'til morning. For now, I'm happy to know you're safe. Come for a Sunday breakfast, around ten. You'll tell me your story, and I have something to show you too."

"We'll be there. But one more thing before I forget." I explained the birthday party dilemma and asked, "Do you have any ideas?"

"I might," she responded. "I'll give Sharon a call."

After a quick dinner, Cat and I picked up where we'd left off, but at a much slower pace. Eventually, we did get to sleep.

In the middle of the night, though, I woke with a start, in a cold sweat. The motion woke her. She sat up and asked, "What's wrong?"

I leaned back on my pillow. "Do you remember that recurring carnival nightmare I told you about?"

"Sure I do. It sounded terrifying."

"When it hit me after the Pentagon march, I wasn't even asleep. But it hasn't returned since we've been together, until tonight. And this time was worse."

"How?"

"I was still four years old in the dream, but I wasn't with my parents. I was with you, like you are now. I was so happy, strolling through the carnival, your hand in my right, an ice cream cone in my left. Suddenly my right hand was empty. When I looked up, you were gone. Vanished. I was all alone. The carnival music turned menacing, and my world collapsed around me." Tears were running down my cheeks.

"Come," she said, lying back and patting her belly. I slid down and rested my head there. She held it with one hand, and stroked my back with the other.

"I'm right here," she repeated softly, over and over. "I'm right here." Before long, we both drifted back to sleep.

Chapter 30

In the morning, before briefing Emma on our adventure, I asked if the birthday problem was solved.

"It's already settled," she announced. "I spoke with Sharon, and the party will be two weeks from yesterday, right upstairs here. And you'll be in charge of the children's games."

Cat volunteered to handle the decorating, and Emma said she'd take care of the food. Then we related Saturday's events. Emma interrupted when I told her I thought we'd been led into a trap.

"That's sure what it sounds like," she commented. "I wouldn't be surprised if Daley was behind granting the permit. I wonder what he's planning for Convention Week."

"I hadn't thought about that," I responded. "Maybe this was a dry run. I never thought the protesters should expect a warm welcome, but yesterday sure put things in a new light."

We continued with our story. Emma loved the part where we borrowed the troop transport. "Now *that* was inspired thinking!" she exclaimed.

While we finished clearing the table, I asked what it was she wanted to show us. She brought over a couple of newspapers.

"First, you've got to see this," she said, opening the Sunday *Tribune* to Page 6, and sliding it across the table. The brief article covered the march on the armory, reporting that twenty-five people got arrested and that tear gas had been used to scatter the marchers. There was no mention of injuries. The National Guard commander admitted the rifles were fitted with bayonets, but claimed they'd been pointed at the sky, not at the marchers. There was no mention of a missing truck.

"Marcellus was right," Cat remarked. "They're covering up the whole thing."

"It isn't the first time," added Emma, "And it won't be the last. In a way, that relates to the main thing I want to show you. But first, listen to this line from the editorial about the riots: 'Here in Chicago, we are not dealing with the colored population, but with a minority of criminal scum.' Colored! Who uses that term anymore? And criminal scum? Disgraceful!"

"Here's something else," she continued. "Friday's *Times* got here yesterday."

She folded the first section in half, and pointed to a headline: "Humphrey Hints He'll Enter Race." We skimmed the first few paragraphs. "Hint" was an understatement. Apparently, a big labor union event in Pittsburgh had been turned into a well-organized campaign rally for LBJ's vice president.

"So, pretty soon," Emma predicted, "there'll be a new front-runner in the contest for the presidential nomination."

"But isn't it too late?" asked Cat. "The primaries have already begun."

"Humphrey will have a big base of support as soon as he announces, which will be soon," Emma explained. "To many liberals, he's been a hero for decades. That's why LBJ put him on the ticket in the first place."

"But he supports the war," I said. "His contradictions are the same as LBJ's. How can he expect to win the primaries?"

"He doesn't need to win any primaries," Emma explained to my surprise. "Only fourteen states choose their convention delegates through primaries. In all the others, it's the party bosses who pick the delegates, not the voters."

"So they'll try to steal this," I groaned, slumping in my seat. "I guess I can see why you read all these newspapers."

"This makes building the antiwar movement even more urgent," Emma argued, "and the demonstration at the convention too. It might be a lot bigger with Humphrey in the picture. Too many people have gotten complacent that either McCarthy or Kennedy will walk in without a fight. But only a powerful grass-roots movement can get us out of Vietnam."

Pointing to the banner headline, she said, "This is the main thing I wanted to show you." It was about the assassination. Pointing next to the byline, she added, "Earl Caldwell is a young Black reporter. He was in Memphis to interview Dr. King. As far as I can tell, he was the only journalist on the scene at the time of the shooting. It's a long article. Take your time."

Cat and I pored over the article. When we finished, I asked which part she wanted to talk about.

"Let's picture the scene," she began. "The balcony where Dr. King got shot is in the back of the Lorraine Motel, overlooking a parking area. Beyond that is a scrubby area overgrown with bushes. Up a hill and behind a wire fence is the rooming house where the police chief says the shot came from. Right?"

"Right," I agreed, "from a second-floor bathroom window."

"And when the shot was fired, what does Caldwell say Dr. King was doing?"

"Leaning over the balcony railing," I replied, "talking to Jesse Jackson and a musician down in the parking lot."

"So you tell me," Emma asked, "how he could've been shot in the front of the neck, if he was looking down and the shot came from above?"

Cat and I turned and looked at each other. "It doesn't seem possible," she said.

"Caldwell says he saw movement in the bushes right after the shot was fired." Emma continued. "That's where Rev. Jackson told the police the shot came from. Doesn't it make more sense that the shot came from there, from below? But it sounds like that possibility isn't even being investigated."

"And there's more," she continued. "Dr. King attracted death threats wherever he went. He always got police protection on high-profile trips like this one, including his first trip to Memphis, the week before. So why weren't any cops there at the time of the shooting? Then, immediately afterward, why was the place instantly swarming with them, as though they were waiting for it to happen? And why did fifteen minutes pass before an ambulance arrived?"

I leaned my elbows on the table, held my head in my hands, and tried to put these pieces together. "So what do you think happened?" I asked, the answer already forming in my brain.

"Martin Luther King," she explained, "had become more than a civil rights leader. Almost exactly a year ago, he came out forcefully against the Vietnam War, in a speech that indicted this nation's whole violent history. And now, he was organizing a Poor People's March on

Washington. Not just Black people, but poor people of all colors. He was pulling together the movements against racism, against war and against economic injustice. He had become *a very dangerous man*. That's why he had to be eliminated."

"So the police did it?"

"They had to at least be involved. But I don't think they were on their own. Probably the FBI directed the whole operation."

"And that's where the cover-up comes in?" asked Cat.

"Yes, and it will be a nice clean one. The police chief says they're looking for a white man who was in the rooming house. They'll find him before long, because they have to make an arrest and close the case. He'll be some poor lost soul, a Lee Harvey Oswald type. They might even get a guilty plea out of him. And that will be the end of it."

"But what about all the contradictions?" I asked. "They're right here in the front-page story!"

"I don't know Earl Caldwell," Emma said, "but he must be a very smart young man. He had to be, in order to break the color line at the *Times*. I'm sure he suspects who was behind this. He put the clues into his story, but he knew that knitting them together would've alarmed an editor. He was only able to do as much as he did because he had the advantage of the story's urgency. There was no time for reading between the lines, like we did. This is the early edition. I wonder if the same story even made it into the late edition."

"Don't you think he'll follow up his own leads?" Cat asked.

"He will if the *Times* keeps him on the story," Emma said. "But that probably won't happen. Soon, they'll assign him to some place far from Memphis."

On our way back upstairs, I commented to Cat, "This weekend has been quite an eye-opener. But I wonder when things like these won't always take me by surprise."

That week, the South Side slowly came back to a semblance of normalcy. It hadn't suffered nearly as much physical damage as the West Side did, thanks to the Black Panthers and the SSO staff being out on the streets. The after-school program resumed on Monday, and more stores reopened each day.

Tuesday's papers summarized the city's human toll. The police arrested 2,150 Black residents, including 368 children. They shot forty-eight people, and killed eleven. On the police side, ninety injuries were reported, none of them serious.

The Army and National Guard troops didn't leave Chicago until a week later. That day, Congress passed the Fair Housing Act, which banned discrimination on the basis of race, religion, national origin or gender. President Johnson, who'd been pushing this law for two years without success, signed it right away. It was no coincidence that the bill suddenly flew through Congress right after the events of the previous week.

Marcellus and I crossed paths at the SSO late Friday afternoon.

"You've recovered from our adventure?" he asked.

"I guess so," I replied, "but there are scenes I'll never forget. American soldiers charging into unarmed civilians with bayonets. Marcellus, what's going on in this country?"

"Nothing that hasn't been going on for a few hundred years. Most white folks have been insulated from it 'til now, though. See, when the system comes down on whites, it's because of things they do, like marching on the Pentagon or an armory. But *we* catch hell because of who we are. Like last Friday night, when so many folks got beaten and arrested. Why? Because they were Black and within reach. There's no escaping that difference."

"I can see that," I agreed. "And there's maybe an assassination cover-up."

"What do you mean?"

I related Emma's analysis of the Earl Caldwell article, concluding, "So the more I think about it, the more I think he was murdered by the cops and the FBI, and that the guy they're hunting is only a patsy. And I also think the shot came from the bushes, not from that rooming house."

"Now that's very interesting," he responded, "in more ways than one."

"It sure is. But the look on your face tells me there's even more to it."

"Remember I told you my mom moved back to Memphis while I was in the Army?"

"Sure."

"Well, we stay in touch by phone. When I called yesterday, she told me something that fits right in with your theory."

"What's that?"

"Yesterday morning, after things cooled down enough, she drove over to the Lorraine. She wanted to see with her own eyes where it happened, and leave flowers from her garden. She said it was still cordoned off by crime scene tape, but a public works crew was working behind the motel."

"Doing what?"

"They were clearing away all the bushes."

"So no more crime scene, no more chance of a real investigation?"

"Right."

"You know, Marcellus, I'm finally starting to *not* be surprised by things like this."

Chapter 31

A few days later, Donnie Dawes, the Mobe's Project Director, spoke on campus. Bespectacled, clean-shaven, soft-spoken and neatly dressed, he could have been mistaken for a Bible salesman.

But he had been to North Vietnam. He gave us a first-hand account of the craters that the B-52s left behind, the villages bombed out of existence, the permanent disfigurement caused by Napalm, which was now falling like rain over the countryside. I was prepared for that, but not for what came next. He reached into a sack and pulled out several twisted scraps of metal.

"These," he explained, "are pieces of anti-personnel bombs. When they hit the ground, sharp steel fragments like these spray everywhere, killing and maiming everyone within range. Their only purpose is to murder, injure and terrorize civilians. Yes, children included. The U.S. government denies it uses these weapons, but they lie, just as they lied for years about the conventional bombing. They lie to the world. They lie to the American people. They lie to you!"

This made me sick to my stomach. I never would have guessed that such weapons were part of the U.S. arsenal. After considering it for a moment, though, I asked myself, *Why the hell not?*

"Johnson says he's suspending some of the bombing," he continued. "That doesn't mean a thing. Even if it isn't a lie, the words he used are 'suspending,' not 'ending,' and 'some,' not 'all.' Bombs still drop from the skies every day. He says he's sending negotiators to a peace conference in Paris. That won't end the war. The only thing that will end it is ending it. Immediate unconditional withdrawal. And it's not enough to end the war either. We have to change the system that produced it. That's why we'll march on the 27th. That's why we'll confront the war-makers in August at the Democratic Convention. Enough of the lying. Enough of this phony, rigged political system. They will hear from us, loud and clear, in cities across the country. And here in Chicago, when the Democrats arrive for their phony coronation party, we'll be ready to greet them."

I resolved to be at both of these events, no matter what.

His talk ended at 5:30. I rushed over to the bookstore to tell Emma and Cat about those bombs. Just as I was getting started, though, the doorbell jingled. My mouth dropped open as Donnie Dawes entered the shop.

"Donnie!" exclaimed Emma with a welcoming smile. "What brings you here today?"

"I couldn't come to Midway without dropping in to see you," he replied.

"You've lost weight," she observed. "I bet you've been too busy to eat. Stay for dinner." Without waiting for a reply, she gave us our instructions.

"Steve, please close up. Cat, call Sal for a pizza. No, two pizzas. Bring them up and join us."

Cat and I looked at each other and shrugged. We both said, "Okay," as Emma led Donnie up the back stairs.

Over dinner, I asked Donnie and Emma how they knew each other.

"I grew up here in Chicago," he began. "Four years ago, after college, I came back. A few of us SDS alumni opened a storefront in the Uptown section, where a lot of poor whites from Appalachia live. We called it JOIN, Jobs or Income Now. The idea was to combine anti-racist political education with community organizing."

"Shortly afterward, one of Midway's SDS members came for a visit," he continued. "She suggested I meet Emma, so I came down here. Emma's been dispensing valuable advice ever since. Without it, JOIN wouldn't have become nearly as successful as it's been. She's taught me a whole lot about community organizing."

"I had good teachers myself," Emma said, "back in the day. But enough about me. How's planning for the march coming along? The 27th is only eleven days away."

"Well, we've got a few problems," he admitted, growing more serious. "The first is that the movement got thrown for a loop by the McCarthy and Kennedy candidacies, and by LBJ's withdrawal. That night, we lost our best, clearest target. Now some people think they can end the war by campaigning, or simply voting, for a peace candidate. They argue that demonstrations and marches are unnecessary now, even counter-productive."

"Americans have a short memory," Emma responded. "They forget LBJ himself ran as a peace candidate. He might even have meant it at the time. If, by some miracle, McCarthy or Kennedy wins, they'll face the same forces, the same pressures, that he did. Eisenhower was right in warning against the power of the military-industrial complex."

Donnie agreed. "The politicians need to face pressure from us too. We need to stay active on the streets, not sit around waiting for the polls to open. But convincing people of that can be an uphill climb."

"But we're facing practical obstacles too," he added. "The mayor's minions have been stonewalling on a parade permit for the 27th. They won't respond one way or the other. If we don't get the permit, the march won't be legal. People could be in danger."

"Daley did this to the Peace Council before," Emma interjected. "He waits until the last minute before he tells his commissioners to issue permits. That way, he fouls up the planning, but he can't be accused of violating anyone's First Amendment rights. You know that."

"Yes, of course, and it may happen that way again. But it sure does foul up the planning. Also, even though we have a signed contract with the Park District to rent their sound system, they haven't taken our calls for three weeks. Even with all the problems, people will show up for this march. But without a sound system, it'll be chaotic. Our closing rally at Civic Center Plaza might not even be possible."

That night, Cat said, "I don't know about this march. I'm still shaking from the last one."

"It'll be fine," I replied. "We'll be with thousands of people. Permit or no permit, they won't be able to stop it."

"No," she insisted. "You thought the armory march would be safe too, and we were just plain lucky to escape that time. If there's no permit, we're not going. It'll be too dangerous."

"I get it, Cat. But let's see what happens. We don't need to decide until the night before."

I was determined to go, permit or no permit, but too tired to argue. Also, the events of the past two weeks, then Donnie's speech and the discussion at Emma's, gave me a lot to think about.

But it was another night of troubled sleep, with visions of children's bodies torn by fragmentation bombs, others melting from the searing heat of Napalm. Flashes of my carnival dream came back too, except that now there were police towering over little four-year-old me, tapping nightsticks against their palms. Knitting it all together was a sickening sense of helplessness.

Chapter 32

In the morning, I noticed that, besides sex, lifting weights was my most effective stress reliever. That relief, however, was transitory. My troubles returned right after reading the morning's war news. These days, I sometimes felt like my head was about to explode.

During a break between classes, I went to see Emma. She was the wisest person I knew, and I needed help badly. Her face registered recognition of my distress right away. She closed the shop, led me to the back, poured us coffee, lit up a Newport, and asked, "What is it?"

"It's the horror of every single day, Emma. I can't stop thinking about the lives we destroy in Vietnam. I keep seeing terrified faces of children. And the shot from out of nowhere that brought down Dr. King. The violent aftermath. Daley's 'shoot to kill' order. The cover-up. And my own helplessness to do anything about any of it. Also, Cat's against our joining the Civic Center march and I don't think I can sit this one out."

"Have you and she talked about this?"

"Not much. I'm sure she senses something's up, but I haven't wanted to talk about it. I don't want to scare her. Keeping it to myself makes it even worse, though."

"First of all," Emma advised, "you must get everything out in the open. She's totally tuned in to you because you're the most important person in her life. So, of course she senses that you're troubled. But now she can only guess at the cause. She might even think you've become unhappy with her. You must open up. If it scares her, you'll comfort one another. You have to trust your love to get you through life's problems. Together. Otherwise, they'll drive a wedge between you."

"I guess I knew you'd say that," I agreed. "And deep down, I know you're right. Okay, I'll have a talk with Cat tonight. It'll be a relief. But what's happening to me? I can't concentrate on school. My classes don't even interest me. I feel like I'm losing my mind."

"This war is insane, Steve, but that doesn't mean you have to be. That's not good for you or anyone around you. It can even threaten your good antiwar work. Look, what you're going through is what I call the Movement Malady. I've been seeing it for forty years, and I've suffered through it myself from time to time."

"What do you mean?"

"Look at it this way. A big part of your life now is conflict. You're questioning everything you were brought up to believe about your country and its history. And you've become what some whites would call a 'race traitor.' Even your parents might think that way now. In a matter of months, the world as you've understood it has been turned upside down. That puts a lot of strain on you."

"I guess so."

"Now, the challenge is to deal with all this *without* losing your mind. You're starting to feel like ending the war is your own personal responsibility. But that will lead you to take on more than you can handle. And then you'll burn out. I've seen that happen, countless times."

"But I don't do enough," I argued. "Look at Donnie. It seems he spends every waking moment on it."

"There's a difference. First of all, his worldview, his ideology, has been set for years. He isn't shocked by new discoveries like those fragmentation bombs. Also, he's at peace, at least for now, with the movement being his whole life. There's plenty of casual sex in it, but for as long as I've known him, Donnie's never been in a serious relationship. And I sometimes wonder if he remembers what fun is anymore."

"It sounds like you're worried about him."

"I do worry. No-one can live the way he does indefinitely. Anyway, your life is different. You have a jewel to cherish, named Cat. You're planning to become a teacher, and we know you're blessed with a gift for that. But first you have to finish school, and for you to stay at Midway, you need to keep up your grades. You have the after-school classes that you and the kids enjoy so much. And you have the Movement. If you don't keep these things in some kind of balance, they'll all suffer."

"I see what you mean," I responded. "It's that 'balance' thing again. That's hard for me, but I know I have to get my priorities back in order. But there's something else too."

"What's that?"

"Tomorrow's my Saran Wrap Thursday. I don't think I can do that right now. I'm too restless and leafleting feels too tame. Also, what if I encounter a shopper who tries to defend the war? I might not be able to control myself."

"So don't do it. The world won't come to an end, and neither will the project. Tell Sabrina you need a sabbatical. Look, Cat's usually with me in the shop while you're leafleting. I'll tell her I won't need help tomorrow. Do something together, something for yourselves. It'll be good for you."

As I got up to leave, Emma added, "Remember, Steve. If you don't take care of yourself, you can't take care of anyone else."

"And that," I responded, gripping her shoulders, "is why you *must* quit smoking!"

That night, after I related my entire conversation with Emma, Cat asked, "Steve, do you trust our love? Do you? Tell me the truth."

"Of course I do."

"Then promise you'll never try to protect me by keeping things to yourself, especially anything that's causing you pain."

"I promise, Cat. This feels so much better."

She came over, sat on my lap, took my head in her hands, and gave me a long deep kiss. Coming up for air, I said, "So we have time for ourselves tomorrow. What would you like to do?"

I knew what I wanted to do, but that wasn't what she had in mind. "I want to get my driver's license," she said. "I'm ready for the road test."

In the morning, I told Sabrina I needed a break.

"No problem at all," she responded. "We'll miss you, but we're getting new volunteers all the time. Since the newspaper article came out, we've had more help than we need. People even interrupted their shopping trips to hand out leaflets. Come back whenever you can, but please don't worry about it."

After classes, we went to the DMV. Cat passed her road test on the first try, and got her license. I traded in my Iowa license too. I wanted my official ID to show my new address, my new home, the home I shared with my beloved Cat.

On the way home, we stopped at a five-and-dime for Arielle's birthday decorations. Cat picked out all girly things. At one point, I asked, "Aren't any boys coming to this party?"

"They'll get over it," she replied. I shrugged and moved on to the Toys and Games aisles.

By Saturday afternoon, we'd transformed Emma's meeting space into Party Central. Arielle looked like a little princess, with her frilly dress and shiny tiara. Unable to contain her excitement, she ran around the room, hugging each of us around the legs.

I spent most of the next two hours with the birthday girl and her friends. We played Pin the Tail on the Donkey, Musical Chairs, Simon Says, Ring Around the Rosie, Pass the Parcel, and Mother, May I, which I changed to Uncle, May I. All the children won prizes. While they played with their new toys, I collapsed on my back, exhausted.

That lasted until Arielle plopped down on my belly and pointed to the ceiling. I knew what she wanted and, after all, she was the birthday girl. I lifted her by the waist and tossed her a few inches up in the air. She giggled and, when I put her back down, she pointed up and said, "Again!"

This drew the attention of the other kids, who each clamored to be next. Marcellus organized them into a line, and then went back to the grownups with a wink and a smile. Each of the kids got two throws. What I didn't notice right away was that, after their turns, they went back to the end of the line. Finally, the lights went out and they ran over for the birthday cake.

I was physically drained. But for those two hours, my troubles had totally vaporized.

Chapter 33

For the next couple of days, I tried to follow Emma's advice, and also hold onto the good mood that came with Arielle's party. Sunday afternoon, Cat took both of us for a drive in the country. On Monday, I enjoyed a particularly lively math class with the South Side kids. As the week wore on, though, keeping my life in balance became more of a challenge.

Wednesday morning, we learned that McCarthy had won the Pennsylvania primary with 71 percent of the vote. This was great news, but it didn't electrify me as much as it might have a few weeks earlier.

The night before the Civic Center march, Cat asked if the permits had been issued. "Not that I know of," I replied. "Either way, we have to go."

"No, we don't!" she exclaimed. "This will be another trap. The whole thing will be illegal. You're looking for trouble."

"We can't let this bully of a mayor keep us from protesting a war that's killing innocent people every week," I argued, my voice rising. "We can't cave in. We have to go!"

"Then you'll go by yourself!" she announced, slamming the bedroom door and turning the lock. I slept poorly on the living room couch, wondering how the pieces of my life that I so treasured could ever fit together. The war was blowing everything apart.

I woke early, to an empty apartment. A note on the kitchen counter read, "JUST BE CAREFUL," but I found no clue to where Cat had gone. Tooter was not where we'd last parked her. I pulled myself together and went to the café for breakfast and a newspaper. The *Tribune* ran a wire service story reporting that students demonstrated against the war that week in Europe, Asia and South America. The schools were closed in Prague, where thousands of students marched on the U.S. Embassy. In Paris, Vietcong flags were hanging from the Sorbonne, the Eiffel Tower and the Arc de Triomphe. There were large demonstrations and hundreds of arrests in Tokyo. Demonstrators in Montevideo marched in solidarity with American draft resisters. We were part of an international movement. I ached to share the excitement with Cat. *Where could she be?*

I tore the article out and brought it with me to Midway's art studio, where Sabrina had organized a production center for sign-making. I painted my favorite slogan: *Vietnam for the Vietnamese!*

Armed with our protest signs, hundreds of us formed a chanting, singing pre-march on our way to the train station. It was a beautiful spring day, and the air was filled with joyful anticipation. I was surrounded by people I knew: Whit and others from The Circle; Sabrina and the Saran Wrap crew; Nicky and the SDS crowd; Jeff Rosen and a bunch of other law students. Even among all those friends and comrades, though, I felt lonely. My mind kept shifting back to Cat. I hated that she was angry with me, and I didn't even know where she was.

We joined over 5,000 people at the staging area in Grant Park. Without a sound system, parade marshals from the Peace Council and the Mobe had to circulate through the crowd with the latest news. It was confusing, but I gathered that, the day before, a judge ordered the city to grant a permit, but only for the first eleven blocks. For the rest of the two-mile march, we'd be confined to the sidewalks. The police were supposed to "facilitate" our progress and keep it orderly.

The most confusing part was what would happen at the Civic Center. The plan had been to hold a rally on its big plaza, but that permit was refused.

"So what are we supposed to do when we get there?" I asked Sabrina.

"I don't know," she said. "Maybe they expect us to go shopping!"

As a small marching band began playing, we followed it onto Columbus Drive. The festive mood was irresistible. We took over the street, chanting and singing. Protest signs waved in the air. This was nothing like the somber mood of the much smaller march three weeks earlier.

As the front ranks reached Michigan Avenue, the police ordered our musicians to stop playing. The parade permit had run out, they said, and loud music violated the noise code. They funneled us onto the sidewalk, creating a tight bottleneck. Very slowly, in fits and starts, we made our way forward.

Now the police filled the street, in riot gear or on horseback, along with patrol cars and military-looking vehicles. They stopped us at every red light. Sometimes, when it turned green, we still couldn't move. Then red again. Green, red, green. Finally, we crossed onto the next block. They packed us in so tightly that people got squeezed off the curb, into the street. The cops grabbed them and threw them into paddy wagons.

An hour later, I made it to the Civic Center. The plaza was cordoned off, but we were allowed onto the sidewalk in front of it. Once that sidewalk filled, the police stopped letting marchers cross the street. People around me yelled for them to join us. Others broke through the ropes onto the plaza. They were clubbed, sprayed with mace and thrown into the reflecting pool. The situation grew increasingly tense. I didn't know what to do and I suspected no-one else, including the police, did either.

After a half-hour standoff, as if on cue, they charged into the crowds on both sidewalks. We spilled out onto the street and ran. They chased us, clubbing anyone they got their hands on and throwing them into police vans. I saw one cop open a van's back door, spray mace inside and slam it closed.

If they wanted to disperse the crowd, it worked. But that wasn't enough. They chased us for blocks, spraying mace and swinging their clubs. I noticed that black tape covered the numbers on some badges. Other badges had been removed. They went after marchers, news photographers, witnesses who were downtown shopping. It was madness.

A woman tripped and fell right in front of me. As I reached down to help her up, a crashing pain exploded in the back of my head. I dropped to my knees. After another blow, everything went dark.

I woke up groggy and confused, being dragged by the armpits across a concrete floor. A creaky steel door slid open, and I was tossed into a big, crowded jail cell. A few people came over and leaned me up against the wall. Soon Nicky was there.

"Are you all right?" he asked as I was coming to.

"I guess so. What about you, Nicky? Your head is bandaged."

"So is yours," he said. I reached up and felt thick gauze wrapped around my head, which throbbed mercilessly.

"What happened?" I asked. "How many of us are in here?"

"Including you, I count sixty-three. They brought the wounded into the infirmary for first aid, and then threw us in here. I saw a cop trying to slap you into consciousness. Or maybe just having fun slapping you around."

"Anyone else from our crowd?"

"Jeff and Sabrina," he replied. "They're not hurt." Looking up, I saw them coming closer.

"And Larry Graff," he added. "Over there." I looked to a corner of the cell and saw Larry, one arm in a sling and bandaged, waving his good arm and making a speech to a small group of listeners.

"So now what?"

"I don't know. I guess we wait."

So we waited. Hours went by. I dozed off once or twice, but someone woke me. He said I might have a concussion, and should try to stay awake.

Finally, they herded us into a courtroom. One by one, we went before a judge. Most of us, including me, were charged with disorderly conduct, some with resisting arrest, Larry and a few others with assault. After the judge set bail at fifty dollars, they took us into another room where we lined up for our one phone call.

Who to call? Not Cat. I wanted to explain this to her in person, not over the phone. I didn't want to wake Emma in the middle of the night. I hadn't seen Whit in the jail cell, so I tried him at home. Fortunately, he answered the phone. I explained the situation, and asked if he could loan me the bail money.

"I'm on my way," he said.

Back in the cell, time dragged by. It seemed an eternity before they started calling names and taking us out. Whit grabbed my arm in an outside hallway and said, "You're all set. Let's get out of here."

I didn't breathe a sigh of relief until we were inside his car. The clock said it was 3 a.m.

"I really appreciate this, Whit," I said. "But what took so long?"

"They kept us waiting," he explained. "I was there for an hour and a half. They didn't even let people sit down."

My head throbbed. I asked if he knew anything about Cat.

"Emma called me last night, around ten, to ask if I knew anything. I told her you'd been arrested, and asked how Cat was doing. Emma said she was right there, but too hysterical to come to the phone."

"Whit, she didn't want me to even go to this march. I don't know what to expect."

Back home, he put a hand on my shoulder, looked up at the apartment, and said, "Good luck."

Chapter 34

I ran up the stairs and went straight to the bedroom. Through the locked door, I heard Cat whimpering.

"Cat," I called, "It's me. Open the door."

"No," she yelled. "Go away!"

"Please, Cat. Let me in!"

"No, no, no, no, no," she sobbed. "Go away!"

It was another night on the couch. But I couldn't have stayed awake any longer if I'd wanted to.

The phone woke me on Sunday.

"Steve, are you all right?" Emma asked. "I've been calling for hours."

"I don't know. I guess. What time is it?"

"1:30. Can you come downstairs?"

"I guess so, but I better shower first. I'll be half an hour."

"Okay. I'll fix you some breakfast. You probably haven't eaten since yesterday morning."

Oh, my God, I thought. *Cat!* I ran through the apartment calling her name. She wasn't there. I looked every place she might have left me a note. There wasn't one.

Emma nearly dropped the coffeepot when I came through the door. I suddenly realized I must be quite a sight with that big bandage wrapped around my head. She motioned to the table, where a plate of toast and scrambled eggs was waiting. Before taking a bite, I asked, "Emma, do you know where Cat is?"

"I'm not sure," she responded while pouring the coffee. "She said she had research to do."

"I have to find her."

"Bad idea, Steve. Let her be for a while. Now eat, before it gets cold."

I really was ravenous, so I followed orders. While I ate, Emma handed me the morning *Tribune*. The headline of a small front-page article read, "Antiwar Protesters Battle Police: 15 Hurt, 50 Arrests." The gist of the story was that the majority of the marchers were peaceful, though noisy, but a small group attacked the police, who handled them professionally. The *Sun-Times* ran a similar story. Neither of these accounts came even close to the truth. By the time I finished skimming them, I was on my third cup of coffee.

"Now," Emma said when I looked up, "tell me what actually happened."

After I told her the whole story, she said, "I was afraid of something like this, after what happened a few weeks ago."

"So was Cat," I responded. "But I thought she was over-reacting. What do you think is happening here?"

"Daley's sending a message. The Democratic Convention will put him and his city on the international stage. He doesn't want anyone spoiling the party."

"So he's trying to scare us away?"

"Yes, and it works on more than one level. First, he's shown what can be expected from his police, and he's provided them with a dry run. More insidiously, by blaming the violence on the marchers, he's given people reason to be afraid of the very demonstrators they'd be joining up with in August. And, of course, he's shown he can control the local press coverage."

"Do you think it'll work?" I asked. "Will it hurt the turnout?"

"It probably will, and that worries me. Now, here's what else you missed."

It was at the top of the front page. Hubert Humphrey had officially declared his candidacy. His speech was filled with meaningless phrases like "the politics of happiness, the politics of purpose and the politics of joy." Not a word about Vietnam. The article said he would pursue a first-ballot victory without entering any primaries, presumably through the party bosses.

I felt like I was drowning again.

"Exactly what you predicted," I said. "But, Emma, I have to find Cat. I need her, and now I'm worried. I haven't seen or heard her since she locked me out of the bedroom."

"I know, Steve. But you have to respect her process. She'll come back when she's ready. Remember, this was a nightmare for her, and she needs time to sort things out."

"What you do need to do," she added, "is get yourself checked out at the E.R. I don't like the look of that bandage." She touched her hand to it, and it came away red. "See?"

I was a little concerned too. My head still throbbing, I walked over to the Midway Medical Center. An hour later, I was led into an examination room. A young doctor soon followed. He introduced himself as Hal Dreyer, a resident.

"You don't have to tell me what happened," he said. "I already know."

"You do?"

"Yes, I was there too."

"You were? Where?"

"First, on the march. Then in the jail cell. You were woozy, but do you remember someone advising you to stay awake because you might have a concussion?"

"Kind of. It's really blurry."

"Sure it is," he said, smiling. "Well, that was me. Now let's have a look."

He kept talking as he unwrapped the bandage, pausing to whistle as the wounds became visible. He carefully cleaned them with what felt like a quart of burning iodine and began sewing.

"I was far back in the march," he explained, "so I didn't get to the Civic Center until all hell had already broken loose. I told the police I was a doctor and wanted to help. They told me to drop dead. I found a pay phone in a drug store, called the E.R. and asked them to send every available ambulance. Outside, I walked right into a bunch of cops and got arrested. They didn't even have to chase me."

"It's a good thing you came in today," he added. "They did a real botch job on you last night."

A half hour later, I had eleven stitches in my head, a much more attractive bandage and a sample bottle of a new painkiller called Tylenol.

"You may have gotten a mild concussion," he said. "But I don't think it's anything to worry about. Now follow the directions on the bottle and come back next week. Ask for me at the desk. We'll see about taking these stitches out."

I shook his hand, thanked him and headed out.

"Stay out of trouble," he called, "and get some rest. You've been through a trauma."

I spent the rest of the day waiting for Cat to come home, growing more anxious by the hour. At around seven, the doorknob turned and my heart leapt. But it dropped as soon as I saw the stern, stoic look on her face. The joyful reunion I'd hoped for wasn't going to happen.

I wasn't sure what to say, so I asked, "Have you eaten?"

"Yes, with Emma," she replied in kind of a detached, robotic voice. "She told me everything that happened to you, and that made up my mind. She said you deserved an explanation, so here I am."

"Made up your mind about what?" I asked.

She headed for the couch and pointed me to the chair. "Steve," she announced, "I can't be with you anymore."

"Why?" I implored, my eyes tearing. "We've been perfect together. This was our first and only fight."

"And that's the reason. I'm not saying it's your fault. But I can't handle the anxiety, the fear. I've been thinking it through, and well, I can start from the beginning if you want." I nodded.

"Do you remember, during the first night we spent together, I told you it was my first time?"

"I'll never forget it."

"Well, that wasn't all. After my parents were killed, I never even went out on a date."

"I bet you had plenty of offers."

"I did, and some were from young men who seemed very nice. That was the problem. I'd resolved not to gamble on letting anyone into my heart, because risking another loss would be too much to bear. Bonding with Emma was the only exception, but that just happened. I made friends, of course, but I never let any of them get too close."

"I understand that. You were grieving for your parents."

"I was. But I was also protecting myself. It worked fine for two years. I stayed focused on my studies, and helped Emma with the store. Then you came along and my wall crumbled."

"How?"

"I don't know for sure. The first time we talked, I sensed you were a good listener. I was comfortable sharing personal stuff with you, but I couldn't talk about the accident. That would've been too painful. In fact, Emma was the only one I'd ever told about it. By the next time, though, I felt compelled to share it with you too."

"It was the way you heard it, Steve. I saw it in your eyes. Empathy. Compassion. They reflected my pain. I felt you connecting with me in my deepest, most guarded level. You said you'd always be there for me, and somehow I believed you. I felt cared for, safe. But I was sliding down a slippery slope."

"Those words popped right out," I said, "from the bottom of my heart. I meant them."

"I know you did, and I knew it then. I still tried to keep my guard up, but I was conflicted. While you were off on the Pentagon march, my feelings rose to the surface, but I still fought to keep them down. The dam broke on Thanksgiving, when you chose to take care of me instead of appeasing your own family. It scared me, and I told you that during the bus ride. By the time we got back, though, I couldn't resist anymore. I had to open my heart."

"The happiest night of my life," I said, "and what a weekend we had. I was already head over heels in love with you."

"And I with you. But I was still conflicted. The deeper I let you in, the more afraid I became of losing you. For two months, I tried all kinds of strategies to protect myself. Then, almost three months ago now, I finally gave in. I had to have you here with me."

"And haven't we been happy together?" I asked. "I love you more each day."

"Oh yes, and every day my being has become more entangled with yours. For a while, my fears even began to subside."

"That's what I wanted," I said. "I'll always love you."

Cat's demeanor softened for a moment. She leaned against the cushions and closed her eyes. Suddenly, she shot straight back up, her brow furrowed in anger, her eyes glistening.

"And then came yesterday! All day, I worried and waited for you to come home. But you didn't. I knew something terrible must've happened. I was already frantic when Whit called and told us you got arrested. The gut-wrenching pain of loss I'd worked so hard to prevent came back with a bang. If it wasn't for Emma, I don't know what I would've done."

"But you must know I wanted to come home, Cat. But I couldn't."

"Getting arrested was bad enough. But you also got beaten. One more blow, and you might never have come home. I can't live like this. The fear is too much. I know I'm hyper-sensitive, but I'm not imagining things. You can be reckless, and then my world falls apart. That's why we have to get away from each other, before it gets any worse. I need to leave you while I still can."

At first, I didn't respond. My head started throbbing again. I leaned back and closed my eyes, feeling the ground beneath me slipping away.

"Steve?" she called out, alarmed. "Are you there?"

I shook my head and opened my eyes. I went to her, dropped to one knee and took her hands in mine.

"Cat, I know I've put you through a lot, and I'm so, so sorry. But please don't do this. I can't live without you. I wouldn't want to. We can work it out. Look at me. Please."

Our tear-filled eyes bore into each other's souls.

"But I don't see how we can work it out," she said. "You crave danger and I need safety. You can't imagine my pain last night, my despair, not knowing if I'd ever see you again. I saw you in my mind's eye lying in the street, your head all bloody. Then Emma told me that was what happened. I can't do it. I can't do it."

"What I need above everything, Cat, is you," I spluttered. "I know I've been unstable lately. I've handled the pressure badly, and I need to do better. It might not look like it, but I really am trying. Really, I am. The one thing I know for sure, though, is that I can't do any of it without you. Stay with me. Please. I'll do anything."

"Anything?"

"Anything."

"If we stay together, Steve, I'll need you to trust my instincts about these marches and demonstrations, about confrontations with the police. That's the only way. But I don't know if you can do that. You need to be in the middle of everything, no matter how dangerous it might be."

"I can do it. Yes, I know it'll be hard at times, but I can do it. I will do it. I promise."

"You really think you can control that restless energy?"

"I have to. I have to keep my priorities straight. You will always come first."

"Oh, I want that so much," she said, starting to cry. "I've been so scared and lonely these past two days..."

"Never again, Cat. I promise."

"Come up here now," she said, "and hold me."

We held each other tight, as I kissed her tears away. Our lovemaking was long and languid. We'd come through the wilderness and found our way back. It was so good to be home again.

But I had to keep my promise. *Never again. Could I really do it?*

Chapter 35

The following Saturday, on my way to get the stitches removed, I picked up a copy of the *Midway Magenta*.

I checked in at the desk, asked for Dr. Dreyer, took a seat in the waiting room and opened the school paper. The banner front-page headline read, **Major Expansion Slated: Physics Institute to Occupy New South Side Campus**. The article, bylined by Barry Wayne, reported that Midway planned to build a new Institute of Applied Physics, housing research labs, offices, staff housing and a conference center.

Inset was a map showing the area that would be incorporated. The intended construction site was six blocks wide, and three blocks deep into the South Side. On its southern edge was the SSO building.

"The target area is now occupied primarily by tenement housing and small businesses," Wayne wrote, "all of which would be demolished. Since Midway currently owns only a small piece of this real estate, university officials have been meeting with city agencies in pursuit of acquisition through eminent domain. If its application is approved, the city will seize control of the affected properties, compensate the current owners, and turn it over to Midway through a long-term ground lease. This is a legal process by which 'redevelopment for the public good' replaces 'blighted' existing uses."

"Asked how renters will be compensated for losing their homes," he continued, "Midway's Director of Development, Horace Masters, replied, "That will be a landlord-tenant matter, and no business of the university.""

The final paragraph read, "The eminent domain application is under consideration by the City Planning Commission, which will hold a required public hearing on Thursday, May 16 at 7:00 p.m., in the City Hall auditorium. It is expected that the commission will vote on the plan immediately following the hearing."

This was a bombshell. Midway planned to bulldoze Black people out of their homes and businesses, with City Hall's connivance. I had to get home and show this to Cat and Emma. I had to call Sharon and Marcellus. Something had to be done.

But as I got up from my seat, a nurse called my name. I'd forgotten about the stitches. Dr. Dreyer was waiting for me. After a quick exam, he pronounced the wounds healed and removed the stitches. Satisfied after I answered a few questions about sleeping and my headaches, he said I could go.

"Any instructions?" I asked.

"You'll still have a small bald patch until the hair grows back. You might want to wear a hat. Or you can consider it a badge of honor." He clapped me on the back and I headed home. Fast.

Cat left me a note. "Emergency BSU meeting," it read. "Home for dinner." She signed it with an arrow-pierced heart. I liked that.

I began boiling water for pasta, opened a book and waited.

Cat came in at 7:30, apologizing for being so late.

"No problem," I replied. "Was it about the *Magenta* story?"

"It sure was."

"Well, come and eat. Tell me everything."

"Okay.That story outraged us all, so we quickly moved on to strategy. Here's what we decided. At the crack of dawn next Friday, we're gonna take over the administration building and barricade the entrances."

"An occupation?

"No, but it'll look that way. What we want is access to the Development Office and the President's Office. We need to find everything they've been keeping under wraps about this physics institute. Once we know what we're dealing with, we can decide what to do."

"That's a great idea. We can get lots of white students to join in."

"No," Cat objected. "We want to do this ourselves."

"I understand. But there must be some way to help."

"There is. We want our white supporters to picket in front of the building entrance, and publicize the inside action as a sit-in against the land grab. We'll prepare the leaflets. If campus security shows up, link arms on the steps and block the entrance. That'll buy us time. If President Kent calls the police, we should be finished with our business by the time they get there."

"Okay," I agreed. "I'll get the telephone tree going."

"And make sure there are no leaks. This has to be a surprise attack. And there's one more thing we want you to do."

"Me?"

"Yes. We'll park Tooter near the building's rear door. While the BSU is inside, and you're out front, keep an eye on Kent's office. That's the second floor on the right. When a window opens, go around back. We'll toss out, or pass out, whatever we've discovered, so you can pack it right into Tooter's trunk. That way, if we do get arrested, the information will still have been liberated."

"Cat, I'm honored to be brought into this plan. But how'd you arrive at it so quickly?"

"We had two hours. During the first hour, we brainstormed the basic strategy. During the second hour, an elected three-person task force worked out the details."

"And you got elected to this task force?"

"Yes. Sharon and Walter Dyson and me. Of course, Marcellus sat in as our advisor."

"Dyson. A little shorter than me, stocky, light skinned?"

"Yes. That's him."

I stopped eating, looked hard at her and said, "I'm so proud of you, Cat. But now I'm the one who's worried. What happens if the timing doesn't work out? Once the cops come, anything can happen."

"Well, we hope this will work the way we've planned it. If it doesn't, we'll have a contingency plan."

"What's that?"

"I don't know yet. Marcellus is meeting with Mr. Watkins tomorrow."

Early the following Friday, we found Emma waiting by the car. "You're coming with us?" I asked.

"Of course," she stated emphatically. "My marching days may be over, but I can still walk a picket line. And this is important."

After parking Tooter in the rear lot, as instructed, I gave Cat a big good-luck hug and she ran ahead to join up with her BSU comrades. Emma and I reached the front entrance as they began streaming into the building. The door closed behind them and wouldn't reopen, we hoped, until they accomplished their mission. As the campus came to life,

Emma and I joined several dozen white students who'd shown up in support. Some of us passed out the BSU's leaflets. The rest marched in a circle, calling out slogans.

"Hands off the South Side!"

"Midway, know your place!"

We didn't try to block anyone from entering the building. There was no need, since the doors were barricaded from the inside. The support staff arrived first. Confused that the doors wouldn't open, they walked back down the steps and stood watching in a group. The deans were more forceful, pounding on the doors and demanding to be let in. After a while, the chief of campus security arrived. His keys turned the locks perfectly, but the doors still wouldn't open. After one of the deans read the leaflet, he gathered the staff together and they left.

For the next three hours, no Midway personnel approached the building. The window I was told to watch remained closed. Then, marching across the quad, came a dozen campus security guards. Some were armed with crowbars, which I hoped were only for prying the doors open.

We quickly gathered on the steps, our numbers up to more than a hundred by then, and linked arms. Emma stood in the center of the front line, a warm grandmotherly smile on her face. As the two forces faced each other, I heard one guard say to another, "We don't get paid enough for this." They soon retreated, and we broke into a chorus of "We Shall Not Be Moved."

We went back to picketing and leafleting. I checked that window every couple of minutes now. After another half hour, it opened and I ran around back. A rear door opened slightly. An arm came through, handing me five big manila envelopes. A voice said, "Hurry." I looked around, saw no-one, opened Tooter's trunk, dropped the envelopes in and locked it.

Back at the front entrance, the doors opened and the Black students came marching out, fists raised in the air. Sharon began making a speech, but things quickly turned ominous.

Horns honking, a bus full of Chicago police, followed by three paddy wagons, drove across the quad, stopping near its center. Ambulances were in waiting across the way. As the cops poured out of the bus, people ran over to see what was happening. Now I was worried, and angry with myself for not talking Cat out of this.

The students stood where they were, hands locked behind their heads, offering no resistance. Violence, I hoped, would be unlikely now with so many witnesses.

The police moved us away from the building, and formed two lines leading to its front steps. A captain strode between the lines and announced, "You're all under arrest. Follow me."

They did as directed, straight to the paddy wagons. I was amazed at how calm they were. As Cat passed by me, I looked at her pleadingly. I so needed to rescue her, but was helpless to do it. She didn't seem concerned, though. She caught my eye, smiled and winked.

Minutes later, something totally unexpected happened. Through the south gate of the campus came a parade, Black people of all ages. In the lead were Marcellus, James Watkins and three men in clerical robes. Directly behind were a dozen Black Panthers, carrying rifles. Behind them, ordinary people were coming and coming. Five deep, they encircled the police vehicles, chanting, "Let our people go! Let our people go!" A group in choir robes sang above the chants:

> *Go down, Moses.*
> *Way down in Egypt land.*
> *Te-ell ol', ol' Pha-aroh,*
> *Let my people go!*

I was awestruck by the spectacle. It wasn't a confrontation; it was a stalemate. The community people weren't going to battle the police, even if the Panthers' rifles were loaded. But the police, outnumbered ten-to-one, weren't going to mow people down either. Watkins and the ministers walked over and spoke with the captain, who said something into his radio. Ten minutes later, a tall, aristocratic-looking man in his late fifties appeared, accompanied by six security guards. The crowd parted for him, and he went directly to the captain. They spoke for a few minutes before he turned and left the scene. *So that's President Kent*, I thought.

The crowd quieted down and the captain told the students, "You're being released with a warning today. But if you try this again, the consequences will be severe." The police were gone within minutes.

Rejoicing broke out. Admirers mobbed the students. Frantically, I looked for Cat. Finding her, I embraced her like she'd been released from prison.

"You knew, didn't you?" I demanded, holding her away by the shoulders.

"Yes, I did, but information was strictly need-to-know."

"Well, we'll have a talk about that, young lady," I said sternly. "But seriously, did you find what you were looking for?"

"We found a lot more than that. Sharon asked me to do a quick preliminary review."

"Can I help?"

"You'd better. But now it's almost time for your after-school class. I'll drive Emma home, and we'll start sorting this out."

At the SSO, I slowly made my way through a festive crowd. No-one seemed surprised to see a white guy in the building anymore. The kids were waiting for me in the training room. One called out, "I seen you there, Mister Steve. Over at Midway."

"That's where I go to school, Robert," I said. "Maybe you will too one day. But how many times have I told you that you don't have to call me Mister?"

"Oh, yeah. Well, okay."

"Now," I began, "let's get the notebooks out. Today, I'll guess each one of your birthdays. Yes, it really is math!"

Chapter 36

"Steve, I don't know if I've ever seen Emma so happy," Cat said. "She was like an excited schoolgirl while we traded our days' experiences. She did need a nap, though, so I came home."

"Good. But what'll happen when they realize this stuff is missing?"

"They won't," she replied. "Nothing's missing."

"Huh?"

"We used their Xerox machine to copy everything we needed. Then we very carefully placed the originals back where we found them. Right now, they're probably wondering what we were even doing there."

"So what do we have here?" I asked.

"The material falls into two broad categories. First, there are architectural plans for the proposed mini-campus. Your job is to analyze them. See what they tell you. But we also found documents, including contracts with the Defense Department. Many of them were stamped, 'Top Secret.' This Institute of Applied Physics they're planning might be aimed at developing a new weapon system."

"Really? What kind of weapon?"

"I'm not sure. I need more time to look the stuff over. All I know now is that it's based on theories developed by a Midway professor named Dietrich von Helsinger. When I mentioned that name to Emma, her face blanched. She said von Helsinger was part of the Nazi death camp machinery. He's a war criminal."

"Doesn't anyone else know that? How can he be at Midway, or even in this country?"

"Emma told me the U.S. intelligence agencies handpicked a few dozen Nazi scientists, including von Helsinger, after the war ended and offered them amnesty if they'd work for us. At Midway, he teaches one graduate seminar and spends the rest of his time on research, which it seems is funded by the Pentagon."

She handed me one manila envelope and asked that I bring it over to the desk. "I'll definitely need the kitchen table," she explained.

Inside were plans for the new buildings, and renderings of how they would appear visually, from the air and from each exposure. The eighteen South Side blocks would be eliminated to form a single superblock, surrounded by an electrified twelve-foot-high fence.

Midway's main campus might be alien to the South Side, I thought, *but nothing like this. What kind of academic facility needs military-grade security?*

I had no architectural training, but I did make some sense of the blueprints and diagrams. The six-story laboratory building was the center of the planned complex. Four of those floors were underground. To meet enormous power demands, one of them was exclusively designated for electrical generators.

After an hour, I called out, "How are you doing?" No response.

"Cat?"

She straightened. "Oh, I'm sorry, Steve. Have you found anything interesting?"

I came over and summarized my findings, which raised more questions than answers.

"Maybe we should use the rendering that shows the security fence," I suggested. "The slogan might be, *'No Fortress Midway.'* But I wish we knew why it's even there."

"There's a clue in here," she told me, waving her hand over the papers strewn on the table, all covered in equations and symbols that meant nothing to me. "But I need help. I can't put the pieces together."

"Help from who?"

"There's a doctoral candidate assisting the professor in my Quantum Mechanics class. His name is Stanislaus Borjevinski, or something like that. He's a genius at relativity and quantum theory, which is what all this is based on. He has no social skills, and I doubt he could write a coherent paragraph, but he lives in the curves of the space-time continuum and comprehends it almost instinctively. His brain is wired differently than ours. He's probably in the physics lab, even though it's Friday night. He almost lives there. I'll call."

After a brief conversation, she reported, "He'll be here tomorrow morning at 9:30. I told him only enough to get him intrigued."

"Are you sure that's the only thing he's intrigued by?" I asked with a burst of concern. "You did invite him to your home. He is a male. He might've gotten the wrong message."

"Don't be silly," Cat laughed. "Stan's passion is theoretical physics, not girls. Anyway, you'll be here too."

Still, I woke unsettled that morning. "Cat, something's bothering me," I said once we got started on breakfast. "Can we talk?"

"Of course. What is it?"

"We've talked a lot about your anxieties," I began, "and I get that."

"I know you do. Is that what's bothering you?"

"No, it's not your anxieties. It's my own."

"About what?"

"When you decided to call this guy, Stan, last night and invite him up here, alarm bells went off in my head. At first, I thought it might be jealousy."

"What?"

"No, no. I realized right away it wasn't that. I don't think anyone can come between us. Look, your deep-down fear is that political violence will somehow take me from you, like at the Civic Center."

"Right," she agreed. "But I'm confused. Does this have something to do with your carnival nightmare?"

"No, it isn't that either. What scares me is the thought of some guy putting his hands on you, hurting you, forcing you. It makes me sick to my stomach, and I sense a murderous rage coming on. That's why I'm always hovering over you at the gym."

"Do you really think I'll get raped at the gym unless you're standing right there to protect me?"

"I know it's crazy, but that's how these things work. Our anxieties aren't always rational, are they?"

"I understand, Steve. What can we do?"

"Well, you wouldn't want to live locked up inside the apartment all the time, or be at the end of a leash when we go out, no matter how comfortable that might make me feel."

"No," she laughed. "That wouldn't be very practical."

"So I'd feel a little better if you learned some self-defense skills. You're in great shape. If you knew jujitsu or something, I'd worry less. I hope so, anyway."

"Well, I did see a flyer announcing a summer self-defense program for women. I'll sign up for it."

"Good," I agreed, glancing up at the clock. "But now you better get dressed. Your boyfriend will be here in a few minutes. I'll clean up." Cat gave me a playful punch on the shoulder and went into the bedroom.

She came back out in jeans, a long baggy shirt and no makeup. I stopped her as she went to answer the doorbell. "If you're trying to not look beautiful," I smiled, "it isn't working."

Stanislaus Borjevinski's eyes lit up, not at the sight of Cat, but at the documents spread out on the table. They immediately got into an animated discussion. Yellow pads were quickly filled with notes and equations. I understood none of it, so I left them alone and spent the day working on my ethics paper. After a few hours, I brought sandwiches to the table, but they didn't even notice until I squeezed Cat's shoulder and pointed to the plate. At dinner time, I went out to get pizza, and put slices right under their noses.

At about eight, I looked over to see Cat sitting by herself, elbows on the table, chin in her hands, staring out over the papers.

"What is it?" I asked. Cat looked up with a frightened expression.

"Stan helped me make sense of this. My guess about a weapons program was right, but I had no idea how terrible it truly is. Compared to this, Napalm is a child's toy. It's worse than a nuclear bomb."

"Can you explain it?"

"I'll try. Von Helsinger's theory is that it's possible, using longitudinal electromagnetic waves, to broadcast space-time curvature engines mimicking quantum patterns over entire populations. These virtual states result in reactions..."

"Wait, Cat," I interjected. "In English, please. What's the bottom line? What's the danger?"

"Okay, sorry. Here's the main thing: If this proves out, something unimaginably horrible becomes feasible. It's based on harnessing the incredible power of quantum energy. Von Helsinger calls it the Quantum Potential Weapon."

"What would it do?"

"It would trick the human immune system into simultaneously fighting one, two, a dozen deadly diseases, resulting in what you might call their shadow states, like a virtual reality. The immune system responds as though these diseases are real, and goes into overdrive to fight them off. It can't sustain such stress for long, though, until it collapses. The body becomes helpless to fight off real diseases. People get sick easily, and die."

"So it's like a death ray that could target someone?"

"Not only someone. It could be directed at a village, a city, even an entire country. It could be worse than the worst plagues you ever heard of. These quantum patterns could be broadcast over a huge area. Everyone in their paths would contract diseases' shadow states. Some would succumb as soon as their immune systems broke down. The rest would have no resistance left to even the tiniest amount of the real thing. The population of an entire nation could be wiped out."

"This sounds like science fiction, Cat. Could it really work?"

"It's what we were trying to figure out today. Stan went over von Helsinger's work, and he said it's at least plausible. But no-one knows for sure. That's why the government is funding the research. To find out."

"And that's what the institute is for?"

"Yes. The space-time curvature engine generator exists only in theory. It would have to be built and tested. It might take years, and a billion dollars, until scientists even develop a prototype. The Pentagon justifies the investment by claiming it could create a weapon so powerful that it ends war as we've known it."

"Or more likely," I said, "a weapon so powerful they could dominate the world."

"Or destroy it," Cat added. "Steve, this is a doomsday machine."

"What can we do about it?"

"I don't know. Let's bring this to the people we trust the most: Emma, Sharon and Marcellus. If we put our heads together, I hope we can come up with something."

Chapter 37

Sunday afternoon, the five of us gathered in Sharon's apartment. Arielle was upstairs, playing with a friend, so I had no pleasant distraction from the grim business at hand. I began with the drawings, explaining the strange underground plans and the ultra-high security. By the time Cat got finished explaining the science, she was still the only one who understood the theory, but we were all horrified at the prospect of what might result.

Marcellus commented, "It sounds like they want to destroy part of the South Side so they can make something to destroy a whole country."

"Or several countries," Emma suggested. "If it works, U.S. imperialism will face no effective resistance. Any country that stands up to it, like Vietnam, could have its entire population wiped out. And without the mess of an actual war."

"Look at what they've done even without such a weapon," Sharon added. "All the elected governments they've overthrown, all the dictators they've installed, in only the past fifteen years: Iran, Guatemala, Congo, Dominican Republic, Ecuador, Brazil, Indonesia, Greece..."

"And now this disastrous war in Vietnam," Emma interjected, "and remember the debacle at the Bay of Pigs. Imagine if they unleashed this thing on Cuba. Cat, who else knows about this besides those directly involved?"

"As far as I know, we're the only ones. Oh, and Stan, the physicist I told you about."

"Will he be talking about it?"

"No, I don't think so. He sees it as an interesting theoretical problem. That's all. He's oblivious to the consequences. And he doesn't talk to many people anyway."

"So the question is," I asked, "what do we do?"

"I know what we shouldn't do," Sharon responded. "And that's tying this death ray thing into the community's campaign against the South Side land grab. We can use the 'fortress' aspect to illustrate Midway's hostility to the community, but not this quantum business."

"Why not?" I asked. "The expansion and the reason for it fit together perfectly. Marcellus summed it up in a single sentence."

"I'll tell you why," she began. "Cat, I believe everything you've told us. I don't understand it all, but I trust you. That's just me, just us. But most people will dismiss it as crazy talk. It won't bring more people into our campaign. It'll scare people away. And anyway, as far as the community's concerned, it doesn't matter what Midway would do with the land they want to steal."

Emma agreed. "The eminent domain issue needs to be kept clean. Standing on its own, unified campus and community opposition has a chance of sinking it. Mixing it with something as difficult to understand as quantum weapons development would confuse people and frighten them. The local press would paint everyone opposing the expansion with a broad brush of lunacy. No, this thing needs to be derailed on a different track."

"What track is that?" I asked.

"Credible exposure. If the project can be discredited, then public pressure, even Congressional pressure, might kill it. This weapon might sound like a great idea in a right-wing think tank, or deep within the bowels of the Pentagon or CIA, but it can never survive the light of day. You know I have my differences with government policy, but I do not believe Americans are that evil."

Cat asked, "But how?"

"We can start with Barry Wayne. But it has to be his story alone. Anyone he mentions as a source can be targeted for serious trouble."

"Okay," I agreed. "But can he be trusted to keep his sources confidential?"

"If you approach him the right way, I believe so. No good reporter will blow a hot story by taking it to the authorities, and he is a good one. He's as persistent as a hound dog, and he'll track it down until the trail ends. Also, he'll be as horrified by what Cat's discovered as we've been."

Marcellus pointed to me and said, "Steve, I think you're the one to approach him. Don't bring Cat into it until you're sure it's safe for her."

So, during my first break between Monday's classes, I went to the newspaper office, where someone pointed Wayne out, talking on the phone at his desk. I walked over and hovered nearby.

Wayne was six-two, medium build, with long sandy-blonde hair. He looked familiar. I was sure I'd seen him before, but couldn't place where. He wasn't in any of my classes, and I didn't remember him from any meetings. When he put the receiver down, I introduced myself.

"I've got a big story for you," I told him. "Can we talk outside?"

He looked at me quizzically. "Sure," he replied, grabbing a pen and a notebook. "A little intrigue will always get a reporter's attention."

We sat on a bench under an oak tree. "Do we know each other?" he asked. "I'm sure I've seen you before."

"I thought the same thing," I replied. "Maybe we'll figure it out. But that's not why I'm here."

"Well then, why are you here?"

"I'm here," I explained, "partly because you did such a great job on last week's story on the expansion, but mostly because Emma Gold said you can be trusted."

"So tell me, what's your story?"

"It isn't my story. I don't even completely understand it. I'm here more as a broker than a source. The first thing I need to know is whether you can protect anonymous sources."

"Well, yes. No-one can force me to give up my sources. And if I promise anonymity, I'll keep that promise. No matter what."

"And documents?"

"That's different. A subpoena can break down all kinds of doors. Even if I hide a document in what I consider a safe place, I can't honestly guarantee its safety. Come on, you've got my attention. What's your story about?"

"Like I said, it's not my story. Your source, who must be kept out of the story at all costs, will be a student named Cat Crawford. Do you know who that is?"

"There's only one Cat," he said. With a flash of recognition, he added, "Wait a minute. You're the guy who works out with her at the gym, aren't you?"

"That's me," I replied, remembering now where I'd seen him before.

"Well," he said with a broad smile, "I would be absolutely delighted to meet with Cat Crawford!"

My alarm bells started ringing full tilt. No way was I going to leave this guy alone with her.

"For security reasons," I said, "this interview has to take place off campus. She lives at 149 High Street, over Emma's bookstore. Can you be there tomorrow morning at 8:30?"

"Okay, I'll be there." he promised as we stood to part ways. "I've taken your bait. But this better be good."

"Don't worry," I called back to him. "It's a blockbuster."

However, I thought, walking to my next class, *you might be a little disappointed with the interview*. I would be right close by.

Over dinner, Cat asked, "How can I give him the story without giving him the documents? They're the evidence, the closest thing to a smoking gun."

"You do need to show them to him," I explained. "But you can't give them to him because he can't protect them. We can't give anyone a solid reason to connect this to the BSU's building takeover. Here's what we can do. First show him the architectural plans, focusing on the high security. That will draw him in. Then show him some of this scientific stuff. Dazzle him. By the time you hint at what it all means, to the dangers it presents, he'll be frothing at the bit for more. But he won't be able to report the story without your help."

"Help how?"

"Tonight, try to write up a short plain-English summary of the whole project and its potential impact on the world. Go easy on the theory, and focus on the weapon. Just don't put your name on it. Your synopsis can be his takeaway from the interview, not the original documents."

"Okay, but what'll we do with the originals?"

"Let's stash them under the mattress for now, until we get a better idea."

Cat went straight to the desk, and started typing.

In the morning, Barry looked disappointed to see me answering the doorbell. I thought, *Well, at least he didn't bring flowers.*

The three of us sat down at the table, but Cat did the talking. She knew he'd already taken the bait, and she reeled him right in.

"I can see a huge story here," he said, "but I'm still not prepared to write it. You won't give me the documents, and the science is way over my head. I don't even have a quotable source."

"Yes, you do," I said, scooping up the documents and handing him Cat's summary. "What you have is 'an anonymous source in the scientific community.' Use this paper however it suits you. You can quote from it, or even plagiarize it. This'll make the whole thing understandable."

He skimmed the summary and agreed. "Yes, very helpful," he said. "But to do the story, I'll need to interview the top people involved, including von Helsinger. This'll take time."

"We don't have much time," I said. "The City Planning Commission meets Thursday night."

"I can't possibly do a credible report in one day. Get me another week, at least."

"Okay," Cat agreed "We'll try."

As Barry raced down the stairs, Cat picked up the phone and called Sharon.

Chapter 38

Cat and I got to City Hall only fifteen minutes before the scheduled start of the Planning Commission hearing. The auditorium was nearly filled by Black South Siders. White men in business suits occupied the last couple of rows. I guessed these were lawyers, lobbyists, real estate developers and maybe architects with other projects on the commission's agenda. *Blacks in the front, whites in the back,* I thought. *A nice reversal.*

Marcellus waved us over. He'd saved seats right in the middle of the community delegation. I was the only white person in the crowd, and no-one did or said anything to make me uncomfortable. My thoughts went back to Thanksgiving, and how my family treated the one person of color I'd brought into their house. I felt more at home now, right where I was sitting.

The seven members of the Planning Commission, all white men, entered from backstage and took their seats behind a long table. The chairman, whose nameplate read, "Hon. Peter A. Donovan," formally welcomed the audience and announced the agenda, which included six matters. Midway's eminent domain application was the last. It looked to be a long, boring night. I wished I'd brought a book to read.

As it turned out, the first five items, which concerned rezoning for commercial development, went quickly. The men in the suits made brief presentations, a commission member made a motion and the projects were approved unanimously. It seemed the fix was in.

When Midway's application came up, the first two rows emptied as people formed lines behind microphones in the two aisles. The chairman glanced at his watch, then announced that each speaker would be limited to three minutes.

"My name is Thelma Washington," began the first. "I hear my apartment building would be torn down to build this Midway thing. I been livin' there ten years, raisin' six kids. Raisin' 'em on my own. You got any idea how hard it is for a single mom with six kids to find an apartment with rent a laundry worker can afford? Are you gonna find me one? I bet you won't. You'll just throw us out on the damn street. Well, let me tell you this. Midway never did nothin' for me, and I ain't givin' up my home for Midway. You'll have to carry us out of there, 'cause we ain't goin' nowhere."

The audience erupted in cheers and applause. Donovan banged his gavel and called for order. It took a few minutes for things to calm down. He said, "Thank you, Miss Washington. Next?"

Thelma Washington rejoined, "You're quite welcome," and returned to her seat. I noticed the person at the end of the third row stand and get on the back of the line. The next speaker was a well-dressed, gray-haired man.

"My name is Obadiah Hamilton," he began. Looking out over the audience with a smile, he leaned into the microphone and whispered, "But you can call me Mister Obie."

Clapping, cheers, whistles rang out. "You go, Mister Obie!"

He continued. "I am the proprietor of the Hamilton Funeral Parlor, and have been since 1945, when I came home from fighting for this country and had to move the family business from Mississippi to Chicago. Why? Because I found out I should've been fighting for democracy back home, not across the ocean. I tried to vote, and they burned my father's funeral home to the ground."

"But that's another story. Here in Chicago, thank the Lord, I've done well. South Side folks trust me to give their loved ones a dignified, respectful homegoing. But that's not the only reason they come to me. The other is that the white undertakers don't want them, and never did."

"And now," he went on, "you want to let Midway University bulldoze the business it took me twenty years to build, and deprive these people of the services I've become known for? Services that every person, at one time or other, will need? Where will I go? More important, where will they go? Have we no rights here? Am I back in Mississippi now?"

Without waiting for a reply, he returned to his seat, waving off an enthusiastic round of applause. A woman on the other end of the third row strode to the back of the other line. Donovan banged his gavel.

"Next," he announced. Now I suspected it was he who was expecting a long, unpleasant evening. For the next two hours, speaker after speaker testified to the injustice Midway's expansion threatened, not only to themselves but to the community as a whole. I saw more clearly that Sharon's instinct to separate the quantum weapon issue from this was quite strategic.

At about ten, as a Mrs. Mae Webster began to speak, Donovan banged his gavel. "This hearing is concluded," he proclaimed. "Thank you for your testimony. The commission will now consider the matter at hand."

The audience wasn't finished, though. People stood and yelled, "We're not done!" After a few minutes, everyone was chanting, "Let her speak! Let her speak!"

Donovan looked flustered. Rubber-stamping Midway's application, in this atmosphere, would be a public relations nightmare. But he also had to know that the hearing might be endless if he allowed it to continue. Instead, he banged his gavel again and angrily announced, "Meeting adjourned. The Commission will consider this matter at its next monthly meeting, on Thursday, June 6th." The members gathered their papers and left the stage.

At first, there was stunned silence. I told Marcellus, "This is big. Wayne said he needed some time to work on the story, and you got him three weeks."

Mrs. Webster, who I later learned was an experienced community organizer, climbed the stage steps and took a seat at the dais. She was quickly joined by Sharon, Marcellus, James Watkins and two pastors.

She announced, "The People's Planning Commission is now in session. The floor is open for testimony."

A few more people spoke, but everyone sensed what was coming.

"The People's Planning Commission," announced Mrs. Webster, "is now prepared to vote. Shall the City of Chicago, using its power of eminent domain, destroy eighteen South Side blocks for the benefit of Midway University? All in favor, say 'aye.'"

Silence.

"All opposed, say 'nay'." This was unanimous, not only from the "people's commission," but from the audience too.

"The application," proclaimed Mrs. Webster, "is denied. Meeting adjourned! Let's go home."

A week later, the campus was buzzing about Barry Wayne's article in the semester's last issue of the *Midway Magenta*. The headline read, "Doomsday Machine Slated for New Midway Institute." I read it aloud to Emma and Cat.

"Documents made available to the *Magenta*," it began, "reveal that the mission of Midway's planned Institute for Applied Physics is to develop a government-funded weapon unlike anything the world has ever seen." He went on to explain Cat's synopsis of the Quantum Potential Weapon. If I didn't know better, I would have thought I was reading science fiction.

>   *According to an informed source in the scientific community who wishes to remain anonymous, this weapon, if successfully developed, would be capable of wiping out the entire civilian populations of targeted areas. No defense could be mounted against it. The actual use of such a weapon would recall the Black Death, the plague that indiscriminately killed millions during the Fourteenth Century.*
>
>   *The theories behind this project are the brainchild of Dr. Dietrich von Helsinger, a research professor in Midway's Physics Department. The professor refused to answer any questions about it, claiming his work is beyond the comprehension of Midway's student body. However, he did volunteer his opinion of the developing community opposition to Midway's expansion. 'The childlike Negro brain,' he asserted, 'is simply incapable of appreciating the import of this work.' When questioned regarding his role in Nazi Germany's scientific apparatus, he abruptly terminated the interview.*
>
>   *Further exploration within Midway's administration was no more revealing. Horace Masters, the Director of Development, claimed his role was limited to the eminent domain application, and he knew nothing about the purpose of the planned facility. President Kent, who agreed to a brief interview after a series of requests, said only that this reporter's information was based on sensitive*

> *classified information. He predicted that
> its source would be "uncovered through
> an FBI investigation and prosecuted to the
> fullest extent of the law."*

"This is wonderful," Emma interrupted. "They must suspect a leak from inside the project. The FBI will interrogate everyone involved. Good for them!"

"There's more," I said, and read on.

> *The Magenta also contacted Dr.
> Bradley F. Bennett, a founding editor of
> the Bulletin of the Atomic Scientists. Dr.
> Bennett said he could not judge the
> project's feasibility based on the limited
> information available, but did state that if
> the project proved successful, "it would be
> more devastating to the planet than a
> dozen hydrogen bombs."*

Emma suggested, "Let's contact this Dr. Bennett. The *Bulletin* is a very credible operation. It was started after Hiroshima and Nagasaki, by a group of scientists who were horrified by the deadly results of their research. The journal's primary mission is to publicize the dangers of nuclear proliferation, and this fits right in with it. Bennett might spearhead another line of attack."

I went to the phone and called Barry Wayne. I congratulated him on the article and asked, "Do you think Dr. Bennett might do something about this if he got his hands on the original documents?"

"I'm sure he'd want to," he replied "The *Bulletin's* primary mission is alerting the world to dangers like this. Write down this number..."

When Bradley Bennett answered the phone, I simply said, "Barry Wayne gave me your number. Do you want to see the documents?" He got the message.

"Yes, I do," he replied. "Very much. But who is this?"

"No names for now. Give me a time and date at a secure location."

I sensed the eagerness in his voice. "I have a summer home in Harbor Country. It's on the Michigan lakeshore, an hour north of Chicago. It'll be a couple of weeks until I can get there, though."

"That's fine," I agreed, knowing Cat wouldn't allow us time for this until finals were over anyway. "How about Saturday, June 15th?"

He said that would be perfect, and gave me the driving directions.

After I hung up, Cat asked, "Why the cloak-and-dagger stuff?"

"Look," I explained, "You're right in the middle of this thing, and that has to be kept within our little circle. So let me handle our security arrangements."

"All right," she replied. "I can see your point. So what now?"

"There's one thing. Sometime before the 15th, go to the library and find out what you can about Bradley Bennett. Look for a clue about how far we can trust him, or whether we should even show up for this rendezvous."

"Okay. I can do that next week."

I didn't say anything about it, but I found myself enjoying what Cat called the "cloak-and-dagger stuff." Probably, it fed into my penchant for risky behavior, but it also felt good to take charge of protecting her. Cat's trust to let me do it felt even better.

Chapter 39

The biggest domestic story that spring was the battle for the Democratic presidential nomination. Humphrey was going around the country making speeches at labor union events and at rallies organized by the big-city party bosses, but his name didn't appear on any of the primary ballots. Whenever he ventured onto college campuses, students booed and picketed. McCarthy's rallies, on the other hand, were mostly held on campuses, where he drew large, enthusiastic crowds. Meanwhile, the Kennedy campaign caught fire, particularly in the urban ghettoes and *barrios*. His antiwar and anti-poverty messages, combined with powerful personal charisma, generated a chemistry no other politician could touch. He waded into crowds of supporters in these communities without bodyguards and was received, as the *Daily Defender* described it, "like the second coming of Dr. King." His supporters' urge to make physical contact resulted in tousled hair and ripped clothing, even missing shoes. I read that he had to buy his cufflinks in wholesale lots.

"Some men see things as they are," he said in his stump speeches, "and ask, '*Why?*' I dream of things that never were, and ask, '*Why not?*'" To millions now, he was "Bobby," the messenger of hope.

McCarthy won the April 30th Massachusetts primary. Coming up next was Indiana, where Kennedy had been campaigning when Dr. King was assassinated. While cities were burning across the country, he faced an angry Indianapolis outdoor crowd. In an extemporaneous speech, he made a connection between his pain and theirs. One memorable sentence was, "My brother was shot by a white man too." The crowd listened intently as he recited the poetry of Aeschylus. No violence erupted there that night. On May 7th, Kennedy swept the Indiana primary.

The two candidates continued sparring throughout the month. Kennedy won Nebraska, but McCarthy carried Oregon. The big prize would be June 4th, the last of the important primaries. Voters in New Jersey, South Dakota and California would cast their ballots that day.

Kennedy told an interviewer he would probably withdraw if he didn't win California.

Meanwhile the war raged on. Two thousand American soldiers lost their lives in Vietnam during the month of May, along with untold numbers of Vietnamese.

The two candidates met in a nationally televised debate on June 1st. At the Saturday night prime-time event, neither delivered a knockout blow. Afterwards, though, Kennedy pulled ahead in the California polls. He challenged Humphrey to debate him in the non-primary states. The vice president ignored the challenge, while racking up delegates in those states without having to risk a either a lost primary or a poor debate performance.

Cat and I stayed up late Tuesday night, eating popcorn and watching the election returns. South Dakota's came in first. LBJ's name was still on the ballot, but any of his winning delegates would be pledged to Humphrey. That ballot line got 30 percent. McCarthy got only 20 percent. But Kennedy got 50 percent.

"Great start for Bobby tonight," Cat remarked.

"Even better than that," I replied. "The vote went more than two-to-one against the war."

New Jersey came in next. Here, McCarthy prevailed by a few points. Again, the two antiwar candidates combined for two-thirds of the votes cast. I exclaimed, "Wow, two-thirds again!"

Cat asked, "Steve, do you *really* think an antiwar politician can get the nomination, win the election and end the war?"

"I know that's probably wishful thinking," I replied. "But what could be better to wish for? Wouldn't a celebration at the convention instead of a protest be so much better? Anyway, it's good to see so many people voting against the war."

"I guess so," Cat muttered thoughtfully, reaching for another handful of popcorn.

The California results were finally announced at almost two in the morning, our time. Kennedy came in first with 46 percent, and McCarthy second with 42 percent. The "unpledged" slate, which was a stand-in for Humphrey, got only 12 percent. California Democrats had voted seven to one against the war! Now Bobby Kennedy had won nearly every major primary election.

The TV coverage moved to a big ballroom in Los Angeles's Ambassador Hotel, packed with cheering Kennedy supporters. The candidate made a short, magnanimous speech, thanking them and reaching out to McCarthy, saying he hoped they would work together now to stop Humphrey. Once again, he challenged the vice president to a series of debates. In closing, he took note of the past year's endemic violence, in Vietnam and in our cities, and pledged to do whatever he could to end it. After he left the stage, the cameras switched to the main kitchen's large pantry area where supporters waited to greet him on his way out of the hotel.

"This has been quite a night," Cat sighed, "and now we can finally go to bed."

I was still too hopped up for sleeping, though. "Let's watch for a few more minutes," I suggested.

Kennedy came through the doors with a few aides, to the sound of cheers. The mood was joyous. But sudden unexpected sounds boomed out. *Crack! Crack! Crack!* People ran, screaming. The party turned to pandemonium. Cat and I jumped up, staring in silence, open-mouthed.

The camera trained on the center of the room. Bobby Kennedy was sprawled on his back, limbs askew. The announcer confirmed the sounds we heard were gunfire. Cat screamed. We slumped back into the couch. I reached over and held her. We both wept. Another dream turned to nightmare.

Neither of us slept much during what was left of that night. Exhaustion must have taken its toll in the morning, though, because it was noon before we struggled out of bed, depressed and deflated. We went through the motions of getting washed and dressed without saying hardly a word. I got the coffee started and, when Cat came in, asked, "Breakfast?"

"Not hungry," she replied. "Is he dead?"

"I don't know. Go turn on the TV. I'll bring in toast and coffee. We have to eat something."

All the networks were on the story, but the only breaking news was that the country had nearly ground to a halt. Kennedy was still in surgery. He'd been shot in both the head and the shoulder. No-one knew any more than that. The reporters filled up time with random interviews, while everyone waited for the doctors' report. The situation looked grim.

After we ate, and stared at the TV a little while longer, Cat jumped to her feet. "What was I thinking?" she exclaimed. "We have to check on Emma!"

I got to the phone first, and called the store. No answer. Under normal circumstances, finals week was a busy time. But nothing that day was normal. Emma answered her home phone, and said she'd love some company.

Disheveled on the couch, she wore a housecoat and slippers. Her ashtray was full, her coffee cup empty. She looked up blankly. Cat ran over and embraced her. They held it a long time. I didn't know what to say, so I asked, "Emma, have you eaten anything today?"

"Yes, you should eat," Cat agreed.

"All right," Emma conceded. "Steve, there's a bowl of fruit in the fridge. And would you please make another pot of coffee?"

Back with the fruit, the coffee and a clean ash tray, I said, "The whole country seems to be in shock. But Emma, I'm surprised to see you taking it so hard. I thought you were kind of cynical about him, about all the politicians."

"People can change, Steve. Sometimes they grow. That speech he gave in Indianapolis, on the night of Dr. King's assassination, was truly amazing. There was no time to have had it scripted, and it struck me as coming straight from the heart. That's the only way he could've communicated the connection he felt between his pain of personal loss and that of his Black audience. If they could believe it, I could believe it. He recited poetry, for God's sake! His campaign evolved into a crusade for social justice after that. And I'm sure he sincerely wanted to get us out of Vietnam. It gave me hope that something good was possible here, without any more violence. Wishful thinking? Of course."

"Steve said almost the same thing last night," Cat remarked. "I guess we'll take a shot on hope wherever we can find it."

Emma turned angry now. She reached for a Newport, but Cat grabbed her wrist and gave her a pleading look. She slumped back and exhaled.

"Was it all an illusion?" she wondered aloud. "In the past five years, we've lost Medgar Evers, JFK, Malcolm, Dr. King, and now Bobby Kennedy. It would take a miracle for McCarthy to get the nomination. But suppose he somehow does. What then? Will he be next?"

We fell silent and turned back to the TV. Still no real news. Emma looked defeated as I'd never seen her before, and her wheezing and coughing was another bad sign. Cat watched her carefully. I was getting restless, though. Catching Cat's eye, I motioned for her to join me in the kitchen.

In a low voice, I said, "I can't stand watching this TV anymore. Nothing's happening and they're filling air time with platitudes. But there's nothing we can do. I can't sit still. My head feels about to explode."

Cat gave me a hug. "Go find a distraction," she said. "Sitting and watching TV isn't healthy for you right now." After a moment's thought, she added, "I know. Get away from all this. Do the laundry or something."

That sounded ludicrous at first, but it did make sense. I needed a distraction, even better a mindless one.

"Okay," I said. "I guess it's time for that anyway. But what about you?"

"I want to stay with Emma. She and I can support each other, and I need to find a way to cheer her up. She's in a bad place right now."

"Yes, and I think she sees all of us heading for a bad place. Anyway, I'll be right across the street if you need me."

Chapter 40

In our informal division of household labor, laundry had early become part of my repertoire. I wasn't very good at cleaning. Cat said I was neat enough, but "couldn't see dirt." At least not like her eagle eye spotted it. She was also much better at grocery shopping and, by far, at cooking.

But I could take out the garbage. And laundry, I could do well. Our Laundromat was designed for studying or socializing while the machines were rumbling. Sometimes, interesting political discussions developed. During the downtimes, I read. The part I liked best was after the clothes came out of the dryer. I made this a mathematical challenge, folding them into geometrical shapes. I particularly enjoyed folding Cat's clothing and took great care to get them right. Along with our laundry bag, I brought my math text and a notebook. I thought reviewing for the final exam, scheduled for Friday, might help get my head out of the day's awful reality.

Crossing the street, bag and books in hand, I noticed an eerie quiet. High Street was mostly commercial, with people coming and going all day, every day. But today, it was almost deserted. I suspected many, many people were doing what Cat and Emma were doing, watching TV and hoping for a miracle.

I was glad to see the Laundromat deserted as well. I needed to get away from the one topic on everyone's minds. I felt irresponsible, even a little guilty, but I had to clear my head. Anyway, I had nothing to offer anyone that could help them. I looked forward to having a big pile of clothes that needed folding. I could do this. *Maybe,* I thought, *this is all I can do right now.*

I got the machines purring and sat down with the math book. Here I found abstraction. More important, certainty. The path from problem to solution might not be obvious, but it was always in there, somewhere. So I dug in. This was what I needed now. Real life, with its ambiguities and gray areas, its uncertainty and despair, could wait.

But it didn't. Concentrating deeply on a quadratic equation, I barely heard the door open and close, and the scrape of a chair moving on the other side of the table.

"Hi, Steve," came a voice I recognized.

I looked up. "Donnie!" I exclaimed in surprise. "What brings you here?"

"Emma told me where to find you. We closed the Mobe office for the day, so I'm catching up on visits."

"It's good to see you. So, how's the planning for the convention protest going?"

"That's what I want to talk to you about. It's kind of a mess."

"What do you mean?"

"We still haven't regained our bearings since LBJ's withdrawal. The Board isn't even united on whether to go ahead with the protest, so we haven't been able to put out an official call. A sizable faction is arguing that demonstrations will hurt the chances of McCarthy or Kennedy winning the nomination, as though that's a real possibility."

"Especially now," I interjected.

"Right. Even if Kennedy survives, his candidacy is over. Some of his delegates will jump onto Humphrey's bandwagon. So that particular objection might drop away. But there's another faction arguing that any action around the convention will be seen as supporting McCarthy."

"What's wrong with that?"

"They say it would validate the Democratic Party. After all, it's the Democrats who've been the war-mongers. The two-party system gives us two wings of the same diseased bird."

"It sounds like you agree with them."

"In a way, I do. But a massive demonstration can challenge the whole system, the whole war machine. We don't want to keep the McCarthy kids from coming. They're against the war, and that's good enough. We want them. We want SDS. We want church groups. We want everyone, even the Yippies."

"Where do they stand on this?"

"They're planning their own thing. A week-long concert in the park. You know: sex, drugs, rock 'n' roll. They say they'll confront the 'Convention of Death' with a 'Festival of Life.' Abbie Hoffman is brilliant at coming up with slogans and pranks. The press loves to cover the Yippies because they always provide a clever line and an entertaining picture. But I can't see the political point of a counter-cultural party. Anyway, they don't want to work with The Mobe. To them, we're too straight."

"Well, you did say it's kind of a mess. Any other big problems?"

"The biggest one of all," he explained, looking around to make sure we were alone there, "is Mayor Daley's Chicago. For this thing to go smoothly, we need cooperation. We'll need permits for marches, for rallies, for camping in the parks. We'll also need to coordinate with the police on security. We're trying for all of that. But so far, we've gotten nowhere. And there's what's already happened here."

"What do you mean?"

"Everyone remembers the 'shoot to kill' order Daley put out after the King assassination. And didn't I hear you took a beating at the Civic Center?"

"I did get a little bloody. But I'm okay now."

"Well, that police riot got reported in newspapers everywhere. The AP dispatch included how the cops attacked people who weren't even part of the march. New York City, by the way, had more than ten times as many marchers that day, and there was no violence at all. I'm hearing from cities and campuses all over that people are fearful of joining a protest here in Chicago. I can't really blame them. It's understandable."

"So it might be called off?"

"I don't know, but I hope not. We can't let Daley scare us away. Anyhow, first we need to overcome our internal factional differences. We'll find out on the 29th, when the Mobe's National Board meets. A decision needs to be made at that meeting. Even if it's a 'go,' we'll have less than two months to get all the pieces in place. That's why I'm here now."

"Here? At the Laundromat?"

"Here, talking to you. I want you to consider joining the staff, even part-time. The pay is paltry, but you could be a big help."

"Why me?" I asked. "And why a paid job? This sounds like something people would volunteer for."

"Oh, we have volunteers all right. They go in and out of the office every day. The problem is, I can't tell which of them are spies from J. Edgar Hoover's FBI and which are from Mayor Daley's Red Squad. For the important things, I need people I can trust."

"Did Emma have something to do with this visit?" I wondered aloud.

He answered with another question. "What do you think?"

"Do you have a specific assignment in mind?" I asked.

"Not yet. A whole range of things will need to be done, and you won't be alone in doing them. We'll need free housing, for example, for what we hope will be a hundred thousand people. That means lining up churches, school gyms and other big places, even parks. In case of injuries, we'll need a medical staff. We'll need to recruit and train marshals to keep order. And we'll need to line up lawyers. A Midway Law student, Jeff Rosen, started working on the lawyers and the parade permits. Do you know him?"

"Yes, he's a good guy. Well-organized, smart, and very committed."

"Good. We need people like you and him to help with the planning and handle the sensitive information. I want to keep the volunteers away from that as much as possible."

"Well, I admit I'm flattered by the offer, and I'd love to help. But I need to talk to Cat before making a commitment."

"Of course you do," leaning back with a smile. "Look, between now and the 29th, I'll be on the road, trying to drum up support and smooth out some factional issues. I'll check in with you when I'm back in town."

I found it difficult to focus on the math after that, as my mind raced with questions about housing, medical care, legal assistance, and other issues which Donnie hadn't even mentioned. I didn't know how to approach any of these, though, and my headache was coming back.

Cat was preparing dinner when I got home with the laundry. I asked, "How's Emma doing?"

"Much better. She was grateful for the companionship. I've never known her to be surprised by big things that happen in the world, but this one really came as a shock."

"Any news on TV?"

"Nothing yet, but it doesn't look good."

"Anything about the election?"

"CBS gave the delegate totals as they stood after California. Humphrey has 561 delegates. The antiwar candidates have a combined 651. But more than half of the delegates still haven't been named, and there are no more primaries. Emma says the party establishment is solidly lined up behind Humphrey, and now even some Kennedy delegates might go along. Politicians want to be on the winning side."

"In other words," I somberly responded, "we're sunk. Ending the war won't even be an issue in the general election. I guess Donnie put it right. 'Two wings of the same diseased bird' was how he described the Democrats and the Republicans."

"When was that?" Cat asked, looking confused.

I summarized our conversation at the Laundromat, leaving out only the problems with the city bureaucracy. I didn't want to worry her, and hoped she would go along with my joining the staff. As a strategic gambit, that didn't last a minute.

"Emma and I discussed the convention protest too," she said. "But can't Daley stop it by holding back the parade permits? He can make the whole thing illegal, and unleash who knows what forces. I don't want you in danger again. You know that."

"Let's not get ahead of ourselves," I argued. "The permit applications won't even be submitted until after the board meets, so let's see what happens. All Donnie wants me to work on is planning and arrangements."

"All right, but that's it. You won't be a parade marshal, and we won't decide whether we'll participate until the permit situation is resolved."

"Okay," I conceded. "Now let's eat."

During dinner, we didn't talk as much as usual. I knew Cat was making a mental list of everything that could go wrong with the protests, while I was fighting off my own knowledge that her worries were justified. But I desperately wanted to do something to end the war, and this was something important. Meanwhile we, like most of the country, were still on edge concerning Kennedy's condition.

Thursday morning, we woke to the news that he was gone. The whole country seemed to be in mourning. Everything was postponed or canceled, including our final exams. The only good news came in a call from Marcellus. A clerk at City Hall called Watkins to tell him the Planning Commission meeting, scheduled for that evening, was canceled. Its next meeting wasn't until September. Now we had more time to kill Midway's land grab and von Helsinger's deadly scheme.

"This makes our meeting with Dr. Bennett even more important," I told Cat. "Did you find out any more about him?"

"Not yet. The rescheduled finals will be over on Tuesday. There'll be plenty of time for research before we go see him next Saturday."

During the next couple of days, we did little besides watch TV, mostly with Emma. Kennedy's body was brought to New York's St. Patrick's Cathedral overnight. The line of people waiting to view it in the morning stretched for more than a mile. Thousands attended the funeral mass Saturday morning. There was music, pageantry and powerful speeches. The one that most struck me was the eulogy delivered by his younger brother, Edward, a senator from Massachusetts:

> *My brother need not be idolized or enlarged in death beyond what he was in life. (He should) be remembered simply as a good and decent man, who saw wrong and tried to right it, saw suffering and tried to heal it, saw war and tried to stop it. Those of us who loved him, and who take him to his rest today, pray that what he was to us, and what he wished for others, will someday come to pass for all the world.*

He saw war and tried to stop it. Those words kept repeating in my mind. *He saw war and tried to stop it.* He tried. *What the hell was I doing?*

Chapter 41

Normal routines began to resume during the following week. Cat and I finished our exams on Tuesday. Final grades posted Thursday morning. Thanks to another C-minus in Western Civ, I barely squeaked by, with a 3.05 grade-point average. I was safe for another semester, though. Cat, to no-one's surprise, got an A in everything.

We'd decided that while she researched Bradley Bennett, I'd help Emma in the shop. Buyback time had arrived, and busy days lay ahead. Before Cat and I parted, though, she surprised me with a question.

"Steve, I'd like to go out tomorrow night. Do you mind?"

"Not at all. Where are we going?"

"No. It's only me."

"Oh," I murmured, already thinking the worst. "Is there something you haven't told me? Or someone?"

"No, it's not that, silly. Sabrina's organizing a 'Girl's Night Out' to celebrate her birthday. Pete's Tavern will have a band playing. Sharon's coming too, plus the girls in the Saran Wrap crew.

"Oh," I said again, only partially relieved. "I'm not sure I like the idea of you being in a bar without me, but I guess there's safety in numbers."

"Oh, it's better than that. Pete hired Marcellus and two of his friends as bouncers for the night. I'll even have an escort walking me home."

"That's good to hear," I said, "but Sharon's too far away to walk. Does she need a ride?"

"No, she's arranged that. But she did ask if you'd babysit Arielle."

"What a great idea!" I exclaimed.

"From the look on your face now," Cat observed, "I guess I'm the one who should be worried about competition, not you!" She pinched my cheek and headed off to the library.

Arielle was waiting for my knock on the door. Already in her pajamas, she grabbed my wrist and pulled me into her room. Sharon laughed and called, "Have fun, you two. But remember, bedtime is 8:30 sharp."

The dolls were lined up on the bed. Tonight, they were the audience, watching the two of us enact a role-play. Arielle had the roles and the costumes all ready. The script would be mostly improvised, but she was the director.

"Let's play p'tend. I'll be Captain Hook's daughter," she announced, putting on her sparkly birthday tiara. "You be Peter Pan... and Captain Hook!" She reached into a box, pulling out a green pointy hat and a broad-brimmed black one. Also, a short stick for a knife and a long one for a sword.

The story was a bit amorphous. Apparently, the daughter had an ambivalent relationship with the Captain, and at least a flirtatious one with Peter. There was much capturing and rescuing, so I had to switch hats every few minutes. Things got quite complicated at times, particularly during duels between Peter and Captain Hook. Arielle took all this very seriously and so, of course, did I.

Eventually, I pointed to the clock and said, "Eight-thirty, sweetheart. Bedtime. That's what Mommy said."

"Not yet," she pleaded. "Two more minutes."

"Okay," I acceded, "but that's it."

In the final scene, Captain Hook realized he'd lose his daughter if he continued his deadly rivalry with Peter Pan. He renounced his evil ways and peace was declared. *Ah, the redemptive power of love!* I thought. The finale ended, somehow, with a group hug.

With the drama concluded, she was ready for bed, though not yet for sleeping. She handed me a little book called, *Millions of Cats*. I read it to her with as much drama as I could muster. Halfway through, though, I got a word wrong and she corrected me. Obviously, she had the whole thing memorized. But still, she wasn't ready for sleeping.

"Tell me a story now. Please, please."

"One more," I agreed. "Which book?"

"No, a story from your head. Your story. Tell me a story about... about a door."

About a door? After a long moment of thought, I came up with a story. It was about a door that traveled the world, looking for the exact right doorway, where it would protect a good little girl from any monsters who might try to enter her room.

Arielle was fading by the end of this one, and so was I, but she had one more request. "Now tell me one about a window."

My window story couldn't have passed a coherence test, but it didn't matter because the princess fell asleep after only a few minutes. I kissed her on the forehead, shut off the lamp, closed the door, and collapsed on the living room couch.

Sharon returned a little after eleven. She asked, "Any trouble?"

"Not a bit," I replied. "We had lots of fun."

"8:30 bedtime?"

"More or less. So did you have a good time?"

"Oh, yes. There was a fun crowd at Pete's, celebrating the end of exams. No-one made any trouble. In fact, the bouncers had almost nothing to do. Marcellus wanted to join us, and he got a bit miffed when I reminded him this was Sabrina's party and 'girls only.' He got over it, but hung close to make sure no other guys tried to invade our space. He'll walk Cat home when she's ready to go."

"She's still there?"

"The party's still going strong. I had to catch my ride, though. Cat will probably be late, but she'll get home safe."

Still, after I'd been home for an hour, I did begin to worry. I knew, in my head, that she couldn't have had a better bodyguard than Marcellus, but I wanted her safe at home. I suddenly understood, in some small way, what she must have gone through the night I was in jail. I promised myself, once more, I'd never put her through that again.

After another hour, I got the jitters, and couldn't sit still. At the same time, though, I was so tired. I kept awake by pacing the floor, pouring cold water on my head, slapping myself in the face.

At around two, I heard footsteps from below. Throwing the door open, I saw Marcellus carrying Cat up the stairs. At the landing, he passed her off to me and said, "She's all yours now, buddy."

Cradling her in my arms, like a baby, I asked, "Are you okay?" Her speech was slurred, but she seemed to be making noises in the affirmative. Her breath reeked of alcohol.

"She's fine," Marcellus offered. "Just a little too much to drink."

Tears welled in my eyes. I said, "Thank you, my friend. Thank you so much for watching over her, for bringing her home to me." I held Cat tight to my body.

Marcellus smiled and slapped me on the back. "My pleasure," he said. "Now you two take care." He went back into the night.

I pulled down the covers and laid Cat, already asleep, gently into the bed. I undressed her slowly and carefully, as though I might have awakened her even if I'd wanted to. I climbed in, cradled her body in mine and covered us with the blanket. Her snoring was music to my ears.

Chapter 42

In the morning, I stumbled my way into the shower, trying to wake myself. I brewed the coffee, brought a cup into the bedroom, and gently woke a very groggy young lady.

"What happened?" were her first words. "My head is splitting."

"Well," I explained, "nothing much. You got a little drunk and passed out."

She struggled to sit up. "More than a little, I guess. I don't even remember coming home. Oh, my head."

"Here, try this," I offered, handing her the coffee and a couple of my leftover Tylenols. "We need to leave soon for our appointment with Dr. Bennett."

"It's Saturday?" she asked. "Oh, I guess it is. I need a cold shower."

I made sure she was steady on her feet and told her, "I'll get breakfast ready."

"Okay, but don't get carried away. Not much of an appetite."

The combination of coffee, Tylenol and cold shower seemed to have done the trick. Afterward, her eyes were clear and she was hungry. My Cat was back.

Once we got on the road, I asked, "So, what do we know about Dr. Bradley Bennett?"

Cat reached into the tote bag where I'd put the five manila envelopes, and took out her notebook.

"Not terribly much," she began, "but probably enough. Emma told us about the *Bulletin of the Atomic Scientists*. Besides warning against nuclear proliferation, though, it also advocates for the peaceful uses of modern physics. Dr. Bennett's done that himself. Fifteen years ago, he and some colleagues founded the Society of Nuclear Medicine."

"What's nuclear medicine?"

"It uses radioactive materials to interact with the human body on the cellular level. Bennett's been a pioneer in using radionuclides to track previously undetectable biochemical processes. He has patents on imaging devices that can detect abnormalities, and diseases that might be brewing, long before any symptoms develop."

"Smart guy, huh?"

"Yes, very smart, and very rich. Each of his patents is worth a fortune, and he has five that I know of."

"So it'll be safe to show him the von Helsinger documents?"

"Well, I haven't uncovered anything to suggest he'd misuse them."

"What about leaving them with him?"

"I hadn't thought about that. Why would we want to?"

"Those five envelopes contain classified material," I explained. "They're a hot potato, a potential danger to anyone connected with them. That's why we've been going to great lengths to distance them from you and the building takeover. If we could pass them on, knowing they'd be used for good purposes and kept safe, then they'll never be traced back."

"This makes sense," Cat agreed. "But let's not decide until we've talked with him. We have to be sure about this."

"Okay. We'll decide before we leave for home. And there's one other thing."

"What's that?"

"Our call to him was anonymous. I thought we'd tell him our names after you'd done your research. But now, I don't see any reason to do that. One more layer of protection. See?"

"Well then, how'll we introduce ourselves? If we don't, it'll be kind of awkward."

"We can make up names," I explained. "But only first names, so it looks like we're still holding something back. You pick the names."

"Okay. I'll be Felicia. And you… well, it's a beautiful sunny day, so how about Sol?"

"Sounds good, Felicia. But if you don't start reading me the directions he gave us, we'll never find the place."

At Cat's final direction, we turned into a driveway that wound through a forest and up a hill. As we neared the top, the redwood-clad house suddenly came into view. A petite, pretty young woman came down the steps to greet us. I registered medium-length curly blond hair, a short upturned nose, wire-rimmed glasses, and a bright yellow sundress.

"You must be our mysterious guests," she said, holding out her hand. "Welcome. I'm Melissa."

I took her hand. "Thank you. I'm, uh, Sol, and this is Felicia."

Leading the way inside, Melissa told us, "Brad's on his way up from the lake. He should be here in a few minutes."

"From the lake?" I asked.

"Sure, come take a look." Melissa led us into in a large living room, decorated in laid-back Western style. Its cathedral ceilings had four large skylights, nourishing half a dozen indoor trees. The back wall had a large fireplace in the center, flanked by sliding glass doors opening to a long, deep deck and, down over the tops of the hillside trees, the vast expanse of Lake Michigan.

"This is fantastic," I gushed. "Absolutely beautiful."

"Yes, we've been very lucky. Come and eat something. You must be hungry after your drive."

We? I wondered. Bennett had to be at least in his mid-fifties, and Melissa couldn't be much past thirty. *A daughter maybe?*

The dining room table was set with a big cobb salad in the center. As we took seats, a deck door slid open, and Dr. Bradley Bennett came through it, apologizing for being late. Bennett was six feet tall, athletically built, tanned and good-looking. I was surprised.

"Oh, you dummy," scolded Melissa. "If you ever got anyplace on time, you wouldn't know what to do once you got there." He pulled her close and kissed her on the lips.

Definitely not a daughter, I thought.

Once Melissa made the introductions, we were all on a first-name basis.

"Brad, this house is wonderful. How long have you been here?" I asked.

"We had it built a couple of years ago, right after the wedding."

That settles that, I thought.

"Felicia" asked how they met.

"That was five years ago at the medical center where I worked, in L.A.," Melissa explained. "I was a radiologist, and Brad was demonstrating his new imaging device."

"Right," Brad added. "And after that, I kept finding excuses for trips out west. What I can't figure out is why it took me so long to propose."

"See what I mean?" exclaimed Melissa. "Always late!" We laughed.

"I've been looking forward to seeing the documents," Brad said. "You've brought them with you?"

"Yes, they're in my tote bag there," Felicia replied, pointing at it.

"It's a lot," I added. "Five big manila envelopes stuffed with papers. I know your interest is in the science, but we brought the contracts too. And we're looking forward to hearing your opinion of the whole thing."

"I can't wait to see them, Sol. But you know what I'm hoping?"

"No, what?"

"I'm hoping the scientific theories turn out to be sheer lunacy. From what Barry Wayne told me, this sounds like a very scary project."

"Do you think it could be lunacy?" Felicia asked.

"Probably not. I've met von Helsinger at scientific conferences. He's a nasty, arrogant fellow, truly disagreeable, but still quite brilliant. I'd be very surprised to find there's nothing to this."

"Felicia, why don't you show Brad what we've got," I said, standing to clear the table. "I'll help with the dishes."

Soon, Brad had the diagrams and equations spread out across the table. He circled around it, rubbing his chin, then took a yellow pad from a side table and began making notes.

"He's into his trance now," Melissa explained. "It'll be a while before he says another word. Why don't you kids go down to the lake? The weather's perfect for swimming today."

"Sounds great," I responded, "but we didn't bring bathing suits."

"No problem," she smiled, pointing out back. "There's a bathhouse at the beginning of the trail. Everything you'll need is in there: blankets, towels, bathing suits in all sizes, even tanning lotion if you want it. Go on out through the deck. You'll see it."

Felicia and I looked at each other, nodded, thanked her, and almost ran to the door.

Chapter 43

The bathhouse was architecturally consistent with the main house, and equally well-appointed. In addition to supplies, it had changing stalls, showers, even a sauna. Finding bathing suits was not a problem.

At the end of the downhill trail, we came to a small sandy beach, totally private, protected on both sides by dunes and tall grasses. The lake looked to me like an ocean. Besides three sailboats way, way out, there wasn't a soul in sight.

Cat grabbed my wrist and pulled me toward the water. It reminded me of Arielle pulling me into her room to play with her dolls. When we stepped into the lake, though, I yelled, "It's too cold!"

"It won't feel cold once we start swimming. Look, let's swim over there," she said, pointing to a wooden raft floating a hundred yards out. She started for it, so I had no choice but to go along.

Cat swam like a fish! She sat on the raft's edge, watching me and smiling for the eternity until I splashed my way out there. I climbed up next to her and asked, "Where'd you learn to swim like that?"

"Oh, I was on the swim team," she explained. "Our little high school had an Olympic-size pool. During my senior year, we even won a state championship."

"A state championship?"

"Not really such a big deal. Our division was a bunch of small private schools, so there wasn't much tough competition."

I stared down at the water, slowly shaking my head. She was just full of surprises. Looking up, I asked, "Is there anything you do badly, or even, like, average?"

"Of course, silly," she answered, laughing and punching me in the shoulder. "Lots of things."

"Okay," I challenged her. "Name three."

"That's easy. I can give you more than three." She rattled off, "Golf. Tennis. Billiards. Playing the piano, or the violin. And then there's Latin, Ancient Greek and Esperanto."

"I see. And did you ever try any of those?"

"Well, no," she admitted, jumping to her feet. She raised her arms toward the sun and called out, "I love this place!"

The sun's rays gave a warm glow to the smooth skin of my scantily-clad Butterscotch Goddess. I loved seeing her so happy. All of a sudden, we didn't have a care in the world. Then she kneeled down and pushed me back into the lake.

"That was a dirty trick!" I yelled. "It's freezing. I'll get you for this!"

"Catch me if you can," she laughed, diving over my head and swimming to shore.

Once we dried off, we spread out the blanket and applied a little tanning lotion. I did her back and she did mine. "Mmm, that feels good," I murmured.

She slapped my behind and asked, "Is that the only thing you ever think about?" We laughed as she laid down next to me. The blazing sun penetrated into my back. After a few minutes, I dozed off.

I don't know how long my nap lasted. I slowly woke to the sensation of Cat's hands kneading the muscles of my back and neck. I groaned in pleasure. She put a finger to my lips and whispered, "Ssshhh."

What I felt next weren't her hands anymore. I realized she was straddling me, and gently brushing her nipples across my back, barely touching it. Then she leaned down, holding my arms outstretched, and pressed her body into mine. It dawned on me that she'd removed her bathing suit.

She sat up, slid down to my knees, reached in between my legs and stroked me. Lifting slightly, she whispered, "Turn over," which I did with some effort. I started to say something, but she shushed me again and pulled off my swimsuit. She took me inside and rode me, slowly. It was over quickly. Too quickly. Then she covered my torso with hers, and buried her face in my neck.

After a while, she rolled off. We lay there on our backs, holding hands and finding animal shapes in the wisps of the clouds drifting through the clear sky. "Wouldn't it be great," I wondered out loud, "if we lived in a place like this?"

"You mean in that big house?"

"No. I mean like right here, on our own private beach. Only the two of us. No TV, no radio, no newspapers, no telephone, no war. Only us, the sand and the surf."

"Well, where would we get food and water?".

"The lake has plenty of fresh water. And fish too. We'd learn to do spear fishing."

After a moment, I added, "And we'd eat coconuts. I've heard they're really healthy."

"Now where would you get coconuts?"

"From the palm trees."

She rolled halfway over, leaned on an elbow and looked down at me quizzically. "Where would you get palm trees?"

I smiled. "From the same place I got our own private beach!"

She squeezed my cheeks, bent down and planted a kiss on my lips.

Lying back again, she asked, "But seriously, would we really be able to ignore what's going on in the real world, like the war?"

After not much thought, I had to admit, "I guess not. I'd probably feel guilty. Maybe even more useless than I sometimes feel now. But it's a wonderful fantasy, a world of just you and me and natural beauty. And love."

"It sure is," she agreed, squeezing my hand.

We fell silent again for a long time, watching the clouds, listening to the breaking waves and the squawks of the seagulls flying overhead, as we soaked up the rays of the sun.

"You know," she said, "we should be getting back to the house. Brad and Melissa might be starting to worry that we drowned out here."

"Well, I guess so," I agreed, although I really didn't want to leave this paradise. Ever.

"But first," she announced, "one more quick swim!" She sprung up and ran, naked, toward the lake, laughing, hair flying in the breeze, arms waving in the air.

Pure joy! I thought, struggling to my feet and running to catch up. I barely managed to tackle her as she dived into the waves.

Eventually, we made our way back to the bathhouse, where we showered and dressed. While Cat dried her hair, I waited outside, reflecting on my fantasy of life on the beach and how quickly that fantasy crumbled once the realities of the world intervened. This led me into contemplating the contradictions of my real life, and the mood swings that came with them.

In so many ways, I knew I led a charmed life. I had great friends, and a wise mentor. I learned something new every day, sometimes even in school. And best of all, I had this incredible woman to love who, even more incredibly, loved me back.

But when images of the war's atrocities invaded my consciousness, when I saw the grinding poverty so many South Siders lived with, when I met children whose lives were already stunted by hunger, violence and terrible schools, I could be consumed by a towering wave of sadness. Following that would come a fit of rage, sometimes collapsing into a hollow, helpless despair, even nausea. Just thinking about this, even after my afternoon in paradise, triggered a return of those very emotions.

My mind traveled back to conversations with Emma about "balance." I brought up her advice from wherever it had been hiding, and told myself I couldn't let these things totally consume me. This brought a moment of peace.

But an inner voice demanded, *What makes you think you deserve such a luxury? Do the Vietnamese have it, wondering from day to day whether this is the one they'll be blown to smithereens by your country's military? Do the draftees have it, plucked from their lives and dropped into hostile jungles, without a clue about what they're fighting for? What makes you so special?*

I struggled for answers to those questions, but found none. Still, I knew that, without some kind of balance in my life, I'd end up in a psycho ward, or someplace worse. The answers would have to wait. Once Cat stepped out of the bathhouse, I told her, "I have an idea."

"An idea about what?" she asked, puzzled.

"I'll tell you on the way home. We better get up to the house now."

We found Brad out on the deck, reading. On the table in front of him were the five manila envelopes, a large pitcher and a few glasses.

"Come, join me," he offered. "Have some of Melissa's lemonade."

Felicia and Sol each emptied a glass quickly. Brad refilled them.

"You know, I was starting to wonder if you were ever coming back up from the beach. I guess you enjoyed it?"

"Oh, we loved it," Felicia replied. "It's such a fabulous setting."

"Yes. What Melissa and I really treasure is the privacy."

"Us too!" Cat and I blurted at the same time. We turned to look at one another, and all three of us laughed.

"But now to business," Brad said. "This material is fascinating. Thank you for bringing it."

"So what do you think?" Felicia asked. "Could this really work?"

"It's so hard to say," he began, "whether or not those space-time curvature engines would be stable or controllable. At the sub-atomic level, the quantum level, the world doesn't work like it does out here."

I almost instantly regretted asking, "What do you mean?"

"In our world," he explained, "something can be either a particle, a tangible thing you might hold in your hand, or a wave, like sound or light. At the quantum level, the electron, zooming around inside the atom, is both. It only assumes an identity as one or the other at the nanosecond it's measured. But, if it's measured again, the result can be the opposite."

"This," I admitted, "is hard for me to wrap my mind around. Felicia's tried explaining it, but I can't seem to get it."

"Yes, it's truly counter-intuitive because we don't live in that world, or think we don't. My point, though, is that von Helsinger's theories can't be verified or disproven without actual experimentation. That's why the Defense Department is willing to fund the new institute. And that's why this thing has to be stopped before it gets off the ground."

"What do you mean?" I asked again.

"Let's suppose they start experimenting, refining the theory along the way, and eventually the experiments succeed. What do you think will happen then?"

"They'll build the weapon?" Felicia speculated.

"Yes, and they'll use it too, with horrific, world-altering consequences. It has to be stopped before the testing, not after, because if the testing succeeds, there might be no way to stop it. It's the same reasoning behind the *Bulletin's* advocacy of a worldwide ban on nuclear testing. That's the only real way to stop proliferation."

"We've been hoping public exposure might be the answer," I suggested.

"Perhaps," Brad replied, "and I'm certainly prepared to write a journal article. Also, I'll be speaking at an international conference next month, and I can make this part of it."

"But we need to stop Midway's land grab," I said, "and we don't have much time for that. The City Planning Commission meets right after Labor Day."

"I understand, and I've thought about that too. I'm willing to bet the presidential candidates are either in the dark about this, or unaware of its horrific consequences. If I can get the signatures of a hundred of the country's top nuclear scientists, a petition might get their attention. We could publish that petition as a full-page ad in, say, the *New York Times* and the *Washington Post*."

"Can you do that?" Felicia asked. "And maybe the *Chicago Tribune* too?"

"I can try. Next month's conference will be the perfect place to get a petition off the ground."

"We hadn't even thought of anything like that," I said. "I'm so glad we came to see you."

"Me too, but I have a big request."

"What's that?"

"I'd like your permission to copy these documents. If they're in my possession, I can't be accused of imagining the whole thing."

"Can you keep them safe?"

"Of course. You can't invent and patent high-tech devices without knowing how to keep materials like these safe and secure."

I looked over at Felicia. She nodded.

"We have a better idea," I said. "You keep the originals. We know they're in good hands. But right now, we better hit the road."

Chapter 44

Once we got on the highway, Cat asked, "So, what's that big idea you mentioned at the bathhouse?" She looked concerned.

"Do you remember Emma's advice about keeping things in balance?"

"Sure I do. Why?"

"Well, while I was sitting out there, all relaxed and everything, I was reminded how that 'balance' thing doesn't come naturally to me. You're always dragging me back from one brink or another. But I do know I need it. Otherwise, I can get overwhelmed by the emotions of the moment and lose perspective. Donnie asked for my help planning the convention protests. I want to do that, but I don't want it to take over my life. Will you help me keep things balanced?"

"How?"

"You're my best medicine. If you see me getting carried away with the work, or getting depressed from it, I want you to intervene. Especially, *especially*, if I'm not paying enough attention to *you*."

"That's a deal. But let's go one step further. Look, it's summertime. Let's promise ourselves to make time for play."

"Having fun with you," I agreed, "is the best thing. If we can't live on a beach, we can still visit some. Chicago has plenty. Maybe we'll even get invited back to Bennett Beach sometime."

"That would be heavenly," she said, echoing my sentiments precisely. "But it reminds me. Why are we still playing cloak-and-dagger with Brad? We trusted him enough to give him the documents, but we haven't told him our real names. If we go back, would we still have to be Sol and Felicia?"

"No need to know. He'll be carrying around enough dangerous secrets without also having to protect who or where we are. This way, those documents can never be traced back to you, the BSU or the building takeover."

"Good thinking," she agreed with a smile.

"Well, I'm very motivated. And anyway, the role-playing was kind of fun, wasn't it?"

"I guess it was." After a pause, she added, "But while we've been working on this von Helsinger thing, I haven't seen any of your big emotional reactions."

"You're right. This is different. The weapon doesn't exist yet, and it's very abstract to me. It's not like seeing children screaming from Napalm burns. Anyway, the campaign to stop it is really your thing, since I don't even understand the science. And the South Side community obviously can mobilize itself against the expansion. My job was something else."

"Something else?"

"I knew from the beginning, from the day we brought those documents home, that you were in danger. My primary mission was to protect you, to keep you from ever being connected to them. Now it's done. Unless, of course, someone talks."

"No-one's gonna talk. I told you why Stan won't, and you handled Barry Wayne. Other than them, and Emma of course, the only ones even aware of my connection to the documents are Marcellus, Sharon and Walter Dyson. I'm not worried about any of them."

"Well, okay," I said, relieved. "You know best."

"Anyway," she asked, "you were able to stay calm and clear-headed the whole time?"

"Yes, and that surprised me a little. Normally, whenever I think of you being in danger, I see nothing but red. But this was different. I had a job to do and I did it, thinking as clearly as I could at each step. But, you know, falling in love with you has kind of opened me up. I keep finding out new things about myself."

Cat squeezed me, high on the thigh, and I felt a stirring a few inches away. With reluctance, I lifted her hand, kissed it and placed it back in her lap.

"I better concentrate on getting us home in one piece," I said. "We can continue this, uh, conversation once we get there."

She curled her feet up on the seat, and leaned against the window. A few minutes later, she dropped off to sleep, a contented little smile on her face. I turned the radio's dial, and the velvet baritone of Nat King Cole poured through the speaker.

What a day this has been,
What a rare mood I'm in.
Why, it's almost like being in love.

I thought, *Nothing "almost" about this, my friend.*

Over breakfast the next morning, I said, "You know, yesterday at the beach was like a whole vacation for me. It felt like a weight was lifted from my shoulders."

Smiling, Cat began to respond, "I'm so glad to hear that. You know..."

The ringing of the phone interrupted her.

"Hi, Steve, it's Donnie. How are you?" I knew right away my little vacation was over.

"Good, Donnie. How about you? Are you back in town?"

"Yes, I'm back, and a little swamped. If you're ready to accept my offer, can you come down to the office tomorrow afternoon?"

After agreeing and hanging up, I filled Cat in and asked if she had an objection.

"No, I don't," she said, "but you have to promise to be careful."

"Nothing to worry about. We'll be preparing for the board meeting. That's all."

"Okay." After a pause, she murmured, frowning, "Just when you were telling me how good it felt to get away from the war..."

The Mobe's office was on the third floor of 407 South Dearborn Street, a small, rundown multi-tenant building in the Loop. Outside its one private office, the open area was filled with old filing cabinets, and desks littered with typewriters, phones, yellow pads, manila files, ash trays and food wrappers. Donnie was busy on the phone, so his office manager, whose name, astonishingly, was Ronnie, showed me around.

Ronnie Moore was a middle-aged woman, by far the oldest person in the place, short and plump but full of energy, with a contagious Irish smile. She introduced me to some of the volunteers. There were a dozen that day talking on the phones, running things off on the mimeograph, clacking away on old manual typewriters, trying to get the coffeemaker and the radio to work. It was crowded, noisy and, even with the few windows wide open, smoky and hot. I suppressed my discomfort.

"People come and go whenever they want," Ronnie told me. "And I've given up trying to keep track. As they come in, I find a place for them to work and assign whatever needs to get done at the moment. What most of them are working on now is finding housing for the protesters. We've given each volunteer a list of phone numbers and a script, but in most cases they have to find out for themselves who the right contact person is."

"What do you do if the staff needs a private conversation?" I asked. "There's no conference room."

"If Donnie's office isn't big enough, we go down the hall. The American Friends Service Committee makes its conference room available to us. They've been very supportive."

"Actually, this is better," she added, "because they're a little less likely to be bugged than we are."

Donnie's office door opened, and he waved me inside. I thanked Ronnie and went in.

"So, I guess you got an idea what's going on. What do you think?" he asked.

"Well, it looks a little chaotic. But I guess reliance on volunteers means you have to take what you can get."

"We have no choice. With the board in disarray, fundraising has been tough, so there's almost no money for real staff. Like I told you, I don't know who most of these people are, so we can't let them in on sensitive information."

"A big problem," I observed.

"You know, every time I think about this," Donnie said, leaning back in his chair, "it reminds me of a little story Abner Mikva often tells."

"Who's that?

"He's in the State Legislature, one of the very few good reps from this city. Anyway, he tells the story of his first experience with Chicago politics, around twenty years ago. He walked into a Democratic Party district office and offered to volunteer for a campaign. The party boss asked who sent him. He answered, 'Nobody sent me.' The boss told him, 'We don't want nobody who nobody sent,' and waved him out of the office."

"That's pretty funny."

"But what's even funnier," Donnie added, "is that now I wish I could afford the luxury of sending away volunteers who nobody sent, and working only with people I trust. It sure feels strange to identify with an old-school political boss."

"I get that. So what do you want me to do? Is the board meeting still on?"

"No, it isn't. Too many doubters. Instead, we'll convene the Steering Committee, which can push the process forward. I've been in touch with the most prominent members, and they're ready to go. We can't wait any longer. Your first job is to get the press here late that afternoon for a formal announcement. I'll ask Ronnie to get space for it at AFSC. Dave Dellinger's people will do the same in New York."

"But I've never done anything like this before. I don't know the first thing about it."

"You're a smart guy," he said with a smile. "I got that on good authority. I know you'll figure it out."

"Well, okay. I'll start on it tomorrow. But I'd rather not do it from here."

"For all I care," he responded, "you can do it from Antarctica, as long as it gets done. So welcome aboard."

Chapter 45

Emma snorted when I described the Mobe's loose setup.

"The Party would never have run anything this way," she responded. "You can't let random people wander in and out of such an important operation's nerve center. Donnie might as well put a sign in the front window that says, *Infiltrators Welcome*."

"What party was that?" I asked.

"Oh, I thought you knew. The Communist Party, of course. I left in '56, after the invasion of Hungary. Now, don't get me wrong. We did make mistakes. But those mistakes did not include inviting spies in through an open door. We at least tried to make it difficult for them."

"Did you ever discuss this with Donnie?"

"Yes, we've talked about it, and he explained the problem to me much as he did to you. He and I respect each other, and he often asks for advice. But anytime I bring up how the Party used to do things, he goes suddenly deaf."

"What's that about?"

"It's a problem with the entire New Left. They want to do everything as opposite as they can from how the Old Left did them. Like Participatory Democracy, which paralyzes SDS with indecision half the time, as opposed to Democratic Centralism, which was an efficient way to establish leadership, make decisions and get things done. The undisciplined openness you described at the Mobe's office is another example."

"Why? Wouldn't they want to learn from past successes and failures?"

"Individually, many do. But organizationally, forget it. You see, even though we accomplished so much for union organizing, civil rights and more, we didn't bring about an actual revolution. They think they will. They don't have the slightest idea how, but they're very sure of it.

Some of this, present company excepted of course, is the arrogance of youth."

"I don't want you to get the wrong impression," she continued. "This is a criticism, not a rejection. These young people have shaken the country out of a deep sleep. Some have sacrificed much of their youth, even their very lives, in the fight for social justice. Anytime they ask for my help, I'll be there. As for the criticism… Well, that's what friends are for."

"So let's get to the bottom line. Emma, do you think we should go ahead with this protest?"

"Absolutely. Like you said, we can't sit by and do nothing."

Cat, her eyes on mine, interjected. "But only if the permits come through. Otherwise, it'll be too dangerous."

That night, rather than return to that uncomfortable conversation, I told Cat about my first assignment. She offered to help.

"I could sure use some help," I said, "since I don't know where to begin."

"We can figure it out together," she responded. "I insist on one thing, though. I have one non-negotiable demand while you're on this job."

"What's that?"

"I *demand* that you end up right here with me, every single night, in one piece, safe and sound, in this bed."

"Your demand," I announced in a deep, pompous voice as she rolled on top, "has been considered and found acceptable." As her tongue met mine, my moment of unease drifted off into the night. For the moment, anyway.

In the morning, I said, "I never got to ask about your afternoon with Emma. How was it?"

"Well, there wasn't much business," Cat began, "since the summer session hasn't started yet. So she brought out an empty carton and took her time filling it with books."

"What for?"

"It's our summer reading. The box is over there in the corner."

"So that's our summer session," I proclaimed, "at the University of Emma!"

"Exactly, and I'm looking forward to it."

"Me too. And the smoking?"

"She did some, but only outside. That's a start, I guess, since it's a little less convenient. She probably went through one pack instead of two or three. Now, do you want to start on your project today?"

"Sure. You have an idea how to approach it?"

"Let's start with the objective. What's the end result you want to achieve?"

"The end result?"

"It's to get the press release on the desk of every reporter and editor who might be covering the convention protests. Right?"

"Well, yeah, I guess so," I mumbled.

I wasn't really as dumb or as helpless as I must have sounded. I just loved seeing Cat take charge of things. She was methodical, efficient and unfailingly effective. Meanwhile, I knew that swirling underneath that practical exterior was intense, passionate emotion. My mind drifted away with these thoughts. It returned when Cat asked in a worried tone, "Steve, are you okay? Why are you smiling? Are you with me?"

"Oh, sorry," I said sheepishly, breaking out of my reverie. "Sure, I'm with you. But let's not play Twenty Questions. Come on. Tell me the plan."

"Okay, here's how I see it. First we'll make the list. We can start with the Yellow Pages. That'll give us the addresses of the local newspapers, and radio and TV stations."

"Some national papers, like the *Times*, must also have news bureaus in Chicago," I added. "Wire services too."

"Of course. Once we've done that, we'll go to the library."

"The library?"

"Sure. The newspaper archive. We'll find every article that covered any of this year's antiwar protests, and write down the reporters' names. Also, let's make sure we catch the local news on all the stations, and get the names of the anchors and reporters. If the press releases are personally addressed, they might get more attention."

"Okay. Then what?"

"This shouldn't take very long," she replied. "We can put together a good list by the time the press releases are ready. Everything will be finished but the deliveries."

That's how we spent most of the next ten days. When I picked up the releases, Donnie invited me to attend Saturday's Steering Committee meeting as a staff observer.

"Thanks for the invitation," I responded. "I'd love to come and see how this works, but I'll have to check with Cat."

"Of course," he smiled. "That I already knew."

After dinner, Cat and I went to work typing labels and stuffing the envelopes. When we finished, I proclaimed with a note of satisfaction, "Good job! Now, let's go to bed."

"Not quite." She pulled a map of downtown Chicago out of a drawer, and spread it out on the table.

"What now?" I asked.

"There are fifty-two envelopes going to nineteen different buildings. If we want to deliver all of them tomorrow, we need to figure out the most efficient route. You read me the addresses, and I'll mark them on the map."

Once she circled each of our destinations, Cat planned out a route that I knew would be the quickest way to cover all the bases. "That was impressive," I commented.

"All this was a simple logical exercise," she explained. "You could've easily done it yourself."

"Oh, I dunno," I murmured. "Anyway, now can we go to bed?"

"I thought you'd never ask," She took my arm in one hand and shut off the lights with the other.

On Friday, Cat did the driving. At each stop, she drove around the block while I ran inside with the deliveries. By early afternoon, we were almost finished.

"It looks like we'll have some time for ourselves today," I said. "What do you want to do?"

In seconds, she replied, "Let's go to the beach. It's a beautiful day, and that's one of the things we promised ourselves."

"Okay. Where?"

"Right near us. Jackson Park has a big beach on Lake Michigan. It was in one of those tourist brochures we picked up last fall."

For the next few minutes, my mind went back to our day at Bradley Bennett's private beach. But when it dawned on me that this beach was a public one, trepidation crept in. As we drove up North State Street, nearing our last stop on East Randolph and passing the enormous Marshall Field department store, I got an idea.

"Let's find a legal parking spot," I said. "I need to buy a bathing suit. Can you deliver this last envelope while I'm doing that?"

"Okay, sure," she agreed, scanning the block.

"Cat Parks the Car" might have been a scene in a Hollywood slapstick comedy. She lined up next to the car in front, shifted into reverse and backed in, or rather into the bumper of the car parked behind. Shifting back into first, she turned the wheel and drove into the car parked in front. Back into reverse. Bang! Forward. I covered my eyes. Bang! Fortunately, all three cars had sturdy metal bumpers, and Tooter's were enhanced with rubber bumper guards. Twice more. Bang, bang, bang. When the engine stalled, we were parallel with the curb, but three feet away and the target of much horn-honking. Cat stared ahead, her hands still on the wheel, looking stunned. Then she reached over, took the envelope from my lap, and opened the door.

"You park the car," she said as she abandoned it. She watched from the sidewalk, frowning, as I completed the process in three smooth moves. I smiled, blew her a kiss, and walked over to Marshall Field's.

"How many bathing suits did you buy?" she asked, staring at the full shopping bag I'd come back with.

"I'll drive home," I replied, "and you can see what's in the bag."

The first thing she pulled out was an ordinary pair of men's swim trunks. Next was a tunic-style, long-sleeved, ankle-length woman's cover-up. She held it up and frowned. Finally, she removed a rubber band and unrolled a very wide-brimmed, floppy straw hat. Her eyes narrowed.

"What's all this?" she asked.

"It's for you," I explained. "So you don't get a sunburn."

"But I want to feel the sun," she argued. "That's half the fun of being on the beach."

"Look, Cat. This is a public beach, and you in a bathing suit will attract too much attention. Those guys sniffing around you at the gym will be nothing compared to what can happen there."

"I won't be the only female in a bathing suit," she objected, "and so what if people look? Like I told you before, ignore them."

"And I told you," I insisted, "that sets off my alarms. I know what's on their minds while they're looking you over. I feel you're being violated."

"Well, I don't. And I'm not gonna hide in a cocoon on a beautiful sunny day."

"Oh, all right," I conceded, trying to avoid a fight. "But let's throw them in the beach bag. You can decide what to do once we get there."

Back home, Cat put on a one-piece bathing suit instead of a bikini, which I took as a concession to my concerns. She also agreed to wear the cover-up, at least until we got close to the water. The big straw hat went into the bag, along with towels, a blanket, sandwiches, and two books from Emma's carton. Cat wanted to start on DuBois's *Black Reconstruction*. For me, she picked out Thomas Kuhn's *The Structure of Scientific Revolutions*. "I read it last year," she told me. "It'll change how you think about science."

Jackson Park Beach wasn't as crowded as I'd expected it to be. But I knew male eyes were checking Cat out. As long as no-one got too close, I resolved to follow her advice and ignore them. This wouldn't be fun if I let my paranoia, if that's what it was, control me.

Once we got our blanket set up, we charged into the surf, where Cat once again swam circles around me. After we dried off, we rolled the towels into neck rolls and stretched out with our books. The combination of the sun's rays, the sound of the waves, and Cat right next to me, was magical. As far as I was concerned, we were the only ones there.

After a while, Cat suggested we go for a walk."

We strolled through the surf holding hands, kicking water and splashing. For this, she agreed to wear the hat, but not the cover-up. Sometimes her decision-making baffled me. I kept my eyes fixed on the water and on her, trying to notice other people only enough to avoid bumping into them.

The afternoon went by quickly. I kept my internal alarms under control and we had a wonderful time. I noticed, though, that as it got close to dinnertime, most people were leaving. I decided that next time we should go later in the day. The beach might be less populated then, so it might not be as difficult to keep those alarms at bay.

Chapter 46

Before leaving Saturday morning, I asked Cat, "Why don't you come with me? I'm sure it'll be okay with Donnie."

"Oh, no," she demurred. "I need to spend today cleaning."

"Cleaning what? Couldn't that wait?"

She waved her arm around the living room. "Look at this place," she insisted. "It's a mess!"

It looked perfectly fine to me. But I knew there was no point in arguing. So, "Okay. I'll be back after the press conference, around six."

"And when are you gonna do the laundry?" she demanded. "The hamper is overflowing!"

I held my hands up, palms out. "Okay, okay. I'll do it tomorrow. Now, can I get a little kiss before I go?" I got a big one, and went out smiling.

The Quaker group's receptionist waved me into a room they'd given us for the day, where David Dellinger, the Mobe's chairman, was calling the Steering Committee meeting to order. I found him just as impressive at close quarters as he'd been at the podium on the Lincoln Memorial, back in October. Though soft-spoken, he guided the discussion with a firm hand until a consensus emerged. Planning for the protests would indeed move forward. Preparations were to begin immediately. No specific plans could be finalized, though, until the full board voted on them. The Chicago staff was assigned to make arrangements for a board meeting on July 20th, three weeks away, in Cleveland.

After the meeting ended, Donnie asked, "Would you mind driving Dave to the airport? He has to get back in time for the New York press conference."

I eagerly agreed, and Donnie introduced us. Dellinger said to call him "Dave."

His bulk barely fit into Tooter's passenger seat. "Sorry for the close quarters," I said.

"Are you kidding?" he laughed. "This is one of the more comfortable places I've been lately."

During the ride, he was friendly and patient with my many questions. He related some of his adventures driving an ambulance for the Loyalists during the Spanish Civil War, the three years he spent in prison as a conscientious objector during World War II, and his more recent trips to Cuba and North Vietnam. He said he'd recently returned from Paris, where the "so-called peace talks" were stalled before they'd really begun.

"I met with Xuan Thuy and his North Vietnamese colleagues," he told me. "All they want is an end to the damned bombing. Then they'd be open to discussing the future of the entire region."

"That sounds reasonable."

"And that's what I told Averell Harriman, the head of the U.S. delegation. But he wouldn't commit to anything. He might not even be authorized to carry on a serious negotiation."

"So the Paris Peace Talks are a sham?"

"I'm afraid so," he sighed. "The so-called negotiators have been in Paris for six weeks, and not a thing has happened. LBJ may have agreed to these talks not to negotiate a peace deal, but to defuse our movement. No real surprise, though. This war won't end around a table."

"How do you see it ending?"

"Even with all its firepower, a U.S. defeat is inevitable," he explained. "The Vietnamese know what they're fighting for, and they've been resisting foreign domination for generations. The U.S. can't even construct a coherent rationale for the war. Its soldiers don't know what they're fighting and dying for. Vietnam will win, but the human cost has been incalculable. That's where we come in."

"You mean the antiwar movement?"

"Right. We can't end the war, but we can help shorten it. The Democratic Convention will be a big opportunity to show the world that the American people are rising in opposition, that we won't sit still while our government kills, murders, drops Napalm in our name. If we don't protest non-violently, though, we'll lose all moral authority." After a pause, he added, "But enough about this. Tell me about you."

I used the time we were stuck in a traffic jam to give him a thumbnail sketch of where I came from, my experiences at Midway, about Emma, Marcellus and Cat, about teaching at the SSO and working with the BSU.

"So," he observed, "this first year of college was quite an educational experience."

"It sure was. Some of it has even been in school."

Eventually, we pulled up to the terminal at O'Hare. The most important person I'd ever met climbed out of Tooter and lumbered into the airport all by himself, carrying only an old briefcase, unassuming and anonymous. *Unless,* I thought, *we've had an FBI tail.* I looked around, not detecting anything out of the ordinary. *But then I wouldn't, would I?*

When I got back, an hour before the press conference, Donnie showed me his draft for the handout. The gist of it was that the antiwar movement will greet the delegates to the Chicago convention, "with or without permits for marches and rallies." It also emphasized that the Mobe will not support any of the presidential candidates, that its faith was in the power of the people in the streets. Our official slogan was now *Confront the Warmakers!*

"Why so much emphasis on neutrality?" I asked.

"This is a message to the Left," he explained. "The hard-core activists we're gonna need, like SDS. If they think we're supporting McCarthy or anyone else, they won't come. And they'd be right to stay away. Besides, by now everyone knows Humphrey has the nomination sewn up."

The ninety-minute press conference was well-attended. Afterward, Donnie congratulated me on my efforts and asked, "Can you come back in tomorrow? We have a lot to do during the next few weeks."

"Well, not tomorrow." Sheepishly, I added, "I promised Cat I'd do the laundry. It's kind of backed up."

"I understand totally," he responded, smiling and rolling his eyes.

I was pleased with the work. It was only an entry-level assignment, but at least I was doing *something.* Over dinner, I told Cat all about my day, trying to reconstruct my fascinating conversation with Dave Dellinger, word for word. She listened intently, responding with only a single question: "What about the permits?"

I had no answer for that, so I said, "I better start getting the laundry organized for tomorrow."

Sunday morning, the skies opened with a vengeance. The hard, driving rain was punctuated by ear-piercing claps of thunder, along with a reminder of why Chicago is known as "The Windy City." A glance out our front window confirmed the uselessness of an umbrella. Concluding it was a good day to stay indoors, I asked Cat, "Couldn't this laundry wait? I'll get drenched before I get across the street." Her stern look answered my question, with no need for words.

"Okay. What about you?" I asked. "Do you have to go anywhere?"

"Not today," she replied. "I spent all day yesterday cleaning and cooking, so today I'll curl up on the couch with Dr. DuBois." Sharing the couch with Cat and a good book seemed like a great way to survive this miserable day. But first, alas, I had to get the laundry going.

So, with a big beach towel over my head and a stuffed laundry bag in each hand, I splashed my way across the street. Once I got the washing machines running, I turned to go back. It dawned on me, though, that the beach towel, which had provided some protection on my way there, was now tumbling around inside one of those machines. Even though I raced back home, I was soaked to the bone and shivering.

Cat looked up from her book and burst out laughing as I came through the door. Still laughing, she led me into the bathroom. She stripped off my clothes and dried me all over with a fresh towel. "When you go back to use the dryers, you might as well bring these with you," she said. She pushed me into the bedroom, where I put dry clothes on. Life seemed good again when I got to the couch with a hot cup of coffee and my new science book.

An hour later, though, I had to go back to the Laundromat. The weather was, if anything, even worse. I found an old oilcloth table covering and draped it over my head for the return trip. I made very sure not to put it into the dryers along with the clean clothes. As soon as I stepped back into the street, though, a gale-force gust of wind tore the oilcloth out of my hands. I got back just as soaked and chilled as the first time.

We repeated the same routine, beginning with Cat's amusement, then the drying and the dressing, then back on the couch with our books. But when it came time to retrieve the clothes from the dryers, the wind and rain still hadn't diminished. I rummaged around the kitchen, and punched air holes in the largest plastic bag we had. Before leaving, I told Cat, "I'll be gone a while this time. I've got a ton of clothes to fold," and put the plastic bag over my head.

She cracked up at the sight. "No." she called through her giggles, "Bring it back here. We'll fold the clothes together."

I never really expected the plastic bag to keep me dry. Once again, I came back soaked and shivering. Cat wasn't laughing this time, only smiling. She took one of the laundry bags from me, and we dumped everything out on the bed. Then she grabbed a couple of big towels from the pile, and led the way into the bathroom.

This time, a steaming bubble bath awaited me. She stripped off my clothes, for the third time, and ordered, "Get in, Buster." I happily obeyed. After watching me for a few minutes, she stripped off her own clothes and joined me. That was even better

After drying each other, we went back to the bedroom. I reached for clothes to put on, but Cat said, "Wait. Let's do this naked."

So that's what we did. Crossing the room to put things away, we both found excuses to rub up against each other, cop a little squeeze or deliver a light, playful spank. It turned out to be my best laundry experience ever. Well before we finished, though, my conspicuous arousal became an impediment to progress. As soon as the bed was clear, I lifted Cat up, dropped her onto the blanket, and jumped in.

The day ended very, very well. Even during its bone-chilling middle, I wasn't consumed by the war. But I did promise myself I'd never get so far behind with the laundry again.

Chapter 47

"Seen the Sunday papers?" Donnie asked Monday morning.

"No, I didn't," I replied. "Between the terrible weather and being busy at home, I never got around to them."

"Oh, I forgot," he said with a knowing smile. "The laundry. Well, the *Tribune* buried our story on Page 10. New York was better, though. Page 3 in the Sunday *Times* isn't bad at this stage of the game. And since you were able to get the wire services here, it's a national story."

"Oh, but here's a little touch of humor," he added, pointing to the last sentence in the *Tribune* article. "Asked whether he will meet with Dawes or other potential protesters," it read, 'Mayor Daley said, 'My door is always open.' "

Donnie introduced me to two full-time staffers: Vernon Grimes, a veteran of both Vietnam and SDS; and Paul Haynes, a former SDS president. Jeff Rosen and Ronnie joined us, and we went down the hall for a staff meeting.

"We have less than three weeks," Donnie said, "to get all our ducks in a row. The better prepared we are for our presentation, the better the chance of a bright green light. We need to show the board we've got everything planned out, and convince them the protests can go smoothly. For now, let's start with our biggest headache, the permits."

The permits were my biggest headache too. If they didn't come through, how would I deal with Cat and her anxiety?

"I was hoping," Donnie went on, "we'd get a meeting with city officials, to discuss and negotiate their terms. For the past month, though, I haven't been able to get through, and no-one returns my calls. They might be under orders from Daley to ignore us."

"Isn't it routine," I asked, "for them to wait until the last minute before they grant the permits? I know they've done that before."

"You're right. But that won't work now. This thing is too big. Also, we need something to show the board in less than three weeks."

"Wasn't there some deputy mayor," Paul asked, "who we were able to deal with once before?"

"Dan Stahl," Donnie replied. "I haven't gotten through to him either."

"Let me try this," Jeff volunteered. "I'll call every day. If he won't take the call and doesn't call back, I'll go to his office and try getting to him directly."

"Good," Donnie responded. "Now, another thing we need to do is stay in touch with all the major peace and New Left groups, keeping them posted on developments and listening to their own thoughts. We can't wait until their reps come to the board meeting. We have to meet with them before the 20th, so they can be involved in the process."

"That's a lot of meetings," Paul observed.

"Yes, it is. Here's how I see it. Dellinger and his staff will cover the Northeast. Paul, I'd like you to cover the Midwest, with special attention to the Chicago Peace Council. Okay?"

Paul agreed.

"And I'll go out to San Francisco," Donnie concluded, "and recruit people to be our West Coast points of contact. Now let's move on. Vern, how about sharing what we've been talking about?"

Vern said, "I'm going to begin recruiting and training parade marshals. If we can get off to a good start, it should make an impression on the board. We'll need a disciplined, well-trained corps to keep things orderly during Convention Week Once I've signed up enough people, we'll start the training."

"Vern's done this before," Donnie explained, "including for October's big March on Washington. So if you, or anyone you know, wants to sign up for the training, please let him know."

Not me, I thought. *Cat would kill me if I signed up for this. But I could make some calls.*

Jeff added, "Coordination of the marshals with the police would make confrontation a lot less likely. I'll add that to my list of calls."

I asked, "What do you want me to do?"

"I was getting to that," Donnie said. "We've talked about the need for housing, legal and medical assistance. Jeff is already working the legal end, but I'd like you to head up housing and medical. You can put volunteers to work on it. Coordinate with Jeff and Ronnie."

I looked over at Ronnie, whose function in these meetings was apparently note-taking. She looked up and nodded.

"Sure," I said. "What else?"

"The last thing on today's list is fund-raising, but I'll ask a few board members to handle that. They're in closer touch with people who can write a check than we are."

"So that's it for now," he concluded. "For those of us in town, let's get together every Monday at ten."

"At last, some organization," Emma commented that afternoon.

"So now it sounds like a good work plan?" I asked.

"Well, it's certainly a start. But you might be over-optimistic about getting City Hall's cooperation. It's no accident that Donnie and Jeff haven't been able to get their calls returned."

"That's what worries me," Cat interjected. "Without the permits, it'll be a war, and the other side has all the guns. People could get killed. If the permits don't come through, Steve, we're not going. You're not going. Remember what happened at the Civic Center."

"Okay, okay," I said. "But let's not get ahead of ourselves. Jeff will be working on this every day."

"All right, we'll wait and see," she conceded, "but remember what I said. And you really didn't volunteer to be a marshal?"

"Really. Housing, medical, planning. That's it for now. Nothing physical."

"Good. Just make sure you stay far away from that."

That night, I called Larry Graff and told him about the need for marshals. As I expected, he volunteered right away. He had little patience for theoretical discussion, always leaning toward physical action. Before we hung up, he asked, "Did you hear grad students are losing their draft deferments?"

"Not until now," I replied. "That's terrible. So, do you have a plan?"

"Nope. I'm staying right here as long as I can."

"But what if you get drafted?"

"Then I'll go. They'll be sorry!" I believed him.

I wasn't so sure about recruiting Nicky Jarvis, but gave it a try. He understood right away the need for marshals, but said, "I don't know, Steve. SDS hasn't staked out a position on this yet. Our members might not even participate. You know what the problem is."

"Yeah, I know. You don't want it to look like you're validating the system. But you can't fight it unless you recognize it. And next month, the war-makers will be right here in Chicago. Could you sit that out? Could you really let them come into our town, have their fun and leave, without confronting them?"

"Steve, calm down. Personally, I agree with you. But the National Council hasn't settled on a position yet."

"So when will it be decided?"

"At a meeting on the 20th in Indiana. That's when the decision will have to be made."

"More bad news," I said. "The Mobe's board is meeting on the same day. It'll have to make its plans without knowing what SDS will do."

"Nothing I can do about that, Steve."

"But you did say you agreed with me about the convention, as an individual. So how about signing up to be a marshal?"

"I promise I'll get back to you," he said, "as soon as things get sorted out."

That call put me in a foul mood. "The country's biggest antiwar organization," I told Cat. "More than a hundred thousand members, and they can't decide on the year's most important demonstration."

"That might be a good thing," she speculated.

"What? How?"

"SDS is always looking for confrontation. If they don't show up, there'll probably be a better chance of keeping it non-violent, like you said Dave Dellinger wants it to be."

I didn't reply. I sat there staring at my shoes with the slogan, *Confront the Warmakers*, running through my mind.

"Anyway, it's getting late and we need to be up early," she said. "Come. Let's see if we can improve on that grumpy mood of yours."

Chapter 48

In the morning, I gave Larry's phone number to Vern and summarized the SDS dilemma.

"That's no surprise," he responded. "They're going through big changes. You know it wasn't so long ago that Donnie, Paul and I were in the leadership. Back then, some people accused us of pulling the organization too far to the left. But now, we might be seen as old conservatives."

"So what do you think about what Cat said?"

"She has a valid point," he replied, "but I don't completely agree. If SDS shows up, it'll be a wild card, bringing its own agenda and its own leadership. So yes, anything can happen. They certainly won't turn the other cheek if they're attacked. But I don't think they'll be the ones provoking violence. No, I'm more concerned about the police and agents provocateurs."

Jeff called out and waved me over to an empty table. "The volunteers did a good job on the churches and synagogues," he told me, pushing over several pages of lists. "They got contact information on almost two hundred of them."

"Glad to hear it. But there's something I have to ask you first. Did you know law students won't be eligible for draft deferments anymore?"

"Sure I know. It's the main reason I won't be coming back in the fall."

"You won't? That must be devastating,"

"Not terribly," he explained. "I found law school a little disappointing, because of all the corporate stuff we had to learn. I would've stayed to finish anyway, but they gave me a leave of absence so I can come back someday if I want to."

"But what'll you do about the draft?"

"I found out that teaching in a ghetto school might get me a deferment, so I'm going back to New York to teach math. There's such a shortage of math teachers that they'll hire anyone who majored in it, like me. And there's this place in Brooklyn called Ocean Hill-Brownsville, where the Black community is trying to do something important about its schools."

"Community control," I said. "I've heard."

"Well, last month, their local elected board got rid of some bad apples, and a few hundred white teachers walked out in protest. The board decided to replace all of them, so that's where I'm going. I'm looking forward to it much more than another year of law school."

"Wow," I said, still a little stunned. "When are you leaving?"

"Right after the convention. But now, let's get to this list. We need to reach all these housing contacts. I'd say 90 percent of the calls can be handled by volunteers. But you should personally visit the pastors of the biggest churches. Ronnie will help make the calls to set up those meetings."

"Okay. Which ones are they?"

"Good question. I guess you'll have to start with some research."

Next, I sat down with Ronnie. She handed me a few pages of contact information with the volunteers' scribbled notations. I asked, "Do they report the results of their calls to you?"

"Not really," she replied. "They make notes in the margins."

"I'd like to reorganize this process a little bit," I said, as though I knew what I was talking about. "Do you mind?"

"Not at all. I'm sure I'd like that too!"

"Good. I'll work on this at home, and we'll talk in the morning."

Cat was reading in the living room. I asked, "How's Reconstruction coming along?"

"Well, this is a long book on a really important and fascinating period. I'm amazed at how much the Reconstruction state governments were able to accomplish in less than a dozen years. The story DuBois tells contradicts everything we ever heard in school about them. But you're home earlier than I expected."

"I did whatever I could there today," I explained. "I've come up with a little project that needs a quieter place to work, and your help if you have the time. Besides, I missed you."

The project had already begun to take shape in my head on my way home. I was pretty sure I could have done it on my own, but I preferred to do it with her.

Cat put the book down and joined me at the table. I explained the housing assignment, and how I wanted to modify the process. Twenty minutes later, we'd designed what we called a "Housing Prospect Sheet." A box at the top called for the site and its address, the name and phone number of the contact person, and the capacity of the space. We filled the rest of the page with lines for recording calls, divided by columns for the date, the caller's initials, and the result of the call.

I slapped the table. "This is exactly what I needed," I exclaimed. "Thank you!"

"I see," Cat said thoughtfully. "And you didn't really need my help, did you?"

"Well..."

"Okay," she said, leaning over to give me a peck on the cheek. "Now you go type this up, all by yourself. I'll make dinner."

The frustrating thing about typing mimeograph stencils was the near-impossibility of correcting mistakes without making a mess. I'd brought four of them home with me, and it was only on the fourth try that I got one suitable for reproduction. I barely finished in time for dinner.

A few bites in, I related what Jeff told me about having to leave law school, and his high hopes about teaching math in Brooklyn.

"This must be difficult for him," she observed.

"I don't know. He seems to be okay with it. You know, if I had my degree now, I'd want to do the same thing, in the same place."

"But," I added, "only if you came with me."

"From what I know of ghetto schools," she said, "you'd be better than most of the teachers out there, even right now. Anything else today? Any news on the permits?"

"Cat, you can't ask me about this every single day. You know we're working on it, and you know I'll tell you as soon as anything develops."

"Anything? Whether it's good or bad?"

"Of course," I answered impatiently. "You know that."

"Okay, I'm sorry," she said, showing signs of a pout. "But, you know, I worry."

"Yes, I've noticed that."

In the morning, I ran off a hundred copies of the Housing Prospect Sheet and brought them over to Ronnie.

"Before calling any prospect for the first time," I explained, "the basic information at the top of the sheet needs to be filled in. The calls and follow-ups get summarized on the lines below. At the end of each day, the sheets end up in your loose-leaf binder, alphabetized by the prospect's name."

"I love this," she said. "It's very efficient. I think it'll make my job easier too."

"One more thing," I added. "The binder must be under lock-and-key unless you're using it. No-one can have access to it besides you and me. And Donnie if he wants to, of course."

In mid-afternoon, I noticed the office was emptying out, and asked Ronnie where everyone was going.

"Holiday weekend," she replied. "Tomorrow's the Fourth of July."

I'd forgotten about that, but it was welcome news. I was more than ready for a little vacation. I headed home, promising myself I'd leave all these problems behind me. Cat and I both looked forward to the SSO's Fourth of July Barbeque and, hopefully, an entire four-day weekend, with each other and without the war.

Chapter 49

We got to Jackson Park in the early afternoon. Wandering through the big meadow looking for our table, we inhaled savory chicken, shrimp and ribs, all drenched in varieties of barbeque sauces. Besides the stationary grills and picnic tables, there were huge rolling grills, dozens of folding tables and hundreds of chairs. There must have been a thousand people there.

Marcellus waved us over. Sitting with him were Sharon and Arielle, along with James Watkins and Hazel Raines, the SSO's director of its pre-school programs.

Watkins looked preoccupied with something. Sitting across from him, I soon learned what that something was. He said, "I'm glad you're here, Steve. You've told me how much you enjoyed your work with the kids, and you have a right to know this."

"Know what?"

"Last Friday, the president signed a new law. It was in the papers on Saturday."

I thought back. "I didn't get to the papers that day," I responded, "because I was beginning my summer job. Actually, I'd like to ask you something about that. Anyway, what's this new law?"

While he spoke, someone put a heaping platter of ribs in front of Cat and me. I looked around, but didn't see anyone to thank.

"For the past year," he explained "LBJ has been pushing for a ten percent income tax surcharge to help pay for the war."

Here's the war again, I thought, *right at the start of the holiday weekend. I can't get away from it.*

"The problem," he continued, "was that he couldn't get it through Congress. Too many liberals have come around to opposing the war, and the conservatives had demands he didn't want to meet. Until last week, that is. He caved in and agreed to cut ten percent from his domestic programs. Because of the way the federal budget is structured, that means big cuts in education and anti-poverty funding."

"How big?"

"The people I spoke to at our funding agencies said it was too soon to tell, but they advised me to start planning for layoffs. I don't know if we'll be able to run an after-school program in the fall. In fact, I don't know if I'll even have a job."

"Goddamn war!" I blurted, adding, "Oh, I'm sorry, Miss Raines. Please excuse the language. It's just that..."

She cut me off. "Don't apologize. This is infuriating. LBJ is sacrificing his civil rights legacy for this war. This stupid war. This *goddamn* war. And, please, call me Hazel."

I needed to change the subject. "This is quite an event," I observed, waving my arm across the field, "but it must've cost a lot. Where'd the money come from?"

Watkins' face brightened. "The staff members are volunteering. No-one gets paid for today. The tables and chairs, and the big grills, are on loan from churches. Everything else – food, drink, decorations, supplies – is funded entirely by sponsors."

"What sponsors?"

"Every spring, since we started doing this," he explained, "our youth groups went from store to store soliciting sponsorships from South Side businesses. In the past, we've been able to cobble together enough contributions to host a bare-bones picnic. But this year was different."

"How so?"

"Remember, during the April uprising, how the Black-owned stores survived intact?"

"Sure. The owners painted 'Soul Brother' on the windows. On some blocks, it seemed they were the only stores not burned or looted."

"That's right," he went on, smiling. "And it gave me an idea. You see, everyone saw those pictures, including the mostly white South Side merchants. So I had big, noticeable decals made, saying 'Proud Sponsor of the South Side Organization,' with our logo in the center. Our young folks making the rounds this year offered those decals to the contributing businesses. We raised three times as much money as last year! Now, there's hardly a South Side storefront that hasn't put our decal on prominent display."

"Kind of a protection racket?" I ventured.

"Oh, no. Never any threats. But it's not my fault if the storeowners saw it as a kind of insurance. This might've been the best idea I had all year."

"Now," he continued, in an obviously better frame of mind, "what's that other thing you want to ask me about?"

"Have you heard about the antiwar protest being organized for the Democratic Convention next month?"

"Sure. I read it in Sunday's paper."

I got a little kick out of that response. He'd actually read the article that came out of our press conference.

"What's your opinion?" I asked.

"I sure can't say I'm against it. But I don't expect people to be pouring out of the South Side to join it."

"Why not? Black men are being drafted, and being killed, way out of their proportion to the population. Isn't antiwar sentiment running high?"

"Oh, it is. But look around this park again. Back in April, the army turned it into a military base. Instead of families having fun, like today, there were soldiers, tents, munitions, even tanks. They turned the South and West Sides into occupied territories. Black folks got beaten and arrested right in front of their own homes. We know from hard experience what a "shoot to kill" order means out of this mayor. No-one wants to invite another military occupation. Remember, we have to live here. I hope these Mobilization folks know what they're doing, though, and no-one gets hurt."

Cat, who'd been listening intently, poked an elbow, hard, into my ribs. I pretended not to notice.

"I understand what you're saying," I said, "and I appreciate the explanation. You see, that's what I'm working on, my summer job. One of my assignments is to line up overnight accommodations for out-of-town protesters, and I thought you might be able to help."

"How? You know we don't have that kind of space."

"Well, on the day of the BSU building takeover, I noticed a couple of pastors with you leading the march on Midway. If their churches have any large open spaces that they might possibly make available for a few nights, I was wondering if you would ask them to meet with me."

"The person you should talk to is Reverend Marshall," he responded. "Ebenezer Baptist. I'll be glad to give him a call."

We were interrupted by an amplified announcement: "Kids of all ages, the games are about to begin! Children at the flagpole with Miss Raines. Grownups in the outfield with Mr. Sparrow."

Hazel stood and asked, "Ready, Arielle?"

Arielle took her hand. After just a few steps, though, she turned and raced back to the table. Grabbing my arm, she pleaded, "Come on, Uncle Steve. Let's play!"

Two of Hazel's staff members brought out supplies for the games, and she divided the children into age groups. My cohort was a dozen four and five-year-olds. This made Arielle feel quite important. She appointed herself my assistant. For the next two hours, I was completely absorbed in potato-sack and three-legged races, Capture the Flag, Simon Says, Uncle May I, a Tug o' War and the like. Sometimes, it was a challenge to keep the kids focused, but they, we, all had a fun time.

During a rare quiet moment, I glanced over toward the "grown-up" games, and spotted Cat in a Water Balloon Toss. She, along with all the other players, was getting soaked, but she seemed to be having a great time. I loved watching her laughing and having fun.

Game Time ended as the jingle of bells signaled the arrival of a Good Humor truck. Through the bullhorn came an announcement: "Free ice cream, kids. Come and get it!" The rapidity with which the line formed at the truck made me smile. As we packed up the supplies, Hazel said, "You know, that reminds me of something Sharon said about you, earlier today."

"About me?"

"Yes. She said whenever she sees you with Arielle, you never stop smiling."

Chapter 50

Out of the corner of my eye, I noticed Cat slowly walking back toward the tables. And then it happened: My worst waking nightmare. A skinny six-footer came up from behind and wrapped his arms around her, pinning her arms to her sides. As she wriggled to break free, my alarm bells sounded and I jumped to my feet. Those alarms turned to shrieking sirens when he raised his hands to grab her breasts and lifted her off the ground.

I sensed movement in the crowd, but I was a bullet shooting across the field. Without slowing, I rammed my fist into the predator's right ear. He let go of Cat, and all three of us staggered. Regaining my balance, I threw another punch where I thought his liver might be, and he doubled over. I grabbed his head, jammed his nose into my knee, and pushed him to the ground. Dropping onto his chest, I pinned his arms with my knees, grabbed his neck with my left hand and pummeled his face with my right fist.

From what seemed a mile away, I dimly heard voices. Yelling. Screaming. *"Noooooo!"* Cat's voice? No matter. The red haze that engulfed me was impenetrable. *Bam!* How'd ya like that, muthafucka? *Bam! Bam! Bam!*

Suddenly, though, the haze lifted. I stopped pounding and looked at what I'd done. His nose was pushed to the right, gushing blood. His left eye, purple and black, was swollen and nearly shut. His mouth was a bloody mess, and he'd certainly swallowed a few teeth. I knew he was still breathing because a rotten stench of cheap alcohol still reeked from his mouth. I got off, lost my balance and fell back on my elbows.

Still foggy, I looked around. Hundreds of eyes were focused on this tableau. The silence was deafening. My rage began turning to apprehension. Here I was, maybe the only white guy in the park, who'd beaten this Black guy half to death.

The spell broke as a big woman stepped away from a grill, waving a spatula and walking toward us. "William Simmons," she called out, "you get yo' sorry black ass up outta this heah park! An' I mean now. Right now, or you gon' deal wit' me!" The predator struggled to his feet and limped away. With a smattering of laughing and hooting, people went back to what they'd been doing.

Still dazed and on my elbows, I scanned the crowd, looking for Cat. I found her, face constricted, arms wrapped across her chest, as though she was holding herself together. I wasn't ready to deal with her at that moment, but knew she was in good hands. Sharon had an arm around her, and Marcellus stood behind them with a hand on each of their shoulders. I let my head drop to the grass and tried to get my bearings.

A grizzled elderly man came over and asked, "Is your name Steve?" I nodded, and he reached a hand down. "Here ya go, son," he said, helping me to my feet. "You come have a beer wit' me." He walked me over to a metal garbage can, and pulled a Budweiser out of the ice for each of us. The cold brew started me on the way back to my senses. "I don't understand," I said. "Do I know you?"

"Well, you do now," he replied with a laugh. "I'm Harold Postelthwaite, Brenda's granddaddy, and I been wantin' to thank you."

"Brenda? You mean from my after-school class? Thank me for what?"

At his family's cluster of tables, he motioned me to sit. A woman put a plate of chicken and collard greens in front of me. Brenda waved, smiling. I looked up and recognized her mother. She patted me on the shoulder, said, "Thank you so much," and went back to her cooking.

"Mr. Postelthwaite, I don't understand."

"Listen, Brenda got her report card last week, with an A-plus in math."

"That's not surprising," I responded. "She has an obvious aptitude for it."

"Well, it ain't never happened before," he continued. "She never got an A in nothin', and she always squeaked by in math. Now it's her favorite subject. She's even teachin' it to the little ones. That's why we're so grateful to you."

Everyone at the table was watching this conversation, which made me a bit self-conscious. "I don't know what to say," was all I could get out.

"Don't need to say nothin', my boy. Eat up, before it gets cold." He called out, "Bring this young man another beer. He's lookin' real thirsty!"

I wasn't very hungry, but it would have been impolite not to clean my plate. I did that, washed it down with the cold beer, thanked everyone and made sure to congratulate Brenda. Off I went in search of Cat, not knowing what kind of reception to expect.

She was sitting under a tree with Sharon, listening to an older woman I didn't recognize. She still looked distressed. Before I got near her, though, Marcellus intercepted me. "Give them a little more time," he suggested.

"Well, okay if you say so. But who's that?"

"Maddy Skinner. She's a social worker. Works for the city and volunteers at the SSO, counseling women."

"Oh," was my only response. I couldn't help being apprehensive about what kind of advice Cat might be getting. Marcellus sat me down on a bench.

"I hear the Women's Self-Defense class starts next week," he said with a smile. "From what I saw today, I'm wond'rin' if you're the one who ought'a be teachin' it!"

"That wasn't self-defense," I exclaimed. "That was attempted annihilation! I don't know what got into me. I scared the hell out of myself."

"Hey, I might've done the same thing. Don't beat yourself up for protecting your woman."

"But this went way beyond that," I countered. "I've been in fights, but I never did anything like this before. I don't know where it came from. I don't even have a clear memory of it. Do you know this guy, Simmons?"

"Oh, yeah. A neighborhood knucklehead. Gets drunk and gets stupid around women."

I stared at the ground shaking my head. "Tell me about Cat. How is she?"

"This was tough for her," he explained. "First, she got traumatized by the groping. Then she was terrified for you, literally shaking with fear. That's why I asked Mrs. Skinner to talk to her."

Sharon joined us. She gave me a little hug and asked, "Are you all right?"

"I guess so. What about Cat?"

"She's waiting for you now. Go on."

Under the same tree, she sat by herself, her face streaked from wiping away tears. I sat down next to her. For the first few minutes, we both stared ahead, not saying a word. Then I put my hand on her knee and said, "Cat, I'm sorry. I couldn't help myself."

She looked up and said, "You warned me something like this could be triggered, but I never thought you were capable of what I saw today."

"Neither did I. This was a first. But whenever I even imagined some creep putting his hands on you, a fury I'd never known before grabbed hold of me."

"The first punch probably would've been enough," she murmured, looking down.

"I guess so. But I couldn't stop myself. It wasn't enough to get him off you. I wanted to obliterate him."

Looking up at me, she said, "I know you wanted to protect me. In fact, now I understand how you feel about the guys at the beach and the gym. But you really scared me."

"I can see that. But why? The guy never touched me."

"Part of it," she explained, "was seeing you so out of control."

"Well, that scared me too. Anything else?"

"Yes. Think of what might've happened. Suppose you did kill him? How would you feel about that? Even worse, what if he had a knife in his pocket, or a gun? What if he'd come here with a gang? You might've been the one to end up dead."

The tears started running again. I took her face in both hands and kissed them away. My eyes glistened too. I looked into hers and whispered, "I just love you so, so much."

After we held each other for a few minutes, she let go and stood up. "Come with me," she said. "I need you to do something."

She led me into a wooded area and turned to face me. I asked, "What is it?"

"I want you to come up from behind, and do what he did."

"What? Why would you want to relive it?"

"I need to know how it feels if it's you. Since it happened, I feel so dirty, so violated. Please. Do it. I have to know." Trembling, she turned her back to me and instructed, "Do it now."

"Okay. If you say so." I approached from behind and wrapped my arms around her. She stiffened.

"Tighter." she commanded, "Like I'm trying to get away. Rub up against me."

"Okay."

"Now, put your hands on my breasts. Squeeze a little," she instructed, inhaling deeply and holding it.

I held and squeezed gently. Soon, she exhaled and I sensed her body softening. "Now let go," she said. Released, she turned and held me around the waist.

"Well?" I asked.

"It feels like *you*, Steve. It feels like you and it feels good. I'm all right now."

I pulled her head into my chest and told her, "*We're* all right now."

After a few minutes, she asked, "Can we go home now? I need a good hot shower, and then all I want to do is snuggle with you for a long, long time."

So we said our good-byes and headed for the parking lot. We'd be on our own for that night's Fourth of July fireworks.

Chapter 51

I forced my eyes open Friday morning and glanced at the clock. Three hours past our normal wake-up time, and Cat was still asleep. I pulled on my pajama bottoms, padded into the kitchen and made the coffee. As I returned, she began to stir. I put a cup down on each of our nightstands, and sat back in bed.

"What time is it?" she moaned.

"9:15."

"Ohhh. Let's not go to the gym this morning," she said. "I'm still exhausted from yesterday."

"And from last night," I added. "Where'd you get the energy for that?"

"Mmmmmmmmm," she purred, snuggling up close. "We can make up for it tomorrow."

"What? Make up for last night?"

"No, silly. Make up for missing today's workout."

"How about this?" I suggested. "Let's spend the whole day in bed."

"Well..." she murmured, considering it. But she cut herself off with a sharp intake of breath, sat up and exclaimed, "Look! At your hand!"

I looked at the back of my right hand, and saw what alarmed her. It was badly swollen and several different colors.

"Doesn't it hurt?"

"I guess a little," I mumbled, examining the hand like it was a foreign object.

"You have to get it looked at. It might be infected or broken. You better go right away. I'll go with you."

"No, you rest. No sense in both of us spending half the day in the E.R. waiting room. I'll bring a book, and I'll come straight back." If bad news was coming, I wanted her to hear it from me, not from a doctor.

On my way to the Med Center, I remembered that I'd made a connection there after the Civic Center march. At the packed waiting room, I asked the receptionist for Dr. Dreyer. She picked up a phone and waved me to a seat. I opened *The Structure of Scientific Revolutions*, and began reading how scientific certainties can crumble in the face of experimental anomalies, how new paradigms emerge. *Fascinating stuff,* I thought. *And if science can change, couldn't society change too?*

After only fifteen minutes, though, I heard my name being called. The receptionist pointed to a swinging door and said, "Room 127, down the hall on the right."

Hal Dreyer was waiting for me. "Didn't expect to see you back here," he said. "You're not still getting headaches, are you?"

"No, I'm not, and thanks for seeing me today. It's something else."

"Well then," he asked with a smile, "what kind of trouble have you gotten yourself into this time?"

When I stretched out my right hand, he whistled. "I can only imagine what the other guy looks like. Sit over here, and let's take a peek. What the hell happened?"

While he manipulated my fingers, I told him the whole story. He kept his eyes on my hand and didn't react. Letting it go, he said, "I don't see anything broken, but let's get an x-ray to be sure. Radiology is right down the hall. I'll call ahead, so go there now. Come back when it's finished."

After I followed his instructions, he told me, "I asked the radiologist to call ASAP with her report. In the meantime, let's talk. Have you ever had an explosion like that before?"

"No, never."

"Well, that's good, but it would be even better if it never happens again. Something's been triggered, something out of your control. Look, it might be dangerous. Consider getting some help."

"Help? From who?"

He wrote something on a slip of paper and handed it to me. It had a name and phone number. "Who's this?" I asked.

"A friend of mine, a psychiatrist. He's a good guy. You'll like him."

Before I responded, the phone rang. After listening for a minute or so, he responded, "Okay, thanks. Please send the written report as soon as it's ready."

"That's what I thought," he told me. "There's soft tissue damage, but no broken bones beyond tiny hairline fractures. They'll heal by themselves. The main thing is to prevent infection, so rub this antibiotic salve into the hand a few times a day until it's healed."

"Well, that's good news. Thanks a lot."

Before leaving, I asked, "Do you have a minute for something else?"

"Okay," he replied, looking at his watch. "But it'll have to be quick."

I gave him a nutshell update on the convention protests, concluding, "I'm supposed to be lining up medical assistance in case it's needed. I was wondering if you had any ideas."

"I've got one. I used to be active in the Medical Committee for Human Rights, which might be willing to help. Since this time-sucking residency began, I haven't been able to keep up with anything, including them. Try getting in touch. If you have trouble, give me a call."

"Okay. Thanks again." I headed for the door.

"Wait," he called. "You forgot this."

It was the note with the name and number of his psychiatrist friend. I thanked him again, and left.

Psychiatrist? I thought. *Did I really need a shrink? Was I going crazy?* This was all I could think about on the walk back home. I decided not to mention it to Cat, since it was sure to alarm her. I also discovered I wasn't so sure I wanted to rid myself of this new friend, this wildebeest that rose up from the depths of my psyche, to protect the one I loved. Nearly all I knew of psychiatry was from reading Ken Kesey's *One Flew Over the Cuckoo's Nest*. That story climaxed with electroshock and a lobotomy. I sure didn't want to end up that way.

"It's nothing serious," I told Cat, who was anxiously waiting. "No broken bones. Some damaged soft tissue, tiny hairline fractures and this ugly bruising. The doctor gave me an ointment to keep it from getting infected."

"Nothing permanent? He's sure?"

"Yes, he's positive. X-rays."

"Well, that's good."

"Oh, but wait," she added, pulling a slip of paper out of a pocket. "You have an appointment this afternoon."

An appointment? I wondered. *Was this the psychiatrist? Did Dr. Dreyer think I needed emergency help? Did he call her?*

Apprehensively, I asked, "An appointment with who?"

"Mr. Watkins called," she explained to my great relief. "He made an appointment for you with Reverend Marshall at three. Here's the address."

Ebenezer Baptist was, indeed, a big church. I was directed to Rev. Marshall's private office. Without looking up, he intoned in a deep bass voice, "Welcome, son. Take a seat. I'll be right with you."

Finishing his task, he stood, dwarfing me in both height and girth, and reached out his hand. "So, you're the young man Brother Watkins told me to expect. What can I do for you?"

I extended my right hand, but before we made contact, he took my wrist in both his hands and exclaimed, "Lordy, Lordy, what have we here?"

"I can explain," I said, extending my left hand, which he took. We both sat back down. This wasn't how I'd hoped to start our meeting.

"I was at the SSO barbeque," I began, uncomfortably, "and there was a little trouble..."

"You mean with Willie Simmons?" he interrupted. "You're the white boy who gave him that beat-down?"

"Well, yes," I reluctantly replied, shrinking into my chair. "I guess so." Becoming increasingly uncomfortable, I added, "I don't know how these things work, but I'm willing to repent for the damage I did."

"Hah!" he exclaimed, slamming his hand on the desk. "He's the one who's needed penance, and now he got some. I must've seen two dozen women he molested this year. Every time, we call the cops. Every time, they do nothin'. Oh yes, I've prayed for him, just as I've prayed for his victims, but nothing changes. Now, you've given him something to think about."

"He attacked my girlfriend," I explained, "and I went a little crazy."

"Yes, I heard, and I can understand why. You probably wanted to kill him. But you didn't. So there's always hope for redemption. Now, tell me why Watkins sent you to me."

I wasn't sure which one of us he thought needed redemption, Simmons or me, but I was happy to change the topic. I explained the developing plans for the protests, and the need for sleeping space. He gave me his complete attention, nodding from time to time, but not providing any clues to a reaction. Concluding, I asked if the church had space he could make available during the convention nights.

He leaned back in his chair and looked up at the ceiling, nibbling on a pencil. After a few minutes, he put his elbows back on the desk and said, "Back in '63, we had a West Coast group stop here overnight on its way to the March on Washington. I remember they came on six buses, so we must've fit a few hundred people. Would that help?"

"Sure it would," I said, knowing I was on the verge of making my "first sale."

"But," he added firmly, "there'll be ground rules. I can't have a horde of white hippies takin' over my church and makin' a mess of it."

"Anything you say."

"I'll write this down for you after I've given it more thought, but a few things come to mind right away. No drugs or alcohol, for example, and no sex in this building. I can give them the lower level, but they'll need their own sleeping bags or mats or something. And they have to clean up after themselves. If they leave out the door and the place isn't the way they found it, those doors will be locked up tight if they try to come back."

"No problem," I said. "We can assign our marshals to enforce the house rules."

"Then you can add Ebenezer to your list."

Ebenezer was first on the list, but his mention of that word gave me another idea. I showed him the list Jeff had given me and asked, "Would you look at this and check off the larger houses of worship?"

Going through it page by page, he made notations and handed it back. "I've checked the biggest ones," he said, "and double-checked those where it might be helpful to use my name."

As he showed me to the door, he added, "My advice is to bring up the ground rules early in your conversations. Antiwar protesters and hippies don't have much of a reputation for orderliness, you know. And take good care of that hand."

Chapter 52

"Let's see that hand," Emma demanded as I entered the shop.

"It's fine," I protested, holding it out to her. "Really, it's fine. The doctor told me to treat it with an antibiotic ointment."

I thought this hand was becoming the center of far too much attention. If it didn't heal up soon, I'd be going out with mittens on. I wondered where I could get extra-extra-large mittens in July.

"Did you use the ointment yet?" Cat asked.

"No, not yet, but it's right here in my pocket."

"And what good is it doing in your pocket?" she scolded. "Here, give it to me." She opened the tube and slathered it on.

"Ouch," I complained. "It burns."

"That means it's working, stupid."

"So," I asked Emma, "I guess Cat told you what happened yesterday?"

She nodded.

"What was your reaction?"

Cat interjected. "Emma said I was lucky you were there."

"That's right," Emma responded. "Terrible things have happened to women in that park. In every park, sometimes even at family gatherings. Especially if alcohol is involved, some men just can't keep their hands to themselves."

"That's what I've been trying to tell Cat," I blurted. "But she got mad because I got her a cover-up to wear at the beach."

"Steve, let's not have that argument again," Cat said. "We found a compromise on it, didn't we?"

"I guess so."

Emma shook her head, smiling. "You two are quite a pair," she mused. "The way you worry about each other is, well… adorable."

"Anyway, did Cat tell you I went a little overboard? What did you think about that?" Emma's opinion was always important to me. If she also thought I needed a psychiatrist, I'd have to give it serious consideration.

"The way I see it is this," she explained. "You're young. Your hormones are roaring. You're in love. The woman you love is endangered. That triggers a signal from the 'lizard brain,' your oldest evolutionary remnant. The only surprising thing is that you were able to stop yourself."

So now I had three explanations for what I did. To Marcellus, I was a man with a woman to protect. To Emma, I was acting from prehistoric animal instincts. To Dr. Hal Dreyer, I might be a nutcase. *Was the answer "(d) All of the above?"*

"Listen, kids," Emma said, "I'm a little tired, and we're an hour from closing time. "Would you mind taking it from here?"

"Not at all," we replied in unison. "Go up and rest. We'll be fine."

"Thanks. But I want to make dinner for you tonight."

"Sure. What time?"

"Right after closing. You can pick everything up at Sal's. It'll be ready."

Watching the back door close, Cat wryly observed, "Emma sure has a funny idea of what 'making dinner' means. Anyway, I bet she's going upstairs to smoke."

"Did she light up this afternoon?"

"She did step outside a few times, but that's all. She bought a dozen different flavors of chewing gum to fight the urges, but says she hasn't found one she likes yet."

"Still, that's a big improvement."

Later, over dinner, I told Emma, "I met with Reverend Marshall today. He said the church had room for a few hundred people, but he laid down some ground rules."

"I'm not surprised," she said. "Things like no sex, no drinking, no drugs?"

"That's the idea. Cleanliness too. It makes perfect sense. I only hope I can keep my promise. Things could get a little chaotic. Oh, and there was something else I wanted to mention."

"Sure. Go ahead."

"This morning, I told the doctor about our need for medical backup at the protests. He suggested getting in touch with the Medical Committee for Human Rights. Have you heard of it?"

"Oh, yes," she replied with a smile. "MCHR is a great organization."

"Tell us about it."

"Do you remember Mississippi Freedom Summer, a few years back?"

"Sure I do," Cat replied. "Dad insisted we watch the TV coverage. Isn't that when those three civil rights workers got killed?"

"Yes. Three martyrs: James Chaney, Mickey Schwerner and Michael Goodman, all murdered by the Ku Klux Klan. But the killings didn't scare the others away. A thousand Northerners went down that summer, mostly white and mostly young, to work with local Black activists who'd been fighting racism for years. The focus was on voter registration, but they also opened freedom schools, conducted political education, and started other community institutions. The Mississippi Freedom Democratic Party came out of that effort."

"But where does MCHR come in?" I asked.

"Oh, sorry," Emma responded. "Sometimes I do go on. You see, everyone knew there'd be violence, that civil rights workers would be attacked by the Klan, by the sheriffs, and so on. They'd need medical care that wouldn't be available. The MCHR was formed to provide that care. It sent down over a hundred doctors, nurses and med students who saved lives, working like battlefield medics and running emergency clinics in Black churches. The next year, they returned for the bloody Selma-to-Montgomery March. And they still have people in Mississippi and Alabama, not only providing health care to people who never had it before, but also fighting to desegregate the Deep South's racist health care system."

"That sure is impressive," I responded. "Any idea how we can get in touch?"

"I do. Dr. Quentin Young, the national chairman, lives not far from here. Wait, I'll give him a call."

"You know him?" Cat and I asked in astonishment. But Emma was already in the kitchen, dialing.

A few minutes later, she called out, "Steve, are you free tomorrow?"

"Got nothing planned."

"Now you do," she said, coming back to the table after another minute. "Lunch with Dr. Young, at 12:30. Here's the address."

Before we left, Emma showed us an article from the July 3rd *Times*, which had arrived in the morning mail. It reported on the daily saturation bombing now raining down over North Vietnam's southern three miles. Seventy-five B-52's were each dropping 54,000 pounds of bombs into that relatively small target area. I could do the math. That was more than 2,000 *tons* of bombs every day. *Every. Single. Day.*

Chapter 53

Cat shook me awake Saturday morning. The clock said 6:15. I registered my confusion by asking, "Wha'?"

"We need to get to the gym," she explained. "Here's some coffee, and your ointment."

I obediently sat up and began sipping the coffee. "But isn't today Saturday? We don't work out on the weekends."

"Don't you remember? We skipped it yesterday. Today's our makeup."

I groaned. "Oh, okay. But can I finish this coffee first?"

"Sure, and you'll want a refill too. Take your time, but we should get there by seven." I knew there was no point in asking why. "And use your ointment," she added.

By nine, we were back home having breakfast. I asked if she had plans for the day.

"Supermarket," she replied, "unless you'll need Tooter."

"No. I can walk to Dr. Young's house."

"Okay then. Can you get back by four?"

"I'll make sure to."

"Then that's when I'll get home."

Grocery shopping was in Cat's domain. Partly, this was because I'd told her I hated shopping. But it was also because she was much better at it. And somehow, she always knew in advance what time she'd be back home. Carrying the groceries upstairs and putting them away was the least I could do.

It was an unusually cool and dry day for a Chicago summer, and I enjoyed my walk through the leafy Hyde Park neighborhood. Dr. Young, middle-aged, about my height and a little heavier, with what struck me as intelligent, sympathetic eyes, welcomed me. I extended my left hand, which seemed to confuse him until he glanced at my right. "What's this?" he asked.

I was getting tired of telling that story. I answered, "Oh, I slammed the car door on it. Should've been paying attention."

Raising a doubtful eyebrow, he invited me into the dining room, where lunch was waiting. I thanked him for seeing me.

"Happy to have you," he responded. "I was expecting a call from the Mobe at some point, but I didn't expect it to come through Emma. That was a pleasant surprise."

"How long have you known each other?" I asked.

"We met at an open housing march a couple of years ago. The march was attacked by gangs of rock-throwing thugs. One of them hit Dr. King in the head. I'd been appointed his personal physician during the Chicago visit, so I tended to him. Emma helped. That turned out to be a bonding experience. She and I have stayed in at least occasional touch ever since."

"Do you know she has emphysema now?"

"I can't say I'm shocked to hear it. I don't remember ever seeing her without a cigarette. How bad is it?"

"We've had some scares, but it seems more or less under control for now. And she's finally making an effort to quit smoking, or at least to stop chain smoking."

"I have to go see her, and I will. But that isn't what you came for. You're recruiting medical support for the convention protest. Fill me in on the planning."

I brought him up to date, including our difficulties with the Daley administration. He commented, "You know, it's quite possible you won't get the permits. What then?"

"If there are no permits," I explained, "it won't be as big as we've been hoping. But it'll still happen. We have to do *something*."

"I understand. I'll need to clear this with the board, but I'm sure we can provide medical support. The question is, 'How much?' If the permits come through, we'll have no problem lining people up. If they don't, it'll be more difficult. I'll need to call on our Freedom Summer veterans, and some of the folks working down South now. They're experienced in dangerous situations."

On my way out, he said, "Tell Emma I'll be over to see her soon. And take care of that hand. Use an antibiotic ointment on it." That reminded me to pull the tube out of my pocket.

Later, after I put the groceries away and Cat began preparing dinner, I filled her in on Dr. Young. She had only one question: "If it's gonna be a peaceful protest, why do we need so many medics?"

I gave her some stupid answer, like, "I dunno. Just in case, I guess," which I knew would be unsatisfactory. Hoping to change the subject, I said, "I should start calling those ministers now. Late Saturday afternoon might be a good time to reach them."

I had no idea whether or not it was an opportune time for that, but I did get lucky. By the time dinner was ready, I'd lined up three meetings for Sunday afternoon, and two more for later in the week.

Sunday morning started with the TV talk shows. On ABC's "Issues and Answers," Hubert Humphrey announced that the biggest issue in the presidential campaign was not the war but street violence. I thought his remark was interesting since none of the candidates, to my knowledge, supported increases in street violence.

Of the three afternoon meetings, I got two offers of cooperation, and one "maybe." I didn't get back home until dinner, leftovers from Friday with Emma. Cat looked unhappy, so I asked what was wrong.

"You said you wanted a nice restful holiday weekend," she explained, "with me and not with the war. Instead, first you got into a fight and then you went running around all over the place working on the protests. And you told me this would be a part-time job. And don't you remember what you said on the way back from the Bennetts'? About wanting to have some fun this summer? About wanting not to deal with the war all the time?"

"Okay," I conceded. "You're right, and I'm sorry. I knew I could get overwhelmed by this, and I do want what I said that day. It's why I asked you to help me."

"And that's just what I'm gonna do. You have to go to the office tomorrow?"

"Yes. The Monday staff meetings are important."

"Then make sure you're home by four. You and I are going to the beach."

Cat's self-defense class began the next morning. It was a three-week program, from 10 to 12, Monday through Thursday.

"I'm so glad you're doing this," I told her during breakfast.

"I'm looking forward to it too," she replied. "I'll spend the afternoon in the shop, but only until four. Because we're going to the beach. Right?"

"Right."

"And you'll be home by four?"

"I already said I would."

"Well, don't forget. And don't forget your ointment."

By the time I left for the office, Cat reminded me a dozen more times to use the ointment and to be home by four. After a good-bye kiss, I said, "Cat, I want to go the beach with you. I really do. I'm looking forward to it. You don't have to nag me."

"Well, don't forget," she nagged anyway. "And don't be late."

The greetings I got at the Mobe weren't, "Hi, how was your weekend?" but rather, "What the hell happened to your hand?"

My response was now down to two words. "Car door." I might have added, "You should've seen it a couple of days ago."

"Let's start with reports," Donnie said, convening the staff meeting. "Anything new at City Hall?"

"I only had three days last week because of the holiday," Jeff began, "and none of my calls were returned. I went down there on Wednesday, but didn't get to see anyone. I did get friendly with a secretary, though, and found out something important that I didn't know before."

"What's that?"

"Permit applications must be filed at least thirty days before the event. That'll be only a few days after our board meeting."

"Did you get the application forms?"

"She sent me to a different office to get them, but the clerk said they weren't available. I'll try again today."

"Okay," Donnie said. "If you can pick up those applications and we get board approval, everything can be done before the deadline. Meanwhile, please keep pushing. Paul, have you got any meetings set up?"

"Six peace groups up in Wisconsin and two more in Michigan. I'll be leaving Wednesday and coming back over the weekend. Next week, I'll meet with the Chicago Peace Council's executive committee."

"Terrific. Anything on your end, Steve?"

I reported on my meetings with Rev. Marshall and the three other ministers, and described the system we now had to track the results of the phone calls.

"That's a great start," Vern observed.

"Well, it's a start," I responded, "but I had to assure the pastors we'd provide our own security. We'll need to assign marshals to ensure order at these sites."

Paul added, "Vern, this is serious. We're not a disciplined membership organization. The Mobe is only a loose coalition. We don't know who'll show up or how rowdy they'll get. Some are likely to be looking for trouble."

"Trouble with the cops, maybe," Jeff interjected. "But not with churches and synagogues."

"Possibly. But what about agent provocateurs? You know, people sent into our midst by the Red Squad, by the feds, posing as protesters but looking to provoke confrontation."

"Okay, okay," Vern agreed. "I can see we'll have to make this part of the marshals' responsibilities. But maybe we'll need some kind of screening procedure before sending people to the churches."

"We'll need to work on this, Steve," Donnie said. "But please keep on lining up sites. Anything else?"

"Well, yes. Have you guys heard of the Medical Committee for Human Rights?" They nodded.

"On Saturday, I had lunch with Dr. Quentin Young, its National Chairman," I reported, going on to summarize his response.

"Great news, Steve," Donnie said. "But didn't you say you were taking the weekend off?"

"It didn't quite work out that way. But I do have to be home by four today, no matter what."

He gave me a knowing smile, which I found a little irritating.

"One more thing on the sleeping spaces," Jeff said. "We're getting into a mindset about worst-case scenarios. What about best-case? Suppose tens of thousands do come to Chicago for this? Or a hundred thousand or even more? Could they be accommodated by the sites on your list, even if we get lots of cooperation?"

"I guess we'll need parks, at least as a backup," I replied.

"Right. That means more permits, which is why I brought it up now. Time's running short."

"Okay," Donnie concluded. "How about this? Steve, keep working on spaces at the colleges, churches, synagogues and so on, but also identify city parks for our people to camp out. Jeff, you contact the Park District to facilitate the permit process."

I was getting a headache from all the work that needed to be done, and all the uncertainties we faced. After the meeting, I sat down with Ronnie to get up to date on the Prospect Sheets, then arranged more meetings and left to meet with a rabbi. That encounter was promising, since he was as opposed to the war as I was, but he said he had to bring it to his board. My head was throbbing by the time I got home.

Chapter 54

Cat's face lit up as I came through the door, as though she didn't really expect me to get there on time. She was busy building hero sandwiches.

"Go ahead and get ready," she happily instructed. "I'm almost finished here."

I changed my clothes and came back to the kitchen, asking, "How was your day?"

"I'll tell you later, but now we need to get going. Here, wrap these in aluminum foil and pour some wine into the thermos. I'll go and change."

After I had everything packed up, she emerged in a skimpy two-piece bathing suit. The vision was delectable, but I had my issues. "Is that what you're wearing?" I asked.

"No," she replied, grabbing the long cover-up and shrugging it on. "This is what I'm wearing." She scooped up the big floppy hat and we were on our way.

Driving to Jackson Park, I summarized the staff meeting, concluding, "I'm feeling overwhelmed again.

"I know," she said. "We can work on this together. Okay? We can probably find park information at the beach bathhouse."

"Yes, together," I repeated, feeling almost grounded.

"But not tonight," she declared, "and no looking at any of those brochures. This is our time. Yours and mine. You won't worry about your work, and I won't nag you about the permits."

"That's a deal!" I exclaimed.

As I'd hoped, the beach was sparsely populated by the time we got there. After stopping in the bathhouse to drop brochures into the bag, we walked halfway down to the water, spread the blanket and ate our picnic dinner. All the while, Cat wore her "disguise," which I could tell was uncomfortable. When I suggested, "Let's hit the water," she held her arms out and shrugged. Looking around, I added, "Looks safe to me." In seconds, the hat and cover-up were gone and we were playing in the waves. Back at the blanket, we dropped on our backs to let the sun's rays dry us off.

"Now," I said, "tell me about your self-defense class. How was it?"

"Really good," she began. "The teacher is Mrs. Murchison from the Phys Ed Department. She has some kind of black belt. But she told us this class won't be about winning fights."

"What then?"

"Strictly self-defense. We'll be learning how to stop an attack, and create enough space to make an escape. That's it."

"Makes sense to me. I guess no matter how good you are, it's safer to be out of a fight than in one."

"You should know," she responded, sitting up and lifting my bruised hand. "Anyway, she taught us a few little tricks as an introduction. But that wasn't the most interesting part of the session."

"There was something else?"

"Yes. Before the lesson, she had us sit in a circle, and asked what brought us there. About half the women are from Midway, all white except for me, and the rest are Black South Siders, referred by Maddy Skinner. The women come from two different worlds, but they have one thing in common."

"What's that?"

"Every one of them has been assaulted by men. Molested, beaten or raped. Some by strangers, some by relatives, some by boyfriends, even a few by husbands. Their stories shook me. Anyway, they all said they'd had enough. They wanted to learn to protect themselves."

"So what did you say?"

"I went last, and I didn't put it very well. I said I was there 'to make my boyfriend feel better.' They thought that was hilarious. Well, at least it broke the gloomy mood. After the laughter died down, I explained what happened at the barbeque and they understood what I meant. Mrs. Murchison said that soon I'll know exactly how to get out of a situation like that. By myself."

My relief must have showed. "That really would make me feel better."

We went for another swim. Back on the blanket, we sat and watched the tide inching its way toward us, the sun dropping lower toward the horizon. Cat said, "There's something I've been meaning to ask you."

"What's that?"

"Remember you told me you hated supermarket shopping? I volunteered to do it, since I don't mind it at all. But I never asked why. I'd really like to know what that's about."

"Everything gets under my skin," I explained. "It's too crowded. The aisles are too narrow. There's too much stuff I don't want, and I can't find the things I need. After a few minutes, I feel the walls closing in on me. And after all that comes waiting in line to pay before I can escape."

"Okay, I see what you mean. Is it only supermarkets, or any kind of shopping?"

"You know I'm okay with the little shops on High Street. My problem is with the big ones. Department stores are the worst. Remember the time I ran into Marshall Field's? How long was I in there?"

"Oh, a few minutes."

"Right. And that's pretty much my limit. I was lucky the beachwear display was right near the entrance."

"But why?"

"If I go deep into one of those stores, I get anxious about finding my way back out. Sometimes I break into a cold sweat. One time, I passed out. Big airports like O'Hare trigger the same reaction."

Cat looked concerned. She asked, "Did you ever bring this to a doctor?"

"Yes, once. He said I was borderline claustrophobic."

"I see. Is there anything else I should know?"

"Well, there are my carnival nightmares."

"Of course. Is that it?"

I decided I might as well let it all out. "I do have a problem with heights."

"You mean from looking down off a high cliff, or a tall building?"

"It's more than that. Like driving over a bridge, I get nervous I'll somehow drive right off it, or flip the car over the railing. And anything higher than the second rung of a ladder makes me nervous, sometimes even dizzy. They call this acrophobia."

"I see," she murmured thoughtfully. "You know, maybe we should add another book to our summer reading pile."

"What's that?" I asked, puzzled.

Cat lifted up on an elbow. "A textbook on Abnormal Psychology. We can go through it together, chapter by chapter, and put each of your symptoms and diagnoses on an index card."

Now I was getting concerned. I still hadn't mentioned the psychiatrist I wasn't planning to call. I raised up on an elbow too, and asked, "Then what?"

"Oh, I don't know. Maybe a new card game. No, wait. A game show. That's it. Did you ever see *What's My Line?* on TV?"

"Sure. Regular people come on as guests, and the panel members ask yes-or-no questions trying to figure out their occupations."

"Right," she said, now brimming with glee. "We could call our show *What's Your Problem?*"

I didn't know what to make of this. I stared, wide-eyed, my mouth hanging open. A minute later, Cat burst out laughing. She pushed me down and fell on top, until I rolled her over and began tickling. Her laughter became uncontrollable. Once her face began turning red, I decided my revenge was complete. I let go and rolled onto my back. Cat regained her composure, scooted over and put her head on my chest. I wrapped my arm around her.

"You know, that was a very dirty trick," I whispered in her ear.

"I know. I'm sorry. It just came to me. I guess I was the only one having fun with it."

"It's okay, and it does seem funny now. But I love you so much. I never want you to think I'm some kind of weirdo."

"And I love you too," she cooed, moving up to kiss my neck. "Just the way you are."

The magic of the moment was eventually broken. A voice above us announced, "Beach is closing, kids. Time to go." It was the lifeguard going off duty. Suddenly, I noticed that everyone else had already gone.

"Okay, boss," I responded cheerfully. "We'll need a minute to pack." He nodded and continued on his way.

By the time we got our stuff together and made it into the dunes, a million stars lit the sky. I noticed a small flat clearing, surrounded by high grasses, and said, "Look."

Cat glanced over at the clearing, then up at me, and asked, "Are you thinking what I'm thinking?"

"Come on," I said.

In seconds, our naked bodies were entwined on the blanket. Making love under the night sky, I thought I saw shooting stars. Afterward, I felt so good, so peaceful, that I considered suggesting we spend the night, right there in the dunes. But a rustling in the grasses, not very far away, interrupted my reverie.

"What's that?" Cat whispered.

"I don't know. A squirrel? Another couple of lovers?"

"Or something, or someone, else," she said. "We should go."

With remarkable efficiency, under the circumstances, we very quietly got dressed, folded the blanket and went to the car. On the way home, we promised ourselves more trips to Jackson Park Beach, but agreed it would be best to leave by the time it closes for the night.

Chapter 55

Ronnie called in the morning with two appointments for me. One was with a minister in the Lincoln Park neighborhood, the other with the athletic director at Langley University. Both were in the afternoon so, while Cat got dressed for her self-defense class, I pulled the Park District brochures out of the beach bag and began looking through them. By the time she came out of the bedroom, I had my elbows on the table and my head in my hands.

"What's the matter?" she asked.

"Here's a list of the parks and their addresses. Would you believe there are more than 600 of them? I don't even know where most of these streets are. I have no idea where to begin."

She sat down next to me, put her hand on mine and calmly advised, "Relax. Of course you do." She went to the cabinet, took out her map of Chicago, and sat back down.

"This will help," she said. "What are the most important things you're looking for in narrowing down the list?"

I thought for a minute and replied, "First, I guess, is proximity to the Loop and to the Amphitheater, where the convention will be. And second is big open spaces that can hold lots of people. Wait, let me see your map." I unfolded it and scanned it quickly.

"This'll sure help. The big parks are the big green spaces. I can narrow this down in no time."

"See that? I knew you'd know what to do." She gave me a quick kiss. "Gotta run now. After class, I'll be in the shop."

I wished we were doing this together. I did know what to do once she got me started, though, so I got to work. Grant Park was the obvious standout, since it was located right in the heart of the Loop. I also saw that most of the parks on the list were very small, and not worth bothering with. Lincoln Park was a huge one, but a couple of miles away. Rooting through the drawer, I found a subway map and found how the two sites were connected. I did the same with all twenty-eight of the parks that looked on the map to be well-located and sizable. By lunchtime, I thought I had the whole thing figured out.

Cat and Emma were having pizza downstairs. I showed them the map, and my list of parks with their subway connections.

"That's terrific," Cat said. "You've nailed your first two criteria. But what about bathrooms?"

"Oy!" I exclaimed, deflated. "The brochures feature picnic areas, ball fields, beaches, pools and other things, but not bathrooms. Of course you're right. We'll never get permits if people will be fouling up the parks. But now I'll have to go and look for myself. My report is due next Monday. There's no time…"

"Sure there is," Cat calmly interjected. "Emma, do you mind if I take Friday off?"

"Of course not."

"Then we'll do it together," she continued, "starting early Friday morning. We'll map out a route, and we'll visit every one of the parks on your list. It'll be fun, especially if we have good weather."

This cheered me up considerably. It was hard to tear myself away, but I didn't want to risk being late for my appointments. So I blew kisses and rushed out the door.

The first meeting was with Rev. Donald Blake, a Presbyterian minister whose church faced Lincoln Park. He not only offered us space, but said he'd be joining the protests himself. *A good start.*

Since I was early to the Langley campus, I took a look at the football stadium. This, I thought, would be a perfect place for overnight camping. Lots of space and plenty of bathrooms. I was optimistic going in to meet Coach Bob, the athletic director. But that lasted only about a minute.

"I've been trying to get you on the phone for the past hour," he told me, "but someone in your office said you were out at another meeting."

"Well, I'm here now. What was it you wanted to tell me?"

"Frankly, I wanted to save you the trip. The university's General Counsel called me in this morning. Somehow, he knew you were coming to see me. Anyway, he said allowing overnight camping would violate the terms of our liability insurance. If anything went wrong, we wouldn't be covered against lawsuits. He also seemed quite sure things would go wrong, and instructed me that letting you folks use the field is absolutely out of the question."

Stunned, I asked, "Do you think this is for real, or a cover for his own politics?"

"At first, I thought it was political. But I made a few calls, and his concerns do seem to be legitimate. I'm sorry to have dragged you out here today, but now I don't see any way I can help."

I thanked him for his time, rose and shook his hand. At the door, another thought hit me. I turned and asked, "I'll run into the same problem at every college, won't I?"

"I'm afraid so. Our insurance policies are very similar."

Back on the road, another question nagged at me: *How did that university official know I had an appointment with the coach?*

Later, I told Ronnie what happened. I asked her to have the volunteers stop calling colleges, and to focus instead on the churches and synagogues. As I filled out the Prospect Sheets summarizing my meetings, she inserted them into the loose-leaf. Finally, I showed her the prospects Rev. Marshall had checked off on the list.

"Please make as many appointments with these as I can keep during the next two days," I said. "Friday, I have to work on the parks. And call me with the schedule in the morning, as early as you can."

Too dejected to make any calls myself, I went home, barely beating the afternoon rush.

Cat took one look at me and asked, "What's wrong now? Did something happen?"

I told her what I'd learned about the colleges. "We'll never find enough space in the temples and churches," I explained, "and we have issues with those too. So now we really do need parks."

She put her things down, sat on my lap and took my face in her hands. "We'll work on the parks starting Friday," she reminded me. "I'll draw us a route, and we'll visit every one of them. Once you've collected all the relevant data, you can target the best ones."

Sensing the tension in my body relax, she leaned into me. I squeezed her in tighter, back in touch with the knowledge that I was the luckiest guy in the whole world. I knew, though, that Cat's enthusiasm for the project would only last as long as the permits were still a possibility. I also knew I couldn't live every day with as many mood swings as the past several had brought me.

Ronnie called Wednesday morning before Cat left for her self-defense class. She'd lined up four meetings with ministers recommended by Rev. Marshall, and gave me the driving directions. She asked me to call back before six to get Thursday's appointments.

Cat saw me writing this down and remarked, after I hung up, "It seems this Ronnie is very good at her job."

"She sure is. She coordinates everything. I guess she must have lots of experience. Funny thing is, though, she never seems interested in the politics of what we're doing."

"But if she's that competent," Cat asked, "couldn't she make more money almost anywhere else?"

"She certainly could. We're incredibly lucky to have her."

The four ministers I met with, two Black and two white, asked questions about the protests, and about how we planned to use and supervise the space. In the end, though, they each said the same thing, to the effect of, "If this has Rev. Marshall's seal of approval, that's good enough for me." I did, however, have to promise each of them we'd provide enough trained marshals to keep their churches clean, orderly and drug-free. I had my doubts about how realistic that was, but put them aside for another day. Back home, I checked in with Ronnie, and got my schedule for Thursday.

Cat arrived as I put the phone down. I felt good about getting something done now. She heard it in my voice.

"It looks like you and Ronnie are a good team," she observed.

"I guess we are. She's incredibly efficient."

"That's nice," she murmured, a bit distantly. "Well, tomorrow I'll finish mapping out our route for Friday's tour of the parks."

Was it my imagination, or did I sense a little competition brewing?

Chapter 56

Following three more meetings on Thursday, I filled out my Prospect Sheets and asked Ronnie for a look at the loose-leaf. I was pleasantly surprised to see that the volunteers had lined up some sleeping spaces.

"There are still more on Rev. Marshall's list," Ronnie pointed out. "Should I set them up for next week?"

"It'll be a busy one," I responded, "preparing our presentation to the board. Monday's staff meeting might be long. So please arrange as many as you can for Tuesday and Wednesday, but only until early afternoon. And tomorrow, can you prepare a progress report for the staff meeting?"

"Sure," she agreed. "I'll be happy to,"

Back at the shop, Cat was working with a customer. She nodded toward the back, where I heard voices. I was pleased to see Dr. Young talking with Emma. He'd kept his promise.

"I see you're using your right hand now," he remarked.

"Yes, it's much better. I don't think I mentioned it, but it was Dr. Hal Dreyer who prescribed the treatment. Do you know him?"

"Yes, I do, since he worked with MCHR in the past. Once he finishes his residency, I hope to see more of him. Until then, he's lucky if he even gets to see any daylight."

"So," I asked, "I guess you two had some catching up to do?"

"Yes," Emma replied. "We've been sitting here talking for an hour now." I noticed her ashtray was not only empty, but clean.

"But I also have news for you," Dr. Young added.

"Oh?"

"I met with James Conlisk, the Police Superintendent, yesterday. He agreed to instruct his officers to give clearly identified medics safe passage during the protests. I'm sure we can line up a sizable number of volunteers. They'll wear white lab coats with big red crosses and caduceus symbols. That's the good news."

"That's great news. But there's something else?

"Yes, there is, and it's not so good. Conlisk also confided, off the record, that he's sure Mayor Daley won't cooperate with the Mobe in any way. If permits aren't granted, his orders will be to do whatever's necessary to enforce the law. Things could get ugly."

I signaled for us to lower our voices, and asked Emma, "Does Cat know this?"

"Not yet. She's been busy out front."

Dr. Young looked at his watch and said, "I've got to be going. It's been good seeing you both. And Emma, you take care of yourself."

"I promise I will," she replied. "And I'm sure you've noticed I have two keepers looking after me too."

"Thanks for everything," I added. "Some big meetings are coming up next week, and this information will really come in handy."

After he left, I sat down close to Emma and quietly asked, "So?"

"This is tough, Steve, since the Mobe might be left with two bad choices. The first, of course, is to cancel the protest, which lets the Democrats off the hook and makes the antiwar movement look pathetically weak. The other is to bring a diminished force into what might be a dangerous situation."

"Well, next Saturday's board meeting should be very interesting," I responded. "But, in the meantime, can we not worry Cat with this?"

"Of course. But the time will come when the subject can't be avoided any longer."

As promised, Cat had our tour of the parks all mapped out for the next morning. By her calculations, we'd be able to cover all, or almost all, of the parks on my list well before dark.

"If we don't get to all of them," she asked once we began our tour, "we can finish tomorrow morning. Right?"

"Sure."

"Good!" she exclaimed, looking down at her map. "Wait, make the next left. Okay, so let's save Lincoln Park for tomorrow afternoon."

"Why tomorrow?"

"Because the carnival's coming to town! Right at the next light, and you'll see our first park. I love carnivals. Rides, games, even animals sometimes, petting zoos... Oh wait, your carnival nightmare. Would that set it off?"

"Not at all. The dream gets triggered by my emotional state, not by actual carnivals. I love them too. In fact, I have a better idea. Let's call Sharon, and ask if she and Arielle want to join us."

I parked the car and we walked into the park. Cat suggested I look for restrooms, call Sharon if I found a phone, then meet her back at the entrance. Walking toward high ground, I spotted a building with both of the amenities we needed. Sharon answered on the first ring.

I jogged back. "Yes, we have bathrooms," I reported.

I watched as Cat made notations on the itinerary. I noticed she'd already written "4,260." I asked what that meant.

"It's how many people can fit in this area comfortably, overnight," she responded.

"How do you know that?"

She launched into an explanation of her calculation, based on the square footage each person would need, the circulation required between the bodies, and the amount of open acreage in the park, somehow based on indices like the number of cars parked on the street or in the lot.

"You can explain this another time," I said. "Let's get to the next one."

"Turn right at the next light," she instructed, back in the car. "Did you find a phone?"

"Yes, I did. Sharon said it'll be a huge treat for Arielle. They'll be ready at noon."

"I can't wait," Cat responded. "Oops, we missed a turn. Make the next right and go around the block. Then it's about half a mile."

The tour went much faster than Cat had anticipated, thanks to the efficiency of her itinerary. We'd qualified ten parks besides Lincoln and Grant, both of which were huge. It was a productive day. Now Saturday was free.

The carnival did turn out to be one of the summer's highlights. Arielle wanted me on every ride with her, and the faster they went, the louder she squealed. I drew the line, though, at anything that went too high. For the Ferris Wheel and the (admittedly small) roller coaster, she settled for Cat or Mommy.

In between, she inhaled so much ice cream and cotton candy that Sharon had to put a stop to it before she got sick. All those treats had left their mark on Arielle's now multi-colored face.

At the tent with the petting zoo, I begged off again, telling Arielle I was allergic to animals. Sharon took her inside. Cat said, "I didn't know you had allergies."

"I don't," I replied. "I love being around animals. I don't know why I said that. Maybe the claustrophobia."

We moved on to the games with prizes. I was determined to win at least one stuffed animal for Arielle, hopefully one for Cat too. But it was frustrating. The only things I won were worthless little consolation prizes. But when a pool table came into view, I cheered up.

"Look over there," I pointed. "I can do that one."

"Pool?" Cat asked. "You know how?"

"There wasn't much entertainment back in Waterloo, but we did have a pool hall. That's where I spent a lot of my free time. Come on, we'll give it a try."

First, we watched a few other players. Nine numbered balls were racked in a diamond shape. The player shot the white cue ball to break them up, then had to "run the table," calling each shot. One miss and the game was over. No-one we watched sank more than two or three balls before missing.

I stepped up to the table and paid the man. As I examined the cue stick, Cat whispered in my ear, "The table is slanted toward the left by about five degrees." I nodded and continued examining the stick, which I found had a slight warp a third of the way up from the handle.

"Are you ready?" the carnival guy asked.

"I am now," I said, unscrewing the bottom part of the stick and handing it to him. "Let's go." I broke the rack with the shorter, but now straighter, stick, and surveyed the table.

"Two ball in the corner." Bang.

"Three ball in the side pocket." Bang. The shortened stick made it easier to put spin on the cue ball, positioning it for the next shot. I easily pocketed the next six balls, leaving only one. But I'd made an error that left me out of position. *How to sink that last ball?*

By now, a small crowd had gathered. I walked around the table twice, trying to find an angle. The crowd buzzed, and I heard side bets being made. I found only one possible way to put that ball in a pocket. It had to be a triple bank shot, but I wasn't sure I'd be able to pull it off. I stood behind the cue ball, and patted the corner pocket to my left. The buzzing got louder, but stopped as I lined up the shot. The cue ball hit the nine where I'd aimed it and, I hoped, with precisely the right spin.

The ball caromed off the first cushion, then the second and the third. As it headed toward the corner pocket, though, it was losing speed. I wasn't the only one holding my breath as it rolled, slower and slower, toward the pocket. Just as it seemed about to stop, it dropped in, thanks to the slight table tilt Cat had detected.

A roar went up. I lifted Arielle and told her, "Pick one!" She pointed to a panda that was bigger than she was, and nearly jumped out of my arms when she got it.

I asked Cat, "How about one for you?"

"You can do this again?"

"I can try."

This time, I made no mistakes. It was over in two minutes. She wanted me to pick the prize this time.

I pointed to a giant "Sylvester the Cat." The guy handed it over, but told me, "No more from you. Get lost." It sounded a little menacing, so we moved on.

For the rest of the afternoon, Arielle insisted on carrying her big panda. This slowed us down considerably, but she wouldn't let go, even on the rides. When she began to show signs of fatigue, we called it a day.

Fitting our expanded party into Tooter wasn't easy. The only way was for Cat and Arielle to sit in the back with their new friends. My rear-view vision was partially blocked, but we made it to Sharon's building without incident. She leaned over, gave me a little kiss on the cheek and said, "You've made a little girl very happy today."

"And she made this a great day for us all," I responded.

Arielle was fast asleep. I carried her upstairs, while Sharon brought the panda. Back in the car, Cat lunged over the stick shift to give me an enormous wet kiss on the lips.

"Let's go home!" she exclaimed. I knew what she had in mind, so I shifted into gear and hit the gas.

Chapter 57

Over Sunday's breakfast, I recalled, "Yesterday was so great. Arielle and the carnival pushed the war out of my mind for the entire day."

"Yes, you needed that," Cat observed.

"I guess so. But this morning, I woke up from a dream about the war. The bombs, the killing, the Napalm. Those poor people can't decide to simply shut it out the way we can."

"Look, you can't feel guilty for having a life," she declared. "You're a human being, not a machine."

"I know, I know. Of course you're right. And I certainly would never give back the fun time we've been having together, especially at the beach and the carnival."

"And we should have more of it," she insisted. "We need it. Besides, that's how your batteries get charged."

"Well," I responded with a big smile, "you sure charged them last night!"

"And I thought I drained them!" she laughed, punching me in the shoulder.

"Anyway, it's back to work now. I have to get the park reports ready for the staff meeting."

Ten minutes later, I sat at the typewriter, Cat next to me with her notes. I'd decided to summarize our results in a simple four-column chart. Cat read from her notes the park's name, location, transit connection and approximate capacity. As she read, I typed. The capacity column totaled 61,340, not counting Grant or Lincoln Parks. With 319 acres at Grant and 1,200 at Lincoln, the capacity would be unlimited. We were finished.

"You know, Cat," I said, "I never could've gotten this done without you. The minute I looked at the Park District brochure, I was totally overwhelmed. You showed me how to analyze it, and you led me through the whole project. Can I put your name on the report along with mine?"

"You exaggerate," she argued, "but do whatever you want. I'm just glad you noticed that we make a good team too."

This mystified me. "What do you mean 'too'?"

"You know, that other woman. What's her name, Ronnie? Anyway, let's decide how to spend the rest of the day."

"Wait. Ronnie? Cat, she's just…"

The phone interrupted my explanation. I was surprised by the caller.

"Oh. Hi, Donnie. What's up?" Hearing that, Cat groaned.

"Listen, Steve, we have a fundraiser in Highland Park tonight, a cocktail party. Jeff will be there, but Paul can't make it. We need another staffer. Can you come?"

"Gee, I don't know. I was planning to be with Cat."

"Bring her. And invite Emma too."

"Hold on a sec." I asked Cat, "Want to go to a party?"

"A party? Well, sure, if you want to."

I told Donnie, "Okay, we'll go." He gave me the details, and we hung up.

Cat asked, "What time do we have to leave?"

"Around four, I guess."

"I better start getting ready. You call Emma."

I looked at the clock. It was only a little past one. I was sure Cat would win any beauty pageant she entered with fifteen minutes of prep time, but I also knew she'd use the entire three hours for this. I gave an involuntary shrug of the shoulders and called Emma. She said she'd love to go, but she couldn't talk now because she had to get ready.

I guessed I should "get ready" too, so I looked through the closet for something to wear. I found a sport jacket, a dress shirt, and a pair of real shoes. No dress pants, though, so chinos would have to do. So that was done, and now I had ten fewer minutes to kill.

I retyped my report, with carbon copies just in case I'd need them. I read the rest of the Sunday paper, and the last chapter of the Thomas Kuhn book. At 3:15, I heard Cat migrate from the bathroom to the bedroom. A half hour later, she emerged, a vision from Heaven. A clingy lavender dress accented her creamy butterscotch skin. Her raven hair, partly swept up and partly not, was like a museum sculpture. That, and her hoop earrings, drew attention to her long neck, and to a face that could have sold any movie. I stared for a moment, then squeaked out, *"Amazing!"*

Emma met us downstairs. She looked good too, at least ten years younger than her everyday image, and happy. As the three of us walked to the car, I remarked, "You know, someone might start an investigation tonight."

"An investigation?" Cat asked. "Of what?"

"Of how a *shlub* like me showed up with not one, but two beauty queens!"

We all laughed, and I was rewarded with a punch in each shoulder.

The party was behind a big house, under a tent the size of a ballroom. Well-staffed food tables and two full bars lined the sides of the tent. Servers circulated with trays of drinks and finger foods. Scattered around were candle-lit bistro tables and chairs. A trio played light jazz in a corner.

"Wouldn't it have saved a lot of trouble," I wondered out loud, "if whoever's throwing this bash simply wrote a check to the Mobe instead of to the caterer?"

"No, this is better," Emma explained. "The social interaction is important, and it's also important to have as many people as possible writing checks. Base-building occurs at many different levels. Some of these folks are probably getting involved for the first time tonight, and one or two might host their own fundraiser before this is over."

While I pondered this thought, Donnie caught my eye and beckoned. "Okay?" I asked Cat.

"Sure," she replied. "We'll go check out the food."

Donnie introduced me to Roger Wolfson, a short, thin man with intense dark eyes, and told me, "Roger's our host tonight."

I shook Roger's hand, and thanked him for the party.

"My pleasure," he said. "Very good to meet you. But please excuse me. The caterer needs my attention."

"Who is he?" I asked Donnie.

"Roger's a geek," he explained. "When he was a freshman at MIT, he invented some kind of computer gadget. He formed a company to market them, made a fortune, and finally sold it to IBM for tens of millions. Now he spends his time giving the money away. He hates the war and loves the Mobe. He's not a 'social' person, though. Within half an hour, he'll disappear into the house."

"So what do you want me to do?" I asked.

"Just mingle. Later, I'll need your help with the collection." Someone called to him, and he walked away. I didn't know anything about "mingling," so I headed for the bar.

Before I got there, though, I ran into Dr. Hal Dreyer. "How's the hand from hell?" he asked.

I showed him. "Much, much better, thanks to you. How'd you get released from the Med Center? I thought you were locked in there."

"Finished my residency last week," he announced with a broad grin. "Tonight, I'm celebrating." From the drink in his hand and the tenor of his speech, I guessed he'd been celebrating for quite a while.

"Congratulations!" I responded, shaking his hand. "It's been a long time coming."

"It sure has. Listen, I told Quentin I'm on board for Convention Week. He's right over there, by the way." I saw Dr. Young with a circle of people, Emma among them.

I'd decided on nothing stronger than white wine, since I was in some way "on duty." I got a glass and wandered around. I found Cat lighting up a small group of middle-aged men. No alarms bells went off, though. They looked harmless, and she seemed clearly in charge. I finished my wine and went for food. I wasn't sure whether it was possible to eat and mingle at the same time.

As I began to consider the buffet, a husky female voice addressed me over my right shoulder. "I heard you're on staff at the Mobe. It must be interesting."

I turned to see a strikingly beautiful, elegantly dressed woman, probably in her early forties. She reminded me of my boyhood heartthrob, the actress Lauren Bacall. I guessed this must be my opportunity to "mingle."

"Well," I stammered, "I suppose so. Sometimes. Mostly I'm just lining up support for the Convention Week protesters. Housing, medical, that kind of thing."

"Housing I understand," she replied. "But medical? Are you expecting sick people?"

"Oh, it's not that. You see, we don't know yet what to expect from the cops. They've gone crazy on demonstrators before. If it happens again next month, we'll need battlefield medics on the spot."

"I heard about that. Have you seen it yourself?"

"One time I was in the middle of it. At the Civic Center march a few months ago, I got my head cracked. Could've used a medic then. But it probably wouldn't have mattered 'cause I got arrested and hauled off."

"Really? Would you tell me about it? Wait, let's get a drink and find a table."

"Well, sure," I agreed, thinking now that this "mingling" thing might not be so difficult after all. A platter of colorful, but unfamiliar, delicacies awaited at the bistro table we found, drinks in hand.

"How awful of me. We haven't been properly introduced. I'm Merrie Alexander," she said, holding out a manicured, bejeweled hand. I had a split-second flash of a 1940s black-and-white movie, where I would take that hand to my lips and say something clever, in French, such as "Enchante." The image dissolved, so I simply gave it a little squeeze and introduced myself.

"So what happened that day?" she asked.

I gave her a capsule version of the Civic Center march, but she wanted details. After a while, she also somehow got me talking about the march to the armory, when we got charged with bayonets, Marcellus took out two soldiers and we 'borrowed' the Army truck.

"Steve, that's a wonderful story!" she exclaimed. "Let's have another drink. Where's a waiter?"

I was getting tired of talking about myself, so I asked what brought her to the party.

"Oh, I noticed Roger directing the caterers this morning and got curious. I asked him what was going on, and he invited me. I'm glad he did."

"You were in the neighborhood?"

"I live right across the street," she explained. "The corner house."

She pulled a small piece of paper out of her bag, made a notation on it and folded it in thirds. "Here. Take this," she said, her green eyes fixed on me with an expression I couldn't decipher.

Before I got a chance to unfold the paper, Cat appeared. "Donnie's about to speak," she reported. "We should get up front."

Rising, I slipped the paper into my shirt pocket and said, "It's been nice meeting you, Merrie."

"Yes, I enjoyed it too, Steve. Maybe another time." Turning to leave, I wondered what she meant by "another time."

Donnie made a practiced, effective pitch for contributions. Jeff, Cat and I circulated with collection cans. As the music resumed, we were besieged with questions about Convention Week.

On the way home, I asked, "Did we have a good time?"

"I certainly did," Emma replied. "I ran into a few people I hadn't seen in quite a while. It was good to catch up. What about you, Cat?"

"It was okay, I guess. Except a bit too much attention on little me. At times, it seemed like I was supposed to be the entertainment. But what about *you*, Mister Personality? Who was that blonde you were all huddled up with?"

"Oh, her name was Merrie something-or-other. She wanted to know about this year's protest marches."

"And how'd you like being flirted with?" Emma asked.

"Flirted? Why would someone like her flirt with me? She might be my mother's age, and she's probably rich."

"You might have to get used to this, Steve, because to some people, movement work is sexy, *especially* if it involves a little danger. The edginess can be a turn-on. You might think much of the work you're doing is mundane, but you're in the inner circle of planning something that looks to be huge. And besides, you are a good-looking young guy."

"You mean she was coming on to me?" I exclaimed, baffled.

"Chances are, she was. Who knows where it might've gone?"

"Well, I did notice her face turn a little sour when you came to collect me, Cat. Anyway, I'm glad you did."

"So am I," she replied. "I should've done it sooner."

"I guess the next time we have to mingle," I suggested, "we should do it together. Emma, am I the only one who didn't know about this?"

"You're still new to Movement work," she explained as I parked the car. "But it's no secret among the veterans. Just ask Donnie. I've got a few stories of my own, too."

Upstairs, I asked Cat, "Do you want to hear Emma's stories?"

"Goodness, no," she laughed. "It would be like seeing your grandparents having sex."

Chapter 58

Before Cat left for Monday's self-defense class, she gently reminded me I still hadn't put away the clothes I'd worn to the party. Taking that as a hint, I hung the jacket and pants in the closet. Rolling the shirt up for the laundry, I heard something crinkling and remembered that piece of paper in the pocket. I unrolled the shirt, extracted the paper and unfolded it.

It was a check issued to the Mobe, in the amount of *five thousand dollars*. I sat on the bed and stared at it, wondering first at the amount, then why she'd handed it to me instead of dropping it into our collection can. Suddenly it dawned on me. Printed in the upper left-hand corner was her name, address and phone number, circled in ink. This was a flat-out invitation. *"Maybe another time,"* was the last thing she said.

My reaction was revulsion, not at her but at myself. I felt like a whore, or how I imagined a whore might feel. Dirty. Disgraced. Even worse, I felt I'd betrayed Cat. *But had I really?* No time to sort this out. I needed to get to the office. But a dark cloud hovered over me all the way there.

I handed Donnie the check as soon as I got through the door. He looked at it, whistled, and said, "Wow. You must've really worked her."

"Donnie, please," I pleaded. "I don't want to talk about it." I resolved I never would talk about it. Not with Cat. Not with Emma. Not with anyone. As though it never happened.

Donnie opened the staff meeting saying, "Let's start with some good news. Last night's fundraiser netted the Mobe almost twelve grand, thanks to..." Our eyes made contact, as I vigorously shook my head. "Thanks to the generosity of Roger Wolfson," he concluded, "and, in particular, one anonymous donor." We moved on to reports.

First, I related what Dr. Young had told me at the bookstore. "So my good news is that we'll have medics," I concluded, "and the bad news is... we just might need them."

"All we can do is keep trying to get the permits," Donnie responded. "I'll try reaching Conlisk myself. I'll tell him we can preserve order if we work together."

"Good luck with that," Vern chipped in.

"Either way," Donnie urged, "you've got to get those marshals trained. Anything else, Steve?"

I explained the problem with the colleges, then invited Ronnie to present our report on the progress we did make. She'd totaled the capacity we'd lined up in the churches and synagogues, which was close to 4,900. Then I passed around the copies I'd made of the parks report.

"This is very good," Donnie mused, looking it over. "Let's keep working on the churches, but I can see we'll really need the parks. Jeff, do we have the permit application?"

"We do," Jeff replied, "and I got the name of the Park District superintendent, Thomas Barry. But I still haven't gotten in to see him or anyone else."

"Okay," said Donnie. "How about you two guys work on the application this week, so we can submit it right after the board meeting?"

Jeff and I both nodded. Next, Paul reported on his meetings in Michigan and Wisconsin. "Except for SDS, which is split for now," he concluded, "the New Left is on board. But they want to know what to expect. If there's gonna be trouble, they'll want to be prepared. The pacifist groups are more ambivalent. And the local McCarthy campaigns said they'd take their cue from the candidate."

"That's what I've been hearing from around the country," Donnie added. "The new thing is that Allard Lowenstein now has something called the Coalition for an Open Convention. He dropped in here on Friday, and claimed he can mobilize a hundred thousand McCarthy kids for an anti-Humphrey rally at Soldier Field during Convention Week."

Paul commented. "With his political connections, he just might get a permit for it. And then lots of those kids might join up with us. Anyway, tomorrow night, I'll meet with the Chicago Peace Council. The Yippies will apply for their permits today. They want part of Lincoln Park that week for what they're calling a 'Festival of Life,' plus Soldier Field for a closing rally on the 30th. But I sure wish I knew what SDS had in mind."

"Yes," Donnie responded. "We all do. It's a tough twist of fate that their national leadership is meeting on the same day as ours. Over the weekend, though, they invited us to make a presentation. Paul, you have credibility with them. Can you do it? It'll be in Hammond, only a half-hour drive." Paul nodded assent.

"Jeff is visiting his parents in New York this weekend," he continued. "So, Steve, can you join me at the board meeting? You'll present the reports, and I'll present the plan of action."

I asked, "Can I let you know tomorrow?"

"That'll be fine. By the way, you can tell Cat we'll be flying to Cleveland instead of driving, so you'll be back home early the same night."

"Okay," he continued. "This week, I'll be talking to Steering Committee members so we can come up with a proposal to the board for Convention Week. So far, all we've discussed is the main event: a peaceful march to the Amphitheater on the 28th, the night of the nomination."

Vern asked, "Are we gonna shut it down?"

"We won't have to," Paul interjected. "If we can surround it with enough people, they won't be able to get in or out. They'll have to shut it down themselves. It'll implode."

This was the first I'd heard of that scenario, but it did strike me as a good idea.

That discussion went no further, so I didn't mention it to Cat. But I did tell her most of what happened, and asked if she had a problem with me going to Cleveland.

She asked, "Can you get back that same night?"

"Donnie says we'll fly both ways. We'll be back at O'Hare around dinnertime, maybe just a little later."

"You should go, Steve. It's a big opportunity for you to meet more of the Mobe's leadership. Before you leave, tell me what time you'll be back so I won't have to worry. But can we reserve Sunday for ourselves?"

I agreed to both requests. Then she asked, "Now, what else is on your mind?"

"What else? Nothing else."

"I know there's something. I can see it on your face. Tell me what it is."

"I said there's nothing!" I barked, which I knew gave me away as soon as the words left my mouth.

She kept pounding at it until I gave in. I told her about the big donation, and how sleazy it made me feel.

"So Emma had it right," she observed. "That woman was coming on to you. If I'd been a little later showing up, she might've invited you over, and not for a cup of tea. And you had no idea?"

"Right. I thought we were just having a conversation. I was trying to, you know, mingle."

"But you enjoyed the flattery. After all, you had the complete attention of a glamorous older woman. Admit that."

"Okay," I conceded. "Look, this is all new to me."

"Now suppose you and I weren't together, and she did invite you to go across the street to her house?"

"If you and I weren't together? I hadn't thought about that. To be honest, I guess I might've been intrigued."

"Not just intrigued. You would've been turned on. You would've gone home with her in a heartbeat."

"Gosh, maybe so."

"But you're telling me this exotic creature as much as offered herself to you, and you weren't tempted, even a little?"

"Jeez, no."

"Not even a little fantasy of what it might be like, what it might be like to undress her? To have her undress you? To *fuck* her?"

I'd never heard Cat use that word, not that way. "No," I protested. "Nothing like that. I told you how I felt."

"Okay then. Tell me why. What was the difference?"

"The difference was you, Cat. I don't need anyone else. I don't want anyone else. That phone number on the check violated *us*."

"So why are you beating yourself up?" I had no answer to that.

"Look," she continued, "the only things you're guilty of are naïveté and a typically needy male ego. Not all the predators out there are men, you know."

"Cat," I conceded, "I'm glad we talked this out. I made a huge mistake trying to keep it to myself. Now would you hold me? Please?"

"On one condition. Promise me again never, ever to keep anything from me, especially anything that's causing you pain. You've promised this before, but this time you have to really mean it."

I gave her my promise, stretched out and put my head in her lap. It took much stroking and caressing, though, until the tension in my body found release. While everything I'd told her up to now was the truth, the promise was a lie. Trouble was brewing around the convention, and it weighed heavily on my mind. But I wasn't going to worry her, or get into an argument over it. Not unless, and not until, I absolutely had to.

Chapter 59

The rest of the week flew by. I had five clergy meetings on Tuesday and Wednesday, and lined up space for almost a thousand more people. Jeff and I worked on drafting permit applications until Friday afternoon. I wondered whether we were spinning our wheels with this, since he still hadn't gotten any city officials to return his calls. But we couldn't give them an excuse to deny the permits just because of a late submission.

Before I knew it, July 20th arrived. Cat and I were on our way out to O'Hare. She'd decided to stay with me until I got on the plane in case my claustrophobia kicked in. I was glad she did because, as soon as we got into the airport, I broke into a cold sweat. The noise, the crush of people rushing around, the sheer size of the place, overwhelmed me. She held my arm tight and got me to the boarding gate. With a parting kiss, she turned me over to Donnie. As he and I headed for the plane, she called out to say she'll be watching at the window to ensure it got off the ground safely.

"I'll check with the airline to make sure you've landed okay," she added. "And don't miss your flight coming back. I'll be right here, waiting."

I felt guilty, knowing she'd spend the day worrying whether I would get back safely. The flight took only ninety minutes. Also, the airline had an excellent safety record, which I knew because she'd researched it during the week. But I also knew that wouldn't keep her from worrying. Suddenly I found myself worrying too, about whether she'd be safe driving home through all the traffic. I'd have to call as soon as the plane landed.

A fine pair of neurotics we are, I thought. Anyway, the claustrophobia did dissipate once I got on the half-empty plane.

"This other rally," I brought up when we were in the air, "the one Lowenstein is organizing. If it attracts a hundred thousand McCarthy supporters, like he says, what'll those people be doing overnight?"

"Oh, I don't know," Donnie replied with a sneer. "That's his problem."

"You don't like the guy?"

"It's not that. I don't know him well enough to like him or not. But I do know enough not to trust him." Lowering his voice so only I heard him, he explained. "Look, Lowenstein got his start in politics almost twenty years ago, when he got elected president of the National Student Association. He parlayed that into a job on the staff of (guess who?) Senator Hubert H. Humphrey. In '64, he joined the Freedom Summer Project in Mississippi, where the FBI's undermining tactics included branding its leaders as Communists. He piggybacked on that red-baiting campaign to further his own ambition, selling out great Black leaders like Bob Moses. And then, only a year ago, we found out the NSA, where his career began, was secretly funded and controlled by the CIA."

"I didn't know any of this," I responded. "First I heard of him was his speech at the Blackstone last November, introducing McCarthy. That was one hell of a speech."

"Sure it was," Donnie agreed. "I heard it on the radio. But did you notice how it totally eclipsed the candidate's speech? Whose event was that anyway?"

"That night, I was kind of wondering the same thing. But what do you think about his Soldier Field rally? Those kids might join us afterward. It seems to me that the more people who come to Chicago, the better."

"That might be. But look at it this way. His rally, if it happens, will be on the first day of the convention. If he's had anyone lining up overnight accommodations, you'd know about it by now, wouldn't you? So his people will probably leave Chicago that same night. Our ranks might be smaller, not larger, because of it. His actual main purpose could be to co-opt the antiwar movement. And also to build his own political base. In November, he'll be on the ballot for Congress."

Learning something new every day, I thought.

Inside the terminal, I raced to a phone and called Cat, but got a busy signal. "Let's go," Donnie urged. "We need a cab."

This airport wasn't as big, as crowded, or as intimidating as O'Hare, and we rushed right through it. Right near the front entrance, I spotted another bank of phones.

"I need a minute," I said, running over to one. To my relief, Cat answered on the first ring.

"It's me," I told her, "We've landed. And I already miss you."

"Oh, I miss you too. I just got off the phone with the airline."

"I know. And did I tell you I love you?"

"Oh, really? Then how about a kiss?"

I sent a loud smack through the phone, and she sent one back. We followed that with a couple more. By now, Donnie was growing visibly impatient.

"Steve, let's go!" he insisted.

"Got to go," I said. "Back at 7:30."

"Okay. Be careful. And don't miss that flight. I'll be waiting."

I hung up smiling, and joined Donnie in a mad rush to the taxi stand.

At our destination, we found several dozen people milling around the meeting room, with still more drifting in. I'd had enough mingling to last me awhile, so I went off in search of coffee. Dellinger was getting things started when I got back.

Donnie waved me up front. Where've you been?" he whispered.

"Went for coffee and got a little lost."

"Oh. I thought you went to make a phone call. Anyway, here we go. You'll be up soon."

Ten minutes later, I was summarizing the progress we'd made on housing, marshal recruitment, and medical support. I also gave a short financial report, based on numbers Donnie had given me. I thought I sounded reasonably coherent, painting a picture of a staff that had things mostly under control. As soon as I finished, someone called out, "What about the permits?"

"We've been working on the applications," I explained. "But we can't submit them until you authorize it. The deadline's a week from now, and we'll only need a day or two to finish."

"What do you hear from the city?" another asked.

"Well, not much so far," I admitted. "Dr. Quentin Young of the MCHR met with the Police Superintendent, and got a commitment that the cops will leave his medics alone. Donnie's planning to meet with him too, so maybe we can coordinate security together. We've left messages for other officials, including a deputy mayor, but they haven't called us back yet."

"Right," came another comment. "And they never will."

This turned into kind of a hubbub, and I looked over at Dave pleadingly. "Good job," he commented, standing next to me and nodding to my seat. I couldn't get back to it fast enough.

He held his hands in the air, and everyone settled down. "Now, let's hear the Steering Committee's proposal for Convention Week activities. Then everyone will have their say."

"It's simple," Donnie began. "We're proposing two marches during the week. The first one is through the Loop to Grant Park, our staging area, where we'll hold a rally with speeches and music. The other one, the big one, on nomination night, from the park to the Amphitheater, then another rally right outside the convention. We'll also do some picketing at delegates' hotels. And we're setting up movement centers where your groups can organize your own meetings and workshops. There's no good reason why this can't all go off peacefully."

He stood back, and Dave invited comments and questions. At first, it seemed everyone was calling out at the same time, but he quickly got things orderly again. The debate was passionate, but I found it kind of boring. I'd been hearing the same arguments for months. Some left groups claimed we'd be justifying 'the system' by making a big deal of the convention, and risk being subsumed by the McCarthy campaign. Mainstream liberals worried that any demonstrations would hurt his chances of getting the nomination. (*What chances?* I thought.) Strong voices, though, also spoke in support of the Steering Committee's proposal. As the afternoon wore on, Donnie took the floor again, raising a question to which the protest's doubters had no answer.

"Suppose we cancel the whole thing," he said. "Will that let Humphrey skate through the week without opposition? No, it won't. But who'll become the new voice of the antiwar movement? Allard Lowenstein, that's who!"

At the mention of that name, booing and hissing erupted. Apparently, Donnie had struck a raw nerve. There seemed to be broad agreement on one thing, at least.

"Right," he continued. "We need to be there not only to protest the war, but also to maintain the integrity of our movement. We're not going to Chicago to support any politicians. We're going there to end this fucking war. And the whole world will be watching Americans standing up to their own government, putting their bodies on the line to do it. And yes, with or without Boss Daley's permission."

Through the entire cantankerous debate, Dave Dellinger never once raised his voice or cut anyone off. He also read the room and knew, as I did, that the best result possible would be a limited one. He steered the way to a consensus that preparation would move forward, but everything would be reviewed at another meeting in two weeks, in or near Chicago. We were on a short leash, but still moving ahead.

A half hour into the flight back to O'Hare, I asked Donnie the big question.

"Here's what I'm wondering. You and Jeff have been knocking yourselves out to get cooperation from the city. Zero results. He and I will get the permit applications in this week. But what happens if we don't get the permits?"

"We can't back off," he replied. "You know that."

"I do. But what then? And why? Is there a strategy here, somewhere?"

"Steve, we went into this hoping to make our point through a peaceful protest. We knew that was the only way to get the most people. We wanted families with children to come. We wanted young people, old people, everyone who wants peace and stands for justice. Now Daley is threatening violence to scare away people who can't afford to be locked up or hit over the head, or worse. But if the cops do attack, however many of us there are after all those threats, we'll make an even bigger point."

"A bigger point?"

"Yes. We'll expose the dark heart of this rotten system that disguises itself behind the veneer of a phony democracy. We'll expose the brutal essence of U.S. imperialism, now venting its wrath on *its own* people, for the entire world to see. And thousands of young people will be radicalized for the battles still ahead. Whatever happens, we win."

"We can't fight them," I countered. "They have all the guns. You know what's happened already this year. What would we be leading people into?"

Donnie's eyes blazed. "And what about the Vietnamese? What terrors do they face, day in and day out, night in and night out? Massacres. Bombing raids. Napalm. A whole generation of children lost, disfigured, murdered. *All in our names.* So what makes Americans so special? Do we take a moral stand only when no risk or sacrifice is involved? What the hell is that?"

His outburst stunned me. "Well, yeah, I guess you're right," I murmured, closing my eyes to end the discussion. I tried struggling with his reasoning, but knew he really was absolutely right. *What, after all, is the alternative? But what will I tell Cat?* I was getting a headache. My mind cleared a bit, though, as the airport lights came into view. I had to get off that plane.

Cat and I embraced as though we'd been separated for months. Donnie clapped me on the back and went on his way.

"It's kind of late," Cat mentioned as we came up for air. "Are you hungry?"

Calling up my best Humphrey Bogart impersonation, I growled, "Only for you, baby. Only for you."

Chapter 60

Sunday morning, sipping our wake-up coffee, Cat announced, "Finally a day for us, a day off from the war. Remember, you promised?"

I'd been looking forward to this too, but Cat's words triggered some of Donnie's in my head. *Day in and day out. Night in and night out.* I wondered whether I was entitled to a day off, without at least feeling guilty. But I nodded and agreed. Pointing to the gray skies out the window, I added, "But I guess it won't be a beach day. Looks like rain."

Cat frowned into her coffee cup, muttering, "And now you have another busy week coming up. What about our day for us? I was so looking forward to being at the beach today."

"Look," I responded. "The most important thing I need to do for the Mobe this week is get the permit apps finished and submitted. I'm sure Jeff and I can get this done by Thursday. Then we can hit the beach on Friday. I'll take the whole day off."

Her face brightened. "Okay, that's a date. But today, you still need a break from the war. Let's get some chores out of the way. I'll do grocery shopping and you do the laundry. Tonight, I'll make a special dinner. I'll invite Emma to join us."

"Sounds like a plan," I agreed. "Just tell me what time I should be here for the groceries. And now, I'll make you a special breakfast."

"Okay. I'll be back from the market at 3:30."

Over fluffy Swiss cheese and spinach omelets with home fries, I filled her in on the board meeting. She listened patiently, then commented, "That's enough for today. The war can wait until tomorrow." I was getting comfortable now with a day off from the war, even if it meant doing housework. Laundry was a good distraction.

But it wasn't meant to be. The phone rang right after Cat left on her errands. It was Nicky Jarvis.

"I promised to bring you up to date after the SDS National Council meeting," he said, "so I'm keeping my word. Got time today?"

"Sure," I said, "and thanks for calling. Can you meet me at my office?"

"You're going downtown?"

"No, my other office: The High Street Laundromat."

So today wouldn't be a total escape, but I did need to hear his report. I was glad to see Nicky come through the door a half-hour later.

"The news is mixed," he explained. "Some National Council members came totally opposed, because the last thing SDS wants is to get co-opted into an electoral campaign, for McCarthy or anyone else. We did end up agreeing on a limited participation, though. What made the difference was Paul Haynes' presentation."

"How was that?"

"He made four predictions, which we took seriously since he's inside the Mobe's operation. First, that we'll never get the permits. Second, that protesters will flood in anyway. Third, that Daley will call in the troops and turn Chicago into an armed camp. Fourth, that confrontation is inevitable."

"We're still trying to keep this peaceful, Nicky. But he might very well be right."

"It made sense to me," he continued. "But he also issued a challenge. He argued that SDS has been in the vanguard of the antiwar movement, that Convention Week will mark the apex of that movement to date, and that we'd cast ourselves into irrelevance if we didn't make our presence felt. 'And what national New Left organization,' he asked, 'has more experience fighting the pigs than SDS?' Well, he'd won many of us over by then."

"So what happened?"

"The delegates struggled with competing arguments all day. We ended up agreeing to send our best organizers and street-fighters to Chicago, with two missions. First, organize the McCarthy kids. Show them they're on a dead-end path and get them to join us in the revolution. Second, disrupt the convention with guerrilla actions. Members will make their own individual decisions. But the SDS hard core will be there, and we'll be ready."

After Nicky left, I finished the laundry, brought it home and put everything away, troubled the whole time by his report. It wasn't only the possibility of SDS provocations. The main thing was Paul's analysis, and my sense that he was correct. All we wanted was a peaceful expression of dissent. But Mayor Daley, and now SDS, were gearing up for battle. And Cat was on her way home from the market, under the impression I'd taken a day off from the war.

After we put the groceries away, Cat wanted me to rest. "You didn't sleep well last night and you're tired," she insisted. "Stretch out on the couch. Pour yourself a drink and put on some music. Just relax. I'll get dinner started."

I thought she was being overly solicitous, but I did have a lot to think about, or try not to think about. I turned the radio to the classical station, and pulled a volume of Lenin's essays out of our "Summer Reading" box. The entry that caught my eye was titled, "Revolutionary Adventurism."

It was all Mozart coming from the radio, which seemed to have a calming effect, and the smells wafting over from the kitchen promised something wonderful. I glanced up at Cat in her apron, slicing and dicing, boiling and simmering. What more could I ask for? I put the book down, closed my eyes, and tried to lose myself in the music and the sweet scents of spices in the air. Soon, I drifted off to dreamland.

Cat and I were walking through the park, holding hands on a sunny fall day. Not a cloud in the deep blue sky, not a care in the world. Flowers still in bloom, the grass still green, but the leaves changing, almost before our eyes, toward a blazing landscape of red, yellow and orange. Overhead, birds cheerfully chirped. We wandered into a small clearing in a grove of trees, stretched out on the soft grass and cuddled. I closed my eyes, enjoying the sunshine peeking through the trees and Cat's warm body against mine. A deep sense of peace washed over me.

Suddenly, the ground rumbled beneath us. I opened my eyes and froze in terror. The sky was now an ominous graphite gray, the trees bare of leaves. Thunder boomed in the distance. Or was it something else? Winding through the trees, jogging silently in our direction, then surrounding us, came dozens of massive soldiers, dressed all in black with helmets and gas masks, pointing enormous weapons. Pointing them at us. I looked down at Cat, still lying on the grass with her eyes closed, so innocent, oblivious to the looming threat. I looked back up. They were right on top of us now, their guns' muzzles not two feet away, fingers moving on the triggers. I threw myself on top of Cat, hoping to protect her. But I fell onto bare ground. She was gone, vanished. I was all alone. Alone, frightened and confused. And now, now I was four years old. A thunderclap morphed into a deafening evil laugh.

I jerked up and screamed.

"Steve, wake up!" Cat, at the edge of the couch, shook my shoulders. "Wake up!"

Slowly, fearfully, I forced my eyes open and squeezed out, "What?"

"You were screaming in your sleep. What happened?"

Her face was inches from mine, contorted with worry. Still shaking, I pulled her down into me and sobbed. She held me and kissed the tears away. "It's all right," she murmured. "Everything is okay. I'm here. I'm here for you."

Once I calmed down, she sat up and asked again, "What happened?"

"It was my carnival dream. My nightmare. But a new version, even worse than before." I shuddered, then added, "I'm sorry if I scared you."

"You're soaked in sweat," she observed, lifting me to my feet and leading me to the bathroom. "Take a shower and get fresh clothes on. That should help. Okay?"

"Uh-huh. Yes. Good idea. Wait, did I ruin dinner?"

"No, I'll take care of it. By the time you're out of the shower and dressed, it'll be ready. But leave the doors open, so I can hear you."

With the water streaming nice and hot, I sat down on the shower floor, wrapped myself in my arms and trembled. After a few minutes, the shaking stopped. I stood back up and finished with ice cold water. By the time I got dressed, I did feel better. I hugged Cat and thanked her.

"You're better now?"

"Yes. Much better."

"Good. Everything's ready. Emma will be here any minute."

"Let's not say anything about this," I asked. "Okay?"

She looked deep into my eyes, silently stroking my cheek, before going back to work. I wondered, *What was that?* while I uncorked a bottle of wine and quickly set the table. While Cat brought over her fresh Caesar salad and garlic bread, there was a knock on the door. I welcomed Emma in with a deep, exaggerated flourish.

"Oh, Steve," she laughed, tousling my hair.

As we started in on the salad, Emma announced, "Wonderful news! Ellie won a foundation grant to help her finish the dissertation. They only award one of these each year, in the whole country. And she already has a faculty interview scheduled at UCLA Berkeley. The only problem is that she'll be out there instead of here during Convention Week. But I'm so proud I could burst!"

Cat and I offered a spirited round of applause and congratulations. I proposed a toast, and we clinked glasses. Emma's enthusiasm and joy were so contagious, I'd already forgotten my earlier descent into hell. Or so I thought. The celebration continued as we moved on to the main course, Creole Bouillabaisse.

"So, Steve," Emma asked, bringing us back to business. "How did the board meeting go?"

I gave her a capsule summary of the debate, the same one I'd given Cat in the morning. She listened carefully to my descriptions of how Donnie laid the basis for consensus, and how Dave Dellinger steered it to a decision.

"Dellinger, of course, never disappoints," she commented, "and Donnie knew exactly which buttons to push. You were fortunate to have a front-row seat. It sounds like a master class."

"You're right. I was certainly impressed with them both. But what do you think of Donnie's reasoning?"

"First of all," she explained, "I've always seen Lowenstein as a shameless self-promoter. He's a brilliant man, and he's accomplished many good things along the way, but the advancement of his own career has always come first. It would be bad enough to let the movement be co-opted into the McCarthy campaign, which we know is now doomed. It would be worse, it would be fatal, to turn it over to an opportunist like Lowenstein."

"And what about the Yippies?"

"Oh, they're wonderful. They epitomize the rebellious energy of your generation. They, and the hippie crowd they've come out of, will change American culture for the good. But they have no political program, and the energy they've harnessed isn't sustainable, not with all the drugs. Eventually, it'll burn out. What we need is a political movement with a realistic program for peace and social justice. The Mobe can't be that either, because it's a single-issue coalition. For now, though, it's on the right track. Something new might grow out of Convention Week."

While I hung on Emma's every word, Cat slipped back to the kitchen counter.

"Emma brought us pastries from the bakery," she announced. "Let's have dessert in the living room."

Chapter 61

Cat and Emma settled on the couch, myself in the easy chair, a tray of pastries on the table, and each of us with a steaming cup of fresh-brewed java. I leaned back, inhaled the coffee, and exhaled from a place deep inside. I felt relaxed, comfortable, happy, so recovered from only a short time earlier. But not for long.

Cat finished her cannoli, sat straight up, folded her hands on her lap and demanded, "Okay. Now what's going on?"

"What do you mean?" I stammered, taken aback. "We've been talking about what's going on."

"Not all of it," she retorted. "You're holding something back. Do you think I can't tell? Overnight, you tossed and turned, moaning in your sleep. And then this afternoon, you came close to a nervous breakdown. That scared the hell out of me. So don't tell me there's nothing else."

She began sniffling, and picked up a napkin to wipe her eyes.

"Damn it," she continued, increasingly agitated, "you promised me only last week you wouldn't hold anything back, especially anything that was causing you pain. How many times have we talked about this? How many times have you broken your promise? How many times have you lied to me? *To me?*"

Emma reached out, taking one of our hands in each of hers. "This is the person who loves you most in all this world," she said, fixing her eyes on mine. "If there's anything, and I mean anything, that you don't feel safe sharing with her, you might as well walk out that door right now. Otherwise, there will be3 nothing but more pain... more pain for both of you."

The ultimatum staggered me. Emma dropped our hands and sat back against the cushions, waiting. Cat stared at me, her face dissolving into tears. "Steve," she cried, "why are you doing this to me? What about us?"

I couldn't take it any longer. Without a rock to crawl under, I gave in. I told them about the challenge Donnie posed on the plane, the analysis Paul laid out to SDS, and its decision to join us with a quasi-guerrilla force. My monologue must have gone on for half an hour. "So, we're stuck between a rock and a hard place," I concluded. "Cat, I didn't want to worry you, not as long as there might still be a possibility of heading off violence. And yes, I guess it has been driving me crazy."

Cat's body lost its rigidity as she collapsed against the cushions. "I knew it," she murmured. "I knew it all along. It'll be a bloodbath, and you'll need to be right in the middle of it, won't you?"

I was helpless. She was coming apart before my eyes. But how could I reassure and comfort her while knowing she was right? I did feel I had to be on the front lines. I saw no other moral choice.

"And I knew it," she went on through her tears. "I knew I'd lose you to this. Have I've lost you already?"

Then she delivered the knockout punch. "Oh, what am I doing here? I should've left you after the Civic Center debacle, when I still thought I could!"

Now Emma sat straight up and declared, "Hold on nowm, Cat. Stop this! Why are you here? Because you love this man. And he's here because he loves you. No-one's losing anyone, and neither of you is going anywhere. We just need to think this through."

Cat wiped her face and looked up at her, wide-eyed. "But..."

"But nothing," Emma scolded. "Listen to me, you two. You're not the first people on earth to face such a dilemma. Everyone with a moral core, a social conscience, has to grapple with it at some time or other. If thousands of people didn't risk life and limb, the Civil Rights Movement would've been nothing but hot air. It wouldn't have changed a thing. But what good will it do anyone if we go off looking for ways to risk our lives at every opportunity? What's the answer? Well, there isn't one. You two have to work this out for yourselves. Together. But you both must stop going off the deep end. You have to work with each other from trust, not from fear."

"And secondly," she continued at a slower pace, "nothing is inevitable. You're not on an out-of-control train hurtling toward an abyss, Steve. Lots of decisions will be made in the next five weeks. Made by all the parties involved, including you. There's no need to jump to conclusions. You're still working on the permits, aren't you?"

"Yes. But it seems no-one expects us to get them."

"So first concentrate on making those applications bullet-proof. Work whatever contacts you have at City Hall. Find people who can influence the decisions it makes, from the outside. Take things one step at a time."

"But what if…"

"What if? What if? What if the sun explodes and we all turn to dust? You can't let what-ifs run your lives. You don't need to decide today what you'll do in five weeks. You do need to do whatever you can. Today, tomorrow, this week. You need to stay calm and use your heads."

Emma began panting and coughing. She leaned back and put up her hands. "I'm all right," she wheezed. "Okay, a little tired. A glass of water would help." I ran to get it.

"I have an idea," Cat said, coming back to her practical self. "Why not plan a big event that doesn't require any permits?"

"I don't think anyone's thought of that," I responded. "Any ideas?"

"Not yet, but let's try to come up with something. We'll do it together."

"Now you're talking," Emma responded, downing her water. "But if you don't mind, there's an old lady here who's up past her bedtime and needs her meds. Before I leave, though, I want to see a big hug."

Cat and I stood up and embraced. I felt like I'd gotten a reprieve from execution. We each held an arm out, inviting Emma to join us. We murmured our thanks, until she broke free and said good-night.

While we cleaned up, I guessed, "Emma knew everything, didn't she?"

"Only what I knew, which wasn't much. You really scared me this afternoon. So, while you were in the shower, I called her. That was before you asked me to keep your nightmare between the two of us. Anyway, it was her idea to deal with it after dinner. And it was better that way, wasn't it?"

I had to agree. I was still agitated when we climbed into bed, though, and too depleted for sex. We just noodled together. Nothing calmed me more than Cat's touch. But I had to ask one question.

"Did you really want to leave me?"

"I never wanted to leave." she explained, "But staying, and constantly worrying about you, was driving me crazy. Still, I knew that if I left, I'd be miserable, and I wouldn't stop worrying anyway. I felt I couldn't stay, but I couldn't go either. No good choices."

No good choices, I thought. *Just like the convention.* "Next time, please, throw dishes at me," I pleaded. "Slam me with a frying pan. But don't talk, don't even think, about leaving. I'll try harder. I promise. But we have to work these things out. Together. It would kill me to lose you."

"I couldn't leave you even if I wanted to," she admitted. "I know that now."

"Then I guess we're stuck with each other," I echoed, beginning to settle down.

"And besides," she whispered, nibbling on my ear, "who would take care of my little boy?"

She was only kidding, but she had it right. I sometimes did feel like a little boy: Vulnerable, overwhelmed by forces totally out of my control. But I also felt loved, and that was what allowed me to sleep.

Opening my eyes in the morning, though, I saw only a note on Cat's pillow. I jerked up in panic. *Did she change her mind? Was this her good-bye?* I forced myself to pick it up.

"At the gym," it read. "Back soon." It was signed with our usual arrow-pierced heart, followed by "PS – I have an idea!" I breathed a sigh of relief and looked at the clock. It was past seven. Still a little groggy, I roused myself so breakfast could be waiting for her.

A half-hour later, she breezed in and planted a kiss on my cheek. I wrapped my arms around her, held her head to my chest and rained kisses on it.

"Mmm. That feels good," she purred, "but why the big welcome?"

"You scared me, leaving a note on the pillow. You were gone, Cat, and I didn't know if you were coming back."

She stood away, squeezed my arms and looked me in the eye. "I meant what I told you last night. I'm *never* not coming back. So let's not have any more of that talk. Or that worry."

"Well then," I smiled, "the pancakes are ready. You must be starving."

"Why didn't you wake me?" I asked, once we began eating.

"I didn't have the heart to wake you this morning. You had such an exhausting weekend, and I thought you needed the sleep."

"Well, you thought right. I'm still a little bleary. But I don't like the idea of you being at the gym without me. You know why."

"You can stop worrying about that, Steve. Remember, I've been learning how to handle myself. I've got some good moves now if I need them."

"Well, okay I guess. But did anyone bother you?"

"No, no-one bothered me."

"Good. But your note said you had an idea. What idea?"

"Oh yes. I woke up with it. See, I read in the paper that LBJ's sixtieth birthday is August 27th, the second day of the convention. The bigwigs are planning a big party that night, somewhere nearby."

"What does his birthday party have to do with us?" I asked. "There'll be so much security, we'll never get within a mile of it."

"That's my idea. We can throw our own party: An *Anti*-Birthday Party. The Mobe has a little money now. Right?"

"I guess so. That fund-raiser was very successful."

"Yes, thanks to you-know-who. Anyway, we should find a place for a free antiwar concert. That wouldn't need a permit. It'll get people out of danger, and it can be fun."

"Cat, that's a great idea. I'll bring it up at the staff meeting."

"Good. If it gets a green light, I'll call around and find an available place. Then all we'll need is someone who can produce a good show."

"You're really into this," I observed.

"If it'll help keep you out of trouble." She sent me out the door with a reminder. "Don't forget. Beach date Friday."

Donnie's summary of the board meeting set the tone for the staff. "We have to get all our ducks in a row before the next one," he insisted. "Otherwise, this thing can still be called off."

I offered a quick update on my clergy encounters, but emphasized how much we'll still need the parks. Jeff promised we would get the permit applications done this week, to which I added, "By Thursday." He also reported that the National Lawyers Guild offered to handle calls in case of arrests.

Paul reported that the Chicago Peace Council was already raising money for a bail fund. His report on the SDS National Council was largely as I'd heard it from Nicky, except that he left out his own participation. He said he'd be meeting with more Midwest peace and antiwar groups during the week.

"I'll be travelling for a few days too," Donnie said, "so let's get some more balls in the air. Vern, besides setting up the marshals' training, I'd like you to make arrangements for the next board meeting. Dellinger will be spending that weekend at Wolfson's house, so look for a meeting place in Highland Park."

"Sure," Vern agreed, "and that gives me another idea. Let's try for another fundraiser out there. Dave will be a big draw."

"Great idea. You can start with the guest list from last week's party. With luck, you'll find someone who can put an event together quickly."

"Can I throw in another thought?" I asked.

"Of course. What's that?"

I introduced Cat's idea for an Anti-Birthday Party. Everyone liked it, but Donnie warned, "We can't spread ourselves too thin. Who's gonna work on this?"

"Cat said she'd look for a place," I reported. "I'm sure we'll be able to present something concrete next week. What we'll still need, though, is someone who can line up the talent."

"I know just the person," Paul suggested. "Abbie Hoffman." We looked at him like he'd lost his mind.

"He's running the Yippie festival, not our protest," Donnie said.

"Right," Paul argued, "but he's been booking talent for months. Who knows how many bands he's already got coming to Chicago? For this one event, why can't we work together?"

"All right. I'll get ahold of him. Now, just a few more things. Steve and Jeff, these have to be on you. A press conference on Monday, somewhere in the Loop. Also line up churches, union halls, campuses for Convention Week movement centers. I know this can't all get done this week, so set your own priorities, starting with the permit apps. Ronnie, can you assign volunteers to help with some of this?"

"Of course," she agreed, "and I'll help too."

Ronnie had been so quiet during the meeting that I'd forgotten she was in the room. But there she was, diligently taking notes on everything, so none of us would forget what we were supposed to do. She and Jeff and I huddled after the meeting, and divided up the work. My main assignment, besides the permit applications, was to arrange for the press conference.

Back at the shop, Cat said she'd get to work on party preparations right away. Emma liked that idea too, although she seemed a little concerned about coordinating with the Yippies. Mostly, she looked happy to see Cat and I in a better place than we were in the night before.

"Brad Bennett called the shop today," Cat told me. "Emma knows to hand me the phone if anyone asks for Felicia."

"What did he say?"

"Remember he told us he'd be speaking at an important conference later this month? It turns out it's the annual meeting of the Federation of American Scientists, which took an official position recently against any use of bio-chem weaponry. He'll expose von Helsinger's doomsday machine, and line up opposition. That's coming up next week."

"Sounds terrific. I'm glad to hear it."

"Oh, but it gets better. He said he'd be travelling during most of August, but he wants to give us an in-person update before he leaves. So he invited us up to the country house a week from Saturday. And that's still not the best part."

"Stop the suspense," I pleaded. "Out with it." Cat's excitement was making it hard for her to sit still.

"And he said they'll be leaving after lunch. And we, you and me, could have the house for the rest of the weekend!"

"Wow!" I exclaimed. "Oh, but wait. We'll probably have a fundraiser Saturday night, and the board meeting is on Sunday. I'm supposed to arrange a press conference for the next day. I don't know if I can get away. What did you tell him?"

"Of course, I thanked him for the invitation and said I'd have to talk to you. He said to call back any time. But don't you remember how we loved it up there? The house, the beach, the lake? And it would be just the two of us! And no-one but Emma would know the phone number!"

"I know, I know. Let me try to work things out."

"Oh, alright," she said dejectedly, looking down and twirling her hair with a finger.

As we headed for the door, Emma fixed me with a stare that said, *"Find a way."*

Chapter 62

Jeff and I went to work on the three applications: One to the Park District requesting that it waive its normal 11 p.m. closing time during Convention Week, for twelve specified parks; another to the Department of Streets for an afternoon march on the 28th, from Civic Center Plaza through the Loop to Grant Park, where we would hold a rally; and the third for that evening's march, from Grant Park to the convention itself. This was the most important one, so we included a detailed route, and a diagram showing how our rally wouldn't interfere with the delegates' access to or from the building.

We divided the first drafts between us, then traded them for revisions. We did it again. And again, and again. Thursday morning, Jeff argued, "Look, this is getting ridiculous. We're preparing a few permit applications, not a Supreme Court brief. And we're running out of time. Let's wrap it up."

I had to agree on both points. I desperately wanted those applications to be bulletproof, though, since so many problems would be solved if the permits did somehow come through. Now we had only one blank left to fill: the number of people expected at these events. Of course, we had no idea how many would actually show up and participate. We decided to write random numbers on scraps of paper, put them in a bowl and pull one out. The winning number was a very optimistic 150,000.

Ronnie typed up the final documents. Jeff brought the march and rally applications to City Hall. I delivered the parks application to the Park District office at Soldier Field. The submissions were time-stamped July 25th, a few days ahead of the deadline. The secretary at the Park District even scheduled an appointment for me with the Acting Superintendent, Thomas Barry, for the following Wednesday.

"Our first meeting with a city official," I told Cat excitedly. "We're finally getting somewhere."

"I'd like to think so," she replied with a note of skepticism. "But it's only a beginning, and time is running short. Let's see what happens next week. Anyway, I may have found a good place for LBJ's Anti-Birthday Party. It's the Chicago Coliseum, a big old rundown stadium. It's serviceable, though, and it can hold 10,000 people. It's only a few blocks from Grant Park and it's cheap. I typed up the details."

"Great. Let me see."

"You can read it once, but then you'll put it away until Monday. You're off duty now, and we're going to the beach tomorrow. Right?"

We did spend all Friday afternoon at the Jackson Park Beach. It was a hot day, and the beach was crowded. We started off with our usual negotiation over Cat's cover-up and floppy hat, but she discarded them anyway the minute we got settled.

"Don't you see you're being paranoid?" she demanded. "No-one's bothered me here, and you're always close by anyway. Besides, this is a public beach and I have a right to be here wearing a bathing suit, just like everyone else. Why should I have to hide?"

"I know," I admitted, "and you're right. But I see the guys leering. I know what they're thinking. And I can't forget what happened at the barbeque."

"Neither can I. But that was before my self-defense class, which finished yesterday. Mrs. Murchison says I can handle myself now in a situation like that."

"Okay. Prove it to me. Let's see what you got."

We both smiled as we stood. "I'm going to walk away," she instructed. "You come up from behind, and do what he did."

Following her instructions, I snuck up from behind and pinned her arms. As she wriggled, apparently trying to get away, I noticed we were attracting attention. It looked like I was assaulting her, and rescuers were on their way.

"Now, do what he did next," she instructed.

As I lifted my hands toward her breasts, her heel slammed down on my instep and I let go.

"Ouch! That hurts," I exclaimed, thinking the demonstration was complete.

It wasn't. Cat twirled around, and swept her foot through my Achilles tendons. Next thing I knew, I was flat on my back, with her foot on my chest. Cat reached her hand out and helped me to my feet.

"That was good," I remarked. "I'm impressed."

She still wasn't finished. "Now, come at me from the front, like you're attacking with a knife."

She stepped away, turned to me, bent her knees a little for balance, and beckoned. I did as I was told, charging ahead with an imaginary knife in my right hand. She stood her ground, watching intently. When I got close, she pivoted, grabbed the knife hand and used my own momentum to pull me past her, totally off balance. On my way, she tripped me and gave a little push. I landed with my face in the sand. Our growing audience applauded.

After two more humiliating demonstrations, I held out my hands and pleaded, "Enough!" She helped me to my feet, and we both took a bow.

"I'm really impressed," I marveled. "You've learned so much."

"And is your mind eased some now?"

"I guess so, but I don't really think my alarms will go out of service. My body's a bit sore, though."

"Sorry if I was a bit rough, but I had a point to make. You know, we better go for a swim. You're all covered in sand. Come on. I'll race you."

I got a little revenge by snatching her up and tossing her into the waves, but her screams turned to joyous cackles each time.

The rest of our weekend was quiet. Cat must have asked a dozen times about accepting the Bennetts' invitation. Each time, I had to tell her I wouldn't know until after Monday's staff meeting. That satisfied neither one of us.

On Sunday, Emma showed us a *Times* article that summarized a report issued by the U.S. military command. It said 26,097 American soldiers had been killed since the Vietnam War ramped up, almost 40 percent of them just during the first half of 1968. The corresponding number for "enemy soldiers" was 372,636. It made no mention of the countless civilian deaths, let alone how many of these were women and children.

The U.S. now had 535,000 soldiers stationed in Vietnam. Our B-52s were averaging 120 bombing missions every single day. The war was escalating, and threatening to spread throughout Southeast Asia. Cat and I weren't the only ones wondering whether, in four weeks time, it would come to Chicago as well.

Vern kicked off Monday's meeting, announcing he had good news. "Ronnie gave me a typed-up copy of the Wolfson party's guest list, in alphabetical order, and I only had to get halfway through the A's. We're all set for a Saturday night fundraiser. I lined up a place for the board meeting too."

"Good," Donnie responded. "Where?"

"I found a community college in Highland Park with an active antiwar group. They reserved a meeting space for us. About the fundraiser, the news is even better. If Dave will be staying at Wolfson's house, he'll only have to walk across the street. It'll be at the home of a woman named Merrie Alexander. She's enthusiastic about hosting it."

Donnie gave me a look, and I shook my head. Vern's report made up my mind about the coming weekend.

"That's great," I told them. "I can't make it, though. I have to be out of town. It's an important family thing."

"What about Sunday's board meeting?"

"I'll never get back in time. I'm sorry, but this weekend is out for me. I'll set up Monday's press conference before I leave, though."

"Okay. But we better rent space for it. If you do as good a job as you did the first time, none of the rooms on this floor will be big enough. Here, use this for a deposit." He signed a blank check and handed it to me.

"And here's this," I added, handing him Cat's detail sheet for the Anti-Birthday Party. He nodded, looking it over, and promised to present it to the board.

As soon as our meeting ended, I called Cat. "I've got the weekend off," I reported. "You can call Brad and Melissa."

"You're sure? The whole weekend?"

"It's set in stone." Through the phone, I saw her face brightening.

"I'll call right away. What time will you be home?"

"Well, I'll be meeting with Dr. Young's team at four, so I guess around six."

"Okay. Don't be late. I'll have something special waiting for you."

"There's always something special waiting for me," I mused. "But I have to go now. Lots to do."

I thought a hotel would be the best place to hold the press conference. But finding one in the Loop turned out to be more difficult than I'd expected. The first three I called were fully booked. The next one had a space that sounded perfect, but it suddenly became unavailable when I told the agent I was calling for the Mobe. The same two patterns repeated at a dozen more. Eventually, I found a side-street hotel, the Midland, which had a small ballroom available. I walked over there, checked it out and booked it.

An hour later, Dr. Young introduced me to the doctors and medical students who, along with him, comprised the MCHR's Convention Week Task Force. Their first question concerned the permits. I brought them up to date on the process, concluding, "So it's still too soon to know, but I'll be meeting with the Superintendent of Parks on Wednesday."

"Let's be realistic," one of the doctors responded. "Quentin told us you've been trying for months to get the Daley administration's cooperation. But Superintendent Conlisk told him you most likely will never get it. So what do you really think will happen?"

"We have to take that prediction into account," I replied. "But if the mayor forces us into a confrontation, I think that's what he'll get."

"You'll march on the convention even without a permit?"

"Yes, we will, or at least we'll try. It's the reason people are coming."

"Good," he reacted, completely unfazed. "Then we'll prepare for the worst, and hope it doesn't happen. We just have to give our people fair warning."

"Conlisk did promise, though," I pointed out, "that his cops wouldn't go after the medics."

"Yes, he did," Dr. Young agreed. "But they sometimes get out of control. You've seen that yourself. We need to be ready for anything."

"Right," interjected one of the others. "And this looks as challenging as what we faced in the South. If the crowd is as big as everyone expects it to be, the congestion alone might keep us from reaching people who need our help."

For the next hour, the five of them strategized. I only listened, except to answer occasional questions. Eventually, they decided to station teams of medics at points of likely contact between the police and the protesters, and set up field hospitals in parks and churches. They would send out a national membership mailing, and recruit members within a hundred miles or so by phone. They seemed confident of a sizable turnout, whether or not we got the permits. But they asked me to keep them informed of new developments.

These antiwar doctors impressed me, and I looked forward to telling Cat about the meeting. On the way home, though, I had second thoughts, since discussing preparations for possible injuries would only upset her. But I'd promised not to hold anything back. This was difficult. Hoping to fend off another headache, I decided to focus on what special something she might be cooking up for dinner.

Cat never asked me about that meeting, though. I did get home on time, but the apartment looked empty. Nothing was on the dinner table, nothing was in the oven, and she was nowhere in sight. I was disappointed, and a little worried. Before I could process those thoughts, though, her voice called out from the bedroom, "Appetizer's in here. Come and get it."

I opened the bedroom door, and stood in wonder. There was my Butterscotch Goddess, lying on top of the covers, hands folded behind her head. She was naked, except for the inverted triangle of whipped cream from her breasts all the way down to her own triangle.

"*I said,*" she repeated, "*come and get it!*"

Our actual dinner was late that night.

Chapter 63

As it turned out, finding and booking the Midland Hotel had been the most difficult part of arranging the press conference. I already had my list of press contacts, so all my team had to do was make the calls. Persuasion was no longer necessary. By now, what we were planning, and what the Yippies were planning, had become the talk of the town. Interest and curiosity ran high.

Also, the Mobe's track record was getting mention in the press. Crowd estimates of the October mobilization in D.C. ranged at first from tens of thousands to hundreds of thousands. During the months since, a consensus emerged among the press corps that the Mobe brought at least 100,000 people to Washington that day. So our predictions of that many, or more, coming into Chicago for the convention protests were being taken seriously.

My meeting with Thomas Barry, the Superintendent of Parks, turned out to be a pleasant surprise, since he wasn't at all hostile. He read through our application and suggested a few small changes, which I made by hand. He explained, though, that granting the permits required a vote of the Park District's Board of Commissioners, whose next meeting was scheduled for August 13th. He invited me to make a presentation before the vote. I left there optimistic that we'd get at least some of what we'd asked for, even though we'd have to wait two long weeks to know for sure.

Later, I reported to Jeff and Donnie on that meeting, and on the one with the medics. Donnie said, "That'll be welcome news at the board meeting. Too bad you won't be there to report it yourself."

"Yes, I know," I agreed. "I wish I could, but there's nothing I can do."

"I understand," he said, thankfully not asking what this made-up family emergency was. "But how about an early meeting on Friday?"

"I don't see why not. What is it?"

"I finally heard from Dan Stahl, the deputy mayor whose door Jeff has been banging on for a month. He suggested we meet for breakfast at eight. I'd like both of you to join me."

"Okay. Where?"

"The corner coffee shop. He didn't want to meet in his office, and he didn't want to come up here either."

"It sounds like he doesn't want anyone to know we're meeting," Jeff observed. "A little out of the ordinary, don't you think?"

I also thought it was odd, but it didn't dampen my enthusiasm. I'd be going home with positive news for once.

Cat's response was, "Remember, Emma once told us they always hold back on protest permits until the last minute? Could that be what's happening now?"

"Makes sense," I agreed. "Maybe they figured out the best way to hold the city together during the convention is by granting the permits."

"I hope so," she responded. "But there won't be time for our morning workout that day. We can make up for it on Saturday, because we don't have to leave here until 9:30 or so. Melissa said they'll expect us around eleven, so we can talk over brunch."

Friday morning, Donnie led us into the coffee shop. Spotting Stahl at a booth in the back, he introduced Jeff and me.

"Call me Dan, please," said the deputy mayor. "Let's get our orders in, and then we can talk. By the way, this is on me."

This seemed a promising beginning. Once the waitress took our orders, Donnie laid out our plans for Convention Week. "So as you can see," he concluded as our meals arrived, "most of this will be nowhere near the Amphitheater. And we can work together to make sure everything comes off peacefully."

Dan listened politely. He responded, "Let me be honest with you. I don't think the parks commissioners will let them be used as campgrounds. And marching on the convention is a bad idea, for security reasons. Plan your march somewhere else and I'll get you a permit in no time."

"But on the night of the nomination," Donnie explained, "we have to be outside the convention. That's what this whole thing is about. That's why everyone's coming. You've seen our application, so you know we won't be interfering with the festivities. We just want to exercise our First Amendment rights."

"I'm telling you," Stahl insisted, "it's a bad idea. Find something else to do."

"Look, Dan," Donnie argued, "even if the city doesn't grant the permit, and even if the Mobe doesn't organize the march, people will still descend on the convention. Like I said, that's why they're coming. Wouldn't a well-organized parade to the Amphitheater be better than a quarter million angry people running through the streets, with no planned activity and no place to gather?"

"Well, I guess you'll get your answers soon," Stahl replied. "But these decisions are really up to the Park District, the Police Department and the Department of Streets."

From what even he'd said before, we knew that was bullshit. We knew it would be the mayor making these decisions, but we didn't challenge him. Instead, Donnie proposed, "Dan, I'm one of Mayor Daley's constituents. Get me a meeting with him. I can bring some of our board members. Let's try to work things out."

"I don't know," he answered. "I'll get back to you. But think about what I said."

It was an ominous start to my day. I'd been hoping for an opening, but it sounded instead like a warning.

"What he was really telling us," Donnie predicted afterward, "was to expect trouble if we don't cave in."

"And we can't cave, can we?" Jeff asked.

"No, we can't. But the board has to know."

I couldn't shake the foul mood this put me in. I'd let my hopes soar on the basis of, as it turned out, nothing but wishful thinking. And now I'd have to tell Cat. To avoid taking out my frustrations on the volunteers, I left the office for the weekend.

Emma and Cat looked hopeful as I came through the bookstore's door, but I had to keep my promise. I related the morning's meeting almost word for word.

"We should've known," Cat responded, her eyes tearing. "What are we gonna do now? What will *you* do?"

I berated myself for doing this to her, but I'd promised on my life not to hold anything back. Now I had no answer, though. Fortunately, Emma did.

"Now hold on," she said, taking Cat's hand. "The convention is still weeks away. Lots of things can still happen. But Cat, you know Steve and the staff have been working hard to avert violence. And, this time, he's given you the complete, unvarnished truth of what's happening. Isn't that right?"

They both looked to me, and I nodded.

"You've been so looking forward to this weekend together," she continued. "Don't let some politician take that away. Whatever ugliness you leave in this city will, sorry to say, wait patiently for your return. So go enjoy that paradise you've been talking about, and leave your worries behind."

I saw Cat wavering. I suggested, "Let's do something to separate from this. We missed our morning workout. Let's go to the weight room now. We'll get some stress relief, and we won't need to set the alarm for tomorrow morning."

Emma smiled in approval, and off we went.

"There's something I don't quite understand," I told Cat later that night.

"What's that?"

"We've been together since Thanksgiving. All through the school year, you worked like a dog on your studies, and made sure I stayed on track too. You made rules for the times we could and couldn't be together, when we had to work and when we could play."

"Right," she admitted. "But what's the puzzle?"

"I have trouble understanding how it changed once school ended and I started work at the Mobe. Since then, you've been the one insisting on our play times, and complaining that I'm the one working too hard. How'd that happen?"

"It's funny you bring this up before tomorrow's trip," she responded, "since it was on the drive home from our first visit with Brad and Melissa that you asked me to do just that. Don't you remember?"

"Oh, yeah. I guess I do."

"But that's not all. I would've done it anyway. Balancing priorities is hard for you. When we were first together, you would've let schoolwork fall by the wayside if I didn't lay down some rules. By the way, enforcing those rules wasn't so easy for me either. Then, as soon as you started with the Mobe, you put no limits on your work schedule, or the responsibilities you took on. It's like you think it's your job to stop the war all by yourself. You have this tendency to go off the deep end with whatever you do. That's why you asked for my help."

"You're right, Cat. Whenever I see what's happening to Vietnam, I get pangs of guilt if I take time away from the work. I'm wrestling with that even now. I know I need to find a balance, but you're right. It's really hard."

"Again, that's why you asked for my help," she continued, "and it's what I've been trying to do. It's not that I don't ever go overboard myself. I can do it too. We need to keep each other from flying off the handle. And sometimes, we also need Emma's help. Thank God we have her."

"Okay," I agreed. "I do get it. But you know what? Once our meeting with Brad tomorrow is over, let's turn the balance switch off for this weekend. Let's forget the war and that weapon and everything else. No newspapers. No TV news. For reading, we'll bring only fiction. We'll only do what feels good. Let's be totally unbalanced for a couple of days."

She agreed with a smile, squeezing my leg. "Yes, let's do that. It might be our last chance before the convention."

Chapter 64

"I'm glad you made it here," Brad welcomed us as we dug into a delicious Mediterranean Quiche.

"So are we," I replied, "and your invitation was more than generous. I don't know how we can thank you."

"It's our pleasure, Sol," Melissa insisted. "We enjoy sharing our good fortune. And listen, after we leave, we want you to help yourselves to anything in the house. Food, drink, books, anything. We'll be gone all week, so stay as long as you want. There's a key to lock up with taped under the front step."

I took Cat's arm and asked to be excused for a minute. We stepped out onto the porch.

"Maybe our masquerade has gone on long enough," I proposed. "Look at what they're trusting us with. It's not fair anymore. We need to trust them too."

"Okay," Cat agreed, "I'm glad. I'll be more comfortable without the pretense."

"There's something you should know," I announced, back at the table. I told them our real names, explained the reason for the deception, and apologized if they felt insulted.

"Of course we're not insulted," Melissa responded. "We always suspected Sol and Felicia weren't your real names."

"You were handling top-secret government material," added Brad. "In your position, I would've been very careful too. In fact, I felt honored that you entrusted me with those documents, and I'm even more so now."

"Well, since the cat's out of the bag," I responded with a wink, "we might as well tell you where they came from, and how we got them."

They loved the story Cat related of the BSU's building takeover, how the group covered its tracks by xeroxing and replacing the original files, and how the South Side community prevented any arrests.

"It's too bad all this has to be kept quiet," Melissa commented. "Someone could make a movie out of it."

"Maybe one day," I agreed, "but only if the whole story can be told. And we're a long way from there. In fact, that's part of why you invited us."

"Right," Brad agreed. "Remember I said I wanted to gather the names of prominent scientists on a petition? Well, the breakthrough came this week at the Federation's convention."

Cat asked, "What kind of reception did your speech get?"

"Quite positive. In response to an audience member who asked what could be done, I directed them to a table out in the lobby, where Melissa was set up with copies of the petition."

"After the session ended," she added, "the scientists lined up at the table, some waiting to sign, others taking copies to bring back home for more signatures."

"We'll release it in a couple of weeks," Brad projected, "after we've gathered enough signatures. But there's something else, something that might turn out to be even more significant."

"Really?"

"At a reception after my talk, a young freelance reporter named Seymour Hersh introduced himself and asked for an interview. Talking to freelancers is usually a waste of time. But when he told me he'd been referred by Barry Wayne and was writing an article for the *New York Times Magazine*, I led him to the hotel bar. Since drinks were free at the reception, the bar was a good quiet place for a chat."

"What's he writing about?"

"It'll be an exposé of the enormous, mostly secret, U.S. military programs that are developing chemical and biological weaponry. He's discovered research and testing facilities that are refining and producing fatal nerve gases, new germs and diseases that have no antidotes, plus all kinds of delivery systems, from aerosol sprays to guided missiles. The Army has thousands of people working on these things, along with scientists at seventy universities. They're spending hundreds of millions every year. Some of what he told me I already knew, enough so I found the rest quite credible. This article could raise enough public and Congressional outcries to make the Quantum Potential Weapon a stillborn horror. And it's tentatively scheduled for publication late this month, well before Chicago's Planning Commission meeting."

"Wow, maybe this really can be stopped," Cat wondered hopefully.

"Maybe so," Brad agreed, looking at his watch. "But now we have a flight to catch. I'll keep in touch as things develop."

"Thanks for bringing us up to date," I said. "You go on. We'll clean up here. Have a great trip."

On their way out the door, Melissa warned, "Oh, I almost forgot. Thunderstorms are in tonight's forecast. Up here, that usually means power failures. We keep candles scattered around the house for nights like this. There's a battery-powered lantern and a transistor radio on the fireplace mantle. Feel free to build a fire too. Have fun, kids!"

"Sounds romantic," I remarked while we put the kitchen back together. "Anyway, this was actual good news. If Brad's petition gets results, Cat, you should get the Nobel Peace Prize. I hate that no-one else can know what you've done, how creative and brilliant and brave you've been."

"If the plug gets pulled on this project," she replied, "many people will deserve credit. The important thing is that it happens, and if that credit goes to Brad or to this Seymour Hersh, or to whoever makes the final decision, that's fine with me. For all I care, that stupid, corrupt Planning Commission can take the credit."

"But enough of this," she added, as we put away the last of the dishes. "Now it's time for us to get, like you said, unbalanced. Let's go. Our private beach has been waiting."

After a quick stop at the bathhouse, we were there. It was exactly as I remembered it, beautiful and totally secluded. I spread the blanket while Cat tuned the radio to a program called "Mostly Motown." Marvin Gaye and Tammi Terrell were singing "Your Precious Love." I knew we'd have the Motown artists serenading the two of us all afternoon.

Cat took off her bathing suit, handed me the tanning oil, flopped down on her stomach and commanded, "Do me. All over."

I jumped at the opportunity, massaging the oil into every square inch. Turning over, she directed, "all over" again. She moaned and cooed and finally announced, "Your turn now."

The combination of the sun's rays and Cat's hands softly oiling my back was more than any man deserved. She, too, didn't miss an inch. She slapped my butt and ordered, "Turn over." Vaguely, I heard the Temptations singing "I Could Never Love Another." Now it was she taking her time, and saving the best part for last. I groaned, twisting and bouncing, but she decided her job was finished for now. "Dance with me," she offered.

The music was perfect for slow, sensual dancing, but we had two problems. First, since we were so oiled up, we did more slithering than swaying. And second, the organ she'd aroused insisted on getting in the way. After a few minutes, she laughed and proposed, "We better go for a swim."

The cold water cured that problem right away. We swam out to the raft, Cat gliding through the water, with me splashing after her. We sat on its far end with our arms around one another, facing the enormous lake and inhaling the sun's warm glow.

"We've done it," I observed. "We've left the rest of the world behind."

"What world?" she asked. "Right now, for us, this is all there is."

For us, the words resounded, *this is all there is*.

Overcome with emotion, I buried my face in her neck, furiously kissed it, pushed her down onto the raft and rolled us over. We dropped right into the lake. I screamed from the shock of the cold water, but Cat laughed and yelled, "Catch me if you can!"

She waited patiently on shore while I made my way back. Diana Ross and the Supremes were also waiting, with "What the World Needs Now Is Love, Sweet Love." Cat led me up closer to the radio and whispered, "Now let's dance."

Less slippery than before, we swayed to the music, eyes closed, entwined as one. Cat's body radiated warmth. Soon, my anatomy again asserted itself.

Cat grasped the problem, stroked it and asked, "What's the matter, baby? Do you need to lie down?" I groaned.

Back on the blanket, Cat tortured me for what seemed like hours before she mounted and brought forth what felt like the release of my life. I was done, spent, depleted, and plain dumb happy. We lay there together for who knows how long, until Cat announced, "I'm hungry."

"Not again," I pleaded. "I can't do it again."

"Not that, silly," she laughed, sitting up. "I'm starving for dinner."

Chapter 65

In deference to the lowering sun, we put our clothes back on at the bathhouse and made our way up the hill. We found a bag of colossal shrimp in the freezer. Cat defrosted and seasoned it while I fired up the grill.

Long after finishing off the shrimp, we nursed what was left of the wine, watching the sun turn bright orange as it dropped slowly to the horizon, somewhere out in the endless lake. Much as I wished for this moment to last forever, I would've had no complaint if I never lived another.

With darkness came the first rumblings of thunder, faint and far off. A breeze rustled through the trees. The temperature dipped. It was time to move the party indoors and prepare for what was coming our way.

I got the fire going while Cat lit the candles. After showering, we put on luxurious silk robes that were waiting in our closet and stretched out on the couch, each with a book and a snifter of cognac. I'd brought Philip Roth's recent novel, *Portnoy's Complaint*, and Cat had Kurt Vonnegut's *Mother Night*. From the stereo came the lilting strains of Mozart's "Eine Kleine Nachtmusik." We read, we inhaled the scents from the fireplace, and from time to time we played a little footsy. Perfect. The thunder was still far off.

An hour later, it arrived with a vengeance. The booms were so loud they seemed to shake the house. Lightning bolts laced through the pouring rain. Out went the electricity. With the fire blazing and the candles burning, all I had to do was turn the lantern on. The storm was so dramatic, though, that it pulled us to watch through the glass doors as it pounded over the lake.

We were transfixed by the power and majesty of the storm, yet warm and safe in our cocoon. But soon Cat drew closer to me, trembling and whimpering.

"What is it?" I asked. "Are you cold?"

"No, it's not that," she sobbed. "It was a storm just like this one. It blew off this lake onto the highway, not even far from here. Mommy and Daddy, trapped in their car, pinned by that huge truck. Oh, what a horror it must've been!"

The dam burst, and she began heaving. I held her tight and implored, "What can I do?" My own tears were welling up too, from her grief and my helplessness.

It was a few minutes before she answered. She gathered herself and wiped her face. In a weak, but very determined voice, she said, "I'll never be in a safer place than I am here, with you, now. It's time for me to work through it. I want to experience my fear, explore it, not escape it, and see if I can get through to the other side. It's controlled me for too long."

I wasn't sure I understood this, and didn't know if she did either, so I repeated, "What can I do?"

Cat pulled herself away, picked up the lantern and went over to the bookcase. "I saw something here before," she murmured. "Ah, here it is." She handed me a collection of short stories by H.P. Lovecraft.

"These are horror stories," I blurted, leafing through the book. "They're the last things you need!"

"They may be exactly what I need. I've been pushing my fears away for almost three years now, and they keep coming back. I have to know what happens if I don't try, if I just give in to them."

"Now you're scaring me," I warned.

"I can do this, Steve, because I know you'll pull me back if I go over the edge. So, please. Read to me. Any story in this book. Please."

I sat down on the couch, with my feet on the coffee table. Cat curled into a fetal position with her head in my lap. I rested one hand on her and, with the other, opened the book to a 1923 story titled, "The Lurking Fear." I began to read...

> There was thunder in the air on the night I went to the deserted mansion atop Tempest Mountain, to find the lurking fear. I was not alone, for foolhardiness was not then mixed with that love of the grotesque and the terrible which has made my career a series of quests for strange horrors...

I stopped and asked, "Cat, are you sure?"

She snuggled tighter. "Keep going, please."

I read on. Two of the narrator's compatriots disappear. Another has his face chewed off by unseen forces. Ultimately, we learn that the family who owned the mansion has devolved into some kind of monster race, living and reproducing down in the cellar for many years. The story ends in a scene of unspeakable horror. Throughout, I felt Cat pulling into a tighter position, squeezing further into me, occasionally shivering.

"Okay," I concluded, closing the book. "We've done it."

"Keep going, please. Keep on reading."

Through all this, the force of the storm rattled the windows. Thunder boomed every few minutes. Lightning flashed through the sky.

I kept my right hand resting on Cat's body, with the book in my left. The next story was "The Thing on the Doorstep." It felt like she was burrowing inside me, and the shivering grew more frequent. But still she wanted more. By the middle of "The Doom that Came to Sarnath," I was getting the creeps myself. As I finished reading "The Strange High House in the Mist," though, I sensed her body relaxing, uncoiling. She opened my robe and went inside. I put the book down and turned off the lantern.

Sometime during the night, we made it into bed. I woke on my side facing a bright, clear morning. Cat was wrapped around me from behind, her hand traveling over my torso. Through my morning fog, I asked, "Electricity?"

"Who knows?" she replied as her hand grasped its target. "Who cares? Now shut up and turn over. I want you now."

A half hour or so later, we threw on our robes and stepped out onto the porch. Big branches littered the grounds, but no trees had come down. What the storm did do was clear out the heat and humidity. The air was crisp and cool, more like September than early August.

"No beach now," I muttered. "It's too cold."

"It might warm up later," Cat responded brightly. "Let's explore the town this morning."

"Okay. But first I need coffee."

We had our coffee out on the deck, inhaling the fresh smells that the storm released from the forest. It felt a little strange, Sunday morning without a newspaper. Even after Tooter took us to an inviting little village, the first pile of papers in sight exerted a reflexive magnetic attraction. Cat, reading my mind, pulled me away. I welcomed the intervention.

For breakfast, we found a cute café with a deck overlooking the lake. It seemed everything in this town was kind of "cute." The food was good, though, and the air was fresher than any that had blown through Chicago in, I guessed, centuries.

"Can you tell me what happened last night?" I asked, "with the horror stories?"

"They were just what I needed. But now I wonder what kind of demented mind could've come up with such stuff. How did *he* sleep at night?"

"I wonder about that too. But let's talk about you. Did it really help?"

"Well, it certainly did for the moment. The pain of suddenly losing my mom and dad has colored everything that's happened since. I know it's not fair to lay this on you, but when I see you tempting danger, those are the fears that flood my consciousness. So I decided to throw open the barricades and face them."

"That was incredibly brave," I responded with genuine admiration.

"It was only doable because I felt so safe with you, knowing you were right there if I unraveled. I'm sure you sensed my cringing and shivering, my heartache and tears. After the worst of it, though, there was kind of an explosion inside, and I felt free. And then all I wanted was more of you."

"Cat, I don't know what to say. You never stop amazing me."

"I understand," she smiled as the check arrived. "So now let's do some shopping."

"Shopping? For what?"

"Oh, I don't know. A souvenir. Something cute, to remind us of this weekend."

We found no shortage of cuteness in the souvenir shop next door: hats, t-shirts, sweatshirts, key chains, all manner of paraphernalia. Nearly everything was inscribed, "Harbor Country."

"How about these t-shirts?" I asked. "We can get his 'n' hers."

"They're nice, but let's keep looking."

I didn't see why we needed to keep looking since we'd already found what we'd been looking for, but I followed along. She showed me some adorable coffee mugs.

"Good," I said. "Let's get them too."

Cat looked at them closely, then put them back on the shelf. "I don't know. Let's keep looking."

That meant crossing the street to another store, where we kept looking. Perhaps I missed something, but the stuff we saw in Store #2 seemed to me exactly the same as the stuff in Store #1. But we made sure we didn't miss anything before moving on to Store #3, where everything also looked quite familiar, and which I hoped was the last souvenir shop in the village.

By now, my eyes were glazing over from all the cuteness, so I decided to wait outside. It was past noon and the sun was blazing, just what I hoped might bring this expedition to a conclusion. I went back in and told Cat, "It's getting hot out now. Beach weather."

"Oh, good," she replied, "and I've found just the right things. How about these?"

She showed me his 'n' hers t-shirts and coffee mugs, identical to the ones we spotted back at Store #1.

"Perfect!" I exclaimed. "Good job! Now we can hit the beach."

This time, we didn't even bother with bathing suits. We grabbed our supplies at the bathhouse, raced down to the beach, and plunged right into the waves. The sand was baking in the sunshine by then, but the storm had turned the water even colder than it was the day before. We got used to it quickly, though, swimming out to the raft.

The rest of the afternoon passed very much like the one before. We used a little less oil and did a little more reading, and this time it was my turn to initiate the lovemaking. I drew that out for as long as I was able.

Afterward, I propped up on an elbow, as my index finger gently drew pictures in her belly sweat. My Cat was actually purring. I had everything I wanted in the world, but now I had to bring up an unpleasant subject.

"Do you want to go home before dinner, or after?"

"No," she murmured dreamily.

"What do you mean, 'No?' It isn't a 'yes or no' question. It's a 'before or after' question."

"No," she repeated, "and don't stop doing what you're doing."

I realized I'd paused in my artwork, so I got back to it. "Okay," I conceded, "but I still don't understand."

"What I mean is I don't want to leave today or tonight. I know we have to go back, but I want to make this last as long as we can. Let's stay the night. Your meeting isn't until ten tomorrow, right? We can get up early and go in the morning."

"I guess so. But we'll never get home in time for our morning workout."

"Oh, that's okay," she agreed, smiling. "I've got a few ideas for a workout we can do right here, tonight. I only need to decide where we'll do it."

For a fleeting moment, I wondered how many years, months, weeks, days or hours I had left before she completely and totally wore me out.

Chapter 66

It was hard tearing ourselves away from our Shangri-La Monday morning, but we really did have to return to the city. With only a few weeks left before the convention, I needed to get back to work, Also, Emma had a checkup scheduled, and Cat always insisted on being driver, monitor and chaperone for these. She dropped me off on South Dearborn Street around 9:30.

I waved to Donnie, who was on the phone, and checked my in-box. There was a carbon copy of very professionally typed Minutes of the board meeting. This had to be Ronnie's work, but she was nowhere to be seen.

The first page was a typed copy of the sign-in sheet. Scanning it quickly, I noticed that both SDS and the Yippies were represented as invited guests. I saw this as a welcome development, since it was at least worth a try to get everyone working together.

The meeting had begun with Donnie's staff report, including a detailed agenda for Convention Week activities. He got an easy green light for the Anti-Birthday Party. There was a little discussion about the movement centers and workshops being planned at various places around the city. Those arrangements remained assigned to the Chicago staff. Not surprisingly, the big issue was the pending permits, for the marches and the rallies and the parks, and what would happen if we didn't get them.

From reading the summary contained in the Minutes, I could hear Dave Dellinger's voice, calmly and convincingly explaining why the march to the Amphitheater was absolutely essential. After much discussion, his argument prevailed, but the board cancelled the daytime march through the Loop. Now, all we'd ask for were Grant Park for a rally and assembly point, several parks for sleeping, and the big march to the convention on Wednesday the 28th. None of the other planned actions, such as picketing the delegates' hotels, required a permit.

As I finished reading, Vern came in. I held up the Minutes and said, "Looks like it went well."

"As well as could be expected," he replied. "Everyone seems to be on the same page now. SDS, the Yippies and the Mobe won't be stepping on each others' toes. In fact, SDS will send people to our marshal training."

"When will that start?"

"First one next Tuesday in Grant Park. After that, twice a week at Lincoln Park."

"Oh, that's good. So how'd the fundraiser at Merrie Alexander's go?"

"Only around thirty people, but we raised almost six grand, so it was certainly worth doing."

"And was it any fun?"

"I don't know about anyone else," he explained, "but I had such a good time I stayed the night. Our hostess was very, let's say, hospitable. No, enjoyable."

He smiled and winked. I rolled my eyes.

Paul, Jeff and a few volunteers arrived, and Donnie came out of his office.

"Where's Ronnie?" I asked. "She's always the first one here."

"She gave up her Sunday for the board meeting," he explained, "and came in early this morning to type up the Minutes. I told her to take the rest of the day off."

"I'm a little surprised she accepted."

"She did want to stay, but I insisted."

"She's sure is amazing. I don't know what we'd do without her."

"You're right, but today we'll have to manage."

Once we got settled in the conference room, Donnie asked, "Steve, are we ready for the press conference?"

"Midland Hotel at four. Should be a good turnout."

"Okay. Dave is staying in town for it. And are you up to date on yesterday's board meeting?"

"I guess so. I read the Minutes."

"Good. So we can skip that. Jeff will do the permit modifications, and you can go ahead and book the Coliseum for the 27th. I had a talk with Abbie last night. We'll sponsor the event and make the arrangements, but they'll produce the actual show. If there's one thing the Yippies excel at, it's showmanship."

"This morning," he continued. "I called Dan Stahl and told him we're withdrawing our application for the Loop march. I pushed him to set up a high-level meeting, including Conlisk, since we want to coordinate with the police to keep things cool. I said it was time to stop messing around, and that any open issues can easily be resolved if he puts us in a room with the right people."

"What did he say to that?" Jeff asked.

"Glad you're sitting down. Surprise, surprise! He said he'd set it up for next Monday at two.

The four of us applauded. *Maybe,* I thought, *this is the breakthrough we've been waiting for.*

"There was one sour note, though," Donnie continued. "Stahl told me the subject came up, tangentially, at a Cabinet meeting, where Daley pronounced, 'There'll be no sleeping in the parks.' "

"But Stahl told us that decision was up to the Park District," I exclaimed. "We're supposed to make our presentation to the Board of Commissioners next Tuesday."

"I'm only passing on what he told me," Donnie said. "Well, we've covered everything now. For the next few weeks, every minute counts, so let's get going."

My first stop was the Coliseum. Instantly, I knew why the place was so available. Dusty and drafty, it seemed to be literally crumbling. It had no air conditioning, and we'd need to rent or borrow a sound system. On the other hand, it hadn't been closed down for code violations, it had sufficient electrical power, and it had room for lots of people. Best of all, it was cheap. I completed the paperwork and rushed over to the press conference.

The turnout surpassed my expectation. Between the reporters and the TV apparatus, it was hard to find an extra square inch. I leaned against the back wall, near the exit in case my claustrophobia kicked in.

Donnie began by laying out our planned activities for Convention Week, including "a march to the convention by a hundred thousand people."

"Our purpose," he added, "is to focus world attention on the problems of war and racism here in the United States."

That was as far as he got before the newsmen started shouting out questions. He and Dellinger parried them.

"Are you plotting to shut the convention down?"

"No. We'll stay outside the building, and we won't keep the delegates from entering or leaving. All we want is to make our voices heard."

"Are you trying to force a McCarthy nomination?"

"We won't be there to support any candidate. We'll be there to oppose the war, the war party, and any politician who can stomach continuing this war for even one more day."

"What response do you expect from the police?"

"That's up to them. But we call on Superintendent Conlisk to work with us to preserve order. A corps of trained marshals will be on hand for that very purpose."

"Suppose the city denies you a permit?"

"We will exercise our First Amendment rights to assemble and protest, whether or not Mayor Daley recognizes those rights. The antiwar movement is taking to the streets, and will stay in the streets until U.S. troops are withdrawn from Vietnam."

After that, the questions became repetitive, and the conference drew to a close. I thought it went well, but I was glad it was over. Back at home, I told Cat we had positive news, but first I wanted to hear about Emma's doctor visit.

"It wasn't bad," she explained. "He showed us how her new chest x-ray compared with the last one. It wasn't better, but it wasn't worse either, which he thought was worth noting. Emma told him she'd cut way back on her smoking and, of course, he told her she needed to cut it out entirely. So at least we're holding our own. What's your news?"

I told her about the board meeting, the press conference, and the Coliseum rental. "But are you okay," I asked, "with turning production over to the Yippies?"

"I don't care if the Zippies run it," she replied. "All I care about is people getting together to make a political point, without confronting danger."

"Good. Now here's the big news. We have a meeting next Monday at City Hall. Dan Stahl told Donnie he'd pull together the top officials whose cooperation we'll need to keep our whole program peaceful and orderly. And then Tuesday, we'll make our presentation to the Park District."

My optimism carried over until morning. "Things are turning around now," I told Cat. "We can't stop Humphrey's nomination, but maybe we can push him to at least consider pulling out of Vietnam. Maybe he'll see it's his only way to win the general election."

"A lot to hope for," she replied skeptically. "The first step is to ensure we can make our voices heard without heads getting cracked. I don't want you ever again in the middle of anything like what happened at the Civic Center."

"I know. I know. One thing at a time. Meanwhile, do you need Tooter for your shopping today?"

"No. I can get everything I need from the shops down the street."

"Okay. The car will get me home a little quicker, so I can help out."

"Off you go then," she said, squeezing my cheek. "You don't have to be early, but please don't be late. Remember, we're expecting Emma at six."

At the office, I wasn't the only optimistic one. We'd all seen clips from the press conference on TV news. The *Tribune* buried the story, but we had no reason to be surprised by that.

"Eight paragraphs on page 6," Paul snorted. "But we got thirty-two in the *Times*."

"Right. But it's the *Times* that sets the table," Jeff pointed out. "It's called the 'newspaper of record' because it's followed around the world. The big wire services covered us too. This isn't a Chicago story. It's a national story. An international story."

"You're right," Paul agreed. "Fuck the *Chicago Tribune* and its corporate, war-mongering bullshit!"

Having settled that, we split up to tackle the day's work. I checked my in-box and found half a dozen pink "While You Were Out" slips. They all recorded messages left by pastors, priests and rabbis, saying they'd have to withdraw their offers of overnight accommodations, but weren't authorized to explain why. Their apologies got me nowhere.

I called Donald Blake, the Presbyterian minister who'd been so enthusiastic about supporting, and even joining, the protests. Happily, his enthusiasm hadn't waned.

"I'll be down there," he promised. "You can depend on it. I'll even try pulling together a group of antiwar clergy to create some kind of buffer. The police might think twice before they wade through clerical collars."

"I'm glad to hear that. It's a great idea."

"But I've run into a problem," he continued. "I don't know if we'll be able to house protesters at the church."

"Why not? When we first met, you didn't even need to be persuaded."

"All I can say right now," he explained, "is that something came up. I have to meet with the congregation's leaders, but I'll get back to you soon."

Puzzled and confused, I put my head in my hands, trying to figure out what was going on. "Something came up." *What did that mean?* It was already late afternoon and I hadn't accomplished anything besides giving myself a headache. I decided to go back to where I'd started, and dialed Rev. Marshall's number.

"I've been getting strange phone calls," I told him.

"So have I," he responded. "We should talk, but not over the phone. Let's meet at the SSO, at around five."

The mystery was only deepening, and now I had to call Cat. "There's something I have to deal with," I told her. "I might be a little late for dinner."

"Late? I thought you were planning to be early."

"I know," I tried to explain, "but this is really important. It can't wait."

"But Emma's coming, and I've been cooking, and... Oh!" I heard pots clattering. "What is it anyway?"

"I'll tell you the minute I get home. No time now, though. I gotta run."

The sound of Cat slamming the receiver made my ears ring. *Would anything go right today?*

The rush hour traffic was, of course, heavier than usual, making me a half-hour late to the SSO. Watkins and Marcellus were with Rev. Marshall in the conference room. I wondered what would hit me next.

Chapter 67

After apologizing for being late, I summarized what Brad Bennett had told Cat and me on Saturday, concluding, "Between the scientists' petition and that *Times Magazine* article, maybe this whole Helsinger project can be pre-empted."

"That would be very good," Marcellus responded. "The anger over Midway's land grab has only been building. The young people I been talkin' to have made up their minds to stop it."

"How?"

"Like Malcolm said: 'By any means necessary.' This could be the thing that unites the rival gangs with one other, and with the Panthers. Those eighteen blocks will be defended. And it won't be spontaneous and disorganized like the riots were."

"Well, if it comes to that," I predicted, "you won't be on your own. There are plenty of Midway students who don't want our school carving up the South Side. We'll be there to fight with you, any way you want us to. 'By any means necessary' sounds good to me."

From a corner of my embattled brain, I heard Cat's voice scolding, *There you go again.*

"Let's hope it doesn't come to that," the preacher said. "But Midway's expansion isn't why I suggested we meet today. You said you were puzzled by the phone calls you've been getting. I can clear up that mystery, but this is not for public consumption."

"I sure hope you can. This has been an awful day."

"Last week," he began, "I got an unexpected visit from two men in suits and ties. They identified themselves as FBI agents."

"FBI?"

"Yes. They knew about your visit with me, and my offer to house your people. They even knew the ground rules we agreed to."

My headache was worsening. *How could they have known?*

"They politely advised me to reconsider. 'In your own best interests,' one of them added. 'If any of those hippies break the law downtown, whether it's assault or littering, and find refuge here,' the other one explained, 'then this is where they'll be apprehended.' And the first one chimed in with, 'So you'll face charges of aiding and abetting fugitives. That's a felony.' By then, well, my blood was beginning to boil."

"Tell Steve what you told them," Marcellus suggested.

"To make a long story short, I told them I didn't come up here from Jim Crow Alabama to build the South Side's largest congregation so that outsiders could tell me who I could and couldn't have in my own house. And I warned them that any attack on Ebenezer would be an attack on the South Side community. Finally, I let them know, 'I get my orders from Jesus, not from J. Edgar Hoover,' and invited them to leave."

"That wasn't all, though," he continued. "On their way out, they warned me it would be considered a violation of national security if I told *anyone* about their visit."

I asked, "Have they been visiting the other ministers too?"

"From the calls I've been getting, it seems they have your entire list. They also knew exactly who to contact, intimidate and threaten."

"What you need to do," Watkins told me, "is find out how they got that information. There's a big leak that better get plugged real quick."

My head was splitting by the time our meeting ended. And it was already past seven. I missed Cat's dinner and she was gonna kill me.

Her expression of anger turned to worry as soon as she saw my face. I didn't need a mirror to know how wan and haggard I must have looked.

"Oh my!" she exclaimed. "What's happened to you?"

She sat me down in the living room, where Emma was having coffee. "Are you hungry?" she asked. "Your dinner's warming in the oven."

"I couldn't eat a thing," I muttered glumly.

She pulled another chair next to mine, and sat with a hand on my arm, looking up at me like I might crumble before her eyes. Emma also looked worried.

"What is it?" she asked.

I related the misadventures of the day, concluding, "So they know everything I've been doing on this, but I can't figure out how. Like

Watkins said, we must have a leak. But I can't imagine how. It can't be wiretaps at the office, since I made some of the calls from here."

"I don't think it's a tap or a leak," Emma mused. "More likely a mole."

"A mole?"

"Yes. Someone the FBI planted inside the Mobe to pass them information."

"But that's not possible," I protested. "It's such a small staff. We work together every day, and you think someone's a spy?"

"Let's be analytical, Steve. We're talking about a specific set of data. Can you describe its chain of custody? Was it posted somewhere?"

"No. Nothing like that." I explained the Prospect Sheet system, and how Ronnie kept them in a loose-leaf binder locked in a drawer.

"So, none of the volunteers had access to more than small bits of information?"

"Right. Even if they all were spies, they couldn't have gotten access to the results of the visits I made myself. And those are the ones the Feds seem to be focusing on. They're the biggest ones."

"And did you ever see signs that the locked drawer had been tampered with?"

"Not that I know of. No."

"Who else had access to that binder besides you and this Ronnie?"

"No-one. Not even Donnie ever looked at it."

"Ronnie," Cat thought aloud, in almost a whisper. Then in a firm accusing voice, "Ronnie. It has to be Ronnie." Emma nodded her agreement.

"Ronnie?" I exclaimed. "How's that possible? She's the one who keeps the Mobe's wheels turning! She's been our Mother Hen!"

"Yes," Emma agreed. "And the last person anyone would suspect."

I stared at the floor, shaking my head and reacting badly. "You must be right. It couldn't be anyone else. But then it can't be just the housing arrangements. Ronnie's in the middle of everything. She's been at every staff meeting, taking notes on what we were doing and planning. She even took the Minutes at Sunday's board meeting. This is a catastrophe!"

We paused for a moment, trying to absorb this new information. Then I blurted out to no-one in particular, "I've been a fool, a total failure. From the beginning, I knew I was in over my head. I should've never accepted any important responsibilities. What was I thinking?"

"Just a minute now," Emma commanded. "You can't blame yourself for this. Ronnie was in place before you got there. You had no reason to be suspicious. No reason at all."

"But I got taken in," I complained. "She was so friendly, so competent, so efficient, so cooperative."

"Of course she was. Why would the FBI insert someone who didn't offer all those qualities? That was the whole point. Look, Steve. Donnie is a movement pro, right? And he's the one who hired this Ronnie in the first place. She's also a pro, a con artist, and she's very, very good at what she does. She could've fooled anyone."

Cat took my head in her hands, and peered into my eyes. "It's not your fault," she insisted. "It's not your fault."

"Cat's right," Emma agreed. "No-one can blame you. But really, that doesn't matter now. The question is what to do. You've got to get the FBI out of the information loop."

I knew she was right, but my brain had become a damp dishrag. I'd never felt so useless.

"We need help here," Cat said, looking at our mentor. "Give us a starting point, please, if you can."

"Disinformation," Emma suggested. "That's your weapon now. Use it. But it's time for me to go. I'm fading. You'll know what to do. I'm sure of it. Let's talk tomorrow."

I went to bed depressed and agitated. Cat did her best to comfort me and I did get some sleep, but only in fits and starts. At around 5 a.m., I gave up trying. By that time, though, I had a plan.

Chapter 68

"Good morning," I greeted Ronnie cheerfully. "I didn't get to ask yesterday. How was your day off?"

"Well, it was a little disorienting being home on a Monday," she replied. "But Donnie was very gracious and I did need a day of rest. But you looked preoccupied yesterday. Did I miss anything?"

"All I know," I said, "is that some of the clergy withdrew their offers. And none of them would explain why. It was very odd."

"Yes, it does sound strange. I wonder what changed their minds."

She went back to her paperwork. Stepping into Donnie's office, I said, "We need to go out for coffee."

"We do?" he asked, looking puzzled. "I'm kind of busy."

"Yes, we do," I insisted. "We really do."

Down in the coffee shop, I related everything that happened the day before. "So Ronnie's an FBI mole," I concluded. "There's no other possible explanation."

Donnie was as dumbfounded as I'd first been. "This is unbelievable," he responded, putting his head in his hands. "She's been such a hard worker, so competent and efficient. I never had to ask her twice to do anything. And she never missed a day of work."

"Of course," I explained. "The whole idea was for her to become so indispensable that no-one would think twice about giving her access to our data, our contacts, our plans. How'd she get hired in the first place?"

"As soon as we opened the office," he explained, "we put an ad in the classifieds. It made it clear that the job was temporary, and we could only offer subsistence wages. I was surprised we got any responses, but there were a few. Ronnie was head and shoulders above the others. She had lots of office experience, even references."

"Too good to be true?"

"I guess so. Now, we have to confront her. I have to fire her. Jesus, this is terrible."

"Wait a minute, Donnie. Confronting her will be a waste of time, since she'll only deny it. And, instead of firing her, wouldn't it be better if she quit?"

"Why would she do that?"

"Listen, I was up thinking about this most of the night, and I came up with a simple plan." I told him what I had in mind, concluding, "I bet she'll be gone within a week. In the meantime, we need to find ways to keep her out of the loop."

Donnie agreed and went back to the office. I got Coach Bob on the phone and asked if he would see me.

"I don't know what we might talk about," he said. "You seem to be a nice fellow, and I'm on your side against the war. But, like I told you, Langley University can't get involved because of liability issues."

"Yes, I know, and I'm not coming to twist your arm. There's something else you can do that'd be really helpful. I'll only need a few minutes."

"Okay, but I hope you're not wasting your time again. You can find me at football practice."

At the stadium, we took seats in the empty stands. "Tell me. What could you possibly want me to do?" he asked.

"I need to smoke out a spy, and you can help me do it."

"Me? How?"

"By telling the truth, Coach. That's all."

"Now I'm confused. Are you pulling my leg?"

"No. If you agree, here's what'll happen. Sometime soon, you'll get a visit from the FBI. They'll have information that you found a solution to the insurance problem and offered to host thousands of convention protesters here on campus. They'll warn you not to do it. They'll probably make threats."

"But I've made no such offer."

"Of course not. So you go ahead and tell them the truth, that I came out here last month to ask for your help, but you refused. I need you to be very forceful about it. Outraged even. Convince them they've been fed a load of horseshit."

"Well, you're right," he agreed. "I would be telling the truth. But then what'll happen?"

"Once the feds think their spy is giving them made-up information, she'll become useless to them. It might even raise doubts about everything else that she's given them. Her handlers will have to pull her off the case."

"And that's all you're asking of me?"

"That's all."

"Okay. I'll do it. In fact, I'll be happy to." He agreed to call me at home after the FBI visit.

Back at the office, I gave Donnie a surreptitious thumbs-up and turned to Ronnie, smiling broadly.

"What are you so cheerful about?" she asked, returning my smile.

"Great news. Remember this morning, I told you about those cancellations? Oh, that reminds me. I need to enter them onto our Prospect Sheets. Do you have the loose-leaf handy?"

"Sure." She unlocked the drawer and set the binder on the desk. "But what's your great news?"

"The news is that those cancellations won't matter. Can you find me the Prospect Sheet for Langley University?"

"Here it is." She opened the binder to the "L" tab. "You wrote that they can't help because of insurance problems. I remember how disappointed you were."

"And that's what's changed," I explained enthusiastically. "The athletic director called me at home last night, and asked me to come see him this morning. I just got back from there."

"See him about what?"

"He found out we can purchase our own insurance to cover liability at Langley. That'll get the university off the hook if anything happens. For only a few days, it won't even cost much. He offered us not only the football stadium, but also the soccer field. Space for gazillions of people! It might be all we need. Here, I'll write down the details."

I filled out the Prospect Sheet and handed it back to her. She scanned it and placed it back into the binder. "This sure is wonderful news," she exclaimed with that contagious Irish smile. "Congratulations!"

It took only a day until Coach Bob reported, "It went exactly as you predicted. I even hammed it up a little. I demanded, 'Who the hell told you this? I'm calling our lawyers, and they'll tell me who to sue!' Well, they got all flustered, sputtered something about confidential sources, and hightailed it out of here."

"Perfect. Thank you so much."

"My pleasure. It was fun. Let me know how things turn out."

Ronnie didn't show up for work on Friday. Her home phone was disconnected. We never saw her again.

I breathed a big sigh of relief as the week ended, but its ups and downs had taken a toll on me. It began in paradise, where I hadn't a care in the world. Then good news on Monday. The fundraiser and board meeting were both successful. We were coordinating with SDS and the Yippies. We booked the Coliseum for the Anti-Birthday Party and held a crowded press conference. Perhaps most important, we had a meeting scheduled with city officials.

Then came the clergy cancellations, the callbacks, the confusion. I wanted to crawl into a hole after the truth about Ronnie became clear. The week did end as well as it could have, but I hoped I wouldn't have to endure another one like it.

"Well, we solved one problem. Now, only a couple more weeks until the convention," I told Cat. "After that, all this will be over and we'll be back in school. We can march and demonstrate and organize against the war, and still live some kind of normal life."

"I hope so," she wondered aloud. "I only hope what you'll really want, after all this, is some kind of normal life."

She insisted I rest over the weekend. I was exhausted, more emotionally than physically, and the upcoming week would be a busy one. I took some time to prepare for Monday's City Hall meeting and Tuesday's Park District presentation, but spent the rest of Saturday on the couch, reading and napping.

Cat joined me there after dinner. Following the NBC evening news, "To Have and Have Not," the first collaboration between Bogart and Bacall, was coming on.

The news, though, took us by surprise. Senator George McGovern of South Dakota had jumped into the presidential race. I knew he'd spoken out against the war for years. In his announcement, he called it "the most disastrous political, moral, diplomatic blunder in our history."

"And that war must be ended *now*," he continued. "Not next year or the following year, but now." We applauded. He called for an immediate halt to the bombing and to the "senseless search-and-destroy missions."

"The loss of American youth and the slaughter of the Vietnamese," he said, "should stop now." He called for ending the draft, and "putting an end to the shameful remnants of racism and poverty that still afflict our country."

"That's about as good as it gets," I reacted. "But I don't understand why he's getting into this so late in the game. He must know Humphrey already has it sewn up. Let's see if there's more on another channel."

I rose to turn the dial, but Cat grabbed my arm. "Not tonight. Look, the movie's coming on. Let's just watch it. But while you're up, bring over the popcorn."

So we snuggled up in a corner of the couch, munching popcorn and watching. The movie was romantic, with a political edge, and we both loved it. Spending the evening that way reminded me of our exchange the night before, about living a normal life.

Sunday morning, we joined Emma for the TV talk shows. We learned that McGovern taught political science before entering politics, and flew fighter planes during World War II. He was an actual war hero.

"If he'd gotten into this sooner," I said with some excitement, "we might've joined his campaign. Maybe I never would've gotten involved with the Mobe. If he wins, he'll get us out of Vietnam."

"There you go, getting carried away again," Cat responded as Emma looked on, smiling. "You know better than that. Sure, he could've run an inspired antiwar campaign through the primaries. I like him too. But even if he did, even if he won every primary, the party bosses would still be in charge of picking the candidate. If we've learned anything this year, it's that this whole thing is a farce. What alternate universe are you dreaming about?"

"Oh, sure, you're right," I sheepishly admitted. "More wishful thinking, I guess."

We went back to watching the programs. McGovern himself was interviewed by Lawrence Spivak on "Meet the Press." He speculated that delegates who wouldn't support McCarthy might vote for a different antiwar candidate. Under Spivak's questioning, though, he conceded that Humphrey was still almost certain to win the nomination.

The main thing he wanted to discuss wasn't that, but the Vietnam plank in the party platform. He said he'd introduce a resolution that completely rejects the administration's war policy, and calls for immediately ending the bombing as a first step toward getting us out of the war. This, he thought, had a good chance of getting through the Platform Committee and being passed on the convention floor. His hope was to get a real peace plank into the party's platform so the party's nominee, even if that was Humphrey, would have to run on it.

During a commercial break, I asked Emma, "Does this make sense?"

"Not in the way he described it," she replied. "I don't believe even he really expects Humphrey to pay attention to a platform plank he disagrees with. But it seems to me McGovern's real objective is to force open debate on the floor, and that's a good thing. A platform fight inside the convention, combined with antiwar demonstrations outside, both of them televised, will make Vietnam the overriding issue of the week. Which is what it should be."

Cat asked. "Are there platform fights at every convention?"

"Only rarely. And those are usually nothing but posturing. No-one pays any attention. The last real fight took place twenty years ago. But that was a momentous one."

"About what?"

"Civil rights. Forces at the 1948 Democratic Convention were pushing a resolution to ban lynching and put an end to racial discrimination. It was a huge fight, and the civil rights forces won. A big bloc of Southern Democrats, including the entire Mississippi delegation, walked out. They formed their own party, the Dixiecrats, and ran their own candidate for president. The Dixiecrats won four Southern states, and almost cost Truman the election."

"Did he support the civil rights plank?" I asked.

"Yes, he did. But he didn't lead the fight. The campaign to get the resolution passed was led by a candidate for the Senate whose energy, eloquence, and commitment to civil rights made him a national figure. He gave an electrifying speech that drew the admiration of millions, myself included. Now guess who that was."

Cat and I both shrugged our shoulders.

"At the time, he was still the mayor of Minneapolis," she explained. "His name..." She paused to build suspense, "...was Hubert Horatio Humphrey."

Chapter 69

I was genuinely hopeful that, this week, we'd make some progress with the city. But Cat was skeptical. "If they didn't want to at least negotiate terms for the permits," I asked her on my way out, "why would they have scheduled the meeting?"

"Well, I guess you'll find out soon enough. Good luck. I sure hope you're right."

Dave Dellinger and two other board members met our team on the City Hall steps. We went upstairs to the deputy mayor's office.

Two men we didn't know flanked Dan Stahl at the conference table. He introduced us to Richard Elrod, an assistant corporation counsel, and Al Baugher, who had something to do with the Youth Commission. No-one else. No mayor, no agency heads, no superintendents of anything. We were shocked.

"Where is everyone?" Donnie demanded, red-faced with anger and, I thought, embarrassment after the big buildup for this meeting.

"Must be busy with other things," Stahl mumbled. "We can try again tomorrow if you want."

Elrod looked like a prizefighter and came across like a prosecutor. I recalled it was he who'd commanded the mass arrests during the April uprising. He demanded to know what we'd do if we didn't get the permits.

"We'll cross that bridge if we come to it," Jeff answered coyly. "But our expectation is that we will get them."

Elrod presented three alternative march routes, none of which would bring us anywhere near the convention. Donnie quickly told him they were unacceptable. Next, he tried to interrogate us on what the marshals would be doing, and whether we were planning to break any laws.

I'd never seen Dellinger visibly angry before this moment. "I see where you're going with this," he seethed. "And I can tell you right now we won't obey any order that violates our civil or constitutional rights."

The squabbling continued until the meeting broke up. It had been a complete waste of time.

Back at the office, things got even worse. Paul, who we'd left behind to supervise things, told us, "I got a heads-up from an old friend who's on McCarthy's national staff. At a press conference this afternoon, he'll urge his supporters to stay away from Chicago during the convention, unless they're delegates."

"Why?" I asked. But we knew the answer. The threat of violence was hanging over everything.

"We better go sit down," Donnie said, pointing down the hall.

This day, which I'd anticipated with hope and optimism, had turned into the exact opposite. McCarthy would, in effect, be warning *everyone* to stay away. Daley's scare tactics had hit pay dirt, and we knew what that meant. We'd get little or no cooperation from his administration, and there wouldn't be a hundred thousand antiwar protesters marching through the streets. There would be only a fraction of that.

"Well?" Donnie asked the dejected staff. "Anyone want out?"

"I want to say something," Paul interjected. "We've been building a grass-roots independent antiwar movement for years now. We're in every city and active on every college campus. Without our movement, there never would've even been any primaries. Now it looks like there'll be a platform fight over the war. That might not mean much to us, but it would never have become an issue there if we hadn't been in the streets."

"Okay, but what's your point?" Vern asked.

"My point is this: If we let Daley scare us off, it could be the end of the antiwar movement as an effective force."

"Why would that be?" I asked.

"We express our numbers and our power, we energize our base, by going into the streets. Demonstrations, rallies, marches. So now everyone's watching to see what we do this time. Daley's trying to shut us down, and McCarthy's caving in. If we do the same, if we cancel the highest-profile protest of the year and leave town with our tails between our legs, it won't only be a sign of moral cowardice. It'll be a *huge strategic blunder*. If Daley can make us back down, what's to prevent every other mayor from making the same threats? 'If protesters show up,' they'll think, 'we'll just call out the troops and they'll crawl back into their holes.' This is not only a moral and political decision. It's a strategic decision, an existential one."

It didn't take much discussion for us to agree.

"I've got to bring it to the Steering Committee," Donnie concluded. "But they'll understand what we have to do. We knew all along this might happen, so now it's time to face it. Vern, you're training marshals tomorrow?"

"Yes. Grant Park to start with and then Lincoln Park. We'll run a session every day until the convention. But now we'll focus a little more on crowd defense than on crowd control."

"That makes sense. Steve, see what you can do with the park commissioners tomorrow. However many people are coming, they'll still need places to sleep. We're not folding."

After this little pep rally, I sat at a desk with my head in my hands, trying to sort out my emotions. One part of me was bursting with rage, itching for battle, whether at the convention or at City Hall, consequences be damned. Another part wanted no more than to hide under the blankets with Cat until the smoke cleared.

Before long, it hit me. *Cat. I'll have to tell her.* I felt my head caught in the grip of a vise that it seemed was always nearby, ready to grab hold.

I picked up the phone and dialed the bookstore. Emma answered.

"Can we talk tonight?" I asked. "I need help. Again. And Cat has to be there too."

Emma didn't ask a single question. She simply responded, "My place at six."

I got home with a little time to spare, so I splashed cold water on my face, flopped down on the couch, and considered how to break the news. *How can I tell Cat whatever hopes we'd been hanging onto have all been dashed?* My headache was only getting worse, so I gave up. I had no way to soft-pedal this. I took a deep breath and headed down to Emma's.

The pizza box sat on the living room table. Cat handed me a beer and gave me her worried look, the one I'd come to know all too well. She sat me down and asked, "What happened?"

I was too agitated to stay seated. "First," I said, "let's turn the TV on." As luck would have it, NBC News was showing a clip from McCarthy's press conference. He called for "a peaceful and orderly convention, and an orderly convention city." He warned that any violence or disorder would be "a tragedy for any hurt or arrested, and a tragedy for those of us who wish to give the political process a fair and peaceful test."

"Why don't you tell that to Daley?" I yelled at the TV. Cat shushed me. Then came the line Paul told us to expect:

"I hope that my supporters will conduct any rallies and other public demonstrations of support in their own communities, and *not* in Chicago."

"See? He's scaring everyone away," I exclaimed angrily. "Playing right into Daley and Humphrey's hands!" I shut the TV off, and paced around the room.

"But what if we get the permits?" Cat asked.

"We're not getting them!" My energy seeped out as agitation turned to despair. I fell back into the chair and repeated, "We're not getting them."

Emma asked, "Was your City Hall meeting canceled?"

"No. It was even worse."

Now the anger rose again. I couldn't sit still. I resumed pacing as I related what happened at the meeting. I recited it, almost word for word, acting out the various roles. It must have looked like a one-man play performed by a lunatic. Cat took my arm and led me back to the chair. She pulled up another next to mine, and held my hand in hers. She wanted to comfort me, but I knew I was upsetting her and I felt guilty for laying this on her yet again.

"And back at the office, as if things weren't bad enough," I continued, "Paul told us to expect what we just saw on the news."

Cat asked, "Now what?"

I related Paul's analysis of how the antiwar movement's survival depended on its refusal to fold under the pressure, no matter what military force might come down on us.

"And we all agreed," I concluded. "There was no way around it. But it looks like there will be violence. There will be sacrifice."

Cat grabbed my face in her hands, and turned it to hers. "No," she insisted with tears welling. "No! Not you! No!"

"Please, take it easy," Emma insisted. "The convention is still two weeks away and I know you two will make the right decision. I don't know what it'll be, but, together, you'll find it. Right now, Steve, I want to know what's going on with you."

"It's driving me crazy." I began as Cat took my hand again. "This war goes on, day after day. Thousands of bombs dropping from the sky, from U.S. planes, every single day. Lives ruined. Lives ended. Children! I can't even bear to hear a child cry. In Vietnam, they're screaming in terror, losing limbs, dying. And here I am, far away from it all, safe and sound in Chicago, spending the whole summer playing make-believe."

"It's not make-believe," Cat interjected. "You've been working hard to make something happen, to make a difference."

"No. It's all been a waste of time," I argued. "We had visions of hundreds of thousands of people marching against the war. An enormous show of force, confronting the war-makers, demanding they bring the troops home. Now, we might not even get near the convention. It was a delusion. I feel so damn worthless."

"Not to me!" she exclaimed. "Never to me!"

"Look at you, Cat. There are tears in your eyes. I keep bringing you heartache and worry. You'd be better off without me."

Taking my face in her hands again, and peering into my eyes, she said, "Steve, you bring me a kind of joy I never knew existed. Of course you sometimes scare me, like now. Sure I worry. That's only because I love you so much. I need you so much."

"You shouldn't. You're beautiful and brilliant, and you have all that love to give. You're wasting it on me. You deserve better, and you could have any man you want. You should be with someone who has something to offer, someone who actually accomplishes things, not a dope who chases dreams." I put her hands back in her lap and looked down at the floor.

"I should go away and leave you alone," I murmured. "I'm just messing up your life."

"No!" she cried, beginning to sob. "Emma, help us. Please."

"Can I say something, Steve?" Emma calmly asked.

"Sure you can," I muttered without lifting my eyes. "But it'll be wasted on me. It's all been wasted on me. You'd be better off without me too. You were both better off before I came along."

"That's for us to decide," she responded. "Not you. Look, what you and Cat share comes along once in a lifetime, and only to those who are very, very lucky. You're not stupid enough to walk away from that, and I know you won't."

"I won't let you," Cat interjected.

"You've been betrayed and misled," Emma continued, "first by that Ronnie and now by the deputy mayor. But you blame yourself instead of them. And look at it politically. If you throw yourself in the garbage because of what they've done, you'll be letting them win. You'll be letting Daley win. Is that what you want?"

That got my attention. "Of course not," I replied, shaking my head. "But what can I do? I'm a failure."

"No, you're not," she argued. "You've been doing good work ever since you came to Chicago, and you've put everything you had into it. You've done more than anyone could've asked. Once your head is on straight again, you'll see that. Don't you want to feel better than you do right now?"

"I guess so. But how?"

"Fight back. Two weeks until the convention, and plenty of work still to do. Remember what Paul said today. He was right. The movement needs this demonstration, whatever form it takes, and the Mobe needs you to help make it happen."

"And I need you," Cat added.

"Fight back," Emma repeated. "Don't let the bastards win. That's how you'll find your way back to yourself."

"And back to me," Cat added. She pulled up closer and put her arm through mine.

My depression wasn't powerful enough to withstand the two of them. It began to lift, though ever so slightly, as though a strong rope was dragging me up out of quicksand.

"You're right," I agreed. "We can't let them win. I guess I've been feeling sorry for myself. There are things I can do, and yes, I need to do them. Cat, Emma, I'm so sorry about this."

"Nothing to apologize for," Emma responded, sliding a pizza slice onto a plate. "It's part of movement life. We need to support each other at moments like this." Handing me the plate, she added, "Now you should eat."

Chapter 70

Cat's ministrations once again permitted me to fall asleep, but this night only in snatches. Each time I woke, it seemed she was waiting. Each time I said, "You need to sleep," and she replied, "I've been sleeping. Now close your eyes." Then she stroked my face or my chest.

Fighting through grogginess, I pumped more iron than usual at our morning workout. The pain seemed to offer a kind of release. Cat noticed veins bulging, though, and begged me to stop. We both knew I was still a mess.

As I dressed for work, she asked, "Are you sure you're ready for this? Are you up to it?"

"I have to be. Today's the meeting of the Park District Board. I'm supposed to make a presentation. We might at least get a permit for something out of them."

"Well, okay, but I hope you can come home early. What time is the meeting?"

It suddenly struck me that I didn't know. "I don't remember," I replied. "I must've it written down at the office."

I couldn't find any note at the office, so I called Superintendent Barry. His receptionist said he was on the phone and couldn't be disturbed. I left a message, asking that he return the call. An hour later, I tried again. Now, he was in a meeting. Again, after another hour, the same result. Between calls, I kept myself busy, working with volunteers stuffing envelopes and typing labels for our final pre-convention fundraising appeal.

The next time I called, I apologized for being a pest, and explained the urgency of the situation. "I don't want to be late for the presentation," I explained, "but I need to know what time I'm expected."

"I'm so sorry," she responded with what sounded like genuine concern. "I hope it wasn't my mistake."

We talked for a few minutes. I found out her name was Sue. She was very nice, but she still couldn't put me through. I asked, "If I bring over a note, can you pass it to him?" She agreed.

I spent the next hour drafting, revising and typing a three-paragraph memorandum. It referenced the application I'd submitted, and gently reminded him of the invitation he'd extended two weeks earlier. I ran it over to his office, and gave it to Sue. She promised to get it to him, and even ask him to read it before the meeting started.

I thanked her and asked, "What time will that be?"

"Four o'clock," was her reply.

Walking through Grant Park on my way back to the office, I stopped to watch the marshal training. Vern had recruited two other vets to help, and they were putting fifty young men through their paces. One tactic was to clench fists and link arms, to form a barrier between police and protesters. Another was to hurl themselves across the bodies of cops trying to drag people off. There was no way to role-play this without looking silly, but they did seem to be enjoying themselves. Neither of these tactics looked like they'd be very effective, though, and the fun would be over once real armed cops were in the picture. Still, I felt an urge to join them. For the first time in memory, the thought of violence consciously attracted me. Mindful of my solemn promise to Cat, though, I continued on my way.

Two messages awaited me, both from clergymen withdrawing offers of housing assistance. I crossed them off my list, and watched the minutes tick by on the wall clock.

At four o'clock, I called Sue again and asked, "Were you able to give him the memo?"

"Oh yes," she replied, "and he read it right away."

"But he didn't ask you to call me?"

"No, he didn't say anything."

"And the meeting has already started?"

"Yes, so I can't disturb them now. Maybe he'll call from there."

I waited until six, then called Sue again.

"I guess they ran out of time for presentations today," she told me. "But I'm sure everything will work out. Call me in the morning. I'll have the Minutes and I can tell you what they decided."

I thanked her and went home, at least as dejected as I'd been the day before.

"You've done everything possible," Cat said, "and we can still hope. They haven't denied anything yet." We both knew, though, that even this last ray of hope was fading fast.

First thing Wednesday morning, I checked in with Sue and asked what happened at the meeting.

"Let me get the file," she said. "Ah, here it is." After a long pause, punctuated only by the sounds of paper shuffling, "I'm sorry, but it seems Mr. Barry didn't put your application on the agenda."

"What?"

"Yes. I don't know why, but it never came up for consideration."

I thanked her, hung up and leaned back as energy drained from my body. I'd only been hanging on, and now this. One more time, I'd been played for a fool. I stared at the clock, watching it tick-tock its way toward apocalypse.

Donnie and Jeff, on their way out, stopped to ask, "What's wrong?"

"Park District," I mumbled, my eyes still fixed blankly on the clock. "They met yesterday. The lying, sadistic son-of-a-bitch never even put us on the agenda. Now, we can forget about a permit for the parks."

"Come with us," Jeff offered. "We're on our way to see a lawyer. This might be just what you need."

Unable to think of anything more useful to do, I walked with them a few blocks to a sleek, modern office building on LaSalle Street. We took the elevator to the top floor, which was occupied entirely by the law firm of Pierce, Gates, Warren and Witherspoon.

Jeff introduced himself to the receptionist adding, "We're here to see Mr. Wendell Pierce."

"Oh yes, he's expecting you. Please follow me. He'll be with you in a moment."

The conference room she led us to had a glass wall overlooking the Loop. The chairs were upholstered in rich, tufted, burgundy leather, the table carved from a dark exotic wood I'd never before seen. Coffee and pastries were waiting.

The door opened, and in strode a tall middle-aged man with patrician features, wearing a pinstriped business suit that whispered, "Custom-tailored. Very, very expensive." His appearance and bearing imparted an air of confidence, even command, before he even spoke a word.

"Sorry to be late," he said. "Sometimes, these real estate negotiations are endless. Jeffrey, how are you?"

"A little edgy, I guess," Jeff replied. "Thanks for taking the time to see us."

We stood, and Jeff introduced us to Wendell Pierce, the firm's managing partner. We each received a firm handshake.

"Jeffrey brought me up to date yesterday," he began as we took our seats. "Is there anything else I should know?" Donnie nodded at me.

"Well, one thing," I explained. "The Park District's commissioners met yesterday, and they never considered our application. Superintendent Barry promised me two weeks ago that they would listen to my presentation, but he didn't even put it on the agenda."

"Not surprising," Pierce observed. "Barry must have gotten the word from Daley. It sounds like you're running out of options."

"And we're running out of time," Donnie added. "We're hoping you can help. Can we sue the city to make them grant the permits?"

"This certainly raises some constitutional issues," Pierce mused thoughtfully, "and it's worth a try. But it seems you'll have to get in line."

"Get in line?" Jeff asked.

"After you and I spoke yesterday, I called a friend at the ACLU. He told me they'd filed a suit on behalf of Lowenstein's group. They're challenging the constitutionality of requiring a permit to use Soldier Field, since the stadium is inside a public park. Apparently, Lowenstein wants to go ahead with his rally even though McCarthy won't support it. And the Yippies are suing to get the use of Lincoln Park for some week-long festival. If we jump in, it'll be a busy week at the courthouse."

"Do you think we'd have a chance?" Donnie asked.

"It's a long shot, but we can present a solid First Amendment argument. We can also charge the mayor with violating his oath of office by 'creating conditions conducive to civil disorder.' Yes, that should get their attention."

"Then let's do it," Donnie urged. "It seems to be our last hope."

"I'll get a team working on it right away. In the meantime, I want you to put this letter on your stationery. Hand-deliver it as soon as you can to Joe Woods, the Cook County Sheriff."

We scanned the letter. Only a few paragraphs long, it described the details of our planned march and cited six Supreme Court decisions supporting our right to do it.

"Putting them on notice," Pierce explained, "and giving them something to think about."

Out on the sidewalk, I asked, "Jeff, this guy must be super expensive. Can we afford him?"

"Hell, no. At his hourly rate, we'd be broke by tomorrow. But he's volunteered to work for us *pro bono*, for free. His firm is even covering the court costs."

"Wow. How'd you find him?"

"We didn't. He found us. He contacted one of my professors, who put him in touch with me."

"But why? He's certainly no movement lawyer."

"His only son was killed last year," Jeff explained. "In Vietnam."

Chapter 71

"So, one ray of hope extinguished, one more to go," I told Cat over dinner. During my recap, she watched me intently, concentrating on my facial expressions. She didn't ask any questions, which was unusual. I asked, "Why are you looking at me that way? What's wrong?"

"That's what I'm wondering," she answered. "I'm trying to tell if you're all right. You've had such a tough couple of weeks. Ronnie's treachery, the disastrous City Hall meeting, and now this business with the parks. It's been one thing after another."

"I'm fine," I said, squeezing her hand. "I'm trying to remember what you and Emma were saying, and to not blame myself for things I can't control. And anyway, maybe this lawyer can help us."

"I hope so too," she responded, "and I'm glad you remember our talk. You did scare me, you know."

"I know. Cat, I hate when that happens. But I get overwhelmed."

"That's what we're here for, Steve, to take care of one another. Ow! My hand! Don't squeeze so tight!"

Releasing her hand, I admitted, "Sometimes I want to squeeze you until we melt together. But here I am again, having to say 'I'm sorry.' "

"Don't apologize for things you do out of love."

The phone rang. It was Paul.

"Do you know about the McCarthy rally?" he asked. "It's tomorrow night."

"Uh-uh. I didn't know there was one."

"Neither did I until a little while ago. We should have more contact with the campaign, or at least with the folks who're still depending on him to end the war."

"I guess so, since we're hoping they join us during Convention Week. But their candidate said to stay away."

"That's why tomorrow night's a good opportunity for us. The rally's at the Civic Opera House, starting at seven. It'll give us a chance to talk to some of them."

"Will McCarthy be there?"

"Not exactly. He'll be at Madison Square Garden in New York. But they'll be broadcasting his speech through closed-circuit TV all over the country."

"Oh, okay. I wonder if he's gotten any better at it. Anyway, I guess we should bring leaflets to hand out."

"Yes, we should. You and I can work on writing one. Okay?"

"Sure. See you tomorrow."

After I hung up, Cat asked, "Who was that?"

I told her about the rally and our plan for leafleting, adding, "That's unless you mind me being out tomorrow night."

"Of course I don't. It's a good idea. I'll come too."

Cat let me oversleep Thursday morning, so I didn't get to the office until almost eleven. A project was already well underway. A donor had contributed 10,000 buttons to help promote the convention protests. Almost two inches in diameter, they read:

CONFRONT THE WARMAKERS!
August '68
See You in Chicago!

Jeff had a group of volunteers packing them up for shipment to the Mobe's constituent groups. Passing by, I got a pleasant surprise.

"Sabrina!" I called. She looked up, came over and gave me a hug.

"Does Cat know you're back in town?"

"Yes. I called a little while ago. I told her I couldn't think of a better way to spend the last couple of weeks of summer than to volunteer with the Mobe. She sounded excited to hear it."

"Excited?"

"Yes. She said she was glad I'd be here now. 'To keep an eye on Steve!' was how she put it. But I better get back to work. Jeff says all these boxes have to go out by the end of the day."

Between the metallic rattle of the buttons, the shouts of the people who pricked their fingers packing them up, the jumble of boxes and newspaper wadding, the taping and addressing, there was no place for Paul and me to work on the leaflet.

"This is nuts," he said. "Let's go down the hall."

On our way into the AFSC office, we nearly bumped into Jack Weaver, its executive director.

"I was coming down to your place," he told us. "Is Donnie around?"

"He is," Paul answered, "but I don't think you want to go in there. It's total bedlam. That's why we came down here, to ask if your conference room's available."

"Okay. I wanted to tell Donnie personally that our board directed me to send a mailing to our members, warning that violence appears unavoidable. They're mostly pacifists, and they have a right to know. I also thought you folks had a right to know we were doing it."

"I'm sorry to hear that," Paul responded, "but it's understandable. I'll pass along the message. But does this mean we can't use the conference room anymore?"

"Of course not, and it's free right now. Policy is up to the board, but I decide how we use our facilities. And listen, people will come into town anyway. Pacifists aren't cowards. Quite the opposite in fact."

Paul thanked him and added, "We'll be out of your hair in a couple of weeks."

"Good luck. I hope you get to make your point without anyone getting hurt."

"They're dropping like flies," Paul remarked once we shut the door.

"What if we can get even one permit?" I asked. "So people can come for some event, like a rally, without worrying about the cops."

"That would help a lot. We do have the Anti-Birthday Party at the Coliseum, so let's play that up. It's so contained, though, and too far from the convention. Anyway, let's get going on the leaflet for tonight. I started a rough draft. Take a look."

I skimmed it quickly and said, "Paul, I don't know if this will get them to join us. There's nothing wrong with it, but I don't think it meets them where they are."

"What do you mean?"

"Like here," I tried to explain, "where it calls our electoral system 'corrupt, bankrupt and rigged.' That's not gonna work."

"But it is what it is," he argued.

"Sure it is. You know it, and now even I know it. But they don't. If they did, they wouldn't still be knocking themselves out for McCarthy. So, if we leave that language in, we'll be insulting them, turning them off."

"I see your point," he agreed thoughtfully. "But how do we get them to see it our way?"

"Not by telling them something they're not ready to hear yet. The Democratic Party itself will teach them how corrupt the system is."

"So how would you approach it?" he asked.

"I think we need to make only a few points, and do it without getting too wordy. We should start off by congratulating them on their good work. After all, the antiwar candidates did win the primaries. Then we describe how the party bosses are stacking the deck against them. Finally, we invite them to join us in the streets to protest. We should emphasize that most of what we're doing is perfectly legal."

"I like that, Steve. On the back, we can list the activities we've got planned."

"Yes, with asterisks marking the ones that still require permits. We can give them a phone number to call for updates, even though it'll be all over the news anyway."

"I really do like how you think about this, Steve. Where'd you get that?"

"I've had a great teacher for the past year. Emma Gold."

"Oh, Emma. You know, a few years ago, SDS held a national conference, and Donnie invited her to run a workshop on Community Organizing. Since then, across the country, I keep running into activists who tell me how that workshop changed the way they talk to people. They're all over, organizing tenants, parents, students, poor people. Organizing for community empowerment and against racism and the war. They tell me their touchstone is what they learned from Emma."

"I didn't know that, Paul. But I'm not surprised. Emma has one daughter, but I think she has many, many children."

It took us an hour, passing drafts back and forth, to finalize the text. We decided to emphasize that the march to the convention would be "with or without a permit," but entirely voluntary. Once we agreed on a final draft, I said, "Wait here. I'll be right back."

I returned with Sabrina and a blank pad. Fifteen minutes later, we had a design that Paul said was better than anything the Mobe had ever put out. By late afternoon, we mimeographed a thousand copies. They completed production without me, though. As soon as I stepped back into our office, the commotion triggered my claustrophobia. I went home for an early dinner.

Cat and I got to the opera house at six. Paul and Sabrina were already leafleting the early arrivals.

"Good practice for resuming our Saran Wrap boycott," Sabrina said. "Will you be joining us again in the fall?"

"I sure plan to," I replied. "Cat and I are looking forward to a normal life after the convention, and the leafleting can certainly be part of it." I wasn't certain what my "normal life" would look like while the war still raged, but the sound of those words had a calming effect.

Not unexpectedly, Cat and Sabrina got lots of attention, with knots of young men eager to hang on their every word. Paul and I got into plenty of conversations too, and some spirited debate.

Once the rally began and the latecomers were inside, we compared notes. We'd encountered a variety of attitudes among the McCarthy supporters. Some said they'd walk away from politics if they had to choose between two pro-war presidential candidates. Many said they did see the value of being in the streets and they'd join us for at least some of what we'll be doing, no matter what their candidate advised. Others were in denial, still hoping McCarthy will somehow win the nomination. What they might do once reality intruded was anyone's guess. We didn't encounter anyone willing to transfer their allegiance to Hubert Humphrey.

The experience energized us. If this was a fair sample, plenty of McCarthy supporters would be joining us. We decided to get a taste of the rally.

The Fire Marshall's notice on the wall said the capacity was 2,000 people, and it was packed. We were standing in the rear of the orchestra section, with about a hundred others, when Phil Ochs, the antiwar movement's traveling troubadour, came on stage. For me, everything that followed his renditions of "Draft Dodger Rag" and "I Ain't Marchin' Anymore" was anti-climactic. When McCarthy took the stage at the 25,000-seat Garden, that arena was also filled to capacity. The speech we watched on a big screen was well-received, but to me it came across as flat. I thought the poet in him did come out, though, with this challenge: "Vietnam asks us, as it has for many years, who we really are as a nation."

"I guess we'll get the answer to that in Chicago next week," I suggested to Cat.

The words running through my head on the way home were from Phil Ochs.

> *It's always the old who lead us to the war,*
> *Always the young who fall...*
> *Call it peace or call it treason,*
> *Call it love or call it reason,*
> *But I ain't marchin' any more.*

Chapter 72

Friday morning, when Cat asked about my plans for the day, I replied, "Everything's up in the air. So much depends on our lawsuit, but we won't know about that until next week. Vern is training marshals in the afternoon. If I can get away, I guess I'd like to see some of that."

"You promised you wouldn't be a marshal," she scolded.

"No, no. I just thought I'd watch."

"Good. I'll come watch with you. When and where?"

"Northeast corner of Lincoln Park, at three."

"Okay. Leave Tooter with me, so I can run some errands for Emma. I'll meet you there."

I was a little annoyed that she still didn't trust me about this, but reminded myself how high the stakes were for her. I was sure she sensed the rage and frustration simmering inside me now. The only way out of this mess would be a court decision paving the way to a peaceful, militant march. It wouldn't have to be to the doors of the convention, only someplace close where our voices could be heard. Hopes dimmed, though, early in an impromptu staff meeting.

"Wendell Pierce called," Donnie told us. "He's already filed our case in Federal District Court and arranged for expedited review."

"It's good to have connections," Jeff commented. "That sounds promising."

"But there's more," Donnie continued. "All three Convention Week cases have been assigned to the same judge, William J. Lynch. Do you know who that is?" We shrugged our shoulders.

"Neither did I," he explained, "until Pierce told me. Judge Lynch is the former law partner of Richard J. Daley, our esteemed mayor."

I spent the rest of the morning doing paperwork, answering the phone and trying not to snarl at anyone. Around noon, Donnie handed me a letter he'd written to John M. Bailey, Chairman of the Democratic

National Committee, asking the DNC to intervene with the mayor. One paragraph read,

> *It would be a grave mistake to believe that by withholding permits, the number of demonstrators will be reduced. The people we represent have faced hazards before, and will face them again. The withholding of permits, like the talk of repressive weapons and troops, will only increase the chances for a confrontation which we, at least, do not seek.*

"Good letter," I said. "Want me to mail it?"

"No. I'd like you to mimeograph a hundred copies. Bailey's holding a press conference at the Conrad Hilton in an hour. I'm going to hand-deliver it to him right there."

"And the hundred copies?"

"Those are for you to hand out to the reporters."

Bailey's press conference turned out to be an unexpected opportunity. Donnie even got to tell him, in front of the cameras, how the city administration was stonewalling our permit requests, and to ask the DNC to help us head off the possibility of violence. Bailey said he would speak to the mayor, but didn't commit to anything. Then Donnie handed him the letter, while I distributed the copies. After the press conference ended, the reporters were all over us.

At Lincoln Park, Cat was already watching Vern and his team try to train a motley crew of a few dozen activists, hippies, Yippies and SDS militants. It was a crowd defense maneuver which student demonstrators in Japan called the Snake Dance. I didn't know how this was supposed to work, but what we saw involved linking arms, swaying back and forth, then gathering into a wedge and pushing forward. The idea, apparently, was to split and disorient the police lines. The actual result was people losing their balance because they were linked together, and sometimes falling over one another. There was lots of laughter, though, and the fragrant scent of marijuana wafted through the air.

"This is ridiculous," Cat declared, heading over for a talk with Vern.

He clapped his hands and announced, "Okay, guys. We're shifting gears now to individual self-defense. Cat here is gonna demonstrate a few techniques."

She beckoned me over. "You know what to do," she winked, then turned and walked slowly away. All those male eyes were on her. We recreated the show we'd put on at Jackson Park Beach a few weeks back, except that now, every time she leveraged her 105 pounds to throw my 140 to the ground, I heard whoops and cheers. After the fifth time, Vern divided the group between those who wanted to learn Cat's moves, and those who were still married to the Snake Dance. I moved to join Cat's group, but she stopped me.

"Not you," she insisted. "We agreed, remember? You're not getting involved with this. Just watch."

Now I asserted myself. "You can't teach these moves throwing the air around, and I don't want any of those guys touching you."

Cat conceded to my demand, and I again became her beanbag. During the next hour, she taught five jujitsu techniques, demonstrating each one on me, then pairing the marshals up to try it for themselves. If it wasn't going well, she stopped them for another demonstration, and tossed me around once again.

On the way home, Cat asked, "Tell me the truth. Weren't you tempted to get into the mix with the marshals? Isn't that why you wanted to go and watch the training?"

"I thought it would distract me from waiting for the legal stuff to play out," I explained. "To be honest, yes, it is tempting. But I'd made up my mind not to give in to that."

"Oh, why?" she asked, putting her hand on my shoulder.

"Ow," I groaned. "Isn't it obvious? You would've beaten the crap out of me!"

"Oh, is my baby a wee bit sore?" she asked slyly.

"Only all over."

"Well, I've got the cure for that, just as soon as we get home."

Chapter 73

Saturday morning, Cat gushed, "Yesterday was fun. If you want to observe some more training next week, I'll be glad to come along and keep you company."

"No, thank you," I replied with mock seriousness. "I've already observed more than enough."

During breakfast with Emma, we went through the papers. The Associated Press coverage of Bailey's press conference made front-page news. The lead story was his announcement that floor demonstrations, the sometimes raucous shows of delegate support which traditionally followed presidential nominating speeches, were being eliminated. He claimed the reason for that decision was "efficiency and time management," but we knew better. They were afraid of disruption from antiwar forces not only outside, but also inside the convention hall. Donnie and I were quoted extensively as well. We even got in a plug for our LBJ Anti-Birthday Party.

"This was brilliant!" Emma exclaimed. "Free national publicity for the Mobe, which comes across as the voice of reason. It makes Daley look like an ass."

She focused on me. "Monday night, Steve, you insisted you'd failed in your work at the Mobe. I know you were down in the dumps at the time, but this is something you should never forget. Donnie could've asked any number of people to work with him on this yesterday, but you're the one he chose. Paul could've asked anyone to work with him on Thursday's leaflet, or he could've done it himself. But he asked for your help and he took your advice. You should remember the trust these movement veterans put in you, time and time again. That's because they value your work, and your opinions."

"It isn't that I haven't noticed," I responded, "but it comes as a surprise to me every time."

"Why should it?" Cat asked.

"Maybe it's because they're not seeing the real me. That's how I feel anyway. Like if they knew the real me, I'd be outside stuffing envelopes, not inside our core staff meetings. And I sure screwed up by trusting Ronnie."

"Let's not get into that again," Cat argued. "Everyone trusted Ronnie. She was in a position of trust before you even got there."

"Try to let a little reality in," Emma urged. "During your first year of college, you exercised real leadership on campus. In almost no time, you became a key Mobe staffer. And look at this woman who loves you so much. You don't think you can put very much over on her, do you?"

"Well, I guess you got me there," I admitted.

"And I don't miss much either," she continued. "Look at all you've accomplished in less than a year. It wasn't make-believe. It was real. And if you ever doubt it, stop and check in with one of us. Now, what do you kids have planned for the rest of the day?"

"Nothing really," I replied, pointing out the window. "The weather's kind of nasty."

"A good day for reading," Cat suggested. "I know. How about you read to me? I love that."

"Okay. I do too. And thanks for this morning, Emma. I wish we could do it tomorrow with the *Sunday Times*. With only a week to go before the convention, maybe we'll have another front-page story."

"We can do that."

"How? You usually don't get it in the mail until Tuesday."

"Downtown at Union Station," she explained, "they get the early edition delivered overnight. It'll be on the newsstand in the morning."

"So I'll go and get it."

"Good. And you know what else they have? Real New York bagels."

"They do? I'll get them too."

"All right then. Bagels, papers and talk shows tomorrow morning. Let's say around ten. We'll make it a pajama party. Now you two run along. I need a little nap."

We spent the rest of the day curled up on the couch with Joyce Carol Oates's short stories. It occurred to me at some point that Cat and Emma were conspiring to distract me from the uncertainties facing us in the coming week. But I was loving it.

Sunday morning, before I left for Union Station, Cat asked how I was feeling.

"Pretty good," I reported, honestly. "How about you?"

"Oh, I'm fine. Wondering if you want me to go with you."

"Really, I'm good. I promise not to get into trouble buying newspapers. You relax. Take a long bubble bath. But I better get going. I'll meet you at Emma's in about an hour."

I walked down the block to get Tooter. Driving back past our building, I noticed, out of a corner of my eye, a figure standing in Emma's doorway, holding a lit cigarette. It was her, of course, with one of her beloved, deadly Newports. *Well*, I thought, *at least she took it outside.* It saddened me, though.

After my errand, I changed into pajamas and went down to Emma's, carrying not only the *Times* and bagels, but also scallion cream cheese, Nova Scotia lox, a red onion, a beefsteak tomato and a jar of capers.

"Meet the Press" had begun on NBC. We watched it, ate, divided up the paper, read clips out loud, ate some more, talked back to the TV and made each other laugh. It was an orgy of Sunday breakfast and current affairs.

The *Times* now had a dozen reporters in Chicago for the convention. Its big Page One story, though, focused on us. It was titled, "Dissenters Focusing on Chicago." Emma pointed to the byline and told us J. Anthony Lukas was one of the paper's top reporters. He'd recently won a Pulitzer Prize for his reporting on the social conflicts that were defining the decade.

"Listen to this," I said, "right here on the front page."

> *"I've never seen anything like it," said one veteran of the peace movement. "The spectacle of the Democrats nominating Hubert Humphrey, while so many other guys are being nominated for death in Vietnam, or for quiet oblivion in the ghettos, is just plain grotesque. So a lot of other people are going to be here in Chicago to do some nominating of our own."*

Cat and Emma applauded. I continued...

> *It would be rash to predict how many dissenters will assemble. One hears estimates ranging from a probably conservative 50,000 to a seemingly inflated "over a million."*

"Over a million," Emma laughed. "I wonder where he got that!"

I scanned the text. "It seems he got it from Lowenstein."

"That figures," she snorted. "The egomaniac."

"It would be the demonstration of the century, though," I mused, "and it sure would be great. But the way things are going, we'll be happy if that 'conservative 50,000' turns out to be right." My mood suddenly darkened, and it must have showed. "The way things are going . . ."

Cat shook my arm. "Tell us more. Keep reading."

I snapped out of it, and went back to the article. "He says, 'There will be scarcely a moment when the dissidents in the streets are not vying for attention with the delegates on the convention floor.' And then, 'All the dissidents are committed to non-violence,' and he quotes Daley, promising to enforce law and order on the streets."

"Oh, but get this." I read from further down the long article.

> *Those who have seen the Chicago police in action*
> *– particularly in the uninhibited clash with peace*
> *demonstrators on April 27 – fear clashes during*
> *the convention are almost inevitable.*

Cat watched with dismay as I went on to summarize the reporter's very respectful summary of interviews with Donnie and Dave, with Lowenstein, and with some Yippie leaders. In each case, the issue of the permits rose to the fore. We turned to the article's continuation on page 69, where Cat found something else.

"Here's the conclusion another reporter reached: 'Both of the men most likely to enter the White House next January have committed themselves to liquidating the war.' Really. That's what it says, right here." She held up the inside page.

"What great news!" Emma exclaimed. "Steve, get Donnie on the phone. Tell him the Mobe can fold up its tents. The war is as good as over!"

It felt so good to laugh. We picked all the papers apart in that mood, as well as the hypocrites interviewed on the TV talk shows. Still, the phrase that stuck in my head, from one of the other *Times* articles was, "the total uncertainty of what is likely to come from the cauldron that is heating up in Chicago."

Later, after dinner, I told Cat, "This has been a great weekend, and you made it happen. Thank you."

"Oh, but it's not over."

After a leisurely bout of love-making, I fell asleep like a baby. It wasn't long, though, until I woke with a start. Cat stirred awake, asking, "What? What is it?"

"That damned carnival dream. It gets more horrible every time."

She rose up on an elbow and. "It's only a dream," she said softly, pushing me back onto the pillow. "But tell me."

"It was like that time we marched on the armory and got attacked with the bayonets, and ran through the alley to get away. Except it was different. It was just you and me. We were trapped in the alley. Soldiers with rifles came at us from one end. Cops waving nightsticks from the other. All staring at us, grinning. I turned, needing to wrap my arms around you, to protect you. But you were gone. Vanished. I was all alone, and the brick walls on both sides were moving, closing in on me. And I was a four-year-old boy again."

"Only a dream," Cat repeated, caressing my cheek. "I'm here. I'm right here. Here for you. Everything's okay."

My body heaved and shook as I burst out crying. She held me and rocked me, cooing in my ear, stroking me until finally, mercifully, I calmed down enough to sleep once more.

Chapter 74

From Monday's early papers, we learned that momentum from Thursday's McCarthy rallies had carried right through the weekend, triggering numerous parades and motorcades around the country. Also, the candidate released the text of his proposed Vietnam platform plank. Like McGovern's, it called for an immediate end to the bombings and the search-and-destroy missions. It called for negotiations among *all* contending forces to form a new coalition government. If the South Vietnamese regime refused to participate, the draft implied, we would simply withdraw our forces and leave it to stand or fall on its own. It concluded, "With such a program, we will have attained our only legitimate objective: the self-determination of the Vietnamese people."

Meanwhile, McGovern called for the immediate, unconditional withdrawal of half of our troops. Asked whether he would consider endorsing Humphrey in the election, he replied, "That depends on the platform."

"If only any of this had a chance of meaning something," I muttered.

"You never know," Cat replied hopefully. "Like Emma said, at least there'll be a platform fight. And it should be a good one."

Another story reported that the actual fighting in Vietnam had escalated to its most intense level in three months. And LBJ announced that, no matter what happened at the convention, or even in the election, "I will be the president until next January 20th, so there will be no earlier change in war policy." *Isn't that lovely?* I thought.

While I was trying to make myself presentable for court, the phone rang.

"Hello, Steve." I recognized the voice.

"Uh, hi, Dad. How are you?"

"Fine, thanks. Listen, I'm in Chicago on business and really need to see you. Can we get together for a little while?"

"Well, sure, but I'll be tied up all day. How about tonight, around seven? You can come here."

When the call ended, Cat asked, "What's this about?"

"Who knows? Must be important, though."

"Well, if you want, I can go down to Emma's and leave you two alone to talk."

"Absolutely not. That would be like hiding you. Besides, whatever it is, I want you here with me."

Donnie, Jeff and I joined Wendell Pierce in the courtroom, where the Lowenstein lawsuit was first on the calendar. To no-one's surprise, Judge Lynch dismissed it, ruling that the Park District "may issue or withhold permits as it sees fit," and that its consideration of the Soldier Field permit was "still under review." I wondered how he could say that with a straight face.

During a recess, Lowenstein held an impromptu press conference in the lobby. He announced the cancellation of his group's planned activities in Chicago, adding that he felt "a sense of dread about what might happen next week." Angrily, he charged the mayor with "inviting violence."

"That's him," Donnie said after Lowenstein left. "Cut and run as soon as the going gets tough, after all his wild claims about how many people will come to his rally."

"Well, however many do come in next week," I speculated, "I guess they'll be with us."

"Probably so," he agreed, adding, "It's kind of ironic. Our board had all those debates about needing to distinguish our protests from the McCarthy campaign, and now the McCarthy kids might be joining us. They'll have no place else to go unless they stay home. They won't all do that."

The Yippies came up next. Their lawyers asked the judge to enjoin the city from interfering with their week-long Festival of Life, since it will take place in a public park. Lynch expressed displeasure with "the plaintiffs' manner of dress," and announced he'll issue his ruling on Friday.

Another recess. Out in the corridor, Abbie Hoffman sauntered over to say hello.

Donnie asked, "Do you really expect to get an injunction?"

"Of course not, but it never hurts to ask. Anyway, we have other plans for Friday."

"What plans?" Jeff asked.

"We'll unveil our own presidential candidate down at the Civic Center."

"The Yippies have a candidate?"

"Yup. A flying pig named Pigasus. A real porker."

"The guy sure knows how to attract attention," Donnie commented after Abbie left.

Back in court, Pierce presented our case. He argued that any interference with peaceful marches and demonstrations would violate the protesters' constitutional rights to free speech and assembly, and that the Park District's refusal to keep the parks open during those few nights constituted "a threat to law and order." Judge Lynch announced he would review the briefs, then adjourned our case until Wednesday at ten.

On our way back to the office, I suggested we distribute a version of our rally leaflets to the McCarthy forces. When we got there, Paul checked in with his contact in Washington and got the addresses of their campaign offices around the country.

I got home in time to fill Cat in on the events of the day and grab a quick dinner before the doorbell rang. During the ritual pleasantries, Dad already seemed uncomfortable.

"What's going on?" I asked.

"Uh, I'd hoped this talk would be just between the two of us." This was his first acknowledgement that Cat was in the room.

"There's nothing you can tell me that Cat can't hear," I told him. "We don't keep anything from each other." I glanced over at her, smiled and added, "Not anymore." After a moment of silence, he began.

"It's something you have a right to know. I can see you're making your own life now and it's time you knew the truth."

"Okay. The truth about what?"

"I don't know how to begin… So I guess I'll spit it out. Steve, I'm not your natural father. I'm your Uncle Gary. Your real parents died a long time ago."

"What?"

"You see, I had two brothers. Harry is two years older. Dave and I were twins. We were always very close. He married Susan, and you were born. I married her best friend, Doris. We lived on the same block and spent lots of time together."

"But what happened?" I asked, still in shock.

"It was the summer of '53. Doris was three months pregnant. There was a travelling circus out in the farm country. The minute you heard about live elephants and tigers, you began jumping up and down, begging to see them. So that's where we all went to celebrate your fourth birthday."

"Gee. I don't remember this."

"There's a good reason for that. You see, we were having a great time, especially you…" He paused. "I'm sorry. This is really difficult for me."

"Take your time."

"During the intermission, I took you to the ice cream stand. You got two scoops, one chocolate and one vanilla. Then, while we were walking back to our seats, something awful happened. Something terrible." He stopped and shook his head slowly.

"What happened?"

"The central support buckled. The tent caved in. People screamed in panic. The stands collapsed under the weight. It was horrible. You and I crawled our way out. Somehow, Doris made it too, but she lost the baby. Dave and Susan, and twenty-three others, didn't. They were crushed to death."

Following a long moment of stunned silence, I asked, "But why don't I remember any of this?"

"The doctors predicted you'd block the memory, because it was so traumatic. You never did ask a single question, and we never brought it up. Even Mom, I mean Aunt Doris, and I never talked about it. We simply pretended you were ours. As time went on, it became easy to believe that."

My head was spinning too fast for me to say much of anything. After an awkward round of good-byes, he left. I fell back onto the couch. Cat had me stretch out with my head in her lap.

"I don't know what to make of this," I murmured.

"I know. It must be a huge shock," she responded, stroking my head. "But it explains so much."

"Like what?"

"I'm no psychologist, but it seems to me a deadly tragedy under a collapsed circus tent could certainly trigger claustrophobia in its young survivor. And remember making up a story about allergies at Lincoln

Park, when you wouldn't go with Arielle into the petting zoo tent? But one thing is for sure."

"What's that?"

"Now we know where your terrible carnival nightmares come from."

When Cat fell asleep that night, I threw on a robe and tiptoed out to the living room, wide awake. I racked my brain, trying to remember that fateful trip to the circus. But I came up empty. I tried to remember my real parents, Dave and Susan, with the same result. Not even their faces.

What kind of son was I who'd completely wiped out his parents' memory, parents who died trying to give their little boy a happy birthday? And it was all my fault, wasn't it? If it wasn't for me, they never would have been in that tent. Could I ever sleep again? Did I deserve to?

To torture myself a little more, I reflected on the carnival nightmare. I didn't remember how old I was the first time I had it, but I might have been four. I did remember that I never saw my parents' faces in it. I simply knew they were there, keeping me totally safe and secure until everything fell apart. I reflected on how it had recently evolved. Now, there wasn't even a carnival. My parents weren't at my side anymore. Instead, there was Cat... and then there wasn't. That was the new constant now, through all the plot and scenery changes. My worst nightmare. I wondered if it would plague me for the rest of my life.

Cat came out a while later. Without saying a word, she knelt on the couch and held me to her.

I told her, "You should be sleeping."

"Hey," she said, lifting my chin. "We orphans have to stick together." She kissed me on the lips and pulled my head down into her lap.

"I've been thinking about the nightmares," I said. "They keep getting worse. I keep losing you. I've never been so terrified. And when I wake up, it's always your job to comfort me. I have to stop doing this to you."

"What you have to stop doing," she insisted, holding me close, "is torturing yourself. None of this is your fault. None of it."

For a long while, she held me like that. A few times, I had little bursts of tears. She caressed my face and wiped them away. Eventually, she urged, "Come. Let's go back to bed."

I thought I would never fall sleep. But, with Cat stroking my back and whispering in my ear, once again, I finally did.

Chapter 75

Sensing movement, I opened one eye and saw Cat getting dressed for the gym. I groaned, "Is it morning already?"

She sat on the edge of the bed and put her hand on my chest. "Go back to sleep, Steve. You need to rest."

"No," I argued. "No, I want to go with you. If you're not here, I won't be able to sleep anyway."

"Then I won't go. I'll stay here with you."

"No. I'm all right. Really. Let's go. It might help clear my head."

The physical exertion of lifting weights did help a little, but I still wasn't ready to face the world until after a steaming hot, then ice cold, shower. Breakfast was waiting. Scanning the *Tribune*, Cat looked pensive.

"What is it?" I asked.

"Front page story. The Governor already called up the National Guard. Starting Friday, there'll be over 5,000 of them in Chicago. He said he's done it at Daley's request, to 'head off threats of tumult, riot or mob disorder.' "

I stated the obvious, trying to make light of that news while beginning to lose my appetite. "That's a lot of bayonets."

"And that's not all," she continued. "Six thousand regular Army soldiers are getting intensive riot control training down in Texas. And guess what they're calling it? Operation Jackson Park! It says several Chicago parks, probably including some of the ones the Mobe asked for, are being reserved for bivouacs."

"So I guess it's okay for soldiers to sleep in public parks, just not the public. Is that all of it?"

"No. All 12,000 of Chicago's cops will be on twelve-hour shifts. No days off and no vacations. There'll be 2,000 stationed around the

Amphitheater, along with federal marshals, FBI agents and the Secret Service."

"Anything else?"

"Well, it seems they've turned the Amphitheater into a concentration camp. It's already been surrounded by a mile-long chain-link fence, topped with barbed wire. Halsted Street will be closed to traffic. There'll be checkpoints set up to keep anyone without convention credentials from getting within a mile of the building. Even with all that, the doors to the sidewalk will be locked. The only way in will be through heavily guarded entrances from the parking lot. They've replaced the big windows with bullet-proof glass. They're even sealing the manholes!"

I was determined to stay calm and not let any of this get to me. "Now, aren't you glad we went to the gym?" I quipped. "This would've been a hell of a way to start our day."

"Steve, this is serious! Donnie's quoted as saying they're turning Chicago into 'an armed camp in a garrison state.' And Lowenstein's urging the McCarthy kids to stay out of Chicago, because there'll be a 'seven-day moratorium on civil liberties.' Yesterday, undercover cops were filming the marshal training. Two photographers got arrested, but just for a few minutes until they showed Army Intelligence credentials. Can't you see what we're up against?"

"I know, I know. Look, our court hearing is tomorrow morning. Maybe we'll get something out of it. Let's not panic. That's just what they want us to do"

"Oh, and here's something else. Someone started rumors of a plot by 'New Left militants and Negro extremists' to assassinate the candidates, drop LSD into the water supply, and blow up a few police stations."

"Anyone we know?"

"Steve!"

"Okay, okay. We know those rumors were planted by the FBI. That's what they do. But let's wait and see what happens in court tomorrow."

"Just don't forget our deal. You're not getting into any battles, and we're not doing anything that'll put you, us, in danger. Now, what's on for today?"

"The only thing I know for sure is a mailing. I need to finish getting our leaflet out to the McCarthy campaign offices. After this morning's news, that'll be even more important."

"Well, try to come home early. You really need to rest. I'll be in the shop with Emma."

It took longer than it should have to redraft the leaflet. But Sabrina insisted on helping with the mimeograph and the mailing. We also rounded up a few volunteers. "We have to hurry," I told the team. "It's already almost three, and we have to get the stuffed and stamped envelopes to the post office by five."

An hour later, Sabrina took me aside. "Steve, I can handle the rest of this. You should go home and rest. You look terrible."

I didn't doubt that one bit. I didn't feel very well either. "You're sure you're okay with this?" I asked.

"Of course I am. Go on home."

"Okay. But don't give anyone else that list. Take it home with you. And thanks. You're an angel of mercy."

"I'm no angel," she laughed. "But I did promise Cat I'd keep an eye on you."

Back at the shop, Cat was busy helping a customer. I blew her a kiss and walked through to the back.

"Steve," Emma greeted me, looking up from a book. "Come sit down. Here, have some coffee. Last night's visit must've been quite a shock. How are you holding up?"

"Okay, I guess. A little tired."

"Well, you look more than 'a little tired.' I hope you'll rest."

"That's why I left work early. Sabrina kind of threw me out of the office. I wanted to check in first, and let Cat know I was back."

I sipped the coffee and asked, "Has she told you about my nightmares?"

"Yes, she has. They sound terrifying."

"They sure are. Cat has this theory. She thinks that awful day at the circus is where they come from. If she's right, they might leave me alone now. I sure hope so."

"Only time will tell, but her theory does make sense. And I had another thought."

"Really? What's that?"

"One thing Cat and I have both marveled at is your instant rapport with children. That might come from the same place. See, I think your little boy is still with you, somewhere in your subconscious, and you're trying to give him a happier ending to that day at the circus."

"I don't get it. How could I do that?"

"Through other children. By delighting them, by making them laugh and have fun. I think seeing the joy in those little faces soothes the little boy inside you. Cat told me what a wonderful time Arielle had with you at the Lincoln Park carnival. And by the way, how old was Arielle when you two first hit it off, back on Christmas Eve?"

"She was four. Wow, I would've never thought of that! It does feel kind of right. I guess that's not a bad thing, is it?"

"Certainly not. It's a gift, a wonderful one. But look, right now you need to go lie down."

"I'll do that, but first one more thing. Do you know Cat has a birthday coming next week?"

"Only now that you tell me. She hasn't mentioned it."

"It's on Friday, the day after the convention leaves town. I want to give her something special, really special, but I don't know what."

"I don't either, but let's both think about it. You know, she's not very interested in material things. She's never mentioned anything she coveted, or even wished she had."

"I know. That would make it too easy."

"How about a surprise party?"

"That would be fun. But the next ten days are gonna be crazy. We'll never find the time to plan a party. Wait. I have a better idea."

"Tell me."

"Our best times were up on Bennett Beach. This'll be the last weekend of summer. I can try for one more invitation. That would be a great surprise."

"I know she'd love it. Go and call now. Then rest, please."

"Okay, but remember. Not a word."

Now Cat was rearranging a shelf. I grabbed her in a bear hug, and gave her a big, sloppy kiss, followed by, "I love you, Cat Crawford. I had to tell you that before I went upstairs."

"Oh, you silly," she laughed, wiping her face. "I love you too. Now go up and lie down. But don't look in the mirror first. You might scare yourself. I won't be long."

Upstairs, I got Brad on the phone. He had a surprise of his own.

"I was going to call you guys. Seymour Hersh's article will be in this coming Sunday's *Times Magazine*. And I'm sure we're going to like it. The timing is perfect, because the scientists' petition is making the rounds in Washington now."

"That's great news. Thanks for telling me."

"Is that what you called about?"

"Well, no. I'm calling to ask a huge favor."

I told him my idea for Cat's birthday, concluding, "I know it's Labor Day Weekend, but we won't be in the way. We can sleep down in the bathhouse, and no-one will even know we're there."

Brad laughed. "That won't be necessary. We'll be in Paris that weekend. The house is yours. You know where the key is, under the first front step."

My exhaustion was mixed now with exhilaration. I poured a drink, kicked off my shoes and stretched out on the couch. I was intrigued by Emma's theory about the little boy in my subconscious. And I liked the idea of Big Steve taking care of frightened Little Steve.

Brad's offer was exciting. *Finally, something to look forward to.* I realized I was no longer looking forward to Convention Week. That morning's news about local and federal military preparations was no joke. They were gearing up for war, right here in Chicago. My resolve to protest what they were doing to Vietnam, and to America, hadn't wavered. But I wanted this month to be over. I wanted to whisk my birthday girl off to our vacation paradise. On that thought, I dropped off to a welcome, peaceful nap.

Chapter 76

I noticed, when I opened my eyes, I'd been covered with a cotton blanket. *Cat,* I thought contentedly, turning over and closing them again. My next conscious moment was waking up in bed, stirred by the rising sun. Turning to my right, I smiled at the sight of her, facing me on her side, fast asleep. I propped up on an elbow, and watched.

I would have been happy spending the whole day watching the rise and fall of her chest, listening to her breathing, wondering what dreams she might be having. Soon, though, she opened one eye, then the other, and asked, "Did you sleep?"

"Yes," I replied. "I had a good night. In fact, I woke up just a little while ago. It's almost six. How long was I out?"

"More than twelve hours. You needed it. How do you feel now?"

"Better. Much, much better. Talking with you and Emma about what happened to my parents and to me, all that really helped."

I didn't tell her how much it helped me to know our weekend in paradise was only ten days away, how my spirits were lifted by something to look forward to. I was keeping something from her again. But since it was a birthday surprise, I gave myself a pass this time.

"I'm so glad," she responded. "How about some coffee before we get up?"

"Good idea. You stay there. I'll be right back with it."

After a few sips, I mused, "You know, I'm glad the suspense will be over soon. Now, we're in court, and today we might find out about the permits."

She reacted, "I hope so. Then you and I can make our own plans."

At the courtroom entrance, federal marshals searched everyone, including the lawyers. Six armed, uniformed cops stood guard inside.

"I've never seen this," Pierce told us. "Certainly not in a civil proceeding. I guess it's a sign of the times."

The defendants were represented by Raymond Simon, the city's chief corporation counsel. He and Pierce made brief opening statements. Then Judge Lynch called them up to the bench. After a few words were exchanged, the judge adjourned the hearing until Friday. Pierce led us down the hall to a conference room.

"Lynch wants us to try working things out ourselves," he told us. "Let's give it a shot."

Simon began the negotiation with an offer Daley had personally authorized. He gave us a choice of five march routes. Since none of them would get us anywhere near the convention, Donnie summarily ruled them out. Simon offered modifications, but none were acceptable. After two hours, both sides agreed to try again the following morning.

Dave Dellinger met us in the lobby, frustrated that his flight had been delayed. Donnie brought him up to date and we went outside, where reporters were waiting with questions. The two leaders emphasized that, "The antiwar movement will be in Chicago next week, with or without permits."

We were sure now that getting an acceptable parade permit was unlikely, and that there was little possibility of being allowed to use the parks overnight. But we still had a good shot at a permit for a daytime rally in Grant Park. In a forced fit of optimism, Jeff and I were assigned to draft another flyer or letter urging people to come to Chicago, even if only for that legal rally. It would go out to the Mobe's big mailing list when and if the permit came through. I suggested we also call our 150 constituent organizations. That became my project too.

The letter we drafted, which Dave and Donnie approved with minor revisions, made clear that we refused to cave in to the government's repressive military tactics. We would exercise our right to march with or without a permit. But it emphasized that the march will be preceded by a massive, totally legal antiwar rally. It urged them to help get the word out, and also invited everyone to Tuesday night's Anti-Birthday Party. Its signoff was our now-standard, "See You in Chicago!"

We assembled two teams of volunteers: Jeff's to handle the mailing, and mine to make the phone calls. Once all these plans were in place, I went home and brought Cat up to date.

Since I had the car the next morning, and didn't have much to do before our 10:30 negotiation, I took a detour to see what the Amphitheater looked like. The security checkpoints were still being assembled, so I was able to drive right up to it. The huge building was surrounded now by a seven-foot-high chain-link fence topped with barbed wire. It looked as though the goal was to keep people inside, not outside.

Simon opened the meeting with his olive branch. We were getting a permit to hold a rally on Wednesday from one until four, using our own sound system, at the Grant Park bandshell. This eased some of the tension in the room, but we were still at an impasse over the parade permit. That negotiation didn't rise much above pretense, since we insisted on marching to the Amphitheater, and Mayor Daley preferred us on another planet.

Soon, there was nothing left to discuss. We wouldn't hear the judge's ruling on our right to march until the following day, but we knew what to expect.

They were giving us the permit for the Grant Park rally, though. Jeff and I got our mailing and telephone teams together. I explained to mine that our job was to (1) emphasize that we had the permit; (2) gather rough estimates of numbers that would be coming from each group; (3) match each group with movement centers we'd lined up for them to meet, plan and regroup in during the week; and (4) ask if they needed places to stay overnight. If they did, I got on the phone and matched them up with our list of places that survived Ronnie's treachery. I also insisted on a commitment from each group to self-enforce the ground rules, in case our marshals are otherwise occupied.

We operated like a well-oiled machine, although we did have to leave messages and make notes for callbacks. I was in kind of a trance, making calls, matching groups with available housing and making sure we stayed on track. When someone held up a receiver and yelled, "It's for you," I thought it was one of my callbacks.

"Oh, you're there," came Cat's voice on the other end. "I didn't know what happened to you. Every time I called, I got a busy signal. I've been worried sick."

"Why? Did something happen?"

"Look at the clock, Steve. What time is it?"

It was past eight. "Oh, I had no idea," I told her. "I'm sorry. We had so much work to do. I can leave now. I'll be home soon."

I found her curled up on the couch.

"You said you wouldn't do this to me," she whimpered. "You promised."

I held her tight and rocked her. "I'm sorry, so, so sorry," I said softly. "I lost track of time. I'm sorry."

One day, I thought, *she's going to stop accepting my clumsy apologies.*

Chapter 77

"The lawyers made their arguments," Donnie told us after Friday morning's court hearing, "and Pierce was really good. Lynch's written ruling will be delivered to their offices this afternoon. But the Yippies withdrew their suit once they found out he and Daley had been law partners."

An hour or so later, I felt myself getting dizzy. Sabrina ran over. "What's wrong?" she asked. "You're white as a sheet."

"Must be the claustrophobia. So many people. So much noise."

"Go out for a walk," she instructed. "Get some air. I'll handle things here 'til you get back."

Outdoors, I quickly regained my balance. I bought a hot dog and wandered over to Civic Center Plaza, where the Yippies were nominating Pigasus for president. They were far outnumbered by reporters and cameramen, and the news-people were outnumbered by the cops. It wasn't much of a ceremony, since the police immediately arrested seven of the leaders and all 200 or so pounds of Pigasus himself. Apparently, the pig's ability to fly had been vastly overrated. It was entertaining, but it seemed to me nothing more than a media stunt. I trudged back to the office.

Donnie already had a copy of our lawsuit's dismissal. In Judge Lynch's opinion, the city had been eminently reasonable in offering alternate routes for a march, while granting the rally permit. He also ruled that the Park District would be acting well within its authority if it chose to enforce normal closing times.

"Well, that's it," Jeff observed. "The die is cast. What now?"

"We have to keep doing what we're doing," Donnie replied. "People need to know we got the rally permit. And we'll picket a few hotels on Sunday. Of course, joining our march to the Amphitheater will be voluntary." I thought I heard him say, "*Our march to Armageddon.*"

I went back to work with my team, calling Clergy and Laymen Concerned, People Against Racism, Resistance, New York's Fifth

Avenue Peace Parade Committee, the Radical Organizing Committee, and on and on. Those I got through to welcomed the news about the rally. I matched groups up with housing as best I could, and tried to make the ground rules clear. Plenty of questions came up, though, regarding what else might happen in Chicago.

Our local director of Women Strike for Peace told me buses from several cities were already on their way, because they had a picket line planned for Saturday at the Conrad Hilton. That was the good news.

"The problem" she explained, "is that on average our buses are less than half full. Most of the women who'd bought tickets have been scared away, especially mothers who planned to bring their children. And grandmothers, whose own children implored them not to court danger."

As the afternoon wore on, I once again found the atmosphere increasingly intolerable. The work was going well, even though the numbers were disappointing, but the place was closing in on me again.

Sabrina pulled me aside at around four. "You've had it," she announced. "You're slowing down and, if you don't stop, you'll start making mistakes. Let me take over. If we don't finish today or tonight, I'll organize a crew to finish over the weekend."

I wondered whether Cat really did ask her to keep an eye on me.

"You're right," I agreed. "I'm shot. But where's your energy coming from? How can you keep going?"

"You've been pounding your head against a wall the whole summer," she explained, "while I've been taking it easy. I need to do this now, but you don't. Go on home."

I thanked her and left. Before heading home, though, I was drawn to Lincoln Park, to watch a little of the marshal training. A hundred enthusiastic young men, and now women too, were seriously drilling in crowd defense, self-defense and mobile defense techniques. It was being filmed by a combination of reporters, police and intelligence agents.

"That's what it'll all be about," said a voice behind me. I turned.

"Paul, where've you been? I haven't seen you for a few days."

"Meeting with SDS," he explained. "A few dozen of its leaders are here. We've been talking strategy over at its movement center, the Church of Three Crosses. Most of them want to keep to the original plan, organizing the McCarthy kids, however many show up. But the gauntlet's been thrown now. So once the cops attack, and they will, the

SDS faction will scatter in small groups, spreading chaos across the Loop, across the city. We can't stop the nomination, but we can damn well stop Chicago."

My only response was, "Oh."

On my way out of the park, I noticed for the first time what a beautiful, sunny day it was. Families were enjoying picnics a hundred yards away. Boys played touch football nearby. Lovers necked on benches under the trees. Down at the beach, bathers romped in the surf. Motorboats whizzed across the waves.

I gazed longingly at the scene. A voice in my head scolded, *Don't these people know there's a war going on, that our country is committing atrocities, claiming more and more victims, every single day?* Then it asked, *And are you becoming one of those victims?*

After I told Cat about the judge's ruling, the phone-calling project, Sabrina's mother-hen help, and Paul's SDS report, she asked, "Is that everything? You're sure?"

"Yes. That's it."

"So now it's time for us to make our plans."

"Can't that wait until morning?" I pleaded. "I'm really beat."

"All right. But I know you'll be back at work tomorrow, and we need to settle this before you go."

"Okay. But there's one other thing."

"What's that?"

"Remember I said I'll be glad when this is over? It was a few days ago."

"I remember. But you didn't say why."

"I've been thinking. This work had to be done, and I've learned a whole lot doing it. But I want to get back to base-building, to talking with ordinary people, not only activists. I want to get back to the Saran-Wrap campaign, and the BSU support work. I want to get back to my after-school classes. I guess I want to get back to school too. But you know what I want most of all, besides you of course?"

"What?"

"I want to stop giving you reasons to worry about me."

After our love-making climaxed that night, Cat was ready to start all over. I wasn't up to it, though. "Sweetheart," I said, "I can't. I'm already falling asleep."

"That's okay. Roll over on your side. Get comfortable."

As I did, she pressed her body into my back. In the morning, that's how I woke, with her arms and legs wrapped around me, as if to keep me from flying out the window.

Saturday morning, the *Tribune* published the final draft that McCarthy and McGovern decided to jointly submit to the Platform Committee. It began by pointing out that more than 25,000 American soldiers had already been killed in Vietnam, that at least 200,000 had been injured, and that over a hundred billion dollars had been spent. It declared that this must come to an end. The essence of the plan was to stop all the bombing now, and negotiate with the North Vietnamese for a phased withdrawal of all foreign forces, including theirs and ours, leaving the South Vietnamese government to deal with the NLF in forming a new governing coalition. It even laid out a new role for the United States in the world, one in which our country respected the rights of others to determine their own destinies. It resolved we would have "No More Vietnams."

"What do you think?" I asked Cat after reading it aloud.

"What I think," she replied, "is that it has as much chance of being adopted as Dave Dellinger has of being elected president. But I guess we'll see."

Another article covered a press conference by the National Guard commander, whose troops were already taking up positions in the armories, Soldier Field and other Chicago locations. Cat summarized this one.

"The general said their orders are 'shoot to kill' only if they have to. But he emphasized that their ammunition is made to kill, not to wound. They're equipped with M-1 rifles, shotguns, tear gas, armored vests and gas masks. The hoods of their jeeps are being outfitted with concertina barbed wire cages for moving crowds.

She riffled through another paper, *Chicago's American*, where Jack Mabley's weekly column caught her eye.

"Well, here's some things being planned that I bet you didn't know about. Mabley says acts of sabotage are being threatened by 'Black and white militants.' Including, get this, 'Scattering hundreds of thousands of nails across the expressways; dynamiting gas lines; drugging or poisoning the food in the delegates' hotel restaurants; LSD in the water supply; Yippie girls disguising themselves as hookers and slipping LSD into delegates' drinks; hijacking a gas tanker and plowing it into a hotel;

cutting the power and phone lines at the Amphitheater; shelling it with missiles…' "

By now, I was laughing so hard I couldn't breathe, and Cat's own laughter kept her from finishing the column. "Obviously," I sputtered, "we've been hanging out with the wrong group!"

Once we calmed down, Cat brought us back to reality. "Enough of the funny papers. You promised we'd make our plans this morning."

"Okay, you're right. How about this? Grant and Lincoln Parks will be our home bases. But we have no reason to stay there after, or even until, the cops come to close them. So that's not an issue. But until eleven, they're open to the public, including us. The Mobe's first event is tomorrow, our 'Meet the Delegates Day.' We'll picket a few of their hotels. We don't need a permit for that. Our next major event is Tuesday night's Anti-Birthday Party. Don't need a permit for that one, either. Wednesday's Grant Park rally has a permit. So we can do all of that without risking confrontation."

"Well, suppose we're in the park at closing time, and people won't leave? What then?"

"If people want to fight over the park," I replied, "that's up to them. We've done everything possible to get permits for overnight camping. We tried and we failed. But we're in this to fight against the war, not to get into a turf battle. Anyone who wants to do that has my blessing. As for you and me, I think we should go home and get some sleep."

Cat looked pleased. I was batting a thousand, but not for long.

"And what about the 600-pound gorilla in the room?" she asked.

"The what?"

"You know. The march to the convention. The one everybody's been saying 'with or without a permit.' And now we know for sure it's without."

This was the one we'd been dancing around for weeks. "Oh, that," I responded, not having a ready reply. "Well, what do you think?"

"Look," she began, "I know that march is what it's been about. 'Confront the War-Makers' and all that. It's the right thing to do. It makes perfect symbolic sense. And yes, it's why people are coming. But it's also why 20,000 armed soldiers and 12,000 cops will be lying in wait. And, as far as I'm concerned, they'll all be gunning for you. So I have to say no, we can't take that risk."

I hated the idea of backing down. I was ready for a fight, and willing to risk the consequences. But to her, nothing that threatened my safety was worth that risk. I came up with an evasive maneuver.

"Let's wait until Wednesday. It isn't like we need a reservation. Compromise is still a possibility. Maybe, to head off a big confrontation, they'll let us march in the direction of the Amphitheater until they turn us around at a checkpoint. The action would still carry symbolic significance, and no-one would get hurt. It's a sensible solution, for the city and for us. Let's wait and see."

"I guess we could wait to decide," she responded thoughtfully. "But remember your promise. You're coming home afterward, safe and sound, no matter what anyone else does. Now, what's on the agenda for today?"

"Probably more calls to make at the office. Then I guess I'll go to Lincoln Park and see what the Yippies are up to."

"Okay. I'll come with you."

"Really? You don't have to."

"Sweetheart," she said, laying a hand on my cheek, "don't plan on going *anywhere* without me now, not until that convention is over. Like I told you, I'm *not* going to sit home and worry. Not again. Not ever again."

Chapter 78

On our way downtown, I said, "You know, Sabrina was a real life-saver yesterday. If she didn't throw me out of the office, I would've been a mess by the time I got home. It's really been great working with her."

"I can understand that," Cat responded. "She's committed, she's smart and so incredibly talented."

"Yes, she is. But for me, none of them is the most important thing."

"You mean you like having her around because of her looks?"

"No, no. The most important thing for me is I know I can trust her. We have to depend on volunteers to help get things done, but we know there are spies and informants among them. Of course, we don't know which ones they are or even who sent them. The FBI claims they have a thousand agents in town already. I'm sure I've been working next to some of them every day. So having Sabrina there really eases the stress."

"That business with Ronnie threw you for quite a loop, didn't it?"

"It sure did. I can still see her in my mind's eye, taking charge of everything, never complaining, always ready to brighten the place with that smile of hers. I still can't get used to the idea that she was actually a treacherous bitch, that she betrayed us every single day."

"Welcome to the zoo!" Donnie exclaimed, greeting Cat with a big smile as we came through the door. "Listen, Steve, reporters and photographers will be all over Lincoln Park today, covering the Yippies' festival and our marshal training. Let's take advantage of that. Dave and I want to hold our own press conference, right in front of the Abe Lincoln statue, at one o'clock. I've got a Steering Committee meeting starting now, down the hall. Do you have your list of press contacts?"

"Sure. It's locked in a file drawer. I'll get right on it."

While I made my calls, Cat joined Sabrina and the other volunteers calling the constituent groups. Jeff handled the incoming. It seemed his phone rang every time he put the receiver down. Whoever was tapping those lines had a very busy day. The joint was jumping.

At the appointed time, I told Cat I was leaving for the press conference. She said, "Wait. I'm coming too." I wondered what kind of trouble she thought I might get into at a press conference, but didn't object. I liked having her with me. I loved having her with me.

A substantial press corps was already milling about. Dave started off by blasting the Daley administration for refusing the permits and bringing in the military might. He said none of it would stop us, though. He expressed a hope that city officials "come to their senses" and issue the parade permit. "If they do not," he declared, "we will proceed with our march, leaving behind those not willing or able to risk injury."

A reporter called out, "You'll go up against the police, the National Guard?"

Dave calmly responded, "We are determined to exercise our constitutional rights, to hold our demonstration and make our voices heard. Yes, even at the risk of bodily harm."

I glanced over at Cat, who was already scrutinizing my face, trying to read my mind. Of course I was torn. For a moment, I also regretted letting her come. But I realized I couldn't have stopped her, and I'd have had to tell her about it anyway.

"Wednesday," I whispered. "We'll decide on Wednesday."

We decided to walk around for a while, getting a sense of the scene. The Yippies' festival wouldn't officially begin until Sunday afternoon, but a couple thousand people had already drifted in. The atmosphere was mellow, like a big picnic, with guitars, bongo drums, singing and dancing. Food, drink and drugs were available, and everything was free. Couples were retreating behind bushes for free sex too. Even the cops appeared to be cool with it.

"This is nice," Cat commented.

"Sure it is. But we're here to stop a war, not to get stoned." I was happy to see the Mobe's literature table, staffed by volunteers.

We continued circulating, and learned everyone arrested at the Civic Center the previous afternoon had already been released on bail, except for poor Pigasus, who'd been transported to an undisclosed location. Seeing a crowd gathering not far away, we strolled toward it.

Hippies, Yippies, other protesters and local kids, along with newsmen, police photographers and federal agents, were observing our marshal training. Vern had equipped the marshals with black armbands, so they'd be recognized once the protests began. They were drilling in the Snake Dance and other crowd protection formations. A helicopter hovered overhead. Abbie Hoffman demonstrated a few karate moves, with which he was obviously not very familiar. But he wore a uniform and headband for the benefit of the cameras.

A hundred yards away, a van screeched up, attracting another small crowd. Three Yippies jumped out, opened the rear door and pulled out a big pig on a leash.

"Meet Mrs. Pigasus!" one of them shouted. "She demands the release of her husband, who has been illegally prevented from continuing his campaign for the presidency!" Freed from the leash, Mrs. Pigasus wandered around, snorting and nibbling the greenery.

It took five minutes for the cops to swoop in and arrest the humans, a little longer to corral Mrs. Pigasus and drag her into a paddy wagon. The crowd watched with apparent amusement. No-one tried to interfere. Another magnet for the media.

"I wonder if the couple will be reunited now," Cat mused with a sardonic smile.

"I certainly wish them well," I responded. "But I've had enough of this. Let's get back to the office and find something productive to do."

There, we found out the local McCarthy campaign had scheduled a noon rally to greet his plane at Midway Airport on Sunday.

"We should go," I suggested. "This'll be an opportunity."

Cat agreed, and we worked up a leaflet listing the week's activities. Sabrina did the artwork. We ran them off, packed them into a box, loaded the box into Tooter's back seat and returned to Lincoln Park. The scene was much the same as earlier in the day, except more people were there. We ran into Nicky Jarvis, who told us the SDS and Yippie leaderships had both decided against trying to hold the park past the curfew.

"That makes sense," I responded. "We're here to protest the war, not to fight the cops over real estate."

"That wasn't exactly the way we looked at it," he explained. "We just don't have the numbers to win that fight. At least not yet."

On our way back home, I said, "See? We've gotten through a whole day without any trouble at all. Maybe the whole week can be like this."

Cat didn't react.

The first thing I looked for in the early Sunday papers was Seymour Hersh's *Times Magazine* cover story. Titled "The Secret Arsenal," it exposed the government's lies about chemical and biological weapons. It also quoted Bradley Bennett at length, detailing the horror of the Quantum Potential Weapon and noting Midway's complicity. This was precisely what we'd been hoping for. I didn't have time to read the whole thing, though, so I skimmed it quickly and put it aside.

There was a big story on our press conference in the front section, which quoted Dave and Donnie extensively. But we took the *Tribune* apart three times, and found not a word about it. The paper did, however, publish an editorial blasting the Mobe and the Yippies for threatening to disrupt the convention and, with it, the city's local economy and international reputation. It praised the mayor for taking resolute steps to "preserve order." Referring to those very steps, the *Times* reported from Chicago, "This city became an armed camp over the weekend."

Both papers carried full-page ads displaying the scientists' petition that Brad had organized.

Hubert Humphrey appeared on "Meet the Press." He said he supported LBJ's war policy because it was "basically sound." Asked about the antiwar platform plank, he confidently stated, "Well, that will not be the platform." We clicked off the TV and left for Midway Airport.

To my surprise, given McCarthy's warnings, at least 5,000 people were waiting for him out on the tarmac, listening to folk music. Many carried signs with slogans such as "America's Primary Hope," and "Lucidity, Not Lunacy." I was stunned to see that spirits were so high, since everyone knew the campaign's remaining days were numbered. We hooked up with Mobe volunteers and spread out to distribute our leaflets. Many people said they'd join our events.

Stepping out of the plane, McCarthy bounded up the stairs to the makeshift stage, took the microphone and began speaking. Quickly, he realized it was dead. He stopped, looked at it quizzically for a moment, and laughed. Beckoning the folk singers back, he called out, "Let's sing!" While staff members fiddled with the electronics, everyone joined in singing, *This land is your land, this land is my land...*

Once the microphone got fixed, he delivered a short, casual, literate speech. Toward the end, he said, "We can build a new society and a new world. We're not asking for much. Just a modest use of intelligence." A roar went up from the crowd.

Soon, we were on our way to picket the Conrad Hilton Hotel, Democratic Party headquarters for Convention Week.

The Hilton faced Grant Park from across Michigan Avenue, but our few hundred pickets were on the sidewalk outside the park, not at the hotel. Vern told me that arrangement resulted from his negotiation with a police sergeant. We joined the picket line, which the marshals kept from spilling into the street. The police had assembled an intimidating presence to guard against any charge on the hotel.

Then, from up the avenue, came Donnie, followed by hundreds marching from Lincoln Park, chanting, *Hey, Hey, LBJ. How many kids did you kill today?* From the other direction came two more busloads of cops. We were more than a thousand now, far too many to still fit on the sidewalk. Donnie led us into the park for a rally.

I saw McCarthy buttons here too, but also the Mobe's "Confront the Warmakers" buttons, Mao Tse-tung buttons and Yippie buttons. There were red flags, Vietcong flags, flags emblazoned with peace symbols and with marijuana-leaves, and American flags too.

After only a few brief speeches, Donnie declared the event a success and we dispersed. It was now on to Lincoln Park, where the Festival of Life's opening concert was scheduled to get underway. Cat became visibly more relaxed, less worried about this whole thing. So did I.

"That was smart, the way Vern and Donnie avoided confrontations back there," I observed. "Don't you think?"

"I noticed too," she responded. "But I hope things stay under control once the big crowds get here."

Chapter 79

Cat and I strolled through the festival grounds. There was a free store, a free medical clinic, and a free food stand. There were kids and balloons in the trees, placards reading "Vote Pig in '68," and lots of drumming and drugs. A few clowns, political and fantastical, roamed the area.

Many of the people there now weren't hippies, Yippies or movement activists. I was a bit surprised by the number of clean-cut, middle-class people wearing McCarthy buttons. We also saw mothers pushing strollers and families, normal park visitors on a pleasant Sunday. Local working-class kids and bikers, apparently attracted by the music, also streamed in. We encountered a small group of the locals pointing at a fence and laughing. I asked what was funny.

"It's those stupid signs, everywhere you look," one of them explained. He pointed to one reading, "PARK CLOSES AT 11 P.M."

"Why's that funny?" I asked. "Isn't that when all the city parks close?"

"All I know," he said, "is on the really hot nights, this is where lots of us, families even, come to sleep. No-one ever gets hassled. If there is a legal curfew, it's never been enforced. And look at those signs. They're all brand new."

The concert faced serious challenges. The Yippies rented a sound system and a flatbed truck to use as a stage, but the city wouldn't allow either of them in the park. Every nationally known band had already canceled, some in advance because of the military threat, the rest at the last minute because they refused to perform with an improvised sound system. Still, some local bands did show up. Without a stage, though, those bands would be visible only by those right up front.

The crowd had grown to five or six thousand by then, far too many to watch a concert without a stage. People were pushing and shoving, jockeying for position. Suddenly, the disputed flatbed drove up behind the band. Dozens jumped onto it. The police swarmed in too, making arrests. Shouts, bottles and rocks came from the crowd. The cops shouted back. "Get the fuck out of town!" and "You fags, go back where you came from!" Many lashed out with their clubs. It was a brief skirmish. They took a few prisoners, impounded the truck, and formed a line back toward the street. The remaining injured were helped to a medical tent. The music started up again.

The energy was changing, though. Many in the crowd were high on rock 'n' roll, and marijuana too, but we sensed something ugly was threatening. Abbie Hoffman, probably sensing it too, announced the concert was over. The crowd dispersed, directionless now. The local families had by then disappeared from the scene.

As the sun began to dip behind the trees, a chill crept into the air. People built little campfires for warmth. From time to time, small bands of cops made the rounds, stamping them out. As soon as they moved on, the fires flared up again. People sitting around them talked about what to do if the police moved in to close the park. Later, a large group gathered on the baseball diamond to debate strategy. Some wanted to stay and fight. Mobe marshals and Yippie leaders circulated, arguing this wasn't the time. A big SDS contingent, several hundred, streamed into the park, some dressed for battle with motorcycle helmets and football gear. They spread out, urging people to leave the park in small groups if that time came, to take to the streets and generate mayhem. *Bring the war home!*

On our way toward the park's perimeter, Cat pointed and exclaimed, "Look!" I followed her gaze. Cops removing their badges meant only one thing.

"Time to go," I told her.

We'd had to park Tooter six blocks away, which turned out to be fortunate. In the dimly lit parking lot, nightsticks were smashing down on cars, shattering windshields and headlights.

Driving home, Cat asked, "Well, were you tempted?"

"Not this time," I replied. "We're only in this to end the war. If they want to fight over sleeping and smoking grass in the park, that's their thing, not mine. And besides..."

"Besides what?"

"Besides, you're with me. I wouldn't do anything that put you in danger." She smiled and squeezed my leg. Her plan was working.

We slept intertwined, feeling safe... until the phone rang. I forced my eyes open and turned on the lamp. It was 2:30.

"We should get it," Cat said. "Maybe Emma needs help."

I staggered into the kitchen and picked up the phone. "Hello?"

"Hey man, can you return the favor?" I recognized Whit's voice and knew right away why he had called.

"Cook County Jail?"

"Yeah, 13th and Michigan."

"Okay. How much?"

"Fifty."

"I'm on my way."

As I got dressed, Cat asked, "What's wrong? Was it Emma?"

"No. Whit got arrested. I have to go bail him out. Everything's okay. You go back to sleep. I'll be home in an hour."

Somehow, I convinced her it would be safe to let me undertake this mission on my own. I grabbed the keys and some cash, and headed downtown.

Things went smoothly at the jail. Whit had a black eye and a bandage on his forehead, but he looked otherwise intact. In the car, he explained, "I'm sorry to drag you out here, but the bail fund ran dry."

"Hey, I'm glad to help. But what happened? I didn't see you in the park last night."

"I saw you guys leaving," he explained. "I should've gone with you. But I was too stoned, and I didn't know what was coming."

"What was that?"

"At eleven sharp, the cops announced they were closing the park. The Mobe's marshals urged people to leave. There was resistance, though. 'The park belongs to the people,' and all that. Lots of arguing. But nearly everyone did finally leave the park. Then the police herded hundreds of us into a big empty lot nearby."

"Then what?" I asked "How'd you get banged up?"

"They wouldn't let us stay there either. Some cops broke their own lines to pull folks out and beat them. We were trapped in a confined space. They shouted, 'Get the fuck out of here!' So we did. We broke through and ran down Clark Street. Then it got really crazy. They chased us, beating everyone within reach. And I mean everyone, even reporters with cameras. Especially reporters with cameras. Our medics got clubbed while they were trying to do first aid. We scattered and they kept on chasing, swinging. We ran through Old Town, the tourist district. All the streets had traffic. Horns were honking. Helicopters hovered right overhead. The cops used Mace and tear gas. Some had shotguns. Man, it was wild. I think they only bothered arresting the people who were lying unconscious in the street, blocking traffic, like me. Let me tell you, man. *They've declared war on us now.*"

Cat stirred as I came back to bed. "Is Whit all right?" she asked.

"Yeah, he's fine. Nothing serious. Let's get back to sleep."

"What do you mean, nothing serious?"

"It can wait until morning. Now, we need to sleep."

I flopped down on the bed, face first. Cat draped herself over my back, and pulled up the covers. Whit's words ran through my mind as, through pure exhaustion, I fell asleep. *They've declared war on us now.*

Chapter 80

Cat was horrified to hear Whit's story in the morning. "The convention doesn't even open until tonight," she responded, "and they're already on the attack. I'm sure glad you were here with me, and not in the middle of all that last night."

But my restlessness was mounting. It wasn't about the park anymore. It was *Them Against Us,* and at least part of me insisted I should have been there, even if only to bear witness.

Jeff called to tell us everyone was gathering back at Lincoln Park's ball field. We joined a large group there listening to various accounts of Sunday night. We learned that clashes had occurred at half a dozen locations. In the largest one, an SDS-led crowd of a few hundred, heading for the Hilton, ran into a police trap. Every report told of cops without badges or nameplates swinging away, with or without provocation, and singling out anyone with a camera. They even attacked bystanders, including residents watching from their front steps. As Whit reported, only those who were in the street, unconscious and blocking traffic, got arrested. The movements out of the park in various directions were spontaneous, but the uniformly brutal police response, it seemed to me, must have been planned in advance. The morning chill had nothing to do with the weather, which was sunny and warm.

Someone came running over with news that Paul was grabbed by plainclothes cops lying in wait outside the SDS movement center. Donnie announced a march to the police station, at 11th and State. Cat agreed we should join it.

At least a thousand of us joined this march. The marshals had to keep us on the sidewalks since, without a parade permit, we'd certainly be arrested, or worse, if we spilled into the streets. We stopped for red lights and obeyed the instructions of the police, who materialized in large numbers along the route. All this obedience sucked out some of the spirit. When the cops squeezed us into half the sidewalk, shouts of "Fuck the cops! Fuck the marshals!" broke out. But no-one broke ranks.

Dozens of cops in riot gear surrounded the police station. There was nothing we could do for Paul, and any confrontation would have set off the brewing powder keg. Somehow, Vern and the marshals maintained control, turning us away from the fortress, up to Ninth Street and then east. Heading into Grant Park, the pent-up emotion burst forth. Coming into sight was a hill, topped by an impressive statue of a Civil War general on horseback. Shouts rang out. *Take the hill! Take the hill!* Hundreds did storm the hill, the earliest arrivals climbing the statue and raising a Viet Cong banner.

Cat and I had enjoyed many walks through Chicago's parks. It was routine to see children climbing on the numerous statues. Sometimes it seemed that was why they came there. Today was different, though. The police created new law on the spot, gathering to take back the hill. Demands to disperse were met with insults and curses. They soon charged, pulling people off the statue and throwing them to the ground. A boy caught his arm in the general's scabbard. Clearly terrified, he grabbed on with the other. A cop pulled from below, breaking his arm. Another smashed his head from above. Once he fell to the ground, a beefy, red-faced cop kicked him in the groin. Others dragged him to a paddy wagon. With police reinforcements arriving, we were helpless to intervene. But news cameras got it all.

Having conquered the hill, the police lost interest in it and retreated. Our forces were in disarray. Donnie and the marshals reasserted themselves, spreading the word to move back to Lincoln Park, but in small clusters less likely to attract notice. Cat, who'd been holding my arm in a steel grip during the battle over the statue, pleaded, "Let's go home now. Please."

"Everyone's going to Lincoln Park," I argued. "Besides, that's where Tooter is."

"Leave the car," she implored. "We can take the train now, and go back for Tooter another time."

Before that, though, Donnie asked me to arrange a press conference, at nine the next morning in front of the general's statue. Cat and I went back to the office to make the calls. Editors were furious over the targeting of their reporters and photographers Sunday night. Attendance would not be a problem. Once we finished the calls, following another futile attempt to overcome Cat's stubbornness, we left for home.

On the train, she retreated into herself, but her expression told me everything. I'd seen it before. I wasn't sure my reassurances would work now. This week, the threat really was imminent, and was I itching to confront it head-on. And *she knew it.*

Back home, I didn't know what to do with myself. I was too restless to concentrate on reading, or even sit still long enough to try. The apartment had never seemed so impossibly small. I paced aimlessly, as though in a prison cell. Nothing Cat did or said could touch this mood. I didn't want to talk. I wouldn't eat. Even her sexual advances were unsuccessful. The sense of confinement became unbearable. I announced, "I'm going out for a walk."

"Okay. I'll come too."

"It's only a walk," I blurted, slamming the door behind me. "I can do it myself!"

That really was all I intended to do. I wasn't going to sneak off to Lincoln Park. Was I tempted? Sure I was. That would have been an irreparable breach of trust, though, and I considered it for only a fleeting moment. Still, I needed to burn off some energy and try to clear my head. I wandered through the campus, where incoming freshmen were trying to find their way around. It was just a year ago, I recalled, that I'd been one of them. I sat on a bench and tried listening to the birds, but grew still more agitated. After a half hour or so, it dawned on me that I'd walked out on Cat, that she was probably terrified about where I'd gone. *How could I have done this?*

I ran back home to find her in a fetal position on the couch. I sat on the edge, put my hand on her shoulder and begged her. "I'm so sorry. Please, please forgive me."

She sat up, her eyes streaked with tears, and stretched out her arms. We embraced as though after a long separation. "I didn't know," she blubbered. "I didn't know where you went. I didn't know if you'd come back."

"I should never have done that. I'm sorry. I just... I just couldn't stand the thought of being in here while everything was happening out there."

"Right after you walked out," she explained, "I called Emma. I was kind of hysterical. She told me not to worry, that you'd come back, that you'd never betray my trust. But she also suggested I try to see it from your point of view. She told me you might never forgive yourself for letting others carry this struggle forward without you. The thing is, I understand. I do. Somehow, history will be made here this week. We're taking our stand against the war, and I don't want to be a bystander any more than you do. But once the smoke clears, I can't be coming home alone while you're lying in the city morgue. The thought of that..."

"Cat, stop. Don't even go there. We can work this out. We can find a way."

"Emma said we'd be able to. So let's give it a try. The curfew is still six hours off. We can go back. But promise me you won't put yourself in harm's way. Like you said, we're in this because of the war, not because of the park."

"Okay. Holding the park isn't our priority. But marching on the convention is. If we don't at least try to do that, none of this will make any sense."

"Again, like you said, we can decide about that on Wednesday. Let's stay calm and take it one day at a time."

The Festival of Life had grown. Music was everywhere: guitars, drums; singing and dancing, much of it topless. A bonfire was the focus of a faux religious ritual dance, apparently improvised on the spot, also clothing-optional. There was a Free Bookstore, with titles ranging from *The Immorality of Marriage* to *Proceedings from the War Crimes Tribunal*, under a sign reading, "Take What You Want. Leave What You Can." Hippies passed out paper bowls of brown rice from twenty-gallon cooking pots. Loaves of bread were somehow being baked and given away. Small crowds gathered to hear soapbox speeches on war and peace, free love, socialism, communism, anarchism. There were workshops on Non-Violent Direct Action, Revolutionary Parenting and Love Secrets from the *Kama Sutra*. Marshals still worked to master the Snake Dance. Joy, sharing, camaraderie, even play, were in the air, along with thick clouds of marijuana smoke. The tension that earlier gripped us evaporated.

People kept coming in: McCarthy and McGovern supporters; Movement radicals; Hippies and Yippies; SDS militants wearing red bandanas; Quakers and other pacifists; local teens. By the time the sun began to set, there were thousands more than the night before. It was exhilarating to see that so many hadn't been scared away.

But as the curfew drew near, cops in riot gear massed on the park's outer edge. People began constructing a barricade. Materials consisted of anything at hand: Tree branches; Planks torn from benches; Entire benches; Picnic tables; Trash bins; Trash. As the wall became noticeable, it captured the imagination of more and more. It grew to six or seven feet high, about a hundred feet wide, and with it grew with the enthusiasm of its scavengers and builders.

"Let's help," I suggested.

"Steve, this barricade is stupid."

"Stupid? Why would you say that?"

"Because, first of all, any big truck could blow right through it. But second, look closely. What do you see?"

"I see what you see. It's a wall, a big barricade between us and the cops."

"And on the sides?"

"On the sides? Nothing. Oh, now I get it."

"Right. They don't even have to touch the barricade. They can simply go around it."

The fact that the barricade had no real military value did not keep it from becoming, for a time, a potent symbol of resistance. Flag-bearers climbed to the top, planting their own symbols: red flags; black flags; VC flags. Protesters taunted the cops from behind it, darting out to throw rocks at the police cars that drew near and then retreated, dented with smashed headlights and windshields. Media lights illuminated this, some of them operated by helmeted newsmen.

Through a bullhorn came the warning. "This park is now closed. Anyone who does not vacate right now is in violation of the law."

But the protesters grew bolder. A chant caught on, and a drumbeat joined to it. "Hold the park! Hold the park!" It was as though, through a force of will, or magic, this one-dimensional barricade had the power to protect them.

Again, from the bullhorn: "You are in violation of the law. Move out of the park! NOW!"

"Hell no, we won't go!" came the response. "The park belongs to the people!"

Still, the cops didn't charge. The builders went back to work, fortifying their fantasy of a fortress. Were they coming? When? Or will they hold off? Word began to spread that we might hold the park after all.

"Maybe they'll simply leave us alone," I speculated.

Cat disagreed. "I don't think so. This is leading up to something. We should go."

"Look at this," I argued. "We can't just walk away from it."

"All right. But let's stay in the rear. Don't throw anything. And stay next to me." I wondered whether I could have broken that grip of hers if I'd wanted to.

Suddenly the area was lit bright as day by searchlights atop police trucks. A metal canister came floating high over the barricade. It bounced on the ground right in front of us and began smoking. *Tear gas!* Cat and I ran, coughing, our eyes burning. We turned back once we'd gotten some distance away to see a rain of canisters, a huge cloud of acrid smoke. Through the cloud, platoons of cops in gas masks charged around the barricade, clubbing people with the butts of their rifles and shotguns.

The only refuge was out of the park. I stopped at a fountain long enough to soak my handkerchief. "Keep your eyes open," someone called. "Don't rub. That'll make it worse." Still running, Cat and I squeezed the water into our eyes to ease the burning.

Thousands of us poured out of the park, onto Clark Street and into Old Town. But cops were everywhere, swinging their clubs. The tear gas cloud drifted into homes and restaurants. People came out onto the street, wheezing and coughing, where they too became targets

Our side fought back now, throwing rocks, bottles, trash, whatever people could get their hands on. Throwing not at store windows, but at the cops, at the patrol cars. They were losing the battle, but still they were fighting back. We stopped a block away, turned and watched in wonder.

Three Black men stood near us, also watching. "White folks fightin' the po-lice!" one of them exclaimed. "Now ain't that somethin'?"

Cat, her hand still gripping my arm, pulled. "Steve," she pleaded, "you promised."

She was right. I spotted an empty street leading away and pointed. "Let's go." Soon we slowed to a casual walk. Behind us, we heard gunfire. But now we were ordinary tourists out for a late-night stroll. By the time we found Tooter, our eyes had cleared and I was able to drive home. I knew I might never have gotten there if Cat hadn't been on my arm that night.

Chapter 81

Cat and I arrived at Grant Park an hour before Tuesday morning's press conference. To my amazement, the area opposite the Hilton was full of protesters with sleeping bags and blankets, some of them still asleep. I approached one who was rolling up his gear and asked, "Were you here overnight?"

"Sure was. We held a little rally and then hung out. The cops never bothered us."

"They never tried to close the park, to throw you out?"

"Well, they did give it a try, one time. We threw stuff at them and they backed off. They didn't come back."

From another camper, a refugee from the battle at Lincoln Park, we learned things had gotten even worse up there after we left.

"They cleared the streets after a while," she explained, "and most of our people went into movement centers and churches. But the cops followed and threw tear gas inside. They ambushed us when we ran back out. I got away with a few friends, but we had nowhere to go. A lady opened her front door and waved us in. That was real nice, but I didn't think anyplace around there was safe. So a lot of us came down here."

"It's as though Chicago had two different police forces last night," I remarked. "At Lincoln Park, they wanted to kill us. Down here, they were cool. I don't get it."

"Look across the street," Cat suggested. "The Hilton. After yesterday's battle at the statue here, the police might've gotten orders to behave themselves in this park, right under the noses of all the delegates and party officials."

"I see. So I guess this is our liberated zone."

"Yes. For now, anyway."

Reporters and TV cameramen from all over the world showed up for the press conference. Some newsmen had visible bruises and bandages.

Donnie's main message was that we wouldn't be intimidated by police brutality. "We will march on the convention tomorrow," he announced, "with or without a permit. And this will be a non-violent march. We are determined to exercise our constitutional rights, but we will do nothing to provoke the police. Or the Army."

"What if they don't see it that way?" a reporter called out.

"I have one message for Mayor Daley and the Democratic Party," Donnie replied, waving his arm toward the TV cameras. "The whole world will be watching."

Donnie was besieged by reporters. He caught my eye and waved me over. "This is Steve Harris, our Director of Press Relations," he proclaimed to my complete surprise. "He'll be glad to answer your questions."

Donnie disappeared, and now I was the one besieged. I had nothing new to add, but I did my best. Answering questions about Wednesday's march, I had no choice but to repeat the party line: "With or without a permit." Cat watched and listened, arms crossed and frowning.

"What was that about?" she demanded once it broke up.

"You mean about the march?"

"Yes. About the march."

"I was speaking for the Mobe, not for me personally. What would you want me to say? That the march was still on, but I might not be in it because my girlfriend won't let me?"

"What do you mean I won't let you? I'll tell you what. You can go and do whatever you damn well please!" With that, she turned and ran away.

"Wait," I called, running after her. Once I got within earshot I shouted, "Cat, wait. Please. I didn't mean it that way. Please. Stop."

She turned, her face streaked with tears. "Oh, really? So then what did you mean by, 'My girlfriend won't let me?' Isn't that what you really think? That I'm holding you back? That I'm holding the movement back? Isn't that it?"

"No, that's not it," I pleaded. "Please, let's sit down and talk." I took her arm and led her to a bench.

"Look," I began, "I got thrown off by all of a sudden getting thrust into being a spokesman. I said what I had to say. Then, when you confronted me, I felt attacked. I didn't mean it. I guess I was hitting back. I'm sorry."

"But that is what you really think, isn't it?"

"No. No, it isn't. We've talked about this so many times. If I was by myself, would I give two hoots about whether or not the march was legal? Of course I wouldn't! But I'm not by myself. And the woman I love is terrified of what might happen to me. Why? Because she loves me. And nothing, nothing is more important than that. So *I've* chosen to avoid danger if I possibly can. That's what I really think. And I also think you know that."

She slid closer, and let me put my arm around her shoulders. "I do know it," she said softly. "I guess the resentments I accused you of are really from my own conflicts. The march is necessary. But we've seen, time and again, the brutality that awaits it. I can't even deal with the thought of you being in the middle of that. I guess I'm being selfish. It's wrong. I know it's wrong. When you threw it back at me, I got defensive. It's me who needs forgiveness, not you. But I'm so confused." She stopped to wipe the tears off her face.

"Okay," I said. "Let's forgive each other and move on. This is complicated. We have the rest of the day to figure it out."

"All right. But what now?"

"It's a beautiful day. Everyone will be at Lincoln Park. We should go there and take as much time to talk things out as we need."

On our way to the car, arms wound around each other, my only thought was, *Just three more days, three more days until I can whisk my sweetheart away to her birthday weekend in Paradise.*

That afternoon, the mood was more subdued. Knots of people exchanged war stories. Medics, many of them bandaged themselves, made the rounds, cleaning and redressing wounds. There was still singing. There was still dancing. But anger hung heavy in the air, along with the fumes.

I spotted Rev. Blake, pastor of Lincoln Park Presbyterian, one of the first ministers I'd met with. I walked over to greet him and introduced Cat.

"If I remember right," I recalled, "you were gonna get back to me about making the church basement available. But I don't think you did call, did you?"

"No, I didn't. The church's lay leadership wasn't able to decide one way or the other, so I had nothing to report."

"Did the FBI visit have anything to do with that?"

"Oh, you know about their threats. Well, yes, it did sort of collapse some of our shaky timbers. But that's all changed now."

"Changed? How?"

"After what happened the last couple of nights, our deacons realized we couldn't close our doors to the protesters. They authorized me to hang a sign over the front door advertising, 'SANCTUARY.' Word got around to the other local clergy and they're doing the same. People need a place to get away from the police, someplace safe, before someone gets killed. Of course, all the work you did assigning groups to particular churches goes out the window since our doors are now open to everyone."

"Don't worry about that. What you're doing is what's needed, and I'm glad to hear it. It's also a brave thing to do."

"Thank you. Tonight, the clergy will gather down here to conduct an ecumenical religious service, with an eight-foot-high cross that's being assembled now. I know it's a long shot, but we're hoping to change the tone, change the atmosphere. Maybe another battle like last night's can be averted."

"Sure sounds worth a try. Cat and I will miss it, though, because of LBJ's Anti-Birthday Party at the Coliseum. Have you heard about it?"

"Sure. People have been passing out leaflets all day. It's a good idea. It'll give folks a way to blow off some steam without risking violence. I'm impressed anyone thought of it ahead of time."

"It was Cat's idea," I proudly announced. She punched me in the arm.

Donnie, standing on a makeshift platform with a portable speaker, called people over. We were a few thousand by then, and looking for direction. Donnie plugged the Anti-Birthday Party, and announced a rally in Grant Park preceding it. Another march would soon be heading down there.

"He's trying to defuse the situation," I told Cat. "It might work."

It didn't appear likely, though. A truck pulled up, and protesters began unloading crates full of smashed-up ceramic tiles. People lined up to cram their pockets with shards and slivers. I asked one what they were for.

He held a wide sliver between thumb and forefinger. "Ever skim a rock across a lake?" he asked.

"Sure."

"Well, tonight the cops won't be the only ones with weapons. And the blood in the streets won't only be ours! Here, you want some?"

I called back, "Thanks, maybe later," as Cat yanked me away.

"Maybe later?" she demanded.

"Just being polite. Look, the march to Grant Park is gathering. Let's go join it."

"No. We'll drive down and park near the Coliseum."

"Why do you want to do that?"

"Because we're saying good-night to Lincoln Park. Everyone coming back here later will be looking for trouble. And you're not one of them. You and I are going home tonight, not here."

Overcoming my reluctance, I agreed. She added, "And we still have to talk about tomorrow."

Chapter 82

The Democratic National Committee had reserved the Hilton's Imperial Suite for President Johnson, and planned a big birthday party for him. It was uncertain, though, whether or not the guest of honor would actually come to Chicago. We hoped he would. His presence would make our demonstration bigger, louder and more sharply focused. We looked forward to giving him a warm, warm welcome.

At the last minute, though, he decided to stay in Washington. Everyone knew why. Any time a president cancels a high-profile birthday celebration and skips his own party's national convention, that's a very big deal. It was because of us: the dissenters; the longhairs; the radicals; the pacifists; the hippies and Yippies; the youth. He might even have gotten a rough reception inside the convention itself. It had been quite a while since he'd made a speech anywhere other than military bases, because he and his war had made him such a magnet for protests. While I was disappointed to hear he bowed out, I felt we'd won this battle of the birthday, and without any violence. Our Anti-Birthday Party became the nation's only public celebration of the occasion.

The event's theme was simple. In the words of the printed program, it was "a tribute to President Johnson celebrating all his achievements, from the first congressional election he stole in Texas to the anti-personnel bombs he's delivered to the peasants of Vietnam." The walls of the lobby were decorated with enlarged photos illustrating Vietnam's gruesome destruction, as well as our own military-occupied communities of color. Speakers included not only movement leaders, but artists, writers and poets. Dick Gregory, the Black comedian and civil rights activist, had the audience in stitches with stinging political satire. Rock bands were interspersed with the speakers.

The highlight for me, once again, was Phil Ochs. Tonight, he had more stage time than he had at the McCarthy rally. He interspersed his lengthy set of songs with commentary on the war and the election. He sang and spoke for our generation, as he talked back to the generals with verses like this:

> *What have we won,*
> *With the saber and the gun?*
> *Tell me,*
> *Was it worth it all?*

Chants of "Hell, No! We Won't Go!" sprang out. Small flames were lit as first a few, then hundreds of draft cards went up in federally prohibited smoke. By the time he left the stage, everyone was standing, roaring, chanting slogans. It was a magical moment. Cat and I weren't the only couple holding each other tight, euphoric with release of the week's tension.

Later, Dave Dellinger announced that, yes, we will march on the convention the following afternoon. Abbie Hoffman declared that the Yippies would join us, that we were "brothers and sisters now." At around midnight, Donnie closed the show, urging everyone to walk, in small groups, the short distance to Grant Park, where we would greet the delegates on their way back from the Amphitheater.

The convention, we later learned, was bordering on chaos that night, and wouldn't adjourn until much later. Before the delegates arrived, we greeted refugees from another night of violence at Lincoln Park. We learned that Rev. Blake's group of ministers had grown to a few hundred. But the police had cleared the park with brute force, clerical collars notwithstanding. They used a machine that sprayed tear gas and then charged in with gas masks, beating any stragglers left behind. Again, battles had raged through the streets. It sounded, though, like the prediction I'd heard earlier was accurate. Not all the casualties were on our side.

As we streamed into Grant Park, some bright light in the police command apparently thought more tear gas might chase us back. The winds were with us, though. East-to-west breezes blew the gas away from the park, across Michigan Avenue and straight into the Hilton.

Campaign workers, gasping for breath, charged across the avenue into the park, receiving a loud welcome. We rushed to soothe their burning eyes with soaking wet cloths, and they joined our growing encampment. They told us the Platform Committee had rejected the Vietnam peace plank. Instead, it reported out a resolution sent in by President Johnson, which was even more belligerent than Humphrey's draft. Many of the new arrivals said they'd had it with the Democratic Party and would join us in the streets.

More than the wind was with us. Outside the Hilton, once the tear gas dissipated, stood a thick row of TV cameras and other media equipment, manned by newsmen who'd already had unpleasant dealings with Chicago's police.

At around 1 a.m., Donnie was summoned to meet with the on-site police commander, who demanded to know if we were going to try storming the Hilton. Donnie assured him we had no such plans, but warned that something worse than Lincoln Park might ensue if the cops tried to enforce the curfew. They made a deal. The police would leave us alone overnight, as long as we stayed where we were and didn't try crossing Michigan Avenue. Grant Park would "belong to the people" for another night.

The impromptu rally went on and on. By Cat's estimate, there were now 7,000 of us. Antiwar delegates returning from the convention added to our ranks. They'd raised some hell of their own when Daley tried to ram the platform through in the middle of the night, after the nation's televisions had been turned off. They'd won that battle, forcing postponement of the debate until Wednesday afternoon. Many were furious over how the party machinery was crippling democracy and how Daley's cops had trampled dissent. One called up to the 25-story Hilton through a portable bullhorn. "Blink your lights if you're with us!" Rows and rows of lights blinked on and off, including all of those on the fifteenth floor, the McCarthy headquarters. The crowd erupted in wild cheers, chanting "Join us! Join us!" More campaign workers bolted from the hotel and into the park.

An hour later, trepidation rippled through the crowd as the Army National Guard came rolling up, armed with bayonet-fitted rifles in barbed-wire-enhanced jeeps. Their commander, though, announced through his bullhorn that they were only there to relieve the police, and that he would honor all previous agreements. He ordered his troops to remove the bayonets. Then the rally turned into a folk concert.

Shortly afterward, it surprised me to hear that a couple of hundred AFSC members had departed from the Quaker Meeting House on their own march, early in the afternoon. Soldiers stopped them at a checkpoint, but didn't attack them or even turn them around. They were still there, even now, picketing and singing. They'd done this independently of the Mobe. But that report, combined with the negotiated occupation of Grant Park, spread a sense of hope.

"You see?" I asked Cat, rhetorically. "We can do this."

"Yes, it is good news," she agreed. "And it's been a long, long day. Now let's go home."

As we left the park, Peter, Paul and Mary led the boisterous crowd in singing, "This Land is Your Land, This Land is My Land," which we'd already sung at least half a dozen times. If we had a Convention Week theme song, that was it.

Chapter 83

It was almost 4 a.m. when we got home, but we were both too wired to sleep. We behaved as though we could hold off the dawning of the fateful day, as long as we kept extending our lovemaking. We squeezed, pounded and held on like it might be our last night together. We both harbored fears of what the new day might bring. It was only when dawn broke through that we succumbed, finally, to exhaustion.

I woke a few hours later, and looked over at Cat. She seemed to be sleeping at peace. I loved watching the gentle rise and fall of her breasts, the slight twitching of her eyes, the rhythm of her breathing. As I took in the sight, the scent, the soft sounds of my Butterscotch Goddess, I had only one thought in mind: *Two more days. Only two more days until we celebrate her birthday with our Weekend in Paradise, and then return to a more or less normal life.* I couldn't wait.

But first we had to get through this. All the work, all the debate, all the planning and organization, would climax this day. I vowed, for the millionth time, to honor my promise and keep us out of harm's way.

The coffee was ready when she opened her eyes. I brought it in and sat on the bed, gently stroking her until she sat up and reached for her cup. "That was some night," I reflected. "I don't know where you got the energy."

"I don't know where either of us did," she responded, already wide awake. "But now we have to prepare for today. Do you have a plan?"

"Sure. We go to the office and do whatever needs to be done. We go to the rally in the park, where the Mobe has a permit for everything. And we join the march on the convention, but only as far as the cops allow. After that, whatever others do, you and I will turn around. No confrontations, no provocations, no fights. Okay?"

"Good. And you'll follow my lead, no matter what the temptation?"

"Like a puppy dog."

"Promise?"

"Promise."

She smiled, leaned up and gave me a kiss. "Good. Now let's have breakfast. I'm starving."

I often wondered how such a small person sometimes ate so ravenously without ever gaining an ounce. I took pleasure in watching, though, because she lost interest in food when she was gripped by anxiety, just as I did during my bouts of depression. I took her healthy appetite as a good sign. It was time now to fuel up for whatever might come our way.

While I scrambled the eggs, Cat called to check in on Emma and then told me, "She wants us to come down before we leave. I don't know, but she sounded a little angry."

"About what?"

"Emma has a right to be angry," she explained. "We've been running around every day and every night while she's been hearing stories about the battles at Lincoln Park, and we didn't check in with her until now. She's probably been worried sick."

"Uh-oh."

Cat's assessment was correct, but Emma's irritation dissolved as soon as we came through the door. We each got a big hug. Then she led us to the couch. "Sit," she directed. "I'll bring over the coffee."

I tried apologizing. "Emma, we're sorry. Things have been so crazy and..."

"It's all right," she interjected. "I'm so glad to see both of you safe and sound. I was getting worried. I called and called, and your phone rang and rang. My imagination began kicking into gear. I even called the hospitals. But you're both okay, so now I'm better. I want to hear everything, but I understand there's no time for that now. I just wish I was healthy enough to join you today. But you know I'll be there in spirit."

It was almost noon, time for us to go. Cat cleared the cups off the table and washed them in the sink. Emma whispered to me, "Please, be safe today. Take care of yourself, and take care of my girl. Call me whenever you get home, no matter how late it is. I'll be waiting."

At the office, Jeff told us, "Everyone's down at the conference room. Big last-minute strategy meeting. It's been going on for more than an hour."

Jack Weaver was at the AFSC reception desk. I asked, "How close to the convention did your group get yesterday?"

"About half a mile. Then they stopped us at a checkpoint."

"Any trouble?"

"None at all. The police didn't bother us, so we kept picketing the checkpoint and singing all night. When the sun came back up, they asked us to leave, so we did. Everyone was tired anyway."

"See that!" I exclaimed, turning to Cat. "No permit, but no trouble either. One more time the city gave in at the last minute."

She regarded me with a raised eyebrow, as if to ask, "Are you kidding?"

"I wouldn't get carried away with optimism," Jack continued. "We were hardly enough people to call it a march. I don't even expect press coverage. For us, this was a simple act of conscience. There's no comparison to what you'll be dealing with today."

We moved on, to see fifteen people seated at the conference table. I recognized them as Steering Committee members, except for one. The stranger had a thick bushy moustache, and sported a cowboy hat and sunglasses. He seemed vaguely familiar, but I couldn't quite place him. Looking on were thirty or forty others, including staff, volunteers, marshals and, I suspected, more than a few police and federal agents. The question being debated was what to do after the rally permit expires at four o'clock.

The stranger took the floor a few minutes after we got there. He predicted mass arrests, whether or not we marched on the convention.

"They won't allow this march," he argued. "And after four o'clock, the rally will be illegal too. We need to get our people out of the park, into the Loop, and shut this city down. Small groups, going this way and that. Hard to predict. Hard to catch. A big mass will be too easy to target."

As soon as I heard his voice, I knew this was Paul. The disguise, I thought, was a little odd, but it did work. I glanced over at Cat, frowning and shaking her head.

"That's not what people came here for," Donnie argued. "You know that. Some, maybe most, of the people in the park today will be there exclusively for the rally, the rally we assured them is legal. And that's all. The rest, we don't know how many, will march as far as we can get. But we didn't invite anyone to come to Chicago in order to trash it."

Everyone at the table had something to say, sometimes all at once. Voices rose. Fingers pointed. A few people walked out. It seemed all the fissures inherent in coalition politics were deepening instead of closing as the moment of truth drew near. Dave Dellinger made his own plea for unity.

"Donnie makes a good point," he began. "Those people in the park, and they're gathering right now while we sit here arguing, are here at our invitation to a legal rally and an optional march. They're human beings who interrupted their lives to stand against the war. Our responsibility is to give them that rally, and give them our best advice about what to do afterward. That's all."

"And the alternatives have to be reasonable," he continued. "Yes, we'll attempt our march on the convention, regardless of the risk, with however many choose to join it. But for those not willing or able to take that risk, I suggest we advise them to disperse in different directions, calmly. To walk, not run. We can tell them the rest of the park is open to the public, so they can stay and enjoy it. They can picket the Hilton if they can get to it safely. They can take other actions as they see fit. But the Mobe will only endorse non-violent actions, including on the march."

A consensus on that plan began to coalesce. Donnie called me over. "We'll need leaflets. Can you do it?"

"We'll do our best," I promised. Cat and I went down the hall to the office. Time was short. I started drafting the leaflet while Cat went back to get Sabrina from the boardroom.

During the next half hour, the three of us finalized the wording. Sabrina turned it into a work of art. We mimeographed thousands of copies. Volunteers offered to help with distribution. Armed with reams of leaflets, we hurried over to Grant Park where Dave had already convened the assembly.

Chapter 84

The sun was bright, the sky clear blue, and the crowd irresistibly festive. As we strolled through it, we noticed it was far more diverse than the previous gatherings. We saw many more middle-aged and older participants and many families with children. The African-American representation was much broader. McCarthy and McGovern buttons were ubiquitous, as were buttons and banners identifying every political tendency in the broad antiwar coalition. This was, by far, the week's largest turnout.

Plainclothes cops passed out their own leaflets, warning that anyone attempting to march on the convention would be arrested. Many hundreds in uniform were lined in formation, behind the bandshell and on the field's two adjacent sides. On the roof of the nearby Field Museum, we saw heavily armed Army National Guard troops. As a precaution, I ducked into a bathroom and soaked the washcloths I'd brought along.

Once Cat and I ran out of leaflets, we settled down on a grassy rise, far enough from the bandshell to survey the activity, but close enough to still hear the speakers. I asked her how many people she thought were there. She scanned the area, did a quick mental calculation, and answered, "Around twenty thousand, I think."

"I guess our press conferences, mailings and phone calls did have an impact," I commented. "Thousands of people came to town once they knew we had a permit for this. But if we'd gotten those permits, for the march and for the parks, if the mayor hadn't scared people away, we would've had ten times as many."

"Look, you did everything possible," she responded. "But Daley was never gonna let it happen."

"I know that now, Cat, and we should've known it from the beginning. His April shoot-to-kill order wasn't only targeting looters and arsonists. It was also directed at us. The National Guard's bayonet charge on our solidarity march the next day? That was another warning.

Three weeks later, the cops went crazy attacking us at the Civic Center. They had no provocation for either of those. Daley wasn't concerned about negative publicity. He wanted it, because it scared people away from coming here this week."

Besides the socializing that goes on at any big event, the crowd's attention was now divided among three focal points. One, of course, was the bandshell, where speakers railed against the war, racism, imperialism, poverty, and the two war-mongering political parties. Another was the intimidating, threatening military presence. The third was the platform debate at the convention which was going on at the same time, broadcast through people's transistor radios.

Two hours into the rally, a murmur went through the crowd. Someone near us threw his radio to the ground. The peace plank had been defeated. A thousand delegates voted to end the carnage. Fifteen hundred voted to continue it. After the vote, an antiwar demonstration broke out right there on the convention floor. Official proceedings were adjourned until evening, when Hubert Humphrey would be named this war party's presidential candidate.

A youngster ran over to the nearby flagpole and tried to lower the flag. Eight burly cops rushed in, beat him mercilessly and dragged him away. A small crowd surged forward and the flag began coming down. People shouted, "Burn it!" "Tear it up!" From the speakers' microphone, someone called, "Half mast! Half mast in mourning!"

Cat wove her arm through mine and we watched as thirty cops waded in, beating everyone in the flagpole's vicinity. Donnie ran over with a band of marshals, trying to create a barrier between the police and the protesters. The cops turned their attention on them. Five pounced on Donnie, beating him bloody and nearly unconscious. Others broke away. The cops chasing them swung their clubs indiscriminately. Cat squeezed my arm with both hands, her eyes welling with tears.

Anger surged through the crowd. The gathering around the flagpole grew larger as battle was joined. With a barrage of rocks, bottles and trashcans, they fought to push the cops back. From behind police lines, a tear gas canister dropped into their midst. Larry Graff picked it up with an oven glove and threw it right back. The police retreated when the cloud of burning smoke erupted.

"They won!" I exclaimed. "The cops are going away!"

"Sure they are," she conceded. "But what's next? And look at poor Donnie. They nearly killed him!"

Whit, Vern and a couple of marshals helped Donnie crawl slowly away, escaping through a hole in a fence.

At the bandshell, a visibly furious Paul took the microphone, shedding his disguise in an instant. "Peaceful protest is now illegal in this police state!" he shouted. "Don't stand there waiting to be slaughtered. Take it to the streets! Form small, mobile groups that can't be easily mowed down. They want a fight, we'll give 'em one. If blood flows in Chicago tonight, don't let all of it be ours. Into the Loop! Now, while we can!"

He stepped down and jogged to one of the walk-bridges that connected the park to the Loop. Several hundred, most of them wearing red SDS bandanas, followed and charged across.

Dave took the mike, and announced the gathering point for the march. "This will be a non-violent action," he declared. "Anyone looking for confrontation should not join in." Marshals circulated through the crowd, telling those armed with sticks and rocks to drop them or to leave. Thousands of us lined up, eight across, arms linked to step off on the much-anticipated march

"This is it," I muttered. "Let's go."

Cat knew I couldn't stand waiting and watching any longer. Frowning, one arm still hooked in mine, she walked down with me to join the marchers.

Before we could even get out of the park, though, a massive police blockade headed us off. The embryonic march stalled, as Dave and other leaders negotiated with the police brass. An hour passed. As time dragged on, the ranks of the marchers, so neatly ordered by the marshals, broke down. Now, we were just thousands of people milling about, waiting to be told what to do, in varying states of restlessness. Chanting and singing continued, but spirits were sagging. The cops barring the way looked equally unhappy. Another hour went by.

The only paths onto Michigan Avenue were over bridges and overpasses spanning sunken train tracks. As far as we could see, all these crossings were now blocked by National Guardsmen with rifles, bayonets and machine guns, even grenade launchers. A few hundred would-be marchers gathered themselves and charged the nearest bridge. Most got beaten back and some just got beaten, but about a hundred made it through. They yelled for more of us to join them. Cat held on tight, feet firmly planted where we stood.

A great many, sick of waiting around, did join them. They ran north, toward the next bridge. We stayed put, but not for long. Tear gas canisters came flying. Within minutes, thick, acrid smoke engulfed our whole area. Now everyone ran to get away, some screaming from burning eyes, others falling to the ground, unable to breathe, many vomiting along the way.

I pulled the wet washcloths out of my pockets, and handed one to Cat. We squeezed the water into our eyes, covered our mouths and noses, and ran like hell. It seemed as though the tear gas cloud was following us. A few blocks north, we came to an unguarded bridge. Thousands of us streamed across before the soldiers and cops got repositioned.

"Are you all right?" I asked Cat. She wiped her eyes, nodded, and hooked her arm back in mine. Others were not all right, coughing, gasping for breath, doubled up in agony.

At that moment, something completely unexpected happened. Coming down Michigan Avenue from the north was a line of police on horseback, followed by three mule-drawn wagons. As the front wagon drew near, I recognized the Rev. Ralph David Abernathy, who I'd seen on TV with Dr. King many times. The mule train was a symbol of the Poor People's Campaign, his last national effort.

Obviously, with the police escort, this little caravan had a permit. And it was heading south. *Maybe,* I thought, *all the way to the convention.* Our dazed, confused crowd suddenly moved with almost military precision, reforming our ranks behind the rear wagon. Now we had a parade, and the police were out in front, leading it! Calls of solidarity rang out between the mostly white antiwar marchers and the Black civil rights workers standing in the wagons.

My hopes suddenly soared. Cat wasn't so sure. "Aren't we putting those people in danger by joining them?" she asked.

"I don't think so. If the cops attack Rev. Abernathy, the country might go up in flames. And they know that." We linked arms with those adjacent and moved slowly forward.

Our march had formed spontaneously, without leaders. Now, the marshals reasserted their authority, keeping the ranks neatly organized and watching out for possible trouble-makers. All week, I thought, they'd proven themselves better trained and more disciplined than I'd given them credit for. At the flagpole, for example, they'd also demonstrated real courage. I experienced another pang of regret that I hadn't been one of them. The chants they started caught on down the line.

"What do we want?"

"Peace!"

"When do we want it?"

"Now!"

After a few blocks, the march stalled. The mule train was barely past the Hilton, where TV cameras were lined atop the sidewalk canopy. But the avenue was blocked by police, who'd apparently regrouped and rushed into the intersection. Fifteen minutes later, the mule train moved forward, but a police brigade swept in to keep us from following. Shouts of support rang out from the wagons as they moved on down the avenue, but we couldn't follow. *What to do?* We'd hit a wall of resistance, but we wouldn't give up. We sat down in the street. We would hold it with a sit-in, the time-honored act of non-violent resistance, until we were permitted to continue. That was a mistake. A big one.

From down the cross-street came the first police charge, right past the Hilton and into the crowd. Clubs swung wildly. People jumped to their feet, only to get knocked back down. The cops in front of the aborted march pulled down Plexiglas face shields and joined in. They weren't trying to clear the intersection, or even make arrests. It was a full-scale assault which the marshals were powerless to prevent. Crowded together and attacked from two sides, there was no effective defense. Police even attacked bystanders. They pushed some elderly people through a plate-glass window and then charged inside, chasing them through a restaurant. People who'd fallen got run over by three-wheeled motorcycles.

Filling the sidewalk outside the park, the huge crowd of people who hadn't yet lined up with us gathered behind police lines, in full view of the TV cameras, chanting, "The whole world is watching! The whole world is watching!"

It seemed the only way out was north, away from the Hilton. With my arm wrapped around Cat, we threaded our way back up the avenue, urging others to do the same. Once we got through the active battle site, the path forward grew easier. We were vulnerable from any direction, though, and had to get out of there.

A few dozen of us broke off, running down a cross-street. Halfway down the block, we saw soldiers waiting at the corner. We turned, ran back and continued north. People ran for their lives, breaking up in different directions, some charging right into traps where there were no TV cameras.

Finally, we came to a cross-street that was well-lit and apparently open. We charged through. We ran a block, then another. All was quiet. We'd escaped.

"Let's slow down now," I suggested. "We'll jump on a train and go home."

The first subway station we came to was guarded by police, obviously itching to crack heads. We moved to the other side of the street, and on to the next station, where we encountered the same scene.

"There's no way out," Cat sputtered dejectedly, "and it's too far to walk."

"Then let's try a way back in," I suggested. "This street is quiet. We can walk south for a while, then circle around and head back to the park from behind the police lines. We should be safe there. The fighting is only in the streets, not inside the park. Then we can walk through the park and find another subway line on the other side."

Without any better ideas, we strode ten blocks south, turned right, and finally back up Michigan Avenue, which was closed to traffic. Arm in arm, we ambled up the street, an innocent couple of tourists out for a leisurely stroll. Soon the Hilton was within sight, surrounded by bedlam. At the edge of the park and on the sidewalk, thousands of people were chanting. *The whole world is watching. The whole world is watching!* Lines of police kept them in place, but they weren't being attacked.

"It looks safe over there," I proposed. "Let's join them."

Suddenly we heard a commotion behind us. Gunshots. Paul and a band of militants wielding primitive weapons ran past. A hundred yards behind chased six cops shooting, I hoped into the air, and yelling. They weren't chasing Cat and me, but they'd grab us if they caught us. I let go of her and shouted, "Run!"

We ran. Those cops were too wide around the middle to catch us, but I didn't know whether they were aiming their guns at us or not. If only we made it to the park, the crowd would swallow and protect us. We ran.

We were only a block from safety when two National Guard jeeps came careening around a corner a few blocks behind us, speeding in our direction.

"Cat! Run!"

Halfway up the block, I tripped and fell. Cat stopped and moved toward me. "No," I pleaded, waving her away. "Run. Please. Run. I'll catch up." She ran ahead, looking back over her shoulder at me. The jeeps were closing in fast. *"Run!"*

I rolled sideways and scrambled back to my feet. One jeep sped over the spot where I'd fallen. I looked ahead. And my nightmare suddenly came horribly true.

The other jeep headed straight for Cat. There was a *thump* and her body was in the air. Another *thump*, as it bounced off an Army truck and dropped to the street.

"No!" I screamed, racing to her motionless form. She was unconscious, her body sprawled unnaturally, somehow twisted. I dropped to my knees and lifted her to me. Her bloody head dropped to one side. I cradled it in my hand.

"Cat! Talk to me. Wake up. Please. Oh my god. Wake up!" Tears running down my face, I tried feeling for a pulse, but hands pulled at me. I resisted. Then I felt a *Thwack!* and everything went dark.

Chapter 85

Gentle ocean breezes rocked the hammock where Cat and I lay snuggled together, gazing at another beautiful sunset. She and I had a magical day on our little tropical island. We swam all the way out to the reef, and rode the waves back to shore. Sun-dried, we made glorious love on the beach. Later, I spear-fished a lovely red snapper to roast over the fire, and Cat's scavenging brought us delicious sides. For dessert, a coconut conveniently dropped from a palm tree. Now, my eyelids were getting heavy. Was it because I'd eaten too much? Or was I being overtaken by this overwhelming sense of contentment? Everything was so right in my world: the rays of the waning sun; the salty sea air; the sounds of the crashing waves; even the loquacious parrots. And, of course, Cat, her warm, nearly naked body curled up in mine, nibbling at my neck and reaching down, as if to see if I really was too sleepy...

But now, a hand held my chin up. I sniffed. This wasn't Cat's scent. *Go away!* I felt something cold on my head. *No, let me be!* Reluctantly, I opened my eyes. *Where am I?* I closed them again, and tried returning to our island paradise, though it was already a fading memory. Then another dream, a nightmare. A barbed-wire jeep, a big truck. Cat, motionless, her bloody head in my hands. Or did it really happen? *No! It can't be!* I shook my head violently.

"Ssssh," came a soft voice. "Try to stay still." Not Cat's voice. My eyes opened again. I saw a young woman holding an icepack. Not Cat. *Where is she?* My eyes darted back and forth. *Where is Cat? Where am I?* The nightmare memory became more vivid. *No!* I jerked up, screamed her name, lost my balance and fell back down.

The woman who was not Cat waved a hand. A man moved in my direction. He looked familiar. *Who is this?* He knelt down, lifted my head and shined a light into each of my eyes. The woman moved away.

"Do you recognize me, Steve?"

Did I? I blinked and looked again. It came to me.

"Dr. Young."

"That's good. It shows your concussion isn't too serious."

"Oh." I looked around, then closed my eyes again. My head hurt too much to keep them open. But I still didn't recognize this place.

"Where am I?"

"McCarthy headquarters at the Hilton. They turned it over to us for a field hospital."

I reopened my eyes. Yes, that explained the other dazed people, the bandages and splints, the men and women in long white coats. But I didn't see the one I was looking for, the one I needed.

"Where is Cat? I don't see her."

"She's not here," he replied. "She's..."

It was coming back, more clearly now. I interrupted. "No! Don't tell me that. Don't tell me she's, she's..." The awful question was stuck in my throat. My eyes filled with tears.

Dr. Young grabbed my shoulders. "No, no. She's alive."

My panic receded. "But where?"

"She needed a real hospital. I had her brought to Midway Medical."

"Oh." I was still so groggy, and my head was pounding. "But isn't that far from here?"

"I had no choice. The ambulance drivers reported that police are guarding the local E.R. entrances. They're snatching kids off gurneys and tossing them into paddy wagons. They invaded a field hospital we set up in a church and dragged patients away. They haven't bothered us here, though, probably because of the politicians and news cameras."

"She was hurt. I remember that. But how bad?"

"She was still unconscious when we put her in the ambulance. We'll only know how serious her injuries are after x-rays and lab tests."

"But she's alive?"

"Yes. She's alive."

I sprang up. "I have to go!" But I was too dizzy to go anywhere.

"When you're a little steadier, I'll have someone drive you. Tell the hospital you're her husband, so they might let you in to see her. They might also want to take a look at you. I'll come down there as soon as I'm finished here."

My mind was beginning to function now. "Emma," I croaked. "Need to tell Emma."

"I already did that. Here. Take these for your headaches, until they go away."

He handed me a vial of Tylenol. I stood up again, a little more stable, and shook his hand. "You're a good man, Dr. Young. Thank you. I think I can go now."

On the way to the hospital, the pills took the hard edge off my headache, but the pounding wouldn't stop. My balance wasn't quite right either. *When will I wake from this awful nightmare?*

"I have to see my wife," I told the receptionist. "She came in a while ago."

"Name?" she asked without looking up.

"Crawford. Cat, no, Ca-taca-taca Crawford. I'm her husband."

"I see," she muttered, fingering through a box of index cards. "Ah yes, here she is. Auto accident..."

"Accident?" I exclaimed. "That was no accident! It was attempted murder!"

"I'm sorry," she said, looking up with alarm on her face. "That's what it says on this card here."

"They tried to kill her!" I continued, my voice rising. "The soldiers. A jeep. Barbed wire. A truck. An Army truck."

I noticed people staring at me now and, more important, I'd drawn the attention of a cop standing nearby. I forced myself to lower my voice.

"I'm sorry," I told the receptionist. "I'm very worried about her. Won't you please tell me where she is?"

"Go to the waiting room at the end of the hallway on your right. I'll call ahead and tell them you're coming."

I did as I was told, and took a seat in the waiting room. Where I waited. And waited. When I couldn't stand it anymore, I went back out into the hallway. On a set of big double doors, a sign read, "TRAUMA CENTER: Authorized Personnel Only." I pushed them open and stepped through. A security guard stopped me.

"You can't come in here," he stated firmly.

"But my wife... I need to see her."

"I'm sorry," he said, holding the door. "Those are the rules." He gave me a little push back out and closed the door.

I paced the hallway, trying to figure out a way in. A doctor came through the door. I hoped he would help.

"I need to see my wife," I told him, blocking his way. "Cat Crawford."

"Oh, she's in radiology now, getting x-rays. Maybe later."

"But is she all right?" I asked, hopefully.

"Too soon to tell," he replied, pushing past me and gesturing toward the waiting room. "You can wait in there."

I sat and held my pounding head in my hands. *Maybe later. Too soon to tell. What did that mean?* I started pacing again. There was no point staying in this room. I moved my pacing back to the hallway. After an interminable amount of time, an orderly came down the hall, pushing a gurney. *Cat!* She was sleeping. I reached out to her, but the doctor walking alongside pulled me away.

"That's my wife!" I cried. "I need to be with her!"

"Not now," he insisted. "Maybe later."

"But is she all right? Tell me she's all right."

"Sorry. It's too soon to tell."

Back in the waiting room, I banged my head against the wall, trying to make it all go away. I did it again. And again.

"Steven!" came a gravelly voice from behind me. "Stop that!"

I turned to see Emma, her face streaked from tears. She led me to a chair.

"How, how'd you get in?" I asked.

"Quentin told me to tell them I'm Cat's grandmother. When I was here earlier, I signed a bunch of papers. But they still wouldn't tell me anything or let me see her."

"They won't tell me anything either. All they say is, 'maybe later' and 'too soon to tell.' What does that mean?"

"They're probably still doing tests," Emma supposed. "I'll wait with you. But you need to calm down. Can you tell me what happened?"

I told her the whole story, from the flagpole incident on. She already knew about the one-sided battle on Michigan Avenue, since the whole thing had been on TV. There were televisions in the convention hall too. Emma told me lots of delegates were up in arms over the attack.

"Senator Ribicoff accused Daley of 'using Gestapo tactics.' From the podium, on national TV. And when the camera switched to Daley, he was holding his middle finger up and shouting."

"What'd he say?"

"The TV didn't pick up the sound, so I tried figuring it out by lip-reading. It was something like, 'Fuck you, you Jew son-of-a-bitch. You lousy motherfucker. Go home!' That's what it looked like. Real classy."

I shook my head and went back to my story. At the part about the speeding jeep, my face collapsed in grief.

"And it was all my fault!" I exclaimed. "It was my fault! This morning, you said, 'Take care of my girl,' and now look what I've done!"

"No, it wasn't your fault," Emma said. "You weren't the one driving that jeep. You were trying to get her to safety."

"But we shouldn't have even been there. Cat insisted all summer that we not try marching on the convention unless we got the parade permit. Why? Because she was worried about me! *Me!* It was *my* idea that we push the envelope to get as far as possible. She went along because I was so fixated on the march, and because she couldn't deal with staying home and worrying. Worrying about me! It was all my fault. If anyone had to get hurt, it should've been me, not her. And now, now I can't even help her. All I can do is sit here, wasting oxygen."

"Cat is a strong-willed person, Steve. It was her decision to be there. You didn't force her to do anything. You have to stop thinking this way. What's done is done. Focus on the future. Cat will need your help to recover from whatever her injuries are. You can't provide it if you're moping around, wallowing in guilt."

I didn't want to talk about this anymore. "I guess you're right. Since we can't do anything but wait, let's turn that TV on and see what's happening at the convention."

The roll call of states would be only a formality since the result was predetermined. But some delegates, angered by the massacre in the streets, were trying to prevent it. The head of the Wisconsin delegation called for the convention to adjourn for two weeks and reconvene in another city. Chants of "Let's go home! Let's go home!" filled the hall. Hundreds of delegates held up "Stop the War" posters.

Eventually, the roll call began, moving inexorably toward its foregone conclusion. Humphrey went over the top when three-quarters of Pennsylvania's delegates gave him their votes, even though McCarthy had overwhelmingly won that state's primary. The band started playing, but booing delegates drowned it out.

When Dr. Young and a nurse came into the room, I stood and turned the TV off.

"I've spoken to the doctors and looked at Cat's chart," he reported. "I assume they haven't told you anything yet?"

"Only that it's too soon to tell. It's driving me crazy. What does that mean?"

"She has cuts, massive bruising and broken bones," he began. "But she's young and remarkably fit. These will heal, and the tests don't show any major organ damage."

"That's it?" I asked hopefully.

"Unfortunately, Steve, that's not it. This is where the 'too soon to tell' comes in. She suffered a traumatic brain injury, and lapsed into a coma."

"What does that mean?" I asked again, nausea rising.

"All we know about comas," he explained, "is that they're like a deep sleep, a state of suspended animation. Neurologists think the brain is trying to reorganize itself, with healthy cells taking over the functions of damaged ones."

"Does that work? How long does it last?"

"Everyone is different. Most people regain consciousness..."

"What do you mean 'most people'?" Now I barely heard him over the sledgehammers in my head.

"I'm sorry, but not everyone comes back. Some go into a vegetative state and, yes, some die. But let's hope for the best."

"Cat will come back," Emma announced with an air of assurance. "But what are the long-term effects?"

"Again, everyone is different. Some people are good as new the minute they wake up. We can certainly hope for that. But others temporarily or permanently lose aspects of their functioning: Memory, hearing, eyesight, reasoning, anything. And there's no way to know until they come out of it. That's why it really is too soon to tell. Comas can last hours, days, weeks, months or even longer. The longer they last, though, the worse the prognosis."

Through my tears, I pleaded, "Can't I just see her?"

"She's in Intensive Care tonight, but you can hopefully visit with her tomorrow. Now, what you need is to go home and sleep. Your own recovery will require rest. I want you to take two of these pills as soon as you get home. You absolutely have to sleep." He handed me another vial.

"All right. But will she even know I'm there tomorrow?"

"No-one can give you a definite answer to that question. But it certainly couldn't hurt."

I closed my eyes and shook my head, but the pounding persisted. Then the nurse spoke for the first time. "There's one more thing," she added. "I'm sorry, but we couldn't save the baby."

My eyes flew open. "Save the baby? What baby?"

"It was only an embryo," she explained, "barely a few weeks in development. She most likely wasn't even aware of it. The impact triggered a miscarriage."

The room spun around. Dizziness and nausea washed over me. I slumped to the floor, threw up and passed out.

Chapter 86

I woke up in a bed, but not our bed. *Where am I now?* My head hurt. I was disoriented. After a few minutes, I realized it was a hospital room, probably at Midway Medical. That meant Cat was here, somewhere. I sprung out of the bed, but nearly fainted. Leaning on the wall for balance, I made my way to the bathroom and washed up. I saw it was daytime, but there was no clock. I found my clothes and began getting dressed. I had to find Cat.

"Where do you think you're going, young man?" A nurse filled the doorway, hands on hips.

"I have to go. I have to find Cat."

"Cat? Your cat? Now sit right down, son. Let me see your chart."

She pulled my chart, murmured "concussion" and told me, "You went into convulsions last night, right here in the building. That was a bad sign, so your doctor checked you in for observation. How do you feel now?"

"Fine. A little headache. Look, I really have to go."

"Not until you get checked out. Dr. Young will be here soon. In the meantime, sit back down. Your lunch is on its way."

"Lunch? What time is it?"

She looked at her watch and said, "A quarter past one," on her way out.

I took my headache pills and finished getting dressed. Someone came in with a tray. I had no interest in eating, so I set it aside. I was not going to wait much longer.

The door opened and Emma came in. "How are you feeling?" she asked.

"A little headache. I'm okay. I need to find Cat."

"I'm coming from her room. If I didn't know better, I would've thought she was peacefully sleeping. Anyway, I found myself saying a prayer. I haven't prayed since I was a child. I don't even believe in God. But there was nothing else I could do."

"What room is she in? I have to go."

"Room 319, on the other side of this floor. But not until Quentin checks you out. You gave us quite a scare last night. Let's make sure you're good to go. I'll wait with you. What's that on the tray?"

"They call it lunch. I'm not interested. You want some?"

"No. You sit down and eat. You probably haven't had anything since yesterday morning."

"But I'm not hungry. Really."

"Eat!"

After I finished forcing the food down my throat, Dr. Young arrived. I asked, "Why am I here?"

"You went into convulsions. It's common after concussions, but serious enough to warrant overnight monitoring. Now, let's take a look."

After examining me, he said, "Well, you made it through the night okay. I'm glad you slept that long. It's safe for you to go now, but take it slow."

"What about my headache?"

"It will subside with a little time. Here are some more pills in case you need them. And no physical exertion. None, until I see you again. Get as much rest as you possibly can."

"Okay. Thanks. I can see Cat now? Have you seen her today?"

"Yes. There hasn't been any change, one way or the other. In some ways, a coma can be a good thing. Her cuts, bruises and broken bones have time to heal while she's not feeling any pain. Awake now, she'd be in serious pain, and might've required sedation. Visiting hours are from 10 to 7, so you can go to her as soon as you're ready. But don't let the equipment scare you. We're monitoring her vital signs, and keeping her fed and hydrated intravenously."

"Do you want me to come with you?" Emma asked after he left.

"Thanks, but no. I need some alone time with her."

"All right then. I'll be in the shop if you need me."

We walked down to the elevator together. As the doors closed, she called, "And don't forget to eat!"

Even though I'd been warned about the equipment, it startled me to see it. Cat was hooked up to all sorts of machines and gadgets. Also, she had bandaged gauze pads all over, plus plaster casts on her left arm, right foot, and rib cage. But she was breathing. She was alive. I sat on the bed, stroked her soft cheek, leaned over, and kissed her as though we were in a fairy tale instead of a nightmare. But my sleeping beauty didn't stir.

"Cat," I said softly, "I'm so sorry." She made no sign of hearing. Before I got any further, I was too choked up to speak. I sat there for a while, a long while, stroking her and gently weeping. My mind went back to our first encounters, almost exactly a year ago, how instantly entranced I was and, soon after, how flattered to be invited to join her for dinner. I remembered how she opened her heart the next time we talked, trusting me with her deepest grief. I recalled the words I'd told her while walking her back home: *I'll always be there for you.* That sentence repeated in my brain, over and over. I remembered the innocent, trusting look on her face as she instantly responded, "Somehow, I know you will." After Thanksgiving, when she poured out her fears of intimate connection, her anxieties over losing another loved one, I somehow convinced her to take a chance on me. Why? *Because I'd always be there for her.* Because I'd never let her down. And now here she was. *Because of me.*

The floodgates opened. Tears flowed so hard that my body heaved. I held my face in my hands. She'd put her trust in me and I'd let her down. I wasn't there for her to keep that Army jeep from breaking her bones and battering her brain. From nearly killing her, which it still might. I wasn't there. I wasn't there for her at the moment she needed me the most. I'd been down on myself before, but this was the first time I wished I'd never been born.

Never been born. Now, because of me, our baby would never be born. I knew we weren't ready to raise a child, that the pregnancy had been an accident, that the embryo was little more than a collision between sperm and egg, but none of that mattered now. This was our baby, our little Kitten, the consummation of our love. Gone. I wasn't there for her either.

All right, I thought, struggling to recover. *I can be here now, for Cat.* Yes, even though I was helpless, at least I could be here. *But what if she doesn't make it? What if she never wakes up?* I would have no reason to live, no excuse for existence.

My thoughts turned to suicide. I considered slitting my own throat, but knew I didn't have the courage for that. On top of everything else, I now realized I was also a coward. People killed themselves with overdoses, but all I had were Tylenol and a few sleeping pills, surely not enough of them. I considered another easy way out, in a bathtub. Drop an electrical appliance into it and electrocute myself. No, better I should slit my wrists and slowly, fully, experience the draining away of my useless life force.

Someone shook my shoulders, a nurse. "Visiting hours ended two hours ago. You have to leave the building now."

"But I have to stay. What if she wakes up during the night?"

"Don't worry," she tried reassuring me. "We'll look after her. That's what hospitals are for."

Reluctantly, I left for home. On the way, I bought a package of razor blades. *Just in case*, I thought. Upstairs, I took a sleeping pill and cried myself to sleep. Alone.

Chapter 87

Friday was Cat's 20th birthday. It was also the day we were to begin our long romantic weekend in paradise. But now she was clinging to life. I forced myself into the shower, threw my clothes on and headed for the hospital.

I asked for a pass at the front desk, but the receptionist refused. The security guard came over when I began making a fuss. "What's the problem here?" he demanded.

"I have to see my wife. She's in 319. She needs me."

"That's all right, but not until visiting hours. They start at ten."

He pointed to a big clock, which registered 8:15. I hadn't even checked the time before I left home. I couldn't sit in that lobby for two hours, so I went outside and roamed until I came to a coffee shop. The sight reminded me I hadn't eaten anything but that hospital food for two days. I wasn't hungry, but went inside anyway, ordered eggs and coffee, and opened the *Tribune.*

The lead article reported on another attempted march to the Amphitheater. The National Guard chased the protesters back to Grant Park, firing tear gas the entire way. At the convention that night, Humphrey was booed from the floor during his acceptance speech.

The police reported arresting 668 protesters on Wednesday, including a dozen delegates. The hospitals reported treating thirty-one newsmen, fifty-two cops and more than a hundred protesters. Many more protesters were injured than arrested though, and only a small fraction got treated in hospitals. Our medics reported that they stopped keeping track after treating the first thousand. Miraculously, no-one, thus far, had been killed. Not a word in the paper about Cat, the only casualty truly on my mind at the moment.

An inside page revealed that conspiracy charges against Donnie, Dave, Abbie and others were already being prepared. The prosecutors leaked their evidence to the paper, probably to begin influencing the jury pool, and the *Tribune* added its own spin. In its telling, everyone involved under thirty or so was a hippie, a Yippie, an anarchist or a "left-wing agitator." Everyone older was "a known Communist." No pacifists, no idealists, no citizens appeared in its coverage of the protests. Our efforts to line up legal and medical teams were offered as evidence of our intent to provoke violence. The story, which turned out to be only the first of a series, included reports from closed meetings of the Mobe, SDS, the Chicago Peace Council and other groups, which had all been infiltrated. It was easy to identify which information had come from Ronnie Moore, the Mobe's chief mole.

As ten o'clock drew near, I tossed the paper into the trash can, where it belonged, and went to be with Cat.

Her condition hadn't changed. She would miss her birthday. Her friends, though, would not. Word had spread quickly. All day long, they streamed in with cards and flowers, candy and balloons. Sabrina directed the room's decoration until it looked like a real party. In the middle of it was poor Cat, oblivious.

Everyone had their own war stories, and some had the bandages, bruises and plaster casts to document them. Whit reported that he spirited Donnie across the state line to an Indiana hospital, where he got thirteen stitches in his head. Jeff said the legal team had been working night and day to get our people out of jail. Two rounds of emergency calls were needed to replenish the bail fund. Nicky pronounced the week a success, though, since the convention was a shambles and thousands of McCarthy kids had been radicalized. I listened to all of this, but my eyes were on Cat. It was no success for her, for us. "Tell me," Phil Ochs challenged in his antiwar ballad, "was it worth it all?"

Barry Wayne came in with another report. "The Defense Department contract got canceled," he told us, "The community opposition, combined with the scientists' public campaign against the new weapon system and its national exposure in the *Times Magazine*, added up to too much pressure. Midway withdrew its eminent domain application, but refused comment. The South Side land grab is dead."

During the round of applause that followed, I whispered in Cat's ear, "You did it, kid. It's too bad we can't tell the world how, but you did it."

Late in the afternoon, with a dozen friends still crowded in, she became the subject of people's stories. Sharon regaled the room with her tale of how Cat tricked the soldiers into letting us steal the Army truck and make our escape from the armory. Emma told of how Cat saved her life after that first bad respiratory attack, getting her to a hospital, this hospital. There was even a professor who told how she dazzled her Advanced Calculus class, during her freshman year, with the elegance of a mathematical proof she presented.

I didn't even know about that one, but the story got me wondering whether she'd be able to do such a thing ever again. How impaired would she be after this? But she also might wake up without any memory of me. *That would be the best thing for her*, I thought. Another wave of despair engulfed me. I slipped out of the room and down the hall, to an empty visitors' lounge where I'd be alone with my misery. I didn't know whether anyone noticed me leave.

A few minutes later, Marcellus took the seat next to mine "You look worse than you did an hour ago," he said. "What is it? I thought being with all these people who care about Cat, about both of you, might cheer you up a little."

"I'm grateful," I explained, "I really am. But these stories started sounding to me like it was a memorial service. Anyway, I don't think I even want to feel better. I don't deserve it, not after letting Cat down the way I did."

"You did not let her down," he argued. "You tried to lead her away from danger, not toward it. Blaming yourself does no good. And if you don't get out of this hole, you won't be any good to her."

"I know. That's what Emma said too. But it's how I feel." I began blubbering. "My god, Marcellus. What if she never wakes up?"

"She will wake up. She will, when she's ready. And then she'll need you more than ever. I know you think you're totally focused on her now. But you're not, 'cause you're too wrapped up with your own guilt. You got to let that go. You got to show yourself a little mercy. And Cat isn't the only one who needs you. Funding for our after-school program came through, and we want you back. Now come with me. There's a birthday party goin' on."

Some guests had gone and others were still arriving. One of the late arrivals was Larry Graff, who'd obviously been seriously beaten. He asked to talk with me alone, so we stepped into the hallway.

"You and me, we both need the same thing," he snarled.

"What thing?"

"How about a cold slice of revenge?"

"Huh?"

"Make the bastards pay. Make them pay for what they did to Cat, to you, to me, to Donnie, to all of us. What they're doing to Vietnam. Make them pay."

"Okay. But how?"

"Not here. I can come to your place around nine. I'll explain then."

Yes, I thought back at home. *Make the motherfuckers pay. Was this what I needed to push the guilt aside, to do something positive? But how?*

Chapter 88

"I've been thinking hard on this," Larry explained that night, "and it's simple. They've got all the weapons. So head on, we can't fight them. The guerrilla actions in the Loop did property damage, sure, but didn't really confront the power. If we want to get revenge, we need to use more stealth. And we need to clearly target the enemy."

Intrigued, I invited him to continue.

"There's a military target on Midway's campus. Right, Steve?"

"Sure. The ROTC Building."

"Right. So here's what we can do. A quick trip to the hardware store, a few bucks worth of ordinary threaded pipe. A snatch of black powder from the chemistry lab. A firecracker or some other simple fuse. And what do we have in, say, twenty minutes? A pipe bomb!" He threw his hands up in the air, as if to mimic an explosion, exclaiming, "BOOM! Bye-bye, ROTC. BOOM!"

The image of a blown-up building drew me in. *Finally*, I thought, *a way to fight back, to avenge what they did to my poor Cat.*

"Okay," I agreed. "But only when the building's empty. I don't want to kill anyone. At least, I don't think I do."

"But I only brought that up as an example," he continued. "We can go bigger. We can target a police station. Lincoln Park would be a good one. Blow it to smithereens. Even better, the Chicago Avenue Armory, home of the fucking National Guard, where they charged us with the bayonets, where the soldier who hit Cat was probably quartered. We can blow that up too."

"We can? It's an armory, for chrissake. It's built to withstand attack."

"I know we can't bring the whole thing down," he countered. "But we can do a hell of a lot of damage. One thing for sure: We can show the whole country, the whole world, that we're fighting back. We'll take it to them. We'll bring the war home."

"How would we do that, attack an armory?"

"ANFO. Ammonium nitrate fuel oil."

"Ammonium what?"

"Look, ammonium nitrate is ordinary fertilizer, the kind they use on farms. The fuel can be heating oil, gasoline, any flammable liquid. Load up a truck with these two, drive it into the armory, even park it outside. Set it on fire and get the hell out."

He threw his hands up in the air again. "Bombs away! Boom!"

My adrenaline was flowing. The National Guard, who charged us with bayonets. The National Guard, who sprayed us with tear gas. The National Guard, who mowed down the most precious person ever in my life. I was helpless to save her now, but here was a way to avenge what they'd done. If soldiers were in the armory, so much the better. *Yes! Bombs away!*

Still, something tugged at me, holding me back. As much as Larry's plan excited me, I wasn't quite ready to sign on. Not yet.

"This is a lot to think about, Larry. You can probably see in my face that I like it. But I need a day or two."

"That's fine. I'll be back, checking in on you and Cat anyway. You tell me when you're ready."

I tried getting to sleep early. Through closed eyes, I saw the armory erupting in flames, soldiers fleeing in terror. And the jeeps, those damned jeeps, melting from the heat of the explosion. My heartbeat quickened. But the pieces didn't quite fit, and sleep refused to come.

I needed someone to talk to, someone I could trust with a secret, someone with an open mind. I had to call Emma. Over coffee, ten minutes later, I told her how much trouble I'd had pushing the guilt aside until I heard Larry's proposal.

"This makes me feel alive," I exclaimed. "I want to shout, 'This is for Cat!' It gets me out of feeling sorry for myself. It gives me something to do. But, somehow, I'm not sure, so..."

Emma interjected, "You want to know if I think it would be justifiable to blow up the armory, or as much of it as you can?"

"Well yes."

"Of course it is. Those armories were originally built to harbor armed forces called in to suppress workers fighting for things like the eight-hour day and a ban on child labor. Now they're used to squash political dissent, to trample on the Constitution. It would be a good thing if they went up in smoke. A very good thing. You get no argument from me on that."

"But what if soldiers are inside?"

"Ah, that's what you have to think about. Who are those soldiers? Young men about your age, who also didn't want to fight in Vietnam. The draft deferment they get is why most of them joined the National Guard. And their attack on the protesters was under military orders. They had no choice."

"But the soldier who drove into Cat... What about that one?"

"You'll never know who that soldier was. All you can do is take collective retribution."

"What am I gonna do, Emma? I sit there waiting, hoping, praying for Cat. But I'm helpless. Along comes a plan to avenge what they did to her. It makes my heart beat faster. But I don't know. Tell me, please, what should I do?"

"I'm not going to tell you what to do, Steve. But I'd like to tell you a little story. Okay?"

"A story? Well, okay, I guess."

"It's from the Cherokee tradition. Here it goes: A little girl is sitting on an old man's lap. He's deep in thought. 'Grandfather,' she asks, 'What are you thinking?' He answers, 'Two wolves are fighting for my heart.' She doesn't understand. 'Two wolves?' she asks. 'Yes, my sweet one,' he explains. 'The Wolf of Love and the Wolf of Hate.' She asks, 'Which wolf will win?'"

Emma peered straight into my eyes, telling me the grandfather's reply: "Whichever one I feed."

"You wanted my advice. Now you've got it. Give some thought to what that wise old man told his granddaughter. Decide which wolf you want to feed. Make whatever decision feels right to you, and put your whole heart into following through. You'll have my support either way."

I did think about those words: *Whichever one I feed.* Which one would I feed, the Wolf of Love or the Wolf of Hate? Which one would get stronger? Which one would win out? I'd been blessed with love, but made a mess of it. The first time I felt alive in two days was hearing Larry's plan for revenge. The Wolf of Hate was roaring. It wouldn't let me sleep. If we were going to do this thing, I wanted to do it now. *Bombs away!*

Or did I? Would it really make me feel better, or would it only make me crave more of the same? If I fed that wolf, would its appetite ever be satisfied? Even if it did make me feel better, would it do anything for Cat? Also, if and when she came back, she might still want me. *Not likely,* I thought, *but possible.* But then, who would I be? If she came back to me, I wanted our lives to be filled with love. Not with anger. Not with hate. No. I needed to feed the Wolf of Love. And I didn't have to wait until she woke up to begin. It might even help bring her back.

What if she didn't come back, though? There was still the other wolf. *Bombs away!* Before I ended my own life, I'd send a few of them on ahead. For now, though, my mind was made up. *I will feed the Wolf of Love.* I fell asleep thinking about how I might do that. It was my first good sleep in about a week.

In the morning, I picked out Doris Lessing's *The Golden Notebook* and a collection of Langston Hughes poetry from our box of summer reading. Cat always loved to be read to. That would be how I'd spend the day. It was still early, so first I swung by Union Station and picked up the *Times.* I wanted to bring Cat up to date on the news without subjecting us to the *Tribune's* offensive drivel. I knew it would probably look crazy, reading to an unconscious person, but I didn't care. I'd be feeding the Wolf of Love.

Taking that decision had calmed me down. Seeing Cat lying there now didn't trigger guilt and self-loathing, maybe because now I was doing something to help her. At least, I hoped I was doing something to help her. First, I sat on the bed, kissed her on the forehead and the lips, whispered, "Good morning, my love," and told her my plan for the day. Of course, she gave no response. I took her face in my hands and kissed her again, this time a long one. After I let go, I sat back and unfolded the *Times.*

I went through the paper, picking out the stories I thought she might find interesting. J. Anthony Lukas's summary of Convention Week began with a report on a spontaneous rally Friday night in Grant Park, where there were still five thousand protesters.

"A whiff of celebration hung with the tear gas," he wrote, "for the young dissidents... had succeeded far beyond their most exotic dreams of a month or even a week ago." He noted that the peak size of our demonstrations was only a fraction of the hundred thousand we were hoping for, and laid that result squarely on Daley's fear campaign. Then he continued, "But within a few days, the actions of Mayor Richard J.

Daley and his blue-helmeted policemen turned almost certain defeat into a startling victory for the dissidents."

Lukas had interviewed many people. He'd picked up on what protest leaders had hoped to accomplish and, in his view, actually did: First, to rally the antiwar movement, which needed a jolt after LBJ's withdrawal in March and the farce of the so-called "Paris Peace Talks." Second, to radicalize thousands of young people, including the McCarthy kids, many of whom now said they'd lost faith in the "corrupt electoral system." And third (here he quoted Dave Dellinger), "to strip the façade of liberal policies from the Establishment, and expose the raw machinery of force and repression beneath it."

Having finished with the paper, I began reading from *The Golden Notebook*. A few chapters in, I heard sniffling behind me and turned. Emma stood inside the doorway, wiping her eyes with a handkerchief.

"This is one of the most beautiful scenes I've ever witnessed," she sniffled as she pulled up a chair beside me.

"It's what we've called our Summer Session at the University of Emma," I explained. "And I thought it couldn't hurt to bring it here for Cat. How long have you been watching?"

"About ten minutes. I didn't want to interrupt you, and seeing this filled my heart."

"In some ways, this was your doing, Emma. You know, the Tale of the Two Wolves. I wrestled with it during the night, and finally chose to feed the Wolf of Love. And you know what? That made me feel better about myself. I know it might sound a little crazy, but feeding that wolf... well... I guess it feels right to me."

Emma's eyes moistened again. "It doesn't sound crazy at all. I can see the difference in your face, and hear it in your voice. You've come out from that dark place you've been in, and I am so relieved. This time, you really had me worried. I was afraid you might do something to yourself."

That brought to mind the razor blades I'd bought, but I decided not to mention them.

"Would you like to hear my thoughts?" she asked.

"Of course."

"I think those two wolves, to keep a good metaphor going, have been fighting inside you for a long time. Your restlessness, your attraction to action, to danger, to risk, to the things that scared the daylights out of Cat? Those were the roars of the Wolf of Hate. And your deep devotion to her, your tenderness and protectiveness, your struggle to keep her from worrying about you? Right there was the Wolf of Love. That's what I think."

"This does kind of put things in perspective," I mused.

"So," she asked, "when have you eaten last?"

I tried to remember. "Yesterday morning, I guess. But maybe I nibbled on snacks that people brought yesterday."

"You go and get some lunch now, Steve. I'll stay here with Cat."

Chapter 89

When I returned from lunch, Emma was out in the hallway with Sharon. Cat's door was closed. Registering the concern on my face, Sharon explained, "Reverend Marshall's in with her now. Praying."

"No!" I blurted. "She's not... She didn't..."

"No, no, not that," Emma interjected. "He came to pray for her recovery. A full recovery."

"I told him what happened," Sharon added, "and he offered to visit. We came over together."

I exhaled and leaned against the wall. Soon, the burly preacher came through the door. I reached my hand out and said, "Thank you for doing this. It's very generous."

He swallowed my hand in one of his, and placed the other on my shoulder, saying, "I do what I can. Now you stay strong, son. If you need me, pick up the phone. And keep the faith. She will come back. I'll keep praying for it. And for you"

Once he and Emma left, Sharon and I went into the room.

"You look different from yesterday," she noticed. "More relaxed. Less tormented."

I explained by repeating what I'd told Emma. I enjoyed telling the Tale of the Two Wolves. In a corner of my brain, I envisioned stopping people in the street to pass it on. It had changed so much for me, and I had an urge to share it. But this was no time to get arrested or thrown into a loony bin. Cat needed me right here.

"That's a great story," Sharon responded. "I bet Arielle would like it too. You know, she asks about you all the time. She adores that giant panda you won for her at the carnival. They sleep together every night. If she doesn't outgrow it by the time she grows a few more inches, I'll have to get them a bigger bed."

"How is the little princess?" I asked.

"She's doing great. She insists I teach her something new every day, so she'll be ready for big-girl school. Say, how'd you like to babysit tomorrow afternoon?"

"I'd love to. But I don't want to leave Cat here all by herself."

"Don't worry. While you're with Arielle, I'll sit with Cat. And if anything changes here, I'll know exactly where to reach you."

After we worked out the details, Sharon said good-bye and I went back to my reading. Other friends interrupted us a few times before visiting hours ended. After that, we were left alone, except for occasional nursing checks. They didn't ask me to leave until almost 9:30. Back at home, I noticed my headache was gone. Within an hour, I was fast asleep.

Sunday morning, I packed a bag of clothes and other things Cat would need before she came home. She would be coming home. I knew it. I didn't know when, but I knew she would. What I didn't know, what I couldn't know, was whether she'd still want to have anything to do with me. She might not even remember me at all. But I could hope. I could hope for another chance to prove myself worthy of her love.

I didn't bother with the Sunday papers. I was anxious to get back to Doris Lessing, whose story I found mesmerizing, and hoped Cat did too. First, though, I climbed into the bed, wriggled through the maze of wires and tubes, and held her the best I could without disturbing anything. I whispered my love into her ear. She didn't respond, not at all. But I did feel her breath, the warmth of her body. That would have to sustain me. I untangled myself, sat up and began reading, pushing aside any thought that she couldn't hear me, that she had no knowledge of what I'd read to her the day before. I simply kept going, feeding the Wolf of Love.

I had a different opportunity to do that after Sharon arrived, and I left for Arielle Time. The neighbor who'd come down to watch her said she'd been asking for me since her mother left. As always, Arielle had something in mind.

"Mommy says Auntie Cat got hurt, and she's sleeping."

"Yes," I replied, "a deep, deep sleep. When she wakes up, she'll be better."

"Let's read a story together," she pronounced, pulling *Sleeping Beauty* off a shelf. For the most part, she read the story to me. I didn't know if she was actually reading it, or if she'd memorized the words. It didn't matter. The Wolf of Love was right there in that room.

Later, after acting out one of her complex dramas of the dolls, I told her the Tale of the Two Wolves. She asked, "Could there be a Panda of Love?"

"Of course. He's right there on your bed."

"And now he's thirsty," she announced. So the three of us had a little tea party.

When Sharon came home, she told me Cat had plenty of company. Much as I'd treasured my time with Arielle, I explained to her that I had to go back now.

"Wait," she said, her eyes scanning the room. She pulled a small stuffed animal off a shelf and said, "Tell Auntie Cat this is from the Panda of Love." I nearly suffocated the poor child with the bear-hug I embraced her with before leaving.

Later, shortly after I began reading, Cat's left eye opened. I also thought she might have squeezed my hand slightly, but couldn't be sure. The eye snapped shut after only a few seconds, but this looked to me like big progress. I told her, "I'll be right back," and ran down to the nurses' station with the news. "She opened an eye! She opened an eye!"

One of the nurses consulted a clipboard and responded, "Her doctor is in the building. We'll page him. Try to keep calm."

Try to keep calm? I wanted to call everyone and tell them about that small miracle, but decided to postpone the announcement until after she got examined. I went back to the book, glancing up after every paragraph to check for signs of change. I didn't see any.

Dr. Young came in. I jumped up and told him what happened.

"Any motor function is a good sign," he explained, "but far from definitive. Have you tried talking to her?"

"All the time. I've been reading to her."

"That might be helping, but we can't know for sure. Have you noticed any response at all?"

"Only what I told you."

"Okay. Let's see." He held each eye open, and shined his flashlight into them. As soon as he released the eyelids, they snapped shut. He took a sharp object out of his pocket and gently pricked her in various places. Sometimes, she reacted by twitching, or squinting.

"Did you see that?" he asked. "Another good sign. People in the deepest of comas don't react to pinpricks at all."

"So she's coming back?" I asked excitedly.

"To be honest, Steve, I can't say. She might be. But people can get stalled on the road back. They only make it part of the way. I know you don't want to hear this, but it's still too soon to tell. It really is. Here's my card. Keep me posted. And how are your headaches?"

"They're gone. I stopped taking the pills yesterday."

"Glad to hear it. If you want to, you can resume your workouts now. It might be good for you. But no running or jumping. Not yet."

Too soon to tell. I prayed I would never hear that phrase again. Back to reading, I continued glancing up hopefully after each paragraph. But nothing happened.

More visitors arrived later. The first was Larry, who asked if I'd decided to join him.

"I'm not doing it," I told him. "At least not as long as there's a chance she'll come back. She opened an eye this morning, and the doctor said that was a good sign."

"But what if, well, what if she doesn't?"

"That'll be a different story."

A little later, Jeff came by. I gave him an update and he wished us luck. "I'm leaving for New York tonight," he explained, "and I wanted to see you guys before I left."

"The teaching job?"

"Right. Ocean Hill-Brownsville. Those schools might be the only ones that open in New York City. The white teachers' union is threatening a citywide strike to kill the Black-led community control experiment. I never thought I'd look forward to crossing a picket line."

Shortly before visiting hours ended, Whit arrived. He told me he needed a few weeks to finish his master's thesis. After that, he'd be off to Canada. "What are your plans for school?" he asked.

"School? I haven't even thought about it since this happened. Registration is this week, isn't it?"

"Right. Tuesday and Wednesday. Classes start on Thursday."

"No way I can deal with school now. I guess I'll drop out. But Cat's only a year from graduation. I don't know what to do."

"Go see the registrar," he advised. "Tell her what's happened. Try to work something out."

I took Whit's advice, early Tuesday morning. The registrar, Mrs. Keene, led me into her office right after I summarized Cat's condition, attributing it to a traffic accident.

"I don't know when she'll be able to return," I explained, "or even if she ever can. And I can't concentrate on anything but her recovery."

"Hold on," she said, walking to a file cabinet and pulling out two folders.

"Miss Crawford has been a straight-A student for three years." she commented, riffling through one of them. "That's no mean feat here at Midway."

"If you ask me," I added, "she's kind of a genius. She's sure a lot smarter than I am."

"You've done quite well here yourself," she concluded after looking through my file. "How about this? I'll put you both on a leave of absence. You'll still be part of the Midway community, and you can go back to your classes when you're ready. In the meantime, you can pay a small fee to use the campus facilities, and also keep the student rate on your group health insurance."

"That sounds great," I replied with as big a smile as I could muster. "But, if we do return, what about our scholarships?"

She looked back at the files and promised, "We can hold them for both of you, but only for a year. Try to return in the spring, or next fall at the latest, if you possibly can."

Chapter 90

Back in Cat's room, I took her hand in mine and opened the Langston Hughes book to a short poem entitled "Love." It began,

> *Love is a wild wonder*
> *And stars that sing,*
> *Rocks that burst asunder*
> *And mountains take wing...*

After an hour or so, we came to his "Love Song to Antonia."

> *If I should sing*
> *All of my songs for you*
> *And you would not listen,*
> *If I should build*
> *All of my dream houses for you*
> *And you would not live in them...*
> *Still I would give you my love,*
> *Which is more than my songs,*
> *More than my houses of dreams*
> *Or dreams of houses.*
> *I would still give you my love...*

Suddenly, at 2:17 p.m., on Tuesday, September 3rd, 1968, a moment I'll never ever forget, Cat's eyes flew open. They darted around the room as I sat staring, my mouth hanging open.

"Where am I?" she asked, agitated and confused. "Why am I hooked up to all these things? What's happened? And what's wrong with you?"

"You're in the hospital, Cat. You got hit by an Army Jeep and went into a coma. We didn't know if you were coming out of it. But you did! You're back!"

"I don't remember anything," she mumbled, calming down but frowning. "Tell me what happened."

"I'll tell you everything," I replied, my voice quivering. "But first I have to ask you something." I took a deep breath and asked, "Do you know who I am? Do you remember me?"

"Of course I remember you. You're the man I love. Why do you ask such a question?"

"Would you still love me if what happened was my fault?"

"Another silly question. I know you'd never do anything to hurt me." My eyes filled with tears, as she opened her arms and said, "Come here, you silly boy."

After I kissed every square inch of her neck and face, I collected myself, wiped my eyes and asked, "What's the last thing you remember?"

Her eyes narrowed in concentration as she tried to think back. She said, "I remember us lining up behind the mule train. Something must've happened after that, but I can't remember what."

I told her everything that happened to us. She responded, "It sounds like you're talking about a different person. I don't remember any of that. What's wrong with me?"

"Look," I explained, "you got hurt real bad. You landed on your head. Dr. Young told me you might have problems with memory. But you're back. You're back. That's the important thing. Wait, we need to tell him."

I pushed the call button. A nurse came in a few minutes later, the same big nurse who'd kept me from leaving my own hospital room Thursday morning.

"So, this is the Cat you were so anxious to find," she remarked. "Now I can see why. Welcome back, young lady. How do you feel?"

"I feel fine," Cat replied. "But I can't remember things. And I'm hungry. No, I'm starving."

"Please call Dr. Young," I asked the nurse. "He'll want to know right away."

A few minutes later, she came back with an orderly. "The doctor ordered x-rays," she explained. "He'll be here in about an hour. We'll bring your wife back well before then."

"Wife?" Cat asked, confused. But I shushed her.

After I saw them to the elevator, I called Emma. The line went silent when I told her what happened. "Emma," I asked, "are you all right?"

"I can't believe it," she answered. "I knew in my heart she would come back, but I'm still in shock. I'll be right there."

"Okay, but please bring her something to eat. She's really hungry."

Emma arrived a few minutes before Cat returned from the x-rays, minus some of the bandages and all of the tubes and wires. After the joyful tears and the hugging, we dug into the pizza Emma delivered from Sal's.

Dr. Young came in while I was cleaning up. He told Cat, "I've seen the x-rays. Most of your fractured bones are already healing nicely. They're only a matter of time now. I'm concerned about your right foot, though. It got badly damaged, and it might not heal as good as new."

Here we go again, I thought. *Too soon to tell.*

"Right now, it's too soon to tell about that," he continued. "In the meantime, you'll need crutches to get around."

"But why can't I remember what happened?"

"That's typical," he explained. "The memory of the specific incident that triggers a traumatic brain injury is nearly always wiped from memory. Sometimes, patients recover everything but that, so I wouldn't worry about it. But now, I'd like to do a complete examination." She nodded assent.

The exam was both physical and mental. He poked and probed, and asked a series of questions. Finishing up, he told her, "You're making an amazing recovery. Besides limited mobility, though, there are a couple of issues that do suggest ongoing problems."

"What issues?" I asked.

"Both of them are common with coma survivors. The first is loss of balance. Physical therapy can be helpful with that, but you must be very careful to prevent any falls. The other is memory, particularly short-term memory. From day to day, Cat, memories might come and go. Don't be surprised if you even forget what you meant to say in the middle of a sentence. This can trigger confusion and agitation, but I want you to try to stay calm whenever it happens. At those moments, stop and focus on your breathing. This may be only a temporary condition. There's still reorganization going on up there, and that takes time. And remember, reasonable physical exercise is good for the brain as well as the body."

"How long will a full recovery take?" I asked, hoping his answer wouldn't be, "Too soon to tell."

"Unfortunately, that isn't something I can accurately predict. Generally, whatever recovery there is happens within six months or so. But during that time, Steve, she shouldn't be left alone. That might be dangerous. Try to get her some help with day-to-day functioning."

"No," I insisted. "I'll take care of Cat."

"We both will," added Emma.

"Okay, Grandma," he agreed with a wink. "In that case, if nothing changes overnight, she can go home tomorrow. I'll leave her prescriptions at the nurses' station. Come see me in the office next week. Meanwhile, remember, you can call anytime."

"You two should be left alone now," Emma said. "I'll come back if you need me. Just call."

Cat's eyes were watery. She began sniffling. I sat on the bed and asked, "What is it?"

The words were hard for her to get out. "Brain damage," she muttered. "I might not, I might never... Oh, it's hard for me to think... I... I might not be me anymore. And I'll be such a burden to you." She turned her head and began sobbing into the pillow.

I lifted her up, shifted her over a few inches, climbed into the bed, took her in my arms and rocked her. "You'll never be a burden to me," I proclaimed, "and I love you just the way you are. Even if I could only have ten percent of you, I'd still be the luckiest man on earth." This made the tears flow even harder. Mine joined them, but those were tears of joy.

"Anyway," I added after a few minutes of clinging to one another, "you will get better. I know you will. You and me, we'll make sure of it."

At seven sharp, the nurse came in and, with a note of indignation in her voice, demanded, "What's going on here?" Cat and I were wrapped together, tighter than a clam. We let go, and I sat up.

"Visiting hours are over," the nurse announced. "It's time for you to go. And we have dinner on the way for this young lady."

Reluctantly, I left. What was I going to do with myself until they let me back in? Our apartment gave me my answer. The place was a mess. I couldn't bring Cat home to this. Fortunately, our Laundromat stayed open all night. By the time I dusted and vacuumed and finished with the laundry, it was past one. I fell into bed and passed out.

I woke at six, bursting with excitement. Cat was coming home! But they wouldn't let me in for four long hours. I brewed the coffee and paced the floor, wondering how to pass the time. Then I noticed little dust balls, things out of place, streaks on the windows. I went back to work.

At the hospital, Cat was already dressed and cleared for discharge. An orderly brought her downstairs in a wheelchair and I helped her into Tooter. A little while later, she managed on her crutches from the car to the front door. I carried her upstairs. We were home!

"Who's been here?" she asked, surveying the room.

"No-one," I replied. "Only me."

"Well, someone's been cleaning, and that couldn't have been you!"

"I was very motivated," I explained, getting her comfortable on the couch.

We were home. Challenges lay ahead, but we would face them together. My nightmare, the one that plagued me since childhood, had come true. But we, Cat and I, with help from Emma and Dr. Young, and especially the Wolf of Love, had beaten it. She'd been snatched away from me, but now I had her back. And I vowed never to risk losing my Butterscotch Goddess ever again.

Epilogue

The next few months were all about Cat's recovery. I took her to physical therapy three mornings a week and she exercised at home every day, working hard at it. As soon as navigating the stairs became feasible, we walked up and down those two flights a dozen times a day. Eventually, the casts came off. Her right foot was still a little twisted, but she was able to get around using a cane for balance. At that point, she discontinued the therapy, complaining it was "too easy," and we went back to our morning weight room routine. Positively Perused was our home base on weekdays. Emma and Cat looked after one another while I taught my after-school classes, joined the Saran Wrap leafleting or ran errands.

Other than the leafleting and the bookstore, we stayed in touch with campus life through visits with friends and gatherings of The Circle. I also brought Cat to BSU meetings, and waited outside for her. They'd made progress with their spring campaign. Black freshman and transfer enrollment was up 20 percent. Four Black professors had been recruited to teach African and African-American History. There was still no Black Studies Department, though, and no requirement that Midway students learn some African-American history. Those fights would continue.

Whenever Emma had doctor appointments, all three of us went. Her condition seemed to stabilize. With great difficulty, she finally quit smoking.

The hardest part for Cat, the most frustrating thing, was memory. It was hard for her to keep from becoming agitated at the moments when it failed. With time, we learned to manage those episodes, sometimes even joking about them. They were also becoming less frequent. Dr. Young confirmed she was making real progress. But I was still reluctant to leave her alone.

We, along with millions of others, sat out the November election. Nixon won it with 43.6 percent of the low-turnout balloting. Humphrey got 42.9 percent, losing by only half a million votes. The segregationist George Wallace candidacy garnered 9.9 percent. Activists and some experts thought Humphrey would have helped himself had he reached out to the antiwar constituency in any meaningful way. As it was, though, since no candidate was credibly committed to ending the war, we were indifferent to the outcome. In any case, Cat and I were still too young to cast a ballot. We'd done our voting in the streets. And we would do a lot more of it once she was able, until the U.S. finally withdrew its forces from Vietnam.

While we snuggled in the wake of love-making one rainy Sunday, I asked the question I'd been saving for the right moment: "Do you remember Dr. Young advised me to tell the hospital people I was your husband?"

"Sure. I remember you told me that. Why?"

"See, when I got there, I was bursting with negative emotions. But when I told the receptionist, 'I need to see my wife,' a little positive charge broke through. I got that charge every time I used or heard that phrase. Well, I want to hear myself say it again, and I don't want it to be a made-up story. I want to wear a ring on my finger that tells the world I belong to you."

I propped up on an elbow, peered into her eyes and asked, "Cat Crawford, will you marry me?"

Those eyes began welling with tears. Her face showed distress. She didn't answer. Not knowing what to make of this, I told her, "You don't have to give me an answer now. You can think about it. But please don't say 'no' right away. Take your time. Make sure you really mean it."

She wiped her eyes. "But I'm not the girl you fell in love with. Not anymore. My foot is crippled. Sometimes it's hard to think straight. My mind might never come all the way back. It wouldn't be fair to you."

"You're getting better every day," I insisted. "We started with word games and crossword puzzles, and now you're already back to your math and physics books. But that's not the point. I told you I'd settle for ten percent. Even if you suddenly stopped making progress, I'd still want to spend the rest of my life with you. You're the love of my life. You're the one I want to spend it with. The only one. Ever."

Now the tears flowed again. "Of course I'll marry you," she blubbered. "Of course I will. Oh, hold me, Steve. Hold me tight."

Saturday, December 7th, 1968, was our wedding day. All our friends came to share it with us. Jeff flew back from New York. Whit risked driving down from Toronto. Donnie and Paul both came in disguise until they were safe inside. Even Brad and Melissa Bennett, and Dr. Quentin Young, were there. Marcellus was my Best Man. Cat was attended by Sharon and Sabrina. The Flower Girl was, of course, Arielle. Emma, as Mother of the Bride, gave her away. Cat needed her cane to walk down the aisle, but no bride was ever more radiant. Even with the bad foot, we were able to jump the broom together.

After Rev. Marshall intoned, "I now pronounce you husband and wife," he nodded to me and added, "You may kiss the bride." The room erupted in applause. As I took Cat in my arms, as we embraced with a long kiss, the applause faded to background noise. A packet of information suddenly exploded inside my head. At that moment, with our lips joined, her body pressed against mine, wedding rings on our fingers, I knew, I just knew, we were going to be *all right*.

I knew Cat would complete her recovery and we'd both go back to school. She'd become a big-time mathematician or scientist. I'd find a path to a teaching license, and bring the joys of math to the masses of children. One day, we would have our own little Kitten, our Tom, maybe a whole litter. And we would spend our lives fighting for peace and social justice *together*. We might even win a few battles along the way.

Nothing had gone as expected since I'd come to Chicago, so I knew I was probably off on some of the details. But what I did know for sure, what I was certain of now, was that we, Cat and me and Emma, our little reinvented family, *we were going to be just fine*.

THE END
and
THE BEGINNING

AUTHOR'S NOTE

My reading of historical fiction often sends me to the Google machine, trying to untangle the real from the fabricated. These few paragraphs might save like-minded readers some time and trouble.

With the exception of Dietrich von Helsinger, Bradley Bennett and Barry Wayne, none of the scientists, mathematicians, journalists, musical artists, authors, poets or philosophers who populate this story are fictional. Nor are their works or accomplishments.

The same is true of the local and national political figures, from Mayor Daley and his subordinate minions to President Johnson. It's true as well of the civil rights leaders and the Vietnamese individuals named in these pages. The actions and words ascribed to each of them are derived from primary and secondary historical sources. Also from such sources are references to specific developments in the Vietnam War, the movement against it, and the federal legislation of the time. The contest for the presidency in 1968 unfolded as described in the story, including the snippets from TV news and talk shows. Except for the fictional Midway and Langley Universities, and High Street, Chicago's landmarks are, or were, also as described.

Other than the South Side Organization, which is a fictional construct based on an actual community group, all the organizations referenced existed as described. Dr. Quentin Young headed the Medical Committee for Human Rights. Abbie Hoffman was the Yippies' chief spokesman and mischief-maker. Allard Lowenstein catalyzed the "Dump Johnson" movement that kick-started the McCarthy candidacy. David Dellinger chaired the National Mobilization Committee to End the War in Vietnam. In portraying each of these, I've strived to be true to their own stories. Donnie Dawes and Paul Haynes, though, are fictional composite mish-mashes of Rennie Davis and Tom Hayden, the Mobe's young Project Directors.

The other characters in this story are creatures of my own fevered imagination.

The wave of urban uprisings and campus revolts occurred largely as described, as did the referenced developments of the Civil Rights, Black Power and Community Control movements. Among the national campaigns to register individual opposition to the Vietnam War, and to the use of Napalm, were the Telephone Tax Refusal and the Saran Wrap Boycott.

All allusions to articles in the *New York Times* and the various Chicago newspapers, other than Sabrina's fictional Saran Wrap interview, appeared in those publications on the dates and pages indicated, including Seymour Hersh's *New York Times Magazine* piece on bio-chemical weapons (except for its fictional reference to the Quantum Potential Weapon).

I've seen claims on the Internet that the Quantum Potential Weapon, as described in the story, does exist today. Evaluating this assertion is far above my scientific pay grade. But I smell conspiracy theory here, so I've cast it into the fiction pile, praying for all of us that this was the correct decision.

"Ca-taca-taca," Cat's full first name, is a Tagalog word that translates as "amazing."

Even with the passing of many decades, there are things we never forget. Memory provided a starting point in narrating the major events around which this story revolves. Historical research, including contemporaneous first-person accounts, helped fill in the details. These events include, among others, the October 21, 1967 March on the Pentagon; the urban uprisings following Dr. King's assassination; the subsequent march on the East Chicago Avenue Armory; the April 27, 1968 march to Chicago's Civic Center; and, of course, Convention Week. Regarding Convention Week, both the planning and the negotiations leading up to the protests, and what happened in Chicago during those dark days and nights, both inside and outside the convention itself, largely transpired as described here.

While I've tried to be meticulous in adhering to the historical record, this is not a "balanced account," whatever that might be. The events are presented from the point of view of the characters I've inserted into them. I must also concede a wee bit of artistic license. This is, after all, fiction. A love story. I hope you enjoyed it as much as I did.

If you did (or even if you didn't), I hope you'll take a moment to post a brief review. I would consider that a huge favor.

Charles S. Isaacs

PARTIAL INDEX OF ACTUAL PERSONS AND PIGS
(excluding entirely fictional references)